Bristol Public Li
D0284322

THE STRANGER HOUSE

Also by Reginald Hill

DALZIEL AND PASCOE NOVELS

A Clubbable Woman
An Advancement of Learning
Ruling Passion
An April Shroud
A Pinch of Snuff
A Killing Kindness
Deadheads
Exit Lines
Child's Play
Underworld
Bones and Silence
One Small Step
Recalled to Life
Pictures of Perfection
Asking for the Moon
The Wood Beyond
On Beulah Height
Arms and the Women
Dialogues of the Dead
Death's Jest-Book
Good Morning, Midnight

JOE SIXSMITH NOVELS

Blood Sympathy
Born Guilty
Killing the Lawyers
Singing the Sadness

Fell of Dark
The Long Kill
Death of a Dormouse
Dream of Darkness
The Only Game

REGINALD HILL

The Stranger House

HarperCollins*Publishers*

This book is a work of fiction. The characters, incidents, and dialogue are drawn from the author's imagination and are not to be construed as real. Any resemblance to actual events or persons, living or dead, is entirely coincidental.

HarperCollins books may be purchased for educational, business, or sales promotional use. For information, please write: Special Markets Department, HarperCollins Publishers, 10 East 53rd Street, New York, NY 10022.

First published in Great Britain in 2005 by HarperCollins Publishers.

FIRST EDITION

Printed on acid-free paper

Library of Congress Cataloging-in-Publication Data
Hill, Reginald.
The stranger house / Reginald Hill.—1st ed.
p. cm.
1. Cumbria (England)—Fiction. 2. Australians—England—Fiction. 3. Spaniards—England—Fiction. 4. Immigrant children—Fiction. 5. Supernatural—Fiction. 6. Historians—Fiction. 7. Villages—Fiction.
I. Title.
PR6058.I448S85 2005
823'.914—dc22

2005040274

ISBN-10: 0-06-082081-0 (alk. paper)
ISBN-13: 978-0-060-82081-7

05 06 07 08 09 ❖/RRD 10 9 8 7 6 5 4 3 2 1

For

Allan, Brian, John and Peter

To his friends a man should be firm in friendship
Sharing gifts and sharing laughter.

"The Sayings of the High One" *Poetic Edda*

AUTHOR'S NOTE

Most of what I know about the incredible scandal of the estimated 150,000 child migrants shipped from Britain to the furthermost corners of its Empire derives from Margaret Humphrey's moving exposé, *Empty Cradles* (Doubleday, 1994; Corgi, 1995), which I recommend unreservedly. But no character in my book is based on any individual involved in any capacity in that sorry tale of abuse of persons and of power.

Australia figures in my story and anything I have got right about matters Australian is almost certainly down to Mel Cain and Christine Farmer of HarperCollins, who organized my only visit to their lovely country and made sure I had a great time. By the same token, anything I've got wrong is down to me, so let me put my hand up now and save you the bother of writing!

But most of the action of *The Stranger House* takes place in Cumbria, England, which is the powsowdy the politicians made thirty years ago of the grand old counties of Cumberland and Westmorland, with segments of Lancashire and Yorkshire stapled on to straighten the boundaries and make it fit more easily into a filing cabinet.

This was the setting of my formative and is the setting of my degenerative years and I feel some natural unease at locating on my own doorstep a story which is full of eccentric people often behaving badly. So let me state without reservation that the valley of Skaddale and its village of Illthwaite are entirely figments of my imagination. Their names, population, history and topography are invented, and they bear no relation other than the most basically generic to any real places.

This means that my dear friends, my excellent neighbors, and indeed all occupants, native or new-come, of this loveliest of landscapes can rest peacefully in their beds.

And so can their lawyers.

My heroine's terms of reference are mathematical, my hero's religious.

No theologian or mathematician I have met provides a model here.

Yet, despite the above disclaimers, it should be remembered that just as theologians and mathematicians use impossibilities, such as the square root of minus one or the transubstantiation of wine into blood, to express their eternal verities, so it is with writers and their fictions.

In other words, just because I've made it all up doesn't mean it isn't true.

Be helpful to strangers who stop at your house,
don't mock or demean them.
It's hard to be certain simply by looking
what kin they may claim.

"The Sayings of the High One" *Poetic Edda*

By dead-man's shore in shadow-land
a hall was raised roofed with serpents
whose venom drips on those who dwell there
killers and defilers. All doors face north.

"The Sibyl's Prophecy" *Poetic Edda*

PART ONE

BLOOD & WINE

Here's some advice a youngster should listen to,
helpful if taken to heart.
Be loud against evil wherever you see it;
never give your enemy an even break.

"The Sayings of the High One" *Poetic Edda*

1

My people

On July 8th, 1992, a small girl woke up in her bed in her family house in the Australian state of Victoria and knew exactly who she was.

Samantha Flood, known to her friends as Sam and her family as Sammy, only child of Sam and Louisa Flood, granddaughter of Vince and Ada Flood, who between them had turned a patch of scrubby farmland on the fringe of the Goulburn Valley into the Vinada Winery which by the end of the eighties was winning golden opinions and medals to match at wine shows up to and including the Royal National Capital.

That morning Sam also knew two new things.

Today she was eleven years old and she was bleeding.

The bleeding was a shock. Not because Sam didn't know what it was. Her ma had explained it all years back, and she'd been taught stuff at school, and the lesson had been complete when her best friend, Martie Hopkins, started not long after she turned ten.

Ten was early. Martie was proud of being the first in their class, just like she was proud of the rest that came early too, the boobs and the bush. Sam was a skinny little thing, not just flat but practically concave. Martie, complacent in her new roundness, once joked in the school showers that you could serve soup on Sam's chest. Sam retorted that at least she wasn't a fat-arse, but secretly she envied Martie. They were always competing for top of the class and neither cared to see the other ahead in anything.

So the bleeding wasn't altogether unwelcome, but on her birthday it seemed lousy timing.

She called to her mother, who came into the bedroom and soon put things right, both inside and out. Lu Flood had a great talent for putting things right. As she sorted her daughter out, she remarked that some of *my people* reckoned it was lucky to start on your birthday. Lu had worked out she was one-seventh Aboriginal and there weren't many situations she hadn't got a bit of *my people* wisdom for. Her husband just grinned and said she made most of it up, while Sam, who loved playing around with numbers, worked out you couldn't be one-seventh something anyway, you had to be half or a quarter or an eighth, because everyone had two parents and four grandparents and so on.

It made no difference to Lu. One-seventh she was, which was a good proportion, seven being a lucky number, and Sam was one-fourteenth, which was twice as lucky.

Maths apart, Sam quite liked all this weird stuff her mother spouted about *my people*. It made her feel connected with that great emptiness outside her bedroom window. And if it got scary, which it did sometimes, the one-seventh (or one-fourteenth) weirdness was more than balanced by the comfortable certainties she got from her father's side of the family.

She used to stagger to Gramma Ada with her great heavy leather-bound photo album and ask to be told about the folk whose faces stared out at her. She liked it best when they got to the old sepia photos where the men had beards or heavy mustaches and the women wore long dresses and everyone looked like they'd been shot and taken to a taxidermist. Gramma knew all their names, all their stories.

With history like this, Sam knew for certain who she was,

so it didn't matter when Ma's stories got a bit frightening, there was nothing in them that those old sepia men with their big mustaches and unblinking stares couldn't deal with.

That morning as Lu cleaned Sam up, she recalled that up north where *my people* came from, when a girl started bleeding, she had to live by herself for a month or so, lying face-down in a hut so she couldn't see the sun, because if she did, her nose would go rotten.

"So there you are, Sam," she said when she'd finished. "Your choice. You can either head out to the old brewhouse and lie flat for a few weeks, or you can take your chances, come downstairs and open your prezzies."

So, no choice. And no change except that Sam was eleven and on a level with Martie.

She had a great day, ate as much chocolate as she liked, which was a hell of a lot, and got to stay up late, watching the telly.

There was only one thing to watch, which was a play everyone had been talking about called *The Leaving of Liverpool.* Sam would have preferred something that had promise of a bit more life in it, but her mother and Gramma Ada wanted to see the play, so that's what they settled down to. Except for her pa. He said he had to check some new vines. If it wasn't cricket or Aussie footie, Pa didn't give a toss for television.

The play (as Sam explained it later to her friends) was about a bunch of English kids who got sent to Australia because they were orphans or at least their parents didn't want them and there was some scheme here to look after them and see they got a proper education. Except it didn't work out like that. They got treated rotten. Worse than rotten in some cases. They got treated like slaves.

It was late when Sam went up to bed but she couldn't sleep. She lay there thinking about the play, and it all got mixed up with the bleeding somehow, and for the first time ever she had a sense of herself as something separate from her context.

Up till now she'd been Samantha Flood who lived with her ma and her gramma at the winery run by her pa and they all loved her. She went to school, she had a lot of friends, she wasn't all that pretty but everyone said she had the loveliest red hair they'd ever seen. And she was really bright, particularly at sums. There was no place further away than Melbourne, no time longer than the months between now and Christmas, nothing sadder in recent years than the death of her kitten, Tommo, who got run over by one of the big drays, and nothing surer than that if anyone was going to live happy ever after with nothing much changing, that person was little Sam Flood.

That was Sam on the inside looking out. That night, the night of her eleventh birthday, for the very first time she found herself on the outside looking in.

It all had something to do with the play she'd seen on the telly. It went round and round in her head till finally she felt like she'd been in it. She realized for the first time just how small she was and that there were things out there bigger even than the dray must have looked to Tommo, which could roll over her and not notice, could pick her up and in the twinkling of an eye drop her on to a boat sailing to the other side of the world.

Finally she fell asleep and when she woke it was light and she felt more like her old self again. When she drew back the curtains and saw the sun, she wondered for a moment if maybe her nose would go rotten, but didn't really worry about it.

That night they showed the second half of the play. Ma tried to send her to bed at her normal time, but Sam chucked a berko and declared she was going to watch whatever anybody said. Her mother yelled after Pa who'd done his usual exit act, and he came back, listened to his wife, looked at his daughter for a moment then said, "Let her watch."

He never wasted words. Use more than six in a sentence, he thought you were yacking.

Other people got worked up by the play too. Next day the

papers were full of it. Sam, after another disturbed night, tried talking about it with her friends, but none of them had seen it, and when she started telling the story, Martie Hopkins stole her thunder by saying, sort of throw-away, "Oh yeah, I know all about those migrant kids. My Aunt Gracie that married Ma's brother, Uncle Trev, she was one of them."

That was Martie's public way of getting back for being knocked off her perch as the only kid in their class to have started her periods. But when privately Sam confided the weird ideas which had started swirling around in her mind, Martie was reassuringly dismissive, saying she'd felt something like that herself when the curse started but it soon wore off.

And she was right. The play was good for a bit of indignation—and Sam was top of the heap when it came to indignation—but soon she found something else to get worked up about. And once she and her mates turned teens, all that stuff on her eleventh birthday got mixed up with everything else that was happening inside and out.

Not that much appeared to be happening outside in Sam's case. At nineteen on her way to Melbourne University she was still the same slight and skinny figure she'd been at eleven. Maybe you could no longer have served soup on her, but prawn cocktail would have taken its time sliding off. If you cared to look deep into her eyes, which not many people did because the intense concentration of her gaze tended to make them feel uneasy, you might be struck by their coloring which was at the slatey end of blue. But the greater part of her adolescent growth and vitality seemed to have gone into her hair which she carried around like a volcanic eruption on top of a matchstick.

As for inside, she knew the world was a much stranger place than she'd once thought, but alongside the rock of her family on which her two small feet were so securely planted she had discovered a shining ivory tower whose staircase spiraled to the stars. Mathematics. By ten she was doing the family accounts and not long afterward her pa was using her to double-check the Vinada books. But already it was clear that her abilities went far beyond mere bookkeeping. Any disappointment her ma and pa felt that she was lost to the family business they kept to themselves, and it was with their blessing and encouragement that she went off to university after a gap year which (unlike Martie who spent it jetting around Europe in the company of well-heeled boyfriends) she devoted to exploring Australia.

Now to the established certainty of her own identity and her growing confidence that anything that couldn't be explained by mathematics probably wasn't worth explaining was added a proud assurance that she lived in one of the most varied and fascinating countries in the world. At that point in her life she could see no reason why she should ever want to leave it.

At university she quickly established herself as one of the brightest maths students of her year. Nor was there any question of geekiness. She worked hard, but huge natural ability plus an eidetic memory meant she had plenty of time to do all the other things a student ought to do, like getting hammered, and getting a suntan, and getting laid, as well of course as getting mad. The first three she did most frequently in the company of another brilliant math student till his chosen specialist path of cryptography got him recruited by government men so anonymous even their suits had no labels. His fatal error was to try and impress Sam by telling her there were things in his work he could no longer discuss with her, upon which Sam completed the square and got very mad indeed, telling him that math was about running naked through the streets, yelling *Eureka!*, not whispering behind closed doors with faceless spooks.

After that for a while she opined that men were a waste of space, except for her pa whom she loved, and her granpa Vince whom she remembered with love, and a visiting professor from

Cambridge, UK, whose mind she loved, and any young man at a party who didn't believe he was God's gift, supported the Demons, and could make her laugh.

So on she wandered toward her inevitable First, more certain than ever who she was and where she was going, and never suspecting, for all her analytical brilliance and eidetic memory, that she was ignoring a message she'd started to hear all those years ago on her eleventh birthday which began in blood and ended in nightmare.

2

Una familia buena y devota

Twelve thousand miles away and some five months before Sam Flood woke to her eleventh birthday, a boy in Jerez de la Frontera in the Spanish province of Cadiz in the region of Andalusia had woken to his sixteenth.

His name was Miguel Ramos Elkington Madero, known to friends and family as Mig.

The Elkington came from his English mother, the rest from his father, also Miguel, as had been all elder sons of the Madero family, whose business records outlining their involvement in the Spanish wine trade went back five centuries.

He and little Sam had absolutely nothing in common.

Except wine.

And blood.

But his was flowing from his hands and his feet.

He rolled out of bed and padded across the cool tiles to the bathroom. The hour was early and his parents and younger brother, Cristóbal, still slept. He stood under the shower and let the water flow over his upraised hands, down his arms and the length of his golden brown body till it washed over his feet, bearing with it the bright red stain.

Finally the water ran clear.

He looked at his palms. Nothing to see, no wound, and the

pain had quickly declined to a faint prickling deep beneath the skin. The same with his feet.

This prickling he had known since infancy, always in the spring around the time of his birthday, steadily growing in strength over the years till it was felt for a few moments as agonizing pain. But never before had there been blood.

As he dried himself, he felt a presence behind him. He turned, thinking his movements had roused somebody else in the house and expecting to see his young brother, or—worse from the point of view of explanation—his father.

Instead he saw standing in the doorway a young man in the black robe of a priest. He had the face of a Michelangelo angel and his fair hair was lifted by some unfeelable breeze into a kind of halo. His expression was serious, almost frowning. He stretched his cupped hands toward Mig. In them lay what seemed to be a trio of eggs, slightly bigger than hens', one white as marble, one slate-blue, the third a sandy red. Then his face relaxed into a smile of great sweetness and he turned and walked away.

Mig made no effort to follow him. This was a vision and there was no point in pursuing visions. His certainty in this matter arose from another of his childish secrets which some instinct had warned him against sharing with adults.

He saw ghosts.

Or rather, in certain places at certain times he felt the presence of departed souls so strongly that it took very little to bring them to the point of materialization. To start with this was a not unpleasant experience, as in the case of his maternal great-grandfather, a jolly old man who used to sit on his bed and talk to him whenever his English mother took him to stay at her family house near Winchester.

Then a couple of years later on a visit to Seville's magnificent Gothic cathedral, he had wandered away from his mother who was dealing with an emergency caused by little Cristóbal's sudden discovery of the pleasures of projectile vomiting. Finding himself in a gloomy and deserted cloister, Mig had become aware of one of what he thought of as his friendly presences. He bent his mind to encouraging it to materialize, which it did, but this time terrifyingly in the form of a wild-eyed and disheveled old man who had come hobbling toward him with clawlike hands outstretched, an incoherent babble of Latin and Spanish and English spilling from his toothless and drooling mouth.

Mig had been so afraid he would probably have fled blindly and got himself utterly lost in the vastness of the old cathedral. But when he turned to run, he saw a young priest standing a few yards away. The man had smiled and beckoned. He had followed, trotting fast in an effort to come up close behind his guide but somehow never getting any nearer. Then they had turned a corner and there were his mother and brother who hadn't even noticed his absence.

When he looked to thank the priest, he had disappeared. But he'd never forgotten that young face with its sweet smile.

And now he had seen it again.

Musing on what this could mean, he returned to his room, where he stripped the stained sheet from the bed, checking that nothing had penetrated to the mattress, then thrust it into the linen basket that stood in the corner. His mother, being English, had been very insistent that her sons were not going to grow up with any *hidalgo* expectation that the world owed them a living. "*Noblesse oblige,*" she said. "Which means you don't expect other people to pick up your dirty washing."

Cristina (née Christine) Madero's elder son now sat on the edge of his bed and contemplated his future. For years the only ambition he'd nursed which ran counter to his preordained lot of running the family business had been to sign on as a striker with, first of all, Sevilla FC and ultimately Man United. At first these strange physical symptoms had only concerned him as possible obstacles to his athletic ambitions. But there seemed to be no long-term effect, and what made him abandon his hoped-for sporting career was the gradual realization that, though he was good, he would never be Best. Anything less had no appeal, and he set aside his football boots with no regrets.

Now it seemed to him that perhaps he had been denied that ultimate sporting edge because another purpose was written for him. To have interpreted this intermittent irritation in his hands and feet as a form of stigmata would have been blasphemously arrogant. But the blood today had changed all that. The blood and the second manifestation of the young priest. The first time the vision had invited him to follow. Now, ten years later, it had offered him a gift. The symbolism of the eggs was not hard to read. In form perfection; in content life. Was not that the essence of a priest's existence, to strive to be perfect and so reveal life's true meaning?

The more he thought about it, the more it seemed to him clear that this was the message he had been receiving for all his short years.

Yet he was in many ways what is called an old-fashioned child, and he knew that getting other important people to accept his sense of vocation was not going to be easy.

Problem one was his own family.

The Maderos were in the eyes of their bishop the very model of a good devout Catholic family—generous in charity, regular attenders at Mass, both their sons serving as altar boys—but never in the five hundred years since they started to make their name in the wine business had a single man of the family offered himself for the priesthood.

Problem two was their family priest.

Father Adolfo was a hardheaded Catalonian who regarded what he called hysterical religiosity with a cold and cynical eye. His reaction to any suggestion that Mig was specially chosen by God as evidenced by the stigmata was likely to be a cuff round the ear, followed by a recommendation to the family that they seek a good child psychiatrist to nip this childish delusion in the bud.

So when Mig sought an interview with him, he limited himself to the unadorned statement that he felt he might have a vocation. He was glad of his discretion when Father Adolfo's reaction was to throw back his head and let out a long booming laugh.

When the echoes had faded, the priest said, "Have you talked to your father about this?"

"No, Father," said Mig.

"Then let's go and see him now. I'm not having a decent generous man like Miguel Madero saying I've been sneaking behind his back, subverting his son and heir."

Miguel Madero's reaction had been one of amazement, which he showed, and horror, which, out of deference to the priest, he tried to conceal. But the shock was too great and it was apparent both to Mig and the priest that Madero Senior could hardly have been more distressed if told his son had ambitions to be a fundamentalist suicide-bomber.

Father Adolfo, though having no desire to appear to encourage what he suspected was an adolescent fancy, was not about to let the dignity of his calling be traduced.

"To be called to the service of God is the greatest honor that can befall a true Catholic," he said sternly.

"Yes, of course . . . I was selfishly thinking of the business . . ."

"The Church's business comes first. You have another son to look after yours," said the priest shortly. "You will want to speak further to Mig. So shall I. Let us both pray to discover the truth of God's purpose."

The next few months saw Mig's infant sense of vocation tested to the full.

His father's motives for opposition were practical and genealogical. Mig had shown a peculiar aptitude for all aspects of the family business, commercial and vinicultural. His flirtation with football apart, he had never seemed likely to divert from his preordained role as head of the firm, the sixteenth Miguel in an unbroken line since the fifteenth century. Sherry is a sensitive creature. It likes calm and continuity. Miguel Senior was so upset that he hardly dared go into the bodega during this period.

His mother's objections were English and social. Behind every great man there is a great woman, telling him he's driving too fast. This was Cristina Madero's role in the family, and she found it hard to accept that her control of her husband did not extend to her son. She also felt things would have been managed better back home. The rich Catholic families of Hampshire provided the Church with money, congregation, and voluntary workers, but saw no reason to provide priests, not when the poor Catholic families of Ireland needed the work.

Only Mig's young brother, Cristo, inspired by a vision of his future which did not involve being perpetually second-in-command, encouraged him.

Father Adolfo was the one who most vigorously questioned his vocation. "It means a calling," he mocked. "Are you sure it's not just an echo of your own vanity?"

Often Mig was tempted to silence him with the revelation of his experience of the stigmata, but a natural reluctance to make such an enormous claim kept him quiet.

But one day when Father Adolfo sneered that he had so far seen precious little evidence of that special spirituality he looked for in a postulant, Mig could not resist the temptation to put him in his place by revealing his other special gift.

Far from being impressed, the priest reacted as if he'd confessed a mortal sin.

"You foolish child!" he cried. "Such trafficking with the alleged spirits of the departed is a common trick of the devil to seduce susceptible minds. Remember Faustus. The Helen he saw was no more than a succuba, a demon that comes in the guise of a naked woman and steals men's seed. Be not deceived, my child. These fancies of yours are the first steps toward the mouth of hell which gapes wide to receive errant souls."

Mig was horrified. Adolfo's words quite literally put the fear of God into him, though he couldn't repress a small regret that so far the demons hadn't come after his seed. For he was already wrestling with that more common danger to a young man with a sense of religious vocation, the tendency for images of naked girls to invade his devotions.

There was no question which was the stronger urge, and after Adolfo's terrifying admonition, there were times when he allowed the lesser sin to divert him from the greater. Lying in bed, he would sometimes feel one of these perilous ghostly presences forming in the darkness, but all he had to do was conjure up an image of some girl of his acquaintance spreading herself before him lasciviously, and it was goodbye ghost!

But this was mere equivocation. In his heart he knew he had to learn to deal with all temptation, great and small.

How he wrestled with his adolescent lust! He mortified the flesh by running till exhausted and he spent so much time under icy showers that he had a permanent cold.

In the end he found less dramatic strategies to master his own body. At the first hint of arousal, he would turn to certain spiritual exercises which sublimated carnal longings into Marian devotion, and if he felt himself backsliding, he would reinforce the sublimation process by adopting positions of great physical discomfort, such as kneeling across the sharp edge of a doorstep. But gradually the need for this reinforcement diminished. The grace of God and his strong human will was enough. And enough also, so it seemed, to save him from that other tendency which had so disturbed Adolfo.

Girls and ghosts. By the end of his teens he believed he had them both under control. His sense of vocation felt strong and real. But still, in deference to his parents who urged him to be absolutely certain before taking the final step, he tested it further. He enrolled at Seville University to study history and laid himself open to all the temptations of student life. With these successfully resisted and a degree in his pocket, he demonstrated that his inner strength was not merely self-denial, which can be a self-congratulatory and ultimately sterile form of virtue, by joining one of the Church's missions to South America as a voluntary helper. Here he spent eighteen months in the rain forest, facing up to the best and the worst in his fellow men, and in himself.

Finally he was ready. His vocation felt powerful and permanent. Every year in the spring the pain returned as strong as ever, though the stigmata had shrunk now to a few spots of blood. Still he kept silent about the experience. When all else failed, this was God's private earnest of the rightness of his choice.

So he entered the seminary in Seville at the age of twenty-three at the same time as eighteen-year-old Sam Flood entered Melbourne University, both convinced they knew exactly who they were and what they were doing and where the paths of their lives were leading them.

And neither yet understanding that a path is not a prospectus and that it may, in the instant it takes for a word to be spoken or a fingerhold to be lost, slip right off your map and lead you somewhere unimagined in all your certainties.

In the cases of Sam Flood and Miguel Madero, this place was situated far to the north.

In a county called Cumbria.

In a valley called Skaddale.

In a village called Illthwaite.

PART TWO

THE VALLEY OF THE SHADOW

Lady, it's madness to venture alone
Into that darkness the dwelling of ghosts.

"The Poem of Heldi Hundingsbani (2)" *Poetic Edda*

1

Hilbert's Hotel

"So why's it called Illthwaite?" asked Sam Flood.

She thought the bar was empty except for herself and Mrs. Appledore but the answer came from behind her.

"Illthwaite. An ill name for an ill place. Isn't that what they say, Mrs. Appledore?"

She turned to see a man emerging from the shady corner on the far side of the chimney breast.

Almost as skinny as she was and not much taller, with a pallid wrinkled face swelling from a pointed chin to a bulbous brow above which a few sad last gray hairs clung like sea grass on a sand dune, he had the look of a superannuated leprechaun, a similitude underlined by the garish green-and-orange checked waistcoat he wore under a dark gray suit jacket, shiny with age. His voice was high-pitched without being squeaky. He could have been anything from seventy to ninety. But his eyes were bright and keen.

"And where do they say that, Mr. Melton? Down at the Powderham, is it, where they've got more tongue than brain?" said the landlady. "If you think silly gossip's worth an extra ten p on your pint, maybe you should drink there more often."

She spoke with a mock menace that wasn't altogether mock.

The old man was unfazed.

"I'll take it under advisement, Mrs. Appledore," he said. "Though we shouldn't forget that the Powderham also offers Thai cuisine and live entertainment, not large incentives to a poor old pensioner, but strong attractions perhaps for a swinging young tourist. None of my business, you say. Quite right. Good day to you both."

He saluted them with an old peaked cap which matched his waistcoat, set it precisely on his head and went out.

"Pay him no heed, Miss Flood," said the landlady. "Ill's nowt to do with sick or nasty. It comes from St. Ylf's, our church, and *thwaite*'s an old Viking word for a bit of land that's been cleared."

"So how come the old boy bad-mouths his own village?"

"Old Noddy Melton's not local," said Mrs. Appledore, as if this explained everything. "He retired here a few years back to follow his hobby, which is getting up people's noses. Poor old pensioner indeed! What he gets now is more than most ordinary folk take home while they're still working. And you need plenty to pay the Powderham's fancy prices, believe me!"

Sam had noticed the Powderham Arms Hotel as she turned into Skaddale. In fact, not knowing what Illthwaite might offer by way of accommodation, she'd tried to get a room there but found it was booked up. The Stranger House on the other hand, despite its unfancy prices, had been able to give her a choice of its two guest rooms, though not before she and her passport had been subjected to the same kind of scrutiny she'd got from Heathrow Immigration who had broken open five of her Cherry Ripes before being persuaded they weren't stuffed with crack.

She must have passed some kind of test because Mrs. Appledore had become quite voluble as she led the way upstairs. Wayfarers had been stopping here at the Stranger for more than five hundred years, she'd proclaimed proudly. Its curious name derived from the fact that it had once been the

Stranger House of Illthwaite Priory, meaning the building where travelers could enjoy the monks' hospitality for a night or two.

"That's fascinating," said Sam without conviction as she inspected the bedroom. For once she was glad she wasn't any bigger. Even at her height, if she'd been wearing her Saturday-night heels, the central low black beam would have been a real danger.

"It's a bit spooky, though," she went on, looking out at the mist-shrouded landscape through the one small window.

"Well, it would be, seeing that we've got our own spook," said the landlady. "But nowt to be afraid of, just this dark fellow, likely an old monk, wandering around still. You'll only ever catch a glimpse of him passing through a slightly open door and you can never catch up with him no matter how fast you move. Go after him, and there he'll be, passing through another door."

"What if you follow him into a room like this, with only one door?"

"They say once you start following the Dark Man, there's always another door, no matter how long you keep chasing."

"Bit like Hilbert's Hotel then," said Sam, trying to lighten things.

"Don't know it, dear. In Windermere, is it?"

"No," said Sam. "It's a made-up place in math that has an infinity of rooms."

"Doing the laundry must be a real pain," observed Mrs. Appledore. "I'm glad I've only got the two to show you. Unless we come across the Dark Man, that is."

She spoke so lugubriously that Sam couldn't help shivering. The pub's low ceilings, shadowy corners, narrow windows and general air of not having been tarted up in living, or dead, memory didn't make the prospect of such ghostly company appealing. What am I doing here anyway? she asked herself. Illthwaite would probably turn out to be a pointless diversion, any chance of real fact lay in Newcastle Upon Tyne, some hundred miles further on. Here all she was doing was chasing one phantom at the risk of sharing a room with another.

Then Mrs. Appledore, a most unspooky lady in her late fifties, with rosy cheeks, broad bosom and matching smile, let out a peal of uninhibited laughter and said, "Don't worry, miss. I've never laid eyes on the bugger and I've lived here most of my life. Bathroom's across the corridor. Come down to the bar when you've cleaned up and I'll make you a sandwich. Or would you like something hot?"

The assumption that she was staying couched in such a friendly way was irresistible. Suddenly the room seemed less constricting. Also she'd been driving through steady drizzle since not long after dawn, and the thought of setting out once more had little appeal.

"A sandwich will be fine," she said.

Ten minutes later she'd descended to the bar to find herself confronted by something resembling a small cob loaf from which slices of ham dangled like the skirts of a hovercraft.

Mrs. Appledore had pushed a half-pint of beer toward her, saying, "First on the house, to welcome you to Illthwaite."

Which had provoked her question about the origins of the name and the old leprechaun's disconcerting interruption.

"Anyway, don't let old Noddy put you off," the landlady concluded. "He's been living by himself too long and that sends you dotty. I should know. Woman on her own running a pub these days, I must be crazy!"

"You're saying he's off his scone?"

"If that means daft but not daft enough to lock up, yes," said Mrs. Appledore cheerfully. "So what are you going to do with yourself while you're here?"

Sam bit into her sandwich and nearly went into toxic shock when her tongue discovered that internally the ham had been coated with the kind of mustard you could strip paint with. She grabbed for the beer and took a long cooling pull, using the pause to consider her reply.

Pa's advice on communication was, "Tell enough to get told what you want to know."

"I'll see the sights, I guess," she said. "What do most visitors do?"

"Most come to go walking on the fells. That's what we call our hills," said Mrs. Appledore. "As for sightseeing, there's not a lot to look at except St. Ylf's, and the Wolf-Head Cross in the churchyard."

"Yeah?" said Sam, carefully chewing at the ham's mustard-free skirting. "The church would be the place where they keep the parish records, right?"

"I suppose so," said Mrs. Appledore. "You interested in that sort of thing?"

"Could be. I think my gran might come from this part of the world," said Sam.

She looked for polite interest and got a blank.

"Is that right? And what would her name have been?"

"Flood, same as mine. Are there any Floods round here?"

"Only in a wet winter when the Skad overflows down the valley. Got in the cellars at the Powderham three years back," said Mrs. Appledore not without satisfaction. "But there's definitely no local family called Flood. So when did your gran leave England?"

"Your spring, 1960. February or March, I think."

"Spring 1960?" echoed the woman.

"Right. Does that mean something?" asked Sam, detecting a note of significance.

"Only that I turned fifteen in the spring of 1960," said Mrs. Appledore rather wistfully. "Mam died the year before and I'd started helping Dad in the pub. Against the law, but I was big for my age, so strangers didn't notice and locals weren't going to complain. Point is, I knew everyone in the valley then. Definitely no local family called Flood. Sorry, dear. You sure it's Illthwaite you're after?"

Sam shrugged and said, "I'm short on detail, so maybe not.

But I'll check the church out anyway. What about the local school? They'll have records too, right?"

"Would do if we still had one. Got closed down three years back. Not enough kids, you see. The few there are get bused into the next valley. When I was a kid, the place was really buzzing. Thirty or forty of us. Now the young couples get out, go where there's a bit more life and a lot more money. Can't blame them."

"Looks like it will have to be the church then. Is it far?"

"No. Just a step. Turn right when you leave the pub. You can't miss it. But you've not finished your sandwich. It's OK, is it?"

"The ham's lovely," said Sam carefully. "I'll take it with me. And one of these."

She helped herself from a small display of English Tourist Board leaflets standing at the end of the bar as she slipped off her stool.

"By the way, I tried my mobile upstairs, couldn't get a signal."

"You wouldn't. It's the fells. They wanted to build a mast but Gerry wouldn't let them."

"Gerry?"

"Gerry Woollass up at the Hall."

"The Hall?" Her mind went back to some of the old Eng. Lit. stuff they'd made her read at school. "You mean he's like some sort of squire?"

"No," said the woman, amused. "Gerry's not the squire. He's chairman of the Parish Council."

And just as Sam was feeling rebuked for her archaism, Mrs. Appledore added, "Gerry won't be squire till old Dunstan, his dad, pops his clogs, which he's in no hurry to do. If you need to phone, help yourself to the one in my kitchen."

"Thanks. I wanted to ring back home, tell them I was still in the land of the living. I'll use my credit number so it won't go on your bill."

"Fine. Through here."

The landlady led her out of the bar and down the hall. The kitchen was a strange mix of old and new. Along the left-hand wall it was all modernity with a range of white kitchen units incorporating a built-in electric oven, fridge, dishwasher and stainless-steel sink. A coal fire glowed in a deep grate set in the end wall and from one of the two massive black cross-beams hung a pair of cured hams on hooks held by ropes running through pulleys screwed into the beam and thence to geared winding handles fixed into the walls. The floor was flagged with granite slabs which bore the marks of centuries of wear, as did the huge refectory table occupying most of the center space. One of the slabs, a rectangle of olive green stone which ran from just inside the door to twelve inches or so under the table, had some carving on it, almost indecipherable now.

"Latin," said the landlady when Sam paused to look. "Old Dunstan says it's St. Matthew's Gospel. Ask and it shall be given, that bit. Sort of a welcome. This was the room that the monks fed the travelers in. Phone's at yon end by the fireplace."

As Sam made her way down the narrow corridor between the table and the units she had to pause to shut the dishwasher door.

"Bloody nuisance," said Mrs. Appledore.

"Why not get something smaller?" asked Sam, looking at the huge table.

"No, not the table, those units," said the woman. "The table's been here since the place were built. The units were Buckle's idea."

"Buckle?"

"My husband."

Sam tried to puzzle this out as she made the connection home.

"Yeah?" said a familiar voice.

"Pa, it's me."

"Hey, Lu, it's Sammy!" she heard him yell. "So how's it going, girl?"

"Fine, Pa. How're things back there?"

"No problems," he said. "The new vines are looking good. Here's your ma. Missing you like hell. Take care now."

This got close to a heart-to-heart with her father. When he said you were missed, it made you feel missed clearer than a book of sonnets. Her eyes prickled with tears but she brushed them away and greeted her mother brightly, assuring her she was well and having a great time seeing a bit of the country before getting down to work.

Despite this, Lu needed more reassurance, asking after a while, "Sam, you sure you're OK?"

"I told you, Ma. Fit as a butcher's dog."

"It's just that a couple of times recently I got this feeling . . ."

"Ma, is this some of your *my people* stuff?"

"Mock my people, you're mocking yourself, girl. I'm just telling you what I've been told. You watch out for a stranger, Sam."

"Ma, I'm in England. They're all bleeding strangers!"

Mrs. Appledore had left the kitchen to give her some privacy. When she finished her call, Sam blew her nose, then headed for the door. The winding gear to raise the hams caught her eye and she paused to examine it. Instead of a simple wheel-and-axle system, it had three gearing cogwheels. Between two blinks of her eye, her mind measured radiuses, turned them into circumferences, counted cogs, and calculated lifting power.

"Real antiques those. As old as the house, they say. Ropes been changed of course, but 'part from a bit of oiling, they're just the same as they were when some old monk put them together," said Mrs. Appledore from the doorway.

"Clever old monk," said Sam. "This is real neat work. Did they have bigger pigs in those days? With this gearing you could hoist a whole porker, if the rope held."

"Bigger appetites maybe. Talking of which, you left your sandwich on the bar. I've wrapped it in a napkin so you can eat it as you walk to the church. And here's a front-door key in case I'm out when you get back. And I thought this old guidebook might help you if you're looking round the village. Better than that useless leaflet."

She proffered a leather-bound volume, almost square in shape.

"That's kind," said Sam, taking the book and opening it at the title page.

A GUIDE to ILLTHWAITE and its ENVIRONS

being a brief introduction to the history, architecture, and economy of the parish of Illthwaite in Skaddale in the County of Cumberland, with maps and illustrations, prepared by the Reverend Peter K. Swinebank DD Vicar of St. Ylf's Church, Illthwaite, assisted by Anthony Woollass Esquire of Illthwaite Hall. Printed at the Lunar Press, Whitehaven mdcccxciv

"Eighteen ninety-four," she worked out. "Isn't this valuable? I'd love to borrow it, but I'm worried about damaging it."

"Don't be daft," said the woman comfortably. "I've loaned it to worse than you and it's come to no harm."

Worse than you. Had to be a compliment in there somewhere, thought Sam.

"Then thank you so much."

"Think nowt of it," said the woman. "Enjoy the church. See you later. Don't forget your sandwich."

"Won't do that in a hurry. See you later!"

Outside, she found the drizzle which had accompanied her most of the way from London seemed at last to have given up. She reached into her hired car parked on the narrow forecourt and opened the glove compartment. There were three Cherry Ripes in there. She'd been incredulous when Martie, whose gorgeous looks had earned her more air miles than most Qantas pilots by the time she left uni, had told her you couldn't get them outside of Oz. Life without a daily injection of this cherry-and-coconut mix in its dark chocolate wrapping had seemed impossible and she'd stuffed a month's supply into her flight bag. Unfortunately the ravages of Heathrow Customs had been followed by the rapine of the Aussie friends she'd stayed with in London, and now she was down to her last three. She slipped two of them into her bumbag, one to eat on her walk to the church, one for emergencies.

Then she took one of them out and replaced it in the compartment.

Knowing yourself was the beginning of wisdom, and she had still to find a way of not consuming every bit of chocolate available once she started.

The landlady had followed her to the front door. In case she'd noticed the business with the Cherry Ripes, Sam held up the cob and nibbled appreciatively at one of the dangling skirts of ham. Then with the Illthwaite *Guide* tucked under one arm, she set off along the road.

Mrs. Appledore stood and watched her guest out of sight, then turned and went back into the Stranger House, slipping the bolt into the door behind her. In her kitchen she lifted the telephone and dialed. After three rings, it was answered.

"Thor, it's Edie," she said. "Something weird. I've got a lass staying here, funny little thing, would pass for a squirrel if you glimpsed her in the wood, skin brown as a nut, hair red as rowan berries. Looks about twelve, but from her passport she's early twenties . . . Don't interrupt, I'm coming to the point. Her name's Sam Flood . . . That's right. Sam for Samantha Flood, it's in her passport. She's from Australia, got an accent you could scratch glass with, and she thinks her grandmother might have come from these parts . . . 1960, spring . . . Yes, '60, so it's got to be just coincidence, but I thought I'd mention it. She's off up to the church to see if there's any records . . . Yes, I'll be there, but not till he's well screwed down. I'll take your word the little bugger's dead!"

2

A turbulent priest

Sam Flood and Miguel Madero saw each other for the first time in a motorway service café to the west of Manchester but neither would ever recall the encounter.

Sam was sitting at a table with a double espresso and a chocolate muffin which was far too sweet but she ate it anyway. She glanced up to see Madero passing with a cappuccino and a cream doughnut. Though he wore no clerical collar, there was something about him—his black clothing, the ascetic thinness of his face—which put her in mind of a Catholic priest, and she looked away. For his part all he registered was an unaccompanied child whose exuberance of red hair could have done with a visit to the barber, but most of his attention was focused on maintaining the delicate relationship between an unreliable left knee and an overfull cup of coffee.

She left five minutes before he did and they spent the next hour only a couple of miles apart in heavy traffic. Then a van blew a tire a hundred yards behind her and spun into a truck. Miraculously no one was seriously hurt, but as Sam's Focus sped merrily north, Madero and his Mercedes SLK fumed gently in the accident's tailback.

From having time to spare for his two o'clock appointment

in Kendal, he was already half an hour late as he reached the town's southern approaches.

On the map Kendal looked to be a quiet little market town on the eastern edge of the English Lake District, but there seemed to be some local law requiring all traffic in Cumbria to pass along its main street, which meant it was after three when he drew up before the chambers of Messrs. Tenderley, Gray, Groyne, and Southwell, solicitors.

Knowing how highly lawyers price their time, he was full of apology as he was shown into the office of Andrew Southwell.

"Not at all, not at all, think nothing of it," said Southwell, a small round man in his early thirties who pumped his hand with painful enthusiasm. "I've been looking forward to meeting you. Professor Coldstream speaks very warmly of you. Very warmly indeed."

"And of you too," said Madero.

In fact what Max Coldstream had said when he mentioned Kendal was, "You're in luck there, Mig. Chap called Southwell, Kendal solicitor, and mad keen local historian. OK, so he's an amateur, but that can be an advantage. Professional historians on the whole are a deceitful, distrusting, conniving and secretive bunch of bastards who would direct a blind man up a blind alley rather than risk giving him an advantage. Enthusiastic amateurs on the other hand may lack scholarship but they often have bucketloads of information which they are eager to share. Painfully eager, if you're in a hurry!"

It only took a couple of minutes for Madero to appreciate Coldstream's warning.

"That's fascinating, Mr. Southwell," he said, interrupting a potted history of the chambers building. "Now, you will recall from my letter I'm on my way to talk to the Woollass family of Illthwaite Hall in connection with my thesis on the personal experience of English Catholics during the Reformation. By chance I came across a reference to a Jesuit priest, Father

Simeon Woollass, the son of a cadet branch of the family residing here in Kendal. I thought it might be worth diverting to see what I could find out about him. A priest in the family must have made the problems of recusancy even greater, as perhaps your researches have already discovered."

This was the right trigger to pull.

Southwell nodded vigorously and said, "How very true, Mr. Madero. But I know you chaps, hands-on whenever possible, so let's take a walk and see what we can find."

Next moment Madero found himself being whizzed down the stairs, past the receptionist who desperately shouted something about not forgetting the partners' meeting, and out into the damp afternoon air, where he was taken on a whirlwind tour.

"It's curious," said Southwell as they raced from the library to the church. "What really got me interested in Father Simeon wasn't you, but this other researcher who was asking questions, must be ten years ago now. Irish chap, name of Molloy. Poor fellow."

"I don't recognize the name. Did he publish? And why do you say 'poor fellow'?"

"He did a few things, pop articles mainly. Not a serious scholar like you, more of a journalist. But nothing on Father Simeon. Never had the chance really. He was something of a rock climber, took the chance to do a bit while he was up here, by himself, very silly, and he had this terrible accident . . . are you all right, Mr. Madero?"

"Yes, fine," lied Mig. Twinges in his still unreliable left knee he was used to, but the other injuries he'd suffered in his own fall rarely troubled him now. This lightning jag of pain across his head and down his spine had to be some kind of sympathetic echo. In fact during his own fall he couldn't even remember the pain of contact . . .

"You sure?" said Southwell.

"Yes, yes," said Mig impatiently as the pain faded. "And he was killed, was he?"

"Died as the Mountain Rescue carried him back. He wasn't so much interested in the background as in what happened when Father Simeon got captured. The book he was writing was actually about Richard Topcliffe—you know about him, of course?"

"Elizabeth's chief priest-hunter, *homo sordidissimus*. Oh yes, I know about him."

"Well, it was Topcliffe's northern agent, Francis Tyrwhitt, who captured Simeon and took him off to Jolley Castle near Leeds to be interrogated. That was Molloy's main interest, torture, that kind of stuff. Ah, here's the church. Note the Victorian porch."

It was clear that, despite his conviction that academics preferred to do their own research, Southwell had already dug up everything there was to dig up about Simeon and recorded it in the folder he carried. Madero was tempted but too polite to suggest that a lot of time could be saved if he simply handed it over. Happily after a couple of hours the man's mobile rang. He listened, then said, "Good lord, is it that time already?"

To Madero he said, "Sorry. Meeting. Lot of nothing, but old Joe Tenderley, our senior partner, tends to get his knickers in a twist. Look, why don't we meet up later? Better still, have dinner, stay the night. Meanwhile you might care to browse through my notes, see if there are any gaps you'd like me to fill."

Madero waited till he'd got the folder firmly in his grip before thanking the man profusely but refusing his kind offer on the grounds that he was already engaged in Illthwaite, which if a bed-and-breakfast booking could be called an engagement was true.

Back in his car, he rejoined the tidal bore of traffic, intending to retrace his approach to the town and take the road which Sam Flood had followed some hours earlier around the southern edge of the county, but somehow he found himself swept away toward somewhere called Windermere. He stopped at a roadside inn, brought up a map of Cumbria on his laptop and saw he could get across to the west just as easily this way. Feeling hungry, he entered the pub and ordered a pint of shandy (England's main contribution to alcoholic refinement, according to his father) and a jumbo haddock. As he waited for his food, he took a long draught of his drink and opened Southwell's folder.

Out of reach of the solicitor's voice and with the evidence of the man's hard work before him, he felt a pang of guilt at his sense of relief at parting company. For every sin there is a fitting penance, that's what he'd learned at the seminary. It would serve him right if his haddock turned out stale and his chips soggy.

It had been a stroke of luck that the man he was interested in had been closely linked to one of Kendal's foremost merchant families during the great period of the town's importance in the field of woolen manufacture which was Southwell's special interest.

Simeon Woollass had been the son of Will Woollass, younger brother of Edwin Woollass of Illthwaite Hall. Will's early history (later a matter of public record in Kendal) showed him to be a wild and dissolute youth who narrowly escaped hanging in 1537 after the Catholic uprising known as the Pilgrimage of Grace. His age (fifteen) and the influence of his brother won his release with a heavy fine and a stern warning.

Undeterred, Will continued to earn his reputation as the Woollass wild man till 1552 when he surprised everyone by wooing Margaret, the only child of John Millgrove, wool merchant of Kendal, and settling down to the life of an honest hardworking burgher.

In 1556 Margaret gave birth to Simeon, and once the child had survived the perils of a Tudor infancy, all looked set fair for the Kendal Woollasses. John Millgrove's commercial acumen meant that business both domestic and export was booming, and with wealth came status. Nor did he let a little thing like religion interfere with his commercial and civil ambitions, and when Catholic Mary was succeeded by Protestant Elizabeth, he readily bowed with the prevailing wind and, like many others, straightened up from his obeisance as a strong pillar of the English Church.

Will, now firmly established as heir apparent of the Millgrove business, was happy to go along with this, which strained his relationship with his firmly recusant brother Edwin. Simeon, however, stayed close to his Illthwaite cousins and it was probably to put him out of their sphere of influence that Will sent his son, aged eighteen, down to Portsmouth to act as the firm's continental shipping agent. He did so well that a year later when a problem arose with their Spanish agent in Cadiz, Simeon, who had a natural gift for languages, seemed the obvious person to sort it out.

Alas for a parent's efforts to protect his child!

Simeon found life in Spain much to his taste. He liked the people and the climate, became fluent in the principal dialects, and presented good commercial arguments for extending his stay. A year passed. Will, suspecting his son had been seduced by hot sun, strong wine and dusky señoritas, and recalling his own youthful excesses, was exasperated rather than angered by Simeon's delaying tactics. Finally however he sent a direct command, which elicited a revelation far more shocking than mere dissipation.

Simeon had been formally received into the Roman Catholic Church.

Missives flew across the Bay of Biscay, threatening from the father, pleading from the mother. In return all they got was news that progressed from bad to worse.

In 1577 Simeon had travelled north into France, ending up at the notorious English College at Douai in Flanders. In 1579 he was ordained deacon and the following year undertook a pilgrimage to Rome, whence in 1582 came the devastating news that he had joined the Jesuit Order and been ordained priest.

All this Andrew Southwell had been able to discover because of the effect it was to have on the Millgrove family's fortunes. John had come close to achieving his great ambition of being elected chief burgess of the town when the smallpox carried him off. It was, however, generally confided that Will Woollass, now head of the firm, would eventually achieve that high civic dignity his father-in-law had aspired to.

But a son and heir who was a Catholic priest was heavy baggage for an upwardly mobile man to carry.

So long as Simeon remained abroad it was easy enough to dismiss rumors. In Kendal they took stories from south of Lancashire with a very large pinch of salt. But the salt rapidly lost its savor when it emerged that Simeon Woollass had joined the English Mission, that band of Catholic priests sent to spread subversion in their native land.

Once sightings of him were reported first in Lancashire then in Westmorland and Cumberland, Will felt obliged to affirm his complete loyalty to the Protestant Church by publicly disowning his son. Despite this the Woollasses suffered the indignity of having their Kendal house searched for signs of the renegade's presence. Will's civic rivals, under guise of protecting the interests of loyal burghers, now made sure that every aspect of his wild youth and his son's treacherous apostasy went on the record.

The inevitable result of such an unremitting bad press was that Will never achieved that eminence in the township of Kendal which had once seemed in his grasp and, with the passing of himself and his wife, the Millgrove firm also died.

"Is there any record that Simeon did ever return to Kendal?" Madero had inquired.

"None, though that of course means nothing," said Southwell. "His father had publicly threatened to turn him in if ever he showed up, but that was probably just PR. When news came of his capture in Chester in '89, Will had a seizure. Understandable reaction when you consider what capture usually meant for a Catholic priest."

Very understandable, thought Madero. Torture, trial, condemnation, the broken body hanged till point of death, then taken down while life was still extant and eviscerated, the bowels thrown to the dogs, the finally lifeless corpse hacked into pieces to be hurled into the river, except for the head which would be stuck on a spike in a prominent place till time and the crows had reduced it to a grinning skull.

No, it was hard to believe a father could do anything which would condemn his own child to such a fate, though in this case Simeon had escaped the ultimate rigors and eventually returned to the Continent in one piece physically if not mentally.

What did it all mean? How could God tolerate a world where men could rip and tear at each other in the name of religion, where such abominations seemed destined to continue as long as mankind survived? Even now as he sat here in this peaceful inn, such horrors were happening somewhere within a few hours' flying distance.

He bowed his head and said a prayer. It was hard to keep an accusatory note out of it, but he tried.

When he looked up his jumbo haddock had appeared.

It was excellent.

Which probably meant his penance was yet to come.

3

Hymn books and hassocks

Mrs. Appledore was clearly not to be trusted. Even making allowance for the fact that her legs might be two or three inches longer than Sam's, the distance to St. Ylf's was not what any honest woman could call a step.

When she'd first tracked Illthwaite down to Cumbria, Sam had pictured a cluster of whitewashed cottages around a village green, their tiny gardens rich with hollyhocks and roses, the whole backed by misty mountains and fronted by a sunlit lake. No cluster here, just an endless straggle with no discernible center. And no whitewash either. Most of the scattered buildings were coated in a dirty gray pebble dash. Garden vegetation consisted mainly of dense dank evergreens with never a hollyhock in sight, though maybe early autumn wasn't the hollyhock season. There was no lake either, sunlit or somber, just the brown-foaming river Skad tracking the road.

The Tourist Board leaflet told her the name Skaddale probably meant the Valley of the Shadow, deriving from the fact that, as winter approached, the high surrounding fells stopped the sun from reaching a good proportion of the land. An alternative theory was that the river got its name from *Scadde*, an ancient dialect word for corpse, referring to its reputation for drowning travelers who tried to ford it downstream at its estuary.

Shadow or corpse, its denizens received the remnants of Sam's caustic cob as soon as the pub was out of sight, and in its place she began to chew on her Cherry Ripe.

The rest of the leaflet confirmed Mrs. Appledore's dismissive judgment. It did its best with the church (old), the Cross (Viking), the pub (haunted), the Hall (not open to visitors) and the village post office (postcards and provisions). But its underlying message to the passing driver seemed to be *Glance out, change up, move on.*

Turning her attention to the chunky *Guide*, she recalled from her school days a hymn beginning *There is a book who runs may read.* Well, this certainly wasn't it. Even trudging, it wasn't easy, and she only managed a glance at the opening page of the lengthy chapter on the church before a stumble in a pothole on the uneven road persuaded her that a twisted ankle was too high a price to pay for the Rev. Peter K's lucubration.

But, as always, a brief glance was enough to imprint the page on her mind.

> *St. Ylf, according to local tradition, was a hermit dwelling in a cave under Scafell who on numerous occasions emerged from mists and blizzards to guide lost travelers to safety. One of these, a footpad whose profession was to prey upon unwary strangers rather than help them, was so grateful for Ylf's help that on reaching the safety of Skaddale, he vowed to abandon his evil life and raise a church here. By the time the church was finished, stories of Ylf's virtue and miraculous rescues had resulted in his canonization and it seemed only fitting that the church be dedicated in his name.*
>
> *Architecturally, St. Ylf's has few conventional attractions, yet it has the beauty of the unique. It was built for one place, yet for all times, providing a rare opportunity*

for the modern Christian to make contact with the simple faith of his distant ancestors and marvel how their hard and often brutish lives did not prevent them from celebrating God's glory and affirming their deep trust in His mercy.

Sam's first thought when some twenty minutes later she rounded a bend and at last saw the church was that it wasn't deep trust in God's mercy it affirmed so much as serious doubts about His weather, particularly the wind which was suddenly buffeting her back like congratulation from an overenthusiastic friend. But it would need more than enthusiasm to move this broad squat building which clung grimly to the ground, its low blunt tower rising from a shallow pitched roof of dull gray slate like the head of an animal at bay, growling defiance. Its muddy brown side walls were pierced by three narrow windows more suited to shooting arrows out than letting light in.

The extensive churchyard was surrounded by a high wall constructed of irregular blocks of stone, or rather roughly shaped boulders bound together by flaking mortar in whose cracks a scurfy ivy had taken hold. To one side of the wall stood a large ugly house, presumably the vicarage. She walked up to the huge wrought-iron gate which looked as if it had come from a Victorian workhouse closing-down sale. It bore a sign inviting visitors to show due reverence on entering the church and due generosity on leaving it, a message reinforced by a peacock screech from the hinges as she pushed it open and stepped into the churchyard.

A forest of headstones rose from close-trimmed turf, and the gardeners were here too, half a dozen sheep, not the snowy Merinos of home, but small sturdy beasts with fleece as gray as the sky they grazed under.

She strolled among the memorials, examining the inscriptions. Infant deaths abounded in the earlier centuries but began to diminish in the twentieth. There were plenty of family groupings, some going back forever, including a long roll-call of Swinebanks with at least one *priest of this parish* every half-century. This got pretty close to the kind of hereditary priest-ship they had at some of the old pagan shrines. Lots of Peters alternating with lots of Pauls. Peter K, the author of the *Guide* had made it to 1939, so he got one war in but missed the other. The next priest (this one a Paul) had died in 1969. Was the present guy yet another Swinebank? Real cozy.

The most elegant headstones in every century belonged to a family called Winander, but when it came to size they had to give best to what looked like a small fortress of black marble, as if someone had felt the peace of the grave was literally worth defending. It marked what must be the very crowded tomb of the Woollass family, the local squires mentioned by Mrs. Appledore, whose own name figured frequently, though Sam couldn't spot a Buckle.

And no sign anywhere of a Flood.

But there was evidence that this was an active graveyard. As she rounded the black fortress she saw ahead of her, near the left-hand wall, a pile of earth as if some giant mole had been at work. A few more steps brought into view the angle of an open grave, sharp and black against the green turf.

Then her heart contracted and she stopped in her tracks as a figure rose out of the dank earth.

It took only a moment to recognize the obvious, that this was the gravedigger who'd been stooping low to remove a large stone which he now deposited on the side.

This done, he straightened up to wipe his brow and looked straight at her.

If his appearance had given her a start, hers seemed to return the shock with interest. He froze with the back of his hand at his forehead, giving the impression of a mariner shading his eyes from the sun as he peered over the bow in search of land. But the expression on his face suggested it was a fearsome reef he saw.

She gave him what she intended as a reassuring smile and moved on toward the church door. Here she glanced his way again and saw he was still staring at her. He was a man in his fifties, square-built and muscular, with a leathery face that looked as if a drunken taxidermist had been stuffing an English bulldog and then given up. But that unblinking gaze belonged to some creature far less cozy than a mere bulldog.

Sam didn't bother with another smile. Why waste it? This felt like the kind of place where not only did they stare at strangers, they probably pointed at the sky whenever a plane flew overhead.

She raised the old-fashioned latch and pushed the door open. Like the gate, its opening was accompanied by a sound effect, this time a groan straight out of a horror movie. Hadn't oil reached Illthwaite yet?

She stepped inside.

When God said let there be light, He must have forgotten St. Ylf's. It was so gloomy in here she had to pause a moment to let her eyes adapt. When murk began to coalesce into form, she found herself standing by a font consisting of a granite block out of which a basin had been scooped deep enough for an infant to drown in. Around its rough-hewn sides a not incompetent artist had carved a frieze of spasmodic dancers doing a conga behind a hooded figure carrying a scythe.

You live in the valley of the shadow, must seem like a good idea to let your kids see early what lies in wait for them, thought Sam. To her left was the space beneath the tower which seemed to be used as a kind of storeroom. The back wall was lined with dusty stacks of hassocks and hymn books, perhaps a reminder of days when the vicar expected a full house at every service. A rickety-looking ladder led up to a trapdoor which stood open, revealing the scudding clouds and admitting just enough light to make the shadowy church even more sinister.

She turned away to face down the aisle where the Gothic experience continued.

At the far end within the chancel on a pair of wooden trestles stood a coffin.

She set off toward it, trainers slapping against the granite floor. As she got nearer, she slowed. This was getting to be too much.

The coffin lid was drawn back to reveal the face of the corpse within.

It was a young face, pretty well de-sexed by death. She looked at the brass plate on the lid. It read *William Knipp—in the seventeenth year of his age.*

Poor sod. He died young.

She thought she heard a noise behind her and turned abruptly.

Nothing.

But there was the sound again. Her keen ear tracked it to the porch, or rather the store space beyond, beneath the tower. She walked back down the aisle and looked up at the open trap. The sky didn't seem quite so dark now.

She called, "Hello! Anyone there?"

Though there was no reply, it felt like there was someone up there, listening.

"Hi," she called. "Sorry to trouble you, but I could do with some help."

Still nothing. She was beginning to feel irritated. While she didn't have much time for priests and such, wasn't it part of their job description that they should be there for you when you needed them?

"OK," she called. "If you're too busy to come down, I'll come up."

Setting the *Guide* on the floor, she grasped the rough wood of the old ladder and began to climb.

She was a good climber, light, supple and nimble. Watching her rapid ascent of the big blue gum overshading the north side of the house at Vinada, her pa had said, "If I'd bought a monkey, I'd sell it."

It only took a few seconds to get to the top of the ladder,

though it felt longer. The higher she got, the more rickety it felt. She glanced down and the floor seemed further away than she would have guessed. Thank God I don't suffer from vertigo, she thought.

Unless vertigo began with a sudden petrifying sense of being *watched*!

The sooner she was off this ladder, the better. She reached her left hand up to get a grip on the floor of the tower.

And next moment the trap came crashing down.

She whipped her hand away, felt the frame graze her finger ends, lost her right hand's grip on the topmost rung of the ladder, and suddenly the floor which had seemed so far away was getting closer far too quickly.

As she fell she had a sense of a darker shadow against the cloudy gray square. Or rather, later she had a sense that she'd had a sense, but for the brief time being all she was registering was her fervent desire not to crash head first on to the unyielding granite slabs.

She knew about falling. She'd always been good on the trampoline. In fact they'd persuaded her to try competitive gymnastics at school, but she'd left the team when it got too serious. Even then she'd known the medals she wanted from life weren't to be got by bouncing. Now, however, all that twisting and turning looked like it might be useful.

First off, she tried a backward somersault to straighten herself up, but all it did halfway through was bring her in violent collision with the back wall.

This however turned out to be her salvation. Instead of sliding down it at great speed to make contact with the floor, she hit the stack of hassocks and hymn books piled there in anticipation of some future full house sellout. The hands of angels might have done a better job at bearing her up, but maybe this kind of divine intercession was the best an Aussie atheist could look for.

This was her last absurd thought before she hit the ground

with sufficient force to drive all the breath out of her lungs but not to kill her. An avalanche of hassocks and hymn books swept down after her, filling the air with swirling dust. She twisted round to protect her face from the holy debris and cried out as it clattered and bounced against her back. Fear of heights she didn't have, but most of her childhood nightmares had been associated with fear of being trapped in a constricted dark place.

The downslide seemed to go on forever. She felt as if she were being buried alive under a mountain of dusty books and cushions. And even when they stopped crashing upon her, through the roar of terrified blood rushing along her veins she seemed still to hear noises: creaking wood, steps, doors opening and shutting.

Till finally these too, whether imagined or real, died away, leaving her to something more frightening than any sound.

The silence of the dark.

4

The Wolf-Head Cross

Later Sam worked out she probably lay there only a matter of seconds, certainly less than a minute. Also that she could have dislodged the hymn books and hassocks simply by sitting up. But at the time it felt as if she lay there an age, fearful that the slightest movement would bring the whole weight of the tower crashing down upon her.

And finally a voice.

"Jesus Christ! Gerry, give me a hand. Miss Flood! Miss Flood! Are you all right?"

Someone was pulling the books and hassocks from her body. Someone who knew her name. Maybe it was God. Though surely the All-knowing wouldn't need to inquire after her health?

She squinted sideways and saw a pair of knees. Would God wear blue denim? She didn't care. She could see, not too clearly, but at least she was out of the dark.

"What happened?" she gasped.

"You fell. Stay still. Gerry, don't just stand there. Get some water."

Gerry? God's second son, maybe. Jesus and Gerry. Now she was being silly. On the other hand this Gerry did seem able to conjure up rain which was now falling in very welcome cool drops on her exposed cheek.

Her mouth felt dry as dust. She swallowed and realized that in fact her mouth was full of dust. She needed to get some of this delicious liquid down her throat. She struggled to turn her face upward.

"No! Don't move till we get help."

Right, of course. She should lie still until experts had assessed the extent of damage and how best to proceed without causing more.

But even as this eminently sensible response was struggling along the self-repairing synapses of her brain, she was twisting round from prone to supine and flexing everything that she felt ought to be flexible.

"I'm OK," she gasped. "Water."

The source of the rain she now traced to a shallow silver platter from which Gerry the Son was flicking water with his finger. God the Blue-jeaned was still kneeling by her. She used his shoulder to haul herself into the sitting position, grabbed the salver, and drained what little water it still contained. Then with the instinct of a thirsty animal in the outback, she pushed herself upright, tottered to the font and buried her face in its cool dark pool. When her mouth was washed clean of dust, she cupped her hands and threw the water against her face and gasped with pleasure as it trickled down her body.

"This is good stuff," she said finally. "Does this mean I've been baptized? My pa will kill me."

The frivolity popped out as it often did at moments of high stress. Her rescuers didn't seem to find it funny.

God was a six-footer, broad-shouldered, barrel-chested, though the barrel showed signs of rolling downhill into a beer gut. Way back he must have been a craggy good looker, but now he was definitely the ancient of days, in his sixties she guessed, his weathered face lined and crinkled. But his eyes still sparkled a bright blue and his thatch of silvery hair was still touched here and there with starts of gold.

The other one, Gerry the rainmaker, was a bit younger,

mid-fifties maybe, his hair still black with only a slight frosting at the edges. His rather chubby face looked as if it could relax into a kind of koala attractiveness, but for now it was set in a blank from which his slatey eyes viewed her more like a strange animal who might be a threat than a young stranger who'd just had an accident. In contrast to God's sports shirt and jeans, he wore a dark suit and a collar and tie.

"I still think we should get you checked out," said God. "That was a nasty tumble you took."

"You saw it?" said Sam.

"No. I came in and saw you lying on the floor under all that crap. It didn't take Miss Marple to work out you must have fallen off the loft ladder, right?"

"It might have tested her to work out what my name was," said Sam.

Before he could reply, the porch door opened and another man came in, this one wearing a priest's cassock and collar. He too was in his fifties, medium height, slightly built, with a salt-and-pepper shag of hair, and a matching tangle of beard, which, if the moistly anxious brown eyes peering out above it were anything to go by, had been cultivated to conceal meekness rather than express aggression.

"Thor," he said. "And Gerry. Hello. What on earth's happened here?"

As he spoke his gaze swung rapidly from the pile of hassocks and hymn books on the floor to Sam, and stuck. His mouth opened and white teeth gleamed through his beard like the moon through a bramble bush in what may have been intended as a welcoming smile but came over more as a grimace.

The man called Thor (right name for a god, wrong religion, thought Sam) said, "I came down to make sure young Billy got screwed in properly. This young lady seems to have slipped off the tower ladder. You should get it fixed. It's a death trap."

"Oh dear. I'm so sorry. Are you all right, Miss . . . ?"

"Flood. Sam Flood," said Sam. "Yeah, I'm fine. Few bruises,

nothing broken. And I didn't slip. Someone slammed the trap shut on my fingers."

Something in what she said robbed the vicar of the power of response for a moment and when he got it back, it hardly seemed worth the effort.

"What . . . ? You're sure . . . ? Who would do such a thing . . . ? It hardly seems likely . . ."

While the vicar was wittering, God ran up the ladder with the casual ease of an ancient mariner and pushed open the trap.

"No one up here now," he declared. "Wind must have blown it shut."

He slid down, landing easily.

"You'd need a bloody gale!" protested Sam.

"Gales are what we get round here," said the man. "Did you actually see anyone?"

"No, not really," she admitted. "But I did hear something. And he had time to come down and get away . . ."

She moved away from the support of the font and was pleased to find she was pretty well back in control of her limbs. Standing under the once more open trap, she peered up at the clouds and recalled that sense of a presence just before it slammed shut. No features, just that frightening feeling of being at the focal point of a predatory stare . . .

"There was a guy outside digging a grave when I arrived," she said. "Was he still there when you arrived?"

She directed this at the man the vicar had called Thor.

"Laal Gowder? Yes, I had a word with him. Why?"

Because I thought it might be him who came in behind me and climbed up to the tower seemed even less sensible an answer than it had a moment ago.

"Just thought he might have seen someone," she said lamely.

"Coming out of the church, you mean? Well, I didn't see anyone. And you were coming up the path behind me, Gerry. You see anyone?"

"No," said the silent man. "Only Gowder."

He spoke the name as if it tasted foul on the tongue. Despite his apparent lack of enthusiasm for her own presence, Sam felt maybe they had something in common after all. She recalled that Mrs. Appledore had mentioned someone called Gerry Woollass. It came back to her. Not God's son, but the squire's son. Same thing round here, perhaps?

Despite beginning to have doubts about her interpretation of events, she wasn't quite ready yet to give up.

"He could have gone out that way," she said, pointing to another door in the wall opposite the main entrance.

"Sorry, no," said the vicar. "That's the Devil's Door."

"Sorry? What was that? The devil's door?"

"Yes. It opens north, which in the Middle Ages was regarded as the direction the devil would come from. In some churches the doorway was actually bricked up. Here at St. Ylf's we're not so superstitious. We merely keep ours locked."

The bramble bush smile flashed again, this time definitely a smile, signaling a joke.

Sam thought of checking the door but didn't. These old farts probably thought she was simply overreacting to the embarrassment of admitting that she, young, fit Sam Flood who held her year's record for scaling the uni's climbing wall, had fallen off a ladder. And they might be right!

She said, "Look, I'm sorry for the bother I've caused. Thanks for all your help."

"Glad to be of service," said God. "I'm Thor Winander, by the way. And this is Gerry Woollass."

Got you right, then, thought Sam, looking at the vicar who, rather reluctantly, said, "And I'm Peter Swinebank, vicar of this parish."

"Same as the guy who wrote the *Guide*? Which reminds me, it must be lying around here somewhere."

It was Woollass who spotted it. He picked it up, dusted it off and handed it back to her, taking the opportunity for a close inspection of her face as he did so.

"Good. Well, I'm glad that no real damage was done," said Swinebank rather stagily. "Once again my apologies. Now I really must get on. People will be arriving for the funeral soon . . ."

"Can I have a quick word first?" said Sam. "It was you I was looking for when I started climbing the ladder. Thing is, I think maybe my grandmother came from these parts. Don't know much else about her except that she made the trip out in spring 1960."

"The trip out where?" inquired Swinebank.

"Have you got cloth ears, Pete?" said Winander. "I should have thought even a deaf man would have picked up our young friend has come hopping along the yellow brick road from Oz."

"Oh, shoot," said Sam. "And all them elocution lessons my ma wasted money on. Anyway, Vicar, any chance you can help me?"

"I don't know," said Swinebank. "What was your grandmother's name?"

"Same as mine. Don't ask me why. It's a long story," she said. "Flood. Samantha Flood. I thought if it was a local family they might be mentioned in the church records."

The three men looked at each other.

"No," declared Rev. Pete. "To my best recollection there has never been a local family called Flood. Right, Thor? Gerry?"

The other two shook their heads.

"No?" said Sam. "Still, if maybe I could glance at your parish records . . ."

"I'm afraid that . . . when did you say she left? Spring 1960, was it?"

"That's right."

"You're sure of that? And that it was Illthwaite?" probed Swinebank.

"I'm sure of the date, and pretty positive it was Illthwaite or something like it."

"Thwaite is a common suffix in English place names," said

Swinebank. "As for the records, I fear we can't help you much there. You see, the church was broken into a few months back and everything valuable stolen. Fortunately the really old records are kept locked in a safe in the vicarage, but most of the postwar books vanished. But, as I say, I'm pretty sure there hasn't been a local family called Flood. Now I really must start getting organized for the funeral. Thor, I presume you've come to see to the coffin?"

"That's right. You can tell Lorna the memorial should be ready tomorrow."

"Excellent. Gerry, Lorna's so grateful you've agreed to say a few words about Billy. The sense of a community coming together is so important at a time like this."

The sense of a community coming close together was very much what Sam was getting. And maybe she was being neurotic, but she felt a sense of relief here too, as at a problem solved or at least sidelined.

She said, "I'll get out of your hair. Thanks again for your help. Have a nice day."

Not perhaps the most apt form of farewell to men about to screw down a coffin and get ready for a funeral, but if it confirmed them in their Pom prejudices that she was an uncouth young Aussie who stuck her nose in where she wasn't wanted and fell off ladders, that was OK by her.

Outside she saw that the gravedigger with the odd name—Laal Gowder, was it?—had disappeared, his job presumably completed. It was to be hoped so, as the church gate now screeched open to admit what were presumably the first of the mourners.

The wind had become intermittent, but a sudden gust strong enough to support Thor Winander's theory sent a chill down her body. She glanced down and realized that the soaking she'd given herself from the font had left her looking like an entrant in a wet T-shirt competition. Not a very strong entrant, in view of her shallow frontage, but hardly what a grieving family might want to encounter so close to the dead boy's grave.

She headed round the back of the church, thinking she might find another way out here. But when she put the building between herself and the road, she pulled up short.

Here, at the center of a quincunx formed with four yew trees which overshaded but did not overpower it, stood what must be the famous cross mentioned by Mrs. Appledore.

It was at least fifteen feet high. Its shaft was ornately carved with intricate knotwork patterns interspersed with panels depicting various human and animal forms. The most striking image, both because of the vigor of the carving and its position at the center of the wheelhead crosspiece, was a wolf's head. Its gaping jaws were wedged open by a sword, but the one huge visible eye seemed to glare straight down at Sam, tracking her hesitant approach, promising that this state of impotence was temporary.

She broke eye contact to look at the *Guide*. This informed her in measured prose that the cross was Viking of the ninth century. Like many similar crosses, it made use of old Norse mythology to convey the new Christian message. The Reverend Peter K. commended the craftsman's skill and gave a detailed interpretation of the symbols used.

The huge snake coiled around the lowest section of the shaft base devouring its own tail was at the same time Satan seducing Eve, and Jormungand, the great serpent which encircles Midgard in the northern legends, while the figure leaning out of a boat and beating the serpent's head with a hammer was both the thunder god, Thor, and Christ harrowing Hell. As for the wolf, this was the beast Fenrir, which the Nordic gods thought they had rendered impotent by setting a bridle round its neck and a sword in its jaws. Eventually, however, it would break loose to join in that destruction of the physical universe called by pagans Ragnarokk or the Twilight of the Gods, by Christians Judgment Day.

Whether this meant the wolf was a good or a bad thing wasn't all that clear.

There were two other problematic areas. One was a front panel from which the image had disappeared almost completely. This defacement, Peter K. theorized, probably occurred in 1571 when a group of iconoclasts toppled the Wolf-Head Cross. It lay in several pieces for nearly twenty years and it was only when it was repaired and re-erected that the second problematic inscription was discovered on the lowest vertical of the stepped base. The symbols revealed didn't look like anything else on the cross. A series of vertical lines with a stroke through them (runic? postulated Peter K.); an inverted V, and another with the lines slightly extended to form a disproportioned cross (Greek?); an oval with two wavy lines through it (hieroglyphic?); and a surround of swirls and whorls.

Sam was amused by the number and variety of "expert" interpretations: a prayer for the soul of a local bishop; a verse from a hymn to an Irish saint; a magical invocation.

That was always the trouble. Like some proofs in math, once you got started, the sky was the limit, but often it was finding the right place to start that was the big holdup.

Illthwaite, she told herself firmly, was a wrong start point. All she could hope was that the dark man at the Stranger House would let her enjoy a good night's sleep, then up in the morning and on to Newcastle.

And if there was nothing new there, then maybe it was time to follow Pa's example and let the dead take care of the dead.

With her back to the church she took a last look up at the Wolf-Head Cross. What had this remote and eerie place been like when those distant inhabitants had decided fifteen feet of carved granite was what they needed to make life comprehensible? Indeed, what had attracted them to settle in this dark and dreary valley in the first place?

Well, whatever it was, it looked like it had worked. Centuries later, and their descendants were still here, though maybe more under the earth than over it.

She shivered at the thought and forced her gaze away from the intricate scrollery of the carving which led you round and round into places you didn't want to go, and eventually, inevitably, back to the eye of the wolf. She checked out the high wall beyond for another exit gate but found none. What she did notice was that the sheep-grazed neatness and order which prevailed elsewhere was scutched here by an outcrop of briar and nettles and rosebay willowherb against a small section of the wall. As the gusting wind moved among this vegetation, out of the corner of her eye she got a brief impression of lines more regular than those provided by the curved stones with their tracery of mortar. She advanced beyond the cross and squatted to take a closer look.

The briar was studded with such ferocious hooks that she could see why the sheep avoided grazing here. It was hard enough for her to brush aside the veiling vegetation but she finally succeeded at the price of several scratches and stings.

Her reward was to discover her glimpse of regularity hadn't been delusive. On a huge base stone someone had carved a quatrain of verse, arranging it in a perfect square.

She read the first line and felt the ground tremble beneath her feet as though the ancient dead were turning in their long sleep.

Here lies Sam Flood

She steadied herself with one hand on the cool damp turf and blinked to bring the stone back into focus. Then she read on.

Here lies Sam Flood
Whose nature bid him
To do much good.
Much good it did him.

Nothing else. No date, no pious farewell, not even an RIP.

She stood up and watched as the wind rearranged the briars and nettles till the carving was once more invisible.

She thought she heard a noise and turned quickly. She was sure she glimpsed a movement on the tower. Well, almost sure. That bloody tower could easily become an obsession. She certainly wasn't going to interrupt the funeral service to take a look. Probably it was pure fancy, and the sound had come from the stomach of a nearby sheep.

But suddenly the cross, the four dark yews, the crouching building, were an insupportable burden.

She hurried round the side of the church and up the path to the gate.

As she reached it, suddenly there was a burst of sound from behind, the voices of what must be a large congregation upraised in a hymn. There didn't seem to be any musical accompaniment but she could make out the words quite clearly.

Day of wrath! O day of mourning!
See fulfilled the prophet's warning!
Heav'n and earth in ashes burning!

Above the church, the wind was shredding the veil of low cloud, and now at last she saw the mountains, much closer than she'd imagined.

The church crouched like a guard dog on their skirts. Back home she'd seen country much wilder and mountains twice as high, but nowhere had she ever felt so out of place.

She turned away and began the long trudge back to the Stranger House.

5

A nice straight country road

The weather had improved considerably when Mig Madero came out of the pub. Gaps were appearing in the clouds and westward the sun was setting in a wash of pink against which the intervening heights lay in sharp silhouette.

He took his laptop off the back seat, plugged it into his mobile, got online and checked his e-mail. He had one message from his mother, reminding him to keep in touch. Realizing he was now past his forecast time of arrival in Illthwaite, he keyed a brief equivocating line saying he had safely arrived in Cumbria. Then he wrote an e-mail to Professor Coldstream.

> Max, thanks for suggesting Southwell—everything you promised—good and bad! Ever hear of a man called Molloy? Some sort of journalist, up here asking questions about Father Simeon a few years back, possibly in connection with a book on Topcliffe and his associates e.g. F. Tyrwhitt. Talking of whom, anything new from your man Lilleywhite in Yorkshire? Off to Illthwaite now. Mig.

His messages despatched, he brought up the map, which confirmed what he knew, that Skaddale with its village of

Illthwaite lay on the far side of those silhouetted heights. The most direct route seemed to be via the next township of Ambleside to a village called Elterwater from which ran what looked like a nice straight country road. With luck, he might at last be able to let the SLK really express itself.

Half an hour later he was beginning to understand why the haddock had been so good. God, being just, had clearly decided that the journey would be expiation enough.

The only traffic he'd met was a slow tractor, but that had been on such a narrow twisty bit of road that overtaking was quite impossible. Nor did things improve when finally the man pulled in at a farm gate. The anticipated long straight empty stretches where he could gun the engine didn't materialize. The road wound onward and upward, so far upward that, despite the clearing skies he'd observed earlier, he found himself running into a patchwork of mist whose threads finally conjoined into an all-enveloping quilt. Full headlights bounced back off the shrouding whiteness. Dipped headlights showed just enough of the road to permit a crawling advance.

Then the road began to go downhill and he thought the worst was over. So much for these so-called mountains, if such low heights deserved the term. Wasn't there another word they used up here? Fells, that was it. Not mountains but fells. A modest little word for modest little eminences.

But even as he relaxed, the road began to climb again. Ten minutes later, as the curves became zigzags and an ever-increasing angle of ascent meant that from his low seat he spent as much time looking up at the sky as down at the road, he recalled his mother's reaction when he'd bought the sporty Merc. She'd objected to almost everything about it but hadn't mentioned he might find himself driving on worse roads than he'd encountered in the Sierra Nevada. God must be really pissed with him!

Soon he was back in the mist. Things weren't helped by the fact that many sheep seemed to regard this twisting ribbon of tarmac as their own personal mattress. Nor were they in a hurry to get out of his way. Slowly they'd rise, stare at him resentfully for a long moment, then step aside with no sign of haste. Some even took a step or two toward the car first and struck an aggressive hoof against the ground.

Dear God, if the sheep were like this round here, how did real wild animals react?

Then at last he was on the flat for a short space before the road began to descend. It was still twisty and narrow and steep but the lower he got, the thinner the mist got, till suddenly he was completely free of it. Above he could see a sky crowded with stars and, even more comfortingly, below he could glimpse the occasional twinkle of house lights.

Soon he was running along a valley bottom, the road still narrow and bendy but at least it was flanked by walls and hedgerows which kept livestock in their proper domain. He met a couple of other cars and, despite the inconvenience of having to back fifty yards at one point to enable safe passage, he was glad of their company. When he saw the brightly lit windows and well-filled car park of a small hotel, he was tempted to turn in. But a glance at his screen told him he was close to his destination now and he pressed on.

The next road to the right should take him into Skaddale. He almost missed it, but was driving slowly enough to be able to brake and turn. There was no signpost but as his map showed no other turnoff for miles, this had to be the one.

After a few minutes his certainty was fading. The road soon grew narrow and serpentine and though he had no sense of rising terrain, he found that once more skeins of mist were winding themselves around his windows. He began to wish he had succumbed to the lure of the brightly lit hotel. To make matters worse, he had begun to experience that strong sense of ghostly presence as he drove up the valley. He resisted it—the last thing a man driving along a narrow road in a mist wanted was the company of ghosts—but the price of resistance was the onset of a bad migraine. It was as if the mist had somehow got into his head where it swirled around wildly, occasionally pierced by dogtooth lines of brightness like the after impression of a lightbulb's filament. The laptop screen was going crazy too. It was all jags of light and swirls of color, no longer a map, at least not a map of any place you wanted to be. He switched it off. It didn't help.

In the end he had to pull up. He felt sick. He lowered the window and leaned forward to rest his forehead against the cool windscreen. He could hear the noise of rushing water, and of wind gusting through trees. And now as his headache eased, there was something else in the wind . . . voices . . . angry voices . . . calling . . . threatening . . . and something . . . someone . . . running in panic . . . cold air tearing at his lungs as weary muscles drove him up the steep slope in his effort to outpace the relentless chasers . . .

This was worse than migraine. He tried to will the headache back. It would not come. But there was pain very close. He could feel it. Very very close . . .

Mig in the car could not move. But there was part of him out there with the fugitive, feeling the cold air tearing at his lungs, branches lashing across his face, runnels of muddy water sucking at his feet . . .

And then he was down . . . stumbling over an exposed root, he crashed to the ground and looked up at the bole of a blasted tree, looming menacingly out of the mist.

And then they were all around him, feet kicking at him, hands clawing him and hoisting him off the ground and binding ropes tightly around his chest and stomach, till he hung from the ruined tree.

For a moment, there was respite.

In the car Mig felt that one last supreme effort would regain the power of movement.

But now came the pain. In his hands, in his feet, not just the familiar prickling, not even the sharp pangs experienced on the few occasions he'd actually bled, but real, piercing, unbearable pain, as if broad blunt nails were being driven through his palms and his ankles . . .

He screamed and threw back his head and tried to fall into blackness away from this agony.

And in the same moment, the pain fled, he opened his eyes and looked up through the windscreen of the Mercedes at a bright and starry sky with not a trace of mist to be seen.

And when he lowered his gaze he saw ahead of him, about fifty yards away, a building with windows aglow and a sign which bore the silhouette of a hooded figure and the words *The Stranger House.*

6

Pillow problems

At eight that evening, Sam descended the creaky stairs of the pub.

On her walk back from the church, her irrational fear had turned to rational anger. Why hadn't Rev. Pete or those other two antiques mentioned the hidden stone bearing her name? Two possible answers . . . no; three. Either they didn't know about it, or they knew about it but were certain it had nothing to do with her, or they knew it had something to do with her but preferred she stayed ignorant.

The first seemed unlikely. It was Swinebank's church; Woollass was the local squire—sorry—squire's son; as for Thor Winander, he gave the impression he'd know everything round here.

The second was the simplest explanation. It was an old inscription that they knew could have nothing to do with her family. Fair enough, though it didn't look all that old, not antique anyway like some of the not dissimilar lettering on the old headstones.

As for the third, that was less likely but more troublesome.

One thing was sure, before she left she needed an explanation. But she'd give them every chance to volunteer one before she started throwing punches.

This decision made, she lay on her bed for ten minutes, which when she opened her eyes had turned into three hours, giving the chance for the shoulder and hip which had borne the brunt of her fall to stiffen up and turn an interesting shade of aubergine.

She headed for the bathroom opposite her bedroom door. The water was piping hot and the old-fashioned bath deep enough to float in. A long soak eased the worst of her stiffness, and now she realized she was very hungry.

At the top of the stairs she heard voices below at the entrance end of the shadowy hallway. Alerted by the unavoidable creakings, the speakers stopped. Then one of the figures moved into the dim light and said, "Here she is now. You can ask her yourself."

It was Mrs. Appledore. And the man she was talking to was Gerry the Son.

"We've just been talking about your accident, dear," said the landlady, her pleasant round face touched with concern. "How're you feeling now?"

"I'm good," said Sam. "No problem, really."

The pub had been empty when she returned and she'd worked out that Mrs. Appledore must have been one of the funeral congregation singing that cheerful hymn.

"That's good to hear," said Woollass. "We were all very concerned."

He sounded sincere enough and his gaze felt less like that of an angler examining a strange fish than it had in the church.

"No need," she said. "Thanks again for your help."

Not that it had amounted to much but, like Pa said, always be polite till you've got good reason not to be.

"Excellent. I hope you enjoy the rest of your stay. Now, I must be off. You'll remember my message, Edie?"

"Ten, not nine-thirty. I think I can just about manage that, Gerry. My best to your dad. It's a long time since we saw him down here."

"He feels very susceptible to cold drafts these days," said Woollass.

"Does he? Well, tell him the only cold drafts he'll find here is the beer," retorted the landlady. "Goodnight now."

As the door closed behind Woollass, she turned to Sam and smiled.

"He's a good man, Gerry, but diplomacy's not his strong point."

"He didn't come here just to inquire after my health, did he?" asked Sam.

"No. He wanted to leave a message, though as you heard it wasn't much of a message. But he was very concerned about you. That's Gerry all over. As someone said, he's got such a bleeding heart, you can hear it squelching when he breathes."

"That wouldn't be Mr. Winander, would it?"

Mrs. Appledore laughed out loud.

"You're the sharp one, aren't you? Of course you met him up at the church."

"That's right. He was very kind. So what's he do for a living?"

"Winanders have been blacksmiths and general craftsmen in the village since way back. Thor's branched out, but. Does arty stuff. And he's a real salesman, so take care. Now you'll be wanting something to eat, I expect. Unless you're planning on going out?"

Memory of the caustic cob had made Sam consider driving down to the fancy-priced hotel in search of dinner, but answers to her questions lay here.

She said, "Yeah, I'm hungry enough to eat shoe leather. What have you got?"

"Anything you like so long as it's sausage or ham."

"Sausage sounds great."

"OK. In you go. I reserved a table for you. I'd better get back behind the bar before the natives get restless."

The ringing of the bar bell and cries of "Shop!" had already been audible from the bar, but all sound stopped for a moment as Sam pushed open the door and stepped inside.

The room was crowded but a path opened up for her leading to a small round table with a handwritten *Reserved* sign draped across an ashtray, and the noise resumed as she sat down. She'd brought the Reverend Peter K.'s *Guide* with her, but before she could open it a pint glass was slammed on the table. She looked up to find Thor Winander smiling down at her.

"A belated welcome to Illthwaite, Miss Flood," he said. "Glad to see you looking so spry after your adventure."

"You're looking pretty spry yourself, considering, Mr. Winander," she replied.

He laughed, showing good strong teeth, and said, "I won't ask, considering what? I'm sorry your family inquiries came to a dead end."

"One man's dead end can be someone else's starting point," she said.

He looked at her speculatively. She met his gaze square on. He wasn't totally unattractive for a geriatric, and he still had a certain Viking swagger to go with his name.

Thought of names made her ask, "You never told me how you knew what I was called. I'd guess you'd been talking to Mrs. Appledore. Right?"

"Quite right. I ran into her and naturally an exotic stranger in our little village was quite a news item. In Edie's defense, I daresay she's been just as forthcoming about me."

"Well, she did say you were a bit of an artist."

"I won't ask what kind," he grinned. "But it's certainly true that few visitors to our fair village escape without paying due tribute to my talents. I look forward to seeing you in my studio before you go. In fact, let's make a date. Tomorrow morning, shall we say?"

"What makes you think I'm in the market for art?"

"What makes you think I'm talking about art?"

Jesus, the old fart was flirting! Did he really think his pillaging and ravishing days weren't altogether behind him?

Perhaps her disbelief showed, for his tone changed from

teasing to something well short of but in the general area of pleading as he said, "It would be good if you could call in. I'm at the Forge, across the bridge and up Stanebank. Enjoy your drink, my dear."

She watched him make his way to a bench by the window where he sat down next to a man Sam recognized as the menacing gravedigger. Or she thought she recognized him till her gaze moved to a third man on the bench, and there he was again.

Her eyes flickered between the two. Same face, same clothes, and the same blank animal stare which though it seemed unfocused she felt was fixed on herself. Twins? Certainly brothers. Bad enough giving birth to one who looked like that, she thought unkindly, but you must really piss fate off to get landed with two!

And now it occurred to her that if there were two, it didn't matter if the gravedigger was still clearly visible outside while she was falling off that bloody ladder. It could have been his mirror image whose petrifying gaze she had felt up on the tower!

Something else to look into. But not here, not now. Here she was the solitary young woman, eating alone. Don't fight it, go with it.

She picked up the *Guide*. It fell open at the last page she'd looked at, the section on the Wolf-Head Cross. She studied a reproduction of the panel showing the god Thor in his boat. It wasn't a detailed portrait but there was a definite resemblance to Winander. She squinted down at the picture and sipped her beer thoughtfully. It was good stuff, slipping down so easily she'd almost got through the pint without noticing.

As if her thought was a command, another glass was set before her.

She looked up to see not the aged Viking but the superannuated leprechaun who'd warned her against Illthwaite.

"Good evening, Miss Flood," he said, his high clear voice pitched low. "I hope you will accept a drink from me in token of apology for any unintentional rudeness I may have shown to you at lunchtime. I should have remembered the scriptures: *Be not forgetful to entertain strangers, for thereby some have entertained angels unawares.*"

"That's nice," she said. "But I wasn't offended. And I'm certainly no angel."

"Angels come in many guises and for many purposes," he said. He didn't smile as he said it but spoke with an earnest sincerity which made her recall Mrs. Appledore's warning that he was a snag short of a barbie.

"I hope you have recovered from your accident in the church," he said.

"Yes, I'm good," she said, thinking, cracked he may be, but he doesn't miss much!

His eyes had strayed down to the open book on the table.

"You are interested in antiquities?" he said.

"In a way," she said. "I was reading about the Wolf-Head Cross."

"Ah yes. The Wolf-Head. Our claim to historical significance. But if you want to find out something of the true nature of Illthwaite, you should read about our other Wolf-Head Cross. Try the chapter on Myth and Legend. But never forget you are in a part of the world where they hold an annual competition for telling lies."

He moved away to what seemed to be his accustomed seat almost out of sight behind the angle of the fireplace.

Her curiosity pricked, she riffled through the pages till she came to a section headed *Folklore, Myth, Legend* which she began reading at her usual breakneck speed.

After an introduction in which the three topics were defined and carefully differentiated, the writer conceded:

> *Yet so frequently do these areas overlap and merge, with invented and historical figures becoming confused, and events which properly belong to the timeless world of the fairies receiving the imprimatur of particular dates and locations, that it is almost as*

dangerous to dismiss any story as wild fancy as it would be to accept all that is related round the crackling fire of the Stranger House on a winter's night as gospel truth. What more likely than that a pious farmer riding home after a night of wassail and ghost stories should mistake a swirl of snowflakes round the churchyard for the restless spirit of some recently deceased villager? When it comes to sharing real and personal concerns with strangers, Cumbrians are a close and secret people, but in launching flights of fancy dressed as fact they have few equals, as those who had the pleasure of meeting the late Mr. Ritson of Wasdale Head can well testify.

As described supra, *in the designs on our great Viking cross can be found a fascinating use of ancient fables to underline and illustrate the awful and sacred truths of Christianity. Had Dr Johnson paused on his journey to the Caledonian wildernesses to view our Wolf-Head Cross, he might have modified his strictures on* Lycidas.

Yet the great doctor was right in asserting that truth and myth may be combined in a manner both impious and dangerous. So in the story of that other cross, which some in their superstitious folly also called "Wolf-Head," we find fact and fiction close tangled in a knot it would take the mind of Aristotle or the sword of Alexander to dismantle.

Here is that story as it is still recounted in the parish, with slight variation and embellishment, according to the nature of the narrator and the perceived susceptibility of the auditor. Be advised, it is not a tale for the faint-hearted . . .

Then her view of the book was interrupted by a large plate and Mrs. Appledore's voice said, "There we go, dear. Tuck in."

Sam smiled her thanks at the woman, then lowered her eyes to the plate and felt the full force of the Reverend's warning. Here was something else definitely not for the faint-hearted. Reminding her of the Wolf-Head Cross carving of Jormungand, the fabled Midgard serpent coiled around the world, on her plate a single monstrous sausage, uninterrupted by twist or crimp, curled around a mountain of chips topped by a fried egg. There had to be enough cholesterol here to give a god or a hero a heart attack. She took a long pull at her beer while she contemplated how to get to grips with it.

Another pint glass was set before her. She looked up to see the old Viking again.

"Thanks, but I've got plenty."

"Perhaps. But I think you'll need a lot more to wash that down," he said. "As we say round here, best way is to pick an end and press on till tha meets tha own behind."

This seemed an impossible journey but she was very hungry and after the first visual shock, she found it smelled quite delicious, so she sawed half an inch off the sausage's tail and put it into her mouth. Fifteen minutes later she was wiping up the last of the egg yolk with the last of the chips. She'd even essayed the merest fork-point of flavoring from a jar of the mordant mustard and found it not displeasing.

She was also nearly at the bottom of her third pint. It really was good beer. It was also beer she hadn't paid for and by the strict rules of the society she'd grown up in, girls who didn't stand their round were signifying their willingness to make some other form of payment. She looked toward the shady corner but there was no sign of Mr. Melton. Winander was still there between the duplicated gravediggers.

She emptied her glass, stood up and went to the bar.

"Ready for pudding?" said Mrs. Appledore.

Shuddering to think how big her puddings might be, Sam said, "No. I'm a bit knackered after all that driving so I think I'll hit the hay. Mr. Melton's gone, has he?"

"Only to the Gents. Why?"

"I just wanted to buy him a drink, that's all. And Mr. Winander too. Put one in the till for them both, will you? And stick it on my bill."

"Of course, dear," said the landlady approvingly. "Us girls need to stand our corner these days."

"We surely do. Talking of which, don't us girls come out to drink round here?"

"Sometimes, but tonight they'll be sitting with Lorna—that's the mam of young Billy Knipp that we buried today. The men leave 'em to it. Sorry if it bothered you, dear."

"Men don't bother me, Mrs. Appledore," said Sam.

"That's all right then," said the landlady. "I never asked you, did you find anything out at the church? About your family, I mean?"

Was this a good moment to ask about the inscription? No, Sam decided. But it might be a good moment to give everyone here the chance to volunteer information.

She said, "No, nothing. Look, as a final fling, would it be all right if I spoke to this lot in the bar, asked them if anyone recalled a family called Flood in these parts?"

Mrs. Appledore glanced assessingly at the assembled drinkers then said, "Why not? It'll make a change from the price of sheep."

She reached up and rang the bell dangling over the end of the bar.

"Listen in, you lot. Let's have a bit of order. This young lady from Australia who's staying with us tonight, she'd like to ask a question about her family. Miss Flood . . ."

Suddenly, looking at all those expectant faces, this didn't seem such a good idea, but if you're stupid enough to go surfing on a shark, you don't let go.

"Hi. Sorry to disturb your drinking, but my name's Sam Flood and it could be that my grandmother who was also called Sam, that's Samantha, Flood came from Illthwaite. It would be back in the spring of 1960 she left. I just wondered if any of you who were around back then could recall anyone of that name round here."

There. Cue for deluge of information. Long pause.

Then a voice, upstage, left. "Weren't there a Larry Flood up Egremont way, used to win the gurning at the Crab Fair wi'out needing to pull a face?"

Second voice, upstage right. "Nay, tha's thinkin' of Harry Hood."

Chorus. "Aye, Harry Hood. That were Harry Hood."

Why was she thinking of this in terms of theater? Sam asked herself.

Because that's how it felt. Like a performance.

"If any of you do recall owt, let me know to pass it on," declared Mrs. Appledore.

The hubbub resumed as she turned to Sam and said, "Sorry, dear."

"No problem," said Sam. "What's gurning?"

"It's making ugly faces through a horse's collar. There's a competition for it at the Egremont Crab Fair. Thought everyone knew that."

"I must have forgotten," said Sam. "A prize for being ugly? Is that where they give prizes for telling lies too?"

"No," said the landlady indignantly. "That's not Egremont. That's at Santon Bridge. Thought everyone knew that too."

"My memory!" said Sam. "I'm off to bed now."

"Hope you sleep well. Don't worry about laying over. The way these boards creak, I'll hear you when you're up."

"Great. By the way, Mrs. Appledore, I don't think I'll be wanting anything cooked in the morning. Way I feel now, a fox's breakfast will do me fine."

"A fox's breakfast? And that 'ud be . . . ?"

"A piss and a good look round. Thought everyone knew that."

Be polite to the Poms. But don't let the buggers get on top of you. Pa's last words at the airport.

We're keeping our end up so far, Pa, she thought as she headed out of the door.

Mr. Melton, presumably just returned from the Gents, was in the hallway.

"Goodnight," she said. "Thanks for the beer. I've left you one in the till."

"No need," he said. "But kind. I understand you are seeking for some local connection with your family."

"That's right. I thought my gran might be from these parts, but I'm beginning to think I might have got it wrong."

He said, "And when did she leave England?"

"March 1960. She was still a kid."

"A kid? In 1960?" He looked at her doubtfully.

He might be dotty but he could still do arithmetic, she thought approvingly.

"Yeah, I know," she said. "She got pregnant not long after she arrived in Oz. My dad was born in September 1961."

"I see," he said. "Interesting. But I'm keeping you from your bed, and this isn't the place to talk. If you care to drop in on me tomorrow, Miss Flood, perhaps I can assist you with your inquiries."

For some reason the phrase seemed to amuse him and he repeated it.

"Yes, assist you with your inquiries. I have . . . connections. I live at Candle Cottage, beyond the church. I'm at home most of the time. Goodnight to you now."

He went back into the bar.

Funny folk! thought Sam as she climbed the stairs. Two invites in a night. Maybe that was the automatic next step if you survived being pushed off a ladder! Anything was possible in a place where Death had his own door, the sausages were six feet long, and they held competitions for telling lies and making faces through a horse's collar . . .

She pushed open her bedroom door and all thought of funny folk fled from her mind.

Someone had been poking around her things. This wasn't feeling but fact. Her eidetic memory didn't only work with the printed page. A postcard home she'd been scribbling was a couple of inches to the left of where she'd set it down on the dressing table, one of the drawers which had protruded slightly was now completely flush, and her rucksack leaned against the wall at an altered angle. And it wasn't just Mrs. Appledore tidying up. The intruder had clearly been inside the rucksack as well as out.

She thought of going downstairs to make a fuss. But there was nothing missing, and anyone in the bar could have come up, or someone who just came into the pub.

She brushed her teeth, got undressed, pulled on the old Melbourne University T-shirt she slept in, and climbed on to the high old-fashioned bed. Usually she launched herself into sleep on a sea of math. She'd started age seven with an old edition of a book called *Pillow Problems* which Gramma Ada had picked up in a secondhand shop. In it the guy who wrote the *Alice* books laid out a variety of calculations he occupied his mind with when he couldn't sleep. By the time she was twelve she'd moved beyond Carroll's problems, but the principle remained. Nowadays she usually played with things like Goldbach's Conjecture which required her to hold huge numbers in her head.

Tonight, however, she turned to the measured nineteenth-century prose of Peter K. Swinebank in search of a soporific.

She found the page she'd reached in the bar and reread the last line:

Be advised, it is not a tale for the fainthearted.

Sam paused and consulted her heart. No sign of faintness there, though a little lower down there was an awareness that sometime in the not too distant future her consumption of all that excellent beer was going to require another trip to the bathroom.

"OK, Rev. Peter K. Swinebank," she said. "I'm ready for you. Do your worst!"

And turned the page.

7

The waif boy

Some time toward the end of the sixteenth century, a waif boy was taken into the care of the Gowders of Foul-gate Farm whose descendants still live and work in the valley.

The boy's age is variously reported as from twelve to sixteen and his origins have been just as widely speculated. Some suggested he was the bastard child of one of the local gentry, kept locked away from public gaze for shame these many years till finally he escaped. Equally popular was the notion that he was a child abducted by the fairies in infancy and returned when puberty rendered him of no further interest to the little people. Some even asserted that he was Robin Goodfellow himself. Such theories at least have the merit of facing up to the supernatural elements of the legend without equivocation.

To my mind the most likely explanation (supported by references to his swarthy coloring and lack of English) is that this youth was in fact a scion of that strange nomadic group misnamed Egyptians who had become increasingly prevalent in Britain during the past hundred years. Perhaps he had been ejected from his tribe because of some fraction of their strange and pagan law. Being young, he was likely to be much more fluent in the Romany tongue than in the English vernacular.

Where all versions agree is that, by taking him in, the Gowders displayed an unwonted degree of Christian charity. Though since somewhat declined, in those days the Gowders of Foulgate were by local standards a well-to-do and powerful family. They were not however famed for their generosity of spirit and their position in the parish seems to have been achieved as much by force of will and arms as agricultural skill.

At the time of our story, the head of the family was Thomas Gowder, a man of about thirty, whose young wife, Jenny, after three years of marriage had yet to provide him with an heir. Also living at Foulgate was Andrew, Thomas's brother, three years his junior, with his wife and two infant sons.

It is maliciously suggested by some that, in taking the waif boy in, the Gowders were inspired less by charity than the prospect of acquiring an unpaid farmhand. Whatever the truth, they paid dearly for it. After some months of living at Foulgate and being nursed back to health, the youth repaid this kindness one night by assaulting Jenny. On being interrupted by her husband, he wrestled the man to the ground and slit his throat from ear to ear, almost severing the head from the neck. Brother Andrew, hearing the sound of the struggle, called to ask what was amiss, upon which the murderous gypsy seized whatever of value he could lay his hands on and fled.

Drew Gowder roused the village, procured help for his sister-in-law, then got together a posse of villagers to go in pursuit of the fugitive.

It was that time of year when spring though close on the calendar seems an age away on the ground. The night was black, the weather foul, good conditions for an outlaw to make his escape. But the pursuers knew their valley stone by stone while the fugitive was a stranger, driven by guilt and panic. His blundering trail up the fell-

side above Foulgate was easy to follow and within a very short time they cornered him attempting to hide in Mecklin Shaw, a small oak wood on the edge of Mecklin Moss.

Trapped, he offered no resistance and they would have bound him and taken him back to the village, but Drew Gowder was so inflamed with grief and rage that he demanded summary justice. A blasted oak stood close by, most of it decayed and fallen away, but what remained was the solid bole, its jagged upper edge in silhouette taking the form of a beast's gaping maw, with the stumps of two branches giving the loose impression of a cross. Pointing to this, Gowder declared that when God provided the means, he was not inclined to reject His bounty. When they understood his meaning, it is to be hoped that some of the others demurred. But Gowder was a strong man, and a deeply wronged man, and it should be remembered that, while the framework of our Common Law was well established, yet in such remote communities as this, the tradition of self-sufficient and local justice was very strong, as indeed it remains to this very day.

So they seized the fugitive murderer and bound him to the blasted tree. At the same time, Gowder had taken himself to a nearby charcoal-burner's hovel and there gathered several scraps of fire-hardened wood which he rapidly shaped into small stakes a few inches long. Then, using the haft of his dagger as a hammer, he drove these stakes through the young man's hands and feet before cutting away the binding ropes, thus leaving him hanging from the tree by those wooden nails alone.

Satisfied with his handiwork, he now led his companions out of the wood and they made their way back to the village, leaving the murderer to die.

That appetite for the macabre still existent in our own day and catered for by the new literature of sensation and the Police Gazette *was at its ravening height in an age when our greatest poet could soil his pen with the foulness of* Titus Andronicus, *and to this we owe the illustrative woodcut of the event reproduced overleaf, which was attached to a broadside ballad allegedly composed by one of the posse.*

(Readers of tender stomach are advised not to raise the veiling tissue.)

Recognizing a come-on when she saw one, Sam turned the page and lifted the sheet of almost opaque tissue paper covering the woodcut. It wasn't pretty, though why one whose profession abounded with images of a man nailed to a cross should have feared that his readers' sensibilities might be offended she couldn't understand. Indeed, it wasn't the crucified man who took the eye, but the representation of the blasted stump to which he was nailed. It was engraved with a vigor that made it look as if its shattered branches were embracing the figure hanging there and drawing into their ripped bark the life that ebbed out of that pierced flesh, while above the executed man the jagged wood metamorphosed into the head of a wolf thrown back to howl in triumph at the moon.

She let the tissue fall and read on.

So far we have a story in which the bare bones of truth are easily detectable. That there was a murder we need not doubt. The grave of Thomas Gowder is still viewable at St. Ylf's, its stela bearing the ambiguous words most foully slain by unknown hand. *And after the murder it is certain a hue and cry was raised and a fugitive cornered in Mecklin Shaw where the enraged Andrew took upon himself the roles of jury, judge and executioner. But now matters become mysterious.*

During that evening the tale of such events would naturally have circulated widely among the community and early next day the parson of St. Ylf's led a large group of villagers back to Mecklin Shaw to recover the crucified man. We have the parson's own account of what it was they found, which in fact was nothing, or rather no one. Some stains there were on the blasted oak which might have been human blood, and some holes which might have been made by wooden nails. But of the fugitive murderer's person, living or dead, they found no trace. Baffled, they returned to the village where neither prayer in the church nor speculation in the alehouse produced any rational solution other than that the man had somehow freed himself and crawled off into the night, only to be consumed by Mecklin Moss which had once, according to tradition, swallowed up whole a horse and cart and the drunken carter who was driving it.

Myself, I think it more probable that Andrew Gowder, as the murderous rage in him declined, began to reflect more coolly on what he had done. As stated supra *while certainly the age was more violent than our own, yet this was by no means a lawless time. Such an action as Drew's, no matter how approved by his neighbors, in the eyes of the guardians of the law would have been judged most culpable, worthy at least of a large fine and religious penance; perhaps the confiscation of land; or even incarceration.*

A further incentive to make Drew Gowder view with unease the possible consequences of his action may have been, as we learn from another source, the presence in the vicinity at that time of a small posse of soldiers under the direction of Francis Tyrwhitt, the northern agent of that most dreadful of Elizabeth's pursuivants, Richard Topcliffe, the notorious rackmaster.

Tyrwhitt by all accounts matched his master in zeal and often outdid him in brutality. A Yorkshireman, and first cousin of the Protestant judge, Sir Edward Jolley, famed for passing swingeing sentences on Catholics, he was permitted use of the dungeons of Jolley Castle near Leeds for his interrogations.

Jolley Castle! Can ever an edifice have been less aptly named?

Thwarted in his main purpose by the discovery of nothing but an untenanted priest-hole at Illthwaite Hall, Tyrwhitt might have been ready to take an interest in any other antireligious practices he chanced on in the district. At the very least he and his posse were a strong visible reminder that even Illthwaite was within reach of the mighty power of the Law.

So what more likely than that Gowder should rise in the middle of the night and return to Mecklin Shaw, perhaps accompanied by a few of his closest confederates, to take down the lifeless body of his victim and hurl it into Mecklin Moss?

A coroner's report of the period tells us no more than Tom Gowder's gravestone, viz. that he was murdered by unknown hand. Of the events in Mecklin Shaw, no mention is made. How should there be? No body was ever found and no witnesses were forthcoming. Even those (probably very few) who had scruples about what had happened would think twice before offering evidence which would incriminate themselves and draw down the wrath of Andrew Gowder, an even more powerful figure in the community now that he was sole owner of the Gowder farmstead.

However, such a general conspiracy to suppress the truth in public record did but provide fertile ground for the growth of those wild chimerical tales we have been examining here. Worse, the gross mimicry of the passion, death and resurrection of our own Beloved Savior contained in the most popular version soon led to the blasted oak stump becoming a focus for forms of worship that were blasphemous and pagan. Imitation of the holy by the unholy has always been a feature of devil-worship, and in this instance there was also an ocular encouragement in that it was possible to see in the jagged edge of the trunk a simulacrum of a wolf's head. The Viking Cross in St. Ylf's churchyard had, as I describe elsewhere, been thrown down by iconoclasts in the 70s. Its sad overthrow probably lent strength to the stories surrounding the stump which soon became known as the Other Wolf-Head Cross. It may also be significant that "wolf-head" was an ancient term for outlaw, dating from the Middle Ages and still in use at this time.

Does this mean that Illthwaite was a center of diabolism? I think not. I doubt if there were more than one or two benighted souls who adhered wholly to what they called the Old Faith. Yet in remote areas full of stone circles and tumuli and other sites once sacred to the gods of the druids, and the Vikings, and the Romans, it would be surprising if some of these simple peasant folk did not occasionally glance back to the old days when a pair of magpies foretold a death and a full moon was the time for curing warts.

Have I not myself seen devout parishioners making their way up the aisle to partake of Holy Communion in a series of strange hops and skips to avoid standing on the cracks between the flagstones? Such foolish superstitions, bred in the bone, are hard to eradicate but it is best to remove their visible objects, and commands were soon given by the Church authorities for the offending stump to be destroyed while at the same time the toppled cross in the churchyard was to be repaired and reconsecrated.

Like many commands from on high, the order for destruction of the stump proved easier to give than to execute.

The first attempts soon ran into difficulties. Experienced woodmen found their axe-edges blunted. Finally Barnaby Winander, the village blacksmith and a man of prodigious strength, swung at the cross with an axe so heavy none but he could raise it. A contemporary account tells us that the razor-sharp edge rang against the stump with "a note like a passing-bell," the shaft shattered, and the axe-head flew off and buried itself in the thigh of a fellow worker.

Winander. Had to be one of Thor's ancestors. Just as the crucifying Gowders had to be the same as the gravedigging Gowders. Nice family. Come to think of it, probably most of the drinkers in the bar had names she'd seen earlier in the churchyard.

Such a sense of continuity in a changing world ought to be comforting.

Somehow it wasn't.

This approach was abandoned and fire was next essayed with the blacksmith and his family to the fore once more. Faggots of bone-dry kindling were set all around the stump, flame was applied, the Winanders got to work with the bellows they had brought up from their forge, and soon whipped up a huge conflagration. Yet when all had died down and the ashes were raked away, there the stump remained, just as it had been before, except a touch blacker.

Myself, I see in this not the hand of the devil but the hands of men, and in particular of the Winanders. This family, whose scions are still the principal craftsmen of the village, have been of inestimable value down the centuries. Examples of their high skill are to be found everywhere in the valley. Yet there are two sides to every coin, and it has been frequently remarked in the character of men of genius that their creative sparks fly out of a fiery temperament which can frequently lead them into scrapes. In each gen-

eration, the Winanders have bred notorious wild men, ever ready for mischief and pranks and more frequent occupiers of the penitent stool in St. Ylf's than the pew. This Barnaby seems to have been such a one. He could have easily ensured the axes were blunted before being used and the stump was thoroughly soaked with water before the fire with no more motive than a delight in preying on the superstitious fears of his gullible neighbors, and of course a desire to discomfort the parish priest.

Yet it should be pointed out that this Barnaby Winander was the same who undertook the repair and raising of the true Wolf-Head Cross, with what success can be judged by its continued presence in our churchyard these three centuries on.

Finally the stump was hauled out of the ground by a team of six oxen and dragged to Mecklin Moss, which it is recorded opened its dark maw to receive this ill-omened timber like a hungry beast that recognizes the foul meat that best nourishes it.

The other trees of Mecklin Shaw have long since vanished too, victims of the peasant need for timber and the charcoal-burners' art, and without their constant thirst to drain the soil, the bog land of the Moss has now consumed the ground where they stood. But the legend of the Other Wolf-Head Cross still persists, with three centuries of accretion, fit stuff to while away a winter's night round the fire in the Stranger House where it may be that it is the tedious repetition of such ancient tales that drives the inn's reputed ghost to slip out of the nearest door.

A joke! Leave them laughing when you go. Bet his sermons were one long hoot, thought Sam.

Time to go to sleep, but not before the forecast visit to the bathroom which, though still not quite essential, had certainly reached the level of desirable.

Finished, and wondering idly how much of the night some ten-pint men of her acquaintance spent in peeing, she came back out into the gloomy corridor, and stopped in her tracks, all thoughts, idle or not, driven from her mind by what she saw.

The door next to hers, the door to the other guest room, was ajar. A figure was passing through it, slender, silent, clad in black. It paused and the head turned, a dark skull-like outline against the darker dark of the room's interior. She felt invisible eyes study her. Then it slipped through the gap and the door closed soundlessly behind it.

Memory of Mrs. Appledore's warning about the danger of pursuing the Dark Man came to Sam's mind, but such things had always been counterproductive. Furious at her fear, she rushed in pursuit, grasped the handle and flung the door open.

Instead of the anticipated darkness, she found the room lit by the ceiling light.

A man wearing black slacks and a black turtleneck was placing a grip on the bed. No ghost, though his hollow cheeks, sallow complexion and shaven head gave him the look of one who'd gone close to the barrier before turning back. Eyes darker than the darkest pure chocolate turned toward her. He didn't speak.

"Hi," she said. "I'm Sam Flood. I'm next door."

He didn't answer. She turned away and left.

Back in her own room she looked at herself in the dressing-table glass, her face flushed, her sun-browned body barely covered by her flimsy Melbourne Uni T-shirt.

I look like I'm on heat! she told herself. What was it I said? *Hi. I'm Sam Flood. I'm next door.* Jesus!

She checked her door. No lock, just a tiny bolt that didn't look strong enough to resist a bailiff's sneeze. Nevertheless she rammed it home and got into bed.

After a while she began to giggle. "Hi, I'm next door," she

said in a breathless little girl Marilyn voice. She choked her giggles into the pillow in case they should penetrate the intervening wall.

And soon sleep brought to an end Samantha Flood's first day in Illthwaite.

8

A bit bloody late

Mig Madero stared at the door for a while after the strange apparition had vanished. Could he have conjured it up himself? Perhaps. To a man who rarely felt the world of spirits was more than an idle thought away, such a thing was not impossible. But the creature's slight body had seemed full of life. A child of the house, perhaps? A girl-child, from the luxuriant red hair, though the loose T-shirt had given little hint of breasts . . .

Firmly he pushed the thought from his mind, finished unpacking, sat down on the bed and stared at the wall.

What was it she had said? *I'm next door.* A weird thing to say. And that accent, made worse by the high pitch of her voice! Definitely a child and not a very bright one.

He was trying to use the interruption to keep at bay memory of what had happened—or hadn't happened—to him earlier. He rubbed the palms of his hands, flexed his feet. No pain, but still the echo of pain. He felt he ought to be tired after the long day's journey. Instead he found he was wide awake.

He'd entered the pub like a fugitive seeking sanctuary. In the bar the landlady had been ringing "time" and trying to persuade her customers to leave. He'd introduced himself briefly from the hallway and followed her directions to his room.

After that nightmare drive, perhaps he should have taken a walk first, got some fresh air, but lights and the closeness of human company had seemed essential.

Now he was back in control. Anyway, if God wanted to frighten the shit out of you, He could just as easily do it in a well-lit crowded room. Night and mist themselves held no fears that man didn't put there. A breath of air would be very welcome.

He stood up, taking care to bow his head so that it didn't crack against the huge crossbeam. This was the kind of room for a man to learn humility in.

Quietly he opened the door and glided silently down the stairs.

He could still hear voices in the bar. The landlady's persuasions must have fallen on stony ground. Or, rather, saturated ground! He went down the narrow lobby and out into the night, pulling the door to behind him.

Little light escaped through the heavily curtained barroom windows and out here it was almost pitch-black till you looked up and saw the breathtaking sweep of stars across the now cloudless sky. The time might come when, either through the inevitable decay of energy, or perhaps because someone had counted all the names of God, one by one the stars would go out.

But here and now, even though his here and now was millennia out of step with some of the stars he was looking at, all he could do was gaze up and feel gratitude for being part of this beautiful creation, and fear at the thought of just how small a part.

Across the road he could hear the tumult of the invisible river. Trees rustled in the still gusting wind. Something moved between him and the stars, a bird, a bat, he could not tell. Nor could he tell whether the distant screech he heard somewhere up the dark bulk of rising ground beyond the river was the sound of birth or the sound of death.

Probably neither. Probably just the noise made by some inoffensive creature going about its inoffensive business. Certainly, for which he gave many thanks, there were no voices in the wind.

Behind him the pub door opened, spilling light on to his darkness, and a trio of men came out. They stopped short as they saw him. Two of them were almost identical, broad and muscular, with heads that looked as if they'd been rough-hewn by a sculptor's apprentice whose master hadn't found time to finish them. They stared at him with an unblinking blankness which, if encountered in certain dubious areas of Seville, would have had him running in search of light. The third, however, a tall man with a shock of vigorous gray hair and a merry eye, addressed him in a reassuringly cheerful tone.

"Good evening to you, sir. A fine night to be taking the air."

"Fine indeed," said Madero courteously. "And a good evening to you too."

"You are staying here, are you, sir? Let me guess. You are the Spanish scholar come to discover why we are the way we are."

"You have the advantage of me," said Madero.

"Sorry. Didn't mean to be rude, but two interesting strangers in one day is enough to distract our simple minds from courtesy. Thor Winander, at your service."

He offered his hand. Madero took it and found himself drawn closer.

"Michael Madero," he said.

"Madero. Like the sherry firm?"

"Not like. The same."

"Indeed! Ah, *el fino Bastardo, delicioso y delicado*."

He smacked his lips as he uttered this rather poorly pronounced version of an old advertising slogan.

Madero withdrew his hand and bowed his head in silent acknowledgment and Winander continued, "It will be a blessing to have some intelligent conversation and news of the outside world. My companions, though excellent fellows in their way, are not famed for their taste or wit. But if you want a ditch cleared or a grave dug, they are nonpareil. Goodnight to you, Mr. Madero."

"Goodnight," said Madero.

The men went on their way, talking in subdued voices and occasionally glancing back at him. One of them had a torch and its beam dipped and danced across the road and over the bridge till finally it vanished in the mass of land rising on the far side.

The light from the still open door made the darkness all around seem even denser now and the stars were nothing but a smear of frost across the black glass of the firmament. He shivered and went inside.

As he reached the foot of the stairs, Edie Appledore appeared.

"There you are," she said. "Found your room all right, did you, Mr. Madero?"

"Yes, thank you. And by the way, it is Ma*the*ro," he said gently, correcting both stress and pronunciation.

"Sorry," she said. "I knew that because that's the way Gerry Woollass says it. Which was what I wanted to catch you for. I forgot earlier, I was so busy, but he left a message asking if you could make it ten o'clock at the Hall tomorrow, not half nine as arranged."

"Thank you. It will suit me very well to have an extra half-hour in bed."

"Been a long journey, has it?"

"From my mother's house in Hampshire."

"That's a right trip. You'll need your rest. Care for a nightcap? Not always easy to sleep in a strange bed, not even when you're tired."

"Thank you. That would be nice."

"Right. No, not in there," she said as he made to step into the bar. "I've seen enough of that place for one night."

She led him down the corridor into a kitchen.

Madero glanced from the huge table to the small windows and the narrow door and said, "How on earth did they get this in here?"

"Didn't," said Mrs. Appledore. "Built it on the spot, they reckon, so it's almost as old as the building. I've been offered thousands for it, and the guy was going to pay for having it dismantled and taken out. I was tempted. Sit yourself down. Brandy OK?"

"That would be fine," said Madero, seating himself on a kitchen chair whose provenance he guessed to be Ikea. "But you resisted the temptation out of principle?"

"No. Superstition. Round here they think you change something, you pay a price."

She opened a cupboard, produced a bottle and two glasses, filled them generously and sat down alongside Madero.

"Your health," he said. "Ah, I see why you don't keep this stuff in the bar."

"They'd not pay what I'd need to ask, and if they did, most of 'em wouldn't appreciate it."

"But they appreciate some old things, it seems," said Madero, running his hand along the top edge of the table then beneath it, tracing the ancient cuts and scars. It was like touching the corpse of a battle-scarred warrior. He got a strong reminder of that pain and fear he'd experienced earlier and withdrew his hand quickly, suppressing a shudder.

"You OK, Mr. Madero?" said the woman.

"Fine. A little tired perhaps. What an interesting old building this is. Was it always an inn?"

"No. There used to be a priory hereabouts and this is what's left of the old Stranger House—that's where visitors and travelers could be put up without letting them into the priory proper."

"And it became an inn after the priory was pulled down by Henry's men?"

"Know a bit about history, do you? I suppose you would.

Not right off, I don't think. But it was so handy placed, right alongside the main road, that it made sense. It's all in the old guidebook the vicar wrote back in the eighteen hundreds. I've got a copy. I loaned it to Miss Flood when she arrived, but you can have it soon as she's done."

"Miss Flood?"

"My other guest. In the room next to yours."

"Oh yes. The red-haired child. I saw her."

Mrs. Appledore laughed.

"No child. She's a grown woman. OK, not much grown, but she's over twenty-one. Says she's looking for background on her grandmother who emigrated to Australia way back. I think she's been steered wrong, so she'll probably be on her way soon. You know how restless young women are these days."

"Are they?" he said. "I haven't noticed."

"No, you'll not have been around them much, I daresay. Whoops. Sorry."

Madero studied her over his glass then said pleasantly, "You seem to know quite a lot about me, Mrs. Appledore."

She said, "All I really know is you're writing a book or something about the old Catholic families, right? No secrets in a village, especially not if it's called Illthwaite."

"So I see. But if you know all about me, it is perhaps fair if I get some inside information in return to prepare myself. What kind of man is Mr. Woollass, for instance?"

"Gerry? He's a fair man, I'd say. Not an easy man, but a good one certainly. There's not many folk in Skaddale won't bear testimony to that. But he's not soft. You'll not get by him without an inquisition."

He noted her choice of word.

"Is there a Mrs. Woollass?" he asked.

She hesitated then said, "Probably best you know, else you could put your foot in it. There was a wife. In fact, there still is in his eyes, him being a left-footer, sorry, Catholic. She ran off a few years back with the chef from the hotel down the valley."

She suddenly laughed and said, "Come to think of it, if I remember right, he was Spanish, so I'd definitely keep away from the subject!"

Her laugh was infectious and Madero smiled too, then asked, "Children?"

"One daughter. She was at university when it happened, but it seems like she sided with Gerry."

"You call him Gerry," he said. "You are good friends?"

"Not so's you'd notice," she said. "But what should I call him? Sir, and curtsy when he comes into the bar?"

"So you are all democrats in Cumbria? It's not quite the same in Hampshire."

"Oh well, but *Hampshire*," she replied as if he'd said Illyria. "It'll be nobs and yobs down there. Don't mistake me, we've got a pecking order. But we've all been to the same school, up till eleven at least, and most families have been around long enough to have seen everyone else's dirty linen. It's not whether you're chapel or Catholic, rich or poor, red or blue that matters. It's what you do when your neighbor's heifer gets stuck in Mecklin Moss on a dirty night or his power line comes down on Christmas Day."

"You make it sound like an ideal community," he said.

"Don't be daft," she said. "We're all weak humans like anywhere else. But for better or worse, we stick together. And Gerry Woollass is part of the glue."

He smiled and finished his drink.

"I too am a weak human, and I think I'd better get some sleep. By the way, I couldn't find a phone point in my room."

"Likely because there isn't one," she said. "Is that a problem?"

"Only if I wanted to get online with my laptop. No problem. I'll use my mobile."

"Not round here you won't," she said. "Had to tell Miss

Flood the same. No signal. But feel free to use my phone here whenever you want, no need to ask."

"Thank you. And thanks also for the drink and the conversation. I look forward to talking with you again."

He meant it. She was a comfortable companion.

"Me too, Mr. Madero," she said, carefully getting it right this time. "Sleep well."

"Thank you. Goodnight."

She watched him leave the kitchen, noting his careful gait. But despite what she perceived as a slight stiffness in his left leg, he moved very lightly, passing up the stairs with scarcely a telltale creak.

Two interesting guests in one day, she thought. The girl she'd be glad to see the back of, but this one was rather intriguing, and sexy too in that mysterious foreign way. Talking to him would make a change from the usual barroom fare of local gossip and tales she'd heard a hundred times already.

She wondered if the monks had felt like this about the strangers who sought shelter here, eating their simple food perhaps at this very same table. Or had they blocked their ears to news from the great world outside, doubting it could be anything but bad? In the long run, they'd been right. Fat Henry's men from London had come riding up the valley and made them listen and told them their way of life was all over. Nowadays they didn't come on horseback. In fact usually they didn't come at all, just sent directives and regulations and development plans. But the message was still the same.

She poured herself another glass of brandy and pulled her chair closer to the fire. The heat had almost died away, only a hollow dome of coal remained, at the heart of which a thin blue flame fluttered one of those membranes of ash which in the old stories always presaged the arrival of a stranger.

"Bit bloody late, as usual," said Edie Appledore, sipping her drink. "Bit bloody late."

PART THREE

THE DEATH OF BALDER

This was the greatest woe ever visited on men or gods,
and after he fell, everyone there lost the power of speech.

Snorri Sturluson *Prose Edda*

If you want to be clever learn how to ask questions
how to answer them also.

"The Sayings of the High One" *Poetic Edda*

1

The last prime number

Next morning Sam woke to sunlight, the first she'd seen since dropping through the clouds over Heathrow four days earlier.

She opened her window wide. What she could see of Illthwaite looked a lot more attractive in the sunshine. In front of her across the Skad the ground rose unrelentingly to a range of hills which looked so close in the clear air that she felt she could trot up there before breakfast. But a glance at her map told her they were four miles away.

She found Winander's house, the Forge, marked on the map. It was on a narrow road, presumably Stanebank, snaking uphill from the humpback bridge almost opposite the pub. Half a mile further on Illthwaite Hall was marked. She raised her eyes again and finally managed to spot an outcrop of chimneys. Their size gave her a proper sense of scale and put paid to any residual notion she might have of a quick walk up to the ridge.

Of the Forge she could see nothing, but a column of smoke rising into the morning air seemed likely to mark its presence.

In the bright light of morning, her discovery of the churchyard inscription felt far less sinister and significant. There was probably a simple explanation and all she had to do was ask. She'd start with Winander. Did his invitation have a more than commercial motive? Then there was the impish little Mr. Melton who'd hinted he might be able to assist her with her inquiries. Finally there was Rev. Pete who'd looked ripe to have any hidden info shaken out of him.

She leaned out of the window and took a deep breath. The air still retained its night coolness, but there wasn't a cloud in the sky and things would surely warm up as the sun got higher. She backed her judgment by putting on shorts. She thought of topping them with her skimpiest halter but decided maybe Illthwaite wasn't ready for that. Also she didn't want to flaunt her bruised shoulder, so she opted for a green-and-gold T-shirt. Might as well fly the colors!

She picked up the *Guide* and ran lightly down the narrow stairs which nonetheless squeaked their tuneless tune, reminding her that she hadn't heard a thing when her mysterious neighbor ascended the previous night. Perhaps he was a ghost after all.

If so, he was a ghost with a good appetite. She found him sitting in the bar tucking into the breakfast version of last night's supper.

She gave him a nod but he didn't even look up.

Mrs. Appledore appeared almost instantly with coffee, cornflakes, and a mountain of thick-cut toast alongside half a churnful of butter and a pint of marmalade.

"Round here, even foxes get hungry," she said, smiling. "It's a grand morning."

"Yeah, a real beaut," said Sam.

She glanced again at the stranger, giving him a last chance to join the human race, and surprised a moue of distaste. Something in his breakfast? Or something in the way she spoke, more like. Well, stuff him!

"So what are you planning to do?" asked the landlady.

Her decision to be more upfront didn't mean she had to lay out her plans, so she answered, "Thought I'd stroll down to the post office and buy some cards to send home."

And dig for a bit of info as well as stocking up on chocolate supplies.

"You'll be lucky. It's shut," said Mrs. Appledore.

"All day, you mean?"

"No. I mean permanent. Since last year. It's happening all over. *Government*!"

She uttered the word with a weary disdain that was more telling than ferocity.

"Don't like the government then?" said Sam. "Shouldn't have thought you'd have been much bothered up here."

"Once maybe, but not anymore. Now you need to move fast as our Dark Man to keep ahead of them. Difference is, if they catch up, it's likely you that dies. Just shout when you want more toast. How are you doing, Mr. Madero?"

She was still careful with the pronunciation.

Mathero, thought Sam. More than just a mysterious stranger, a mysterious foreigner, which somehow made his response to her accent even more offensive.

But his voice when he replied was pure English, purer than hers anyway!

"I'm doing very well, Mrs. Appledore," he said with grave courtesy.

"Good lad. We'll soon get you fattened up."

She left. Sam glanced at Mr. Madero once more and this time caught his eye. She gave the small sympathetic smile of one who was often herself the object of other people's fattening-up ambitions. He returned her gaze steadily but not her smile.

Determined not to risk another rebuff, Sam opened the *Guide* at random and began to read a passage about Illthwaite Hall and the Woollass family. The Reverend Peter K. clearly enjoyed the benefits of their influence and their board and was at pains to stress that, though they were Roman Catholics, this in no wise interfered with the pursuit of their many social and charitable duties as the chief family of the area.

Sam read at her usual rapid pace, her eye devouring the pages as fast as her mouth devoured toast, until her reaching hand encountered emptiness.

She raised her head and became aware of two mysteries. One was that Madero had somehow moved from his table to a stance by her left shoulder without attracting her attention. The second, equally unobserved and therefore far more worrying, was that the mountain of toast had somehow moved from the plate, presumably into her stomach.

"Help you?" she said.

He said, "Mrs. Appledore mentioned the *Guide* to me and I wondered if I could have a look at it, when you're finished, of course."

"Sure," she said. "When I'm finished."

She stood up and, tucking the book firmly beneath her arm, went through the door. In the hallway she met Mrs. Appledore.

"All done, my dear? Sure you don't want something hot? Always start the day with a hot breakfast, my mam used to say. Never know when you'll need your strength."

"I'll just have to take my chances, I guess," she said. "Anyway, your other guest looks like he's eating enough for two."

"Mr. Madero? Well, he needs feeding up. I think he's been ill, poor chap. And I doubt if they feed them much solid grub in them foreign seminaries."

"Seminaries?"

"Oh yes. He was training to be a priest or something afore he got ill. Left-footer, like the squire," said Mrs. Appledore confidentially.

"Catholic, you mean?"

"That's right. You're not one, are you, dear? I mean no offense."

"No I'm not. And you can mean all the offense you like," said Sam.

"All I'm saying is, them drafty cloisters and all that kneeling on cold stones can't do a man much good. At least in the C.

of E. they appreciate a bit of comfort. Even old Reverend Paul—that's our Rev. Pete's dad, who was big on prayer and fasting, and salvation through suffering—kept the vicarage larder well stocked and the boilers well stoked. Rev. Pete likes his grub and his coal fire too."

So, thought Sam. A wannabe priest. No wonder she hadn't liked the look of him.

"Will you be leaving today, dear?" Mrs. Appledore went on.

"Not sure," said Sam. "Can I let you know later? Or do you need the room?"

The woman hesitated, then said, "No, not yet. But if you could let me know soon, in case someone turns up. I'd appreciate it."

"Sure," said Sam. "That's great."

She went outside. A black Mercedes SLK with a small crucifix and a St. Christopher medallion dangling from the rear-view mirror was parked alongside her Focus. No prizes for guessing whose it was. She looked across the bridge to Stanebank. That track looked pretty steep. Best to take some provisions in case she walked off the toast too quickly.

She went to her car, unlocked the door and took her last Cherry Ripe out of the glove compartment. Her Ray-Ban Predators with the red mirror lenses were there too. These were a present from Martie which Sam had accepted with the ungraciousness permitted between friends, saying, "Thanks, but it's Cambridge, England, I'm going to and they say you've more chance of seeing the sun in a rain forest." To which Martie had replied, "It's not the sun I'm worried about, girl, it's those basilisk eyes of yours. How're you going to try out the Pom talent when a single glance from you reminds most men they've got an urgent dental appointment?"

What the hell? she thought. This may be the only time I really need shades.

She put them on and straightened up to discover that once again the pussyfooted Madero had contrived to follow her without making any noise. He was carrying a black briefcase and standing by the Merc, looking dubiously toward the humpback bridge.

Very fond of black, our Mr. Madero, thought Sam. Or perhaps he'd just made a big investment in the color when he was trying for the priesthood.

She strolled across the road on to the bridge where she paused to peer over the parapet. The Skad was no longer tumbling along like brown coffee flecked with milky foam, but moving much more smoothly with nothing but sun starts breaking its surface. She watched for a moment then turned to walk on. There he was again, right behind her.

"You following me, or something?" she said.

"No," he said, surprised. "This is Stanebank, I believe, which I'm reliably informed I need to ascend to reach my destination. It doesn't look a sensible road to take my car up, even if it got over this bridge without scraping the exhaust."

"Why'd you want to drive anyway?" said Sam. "It's only a step."

"So I've been told."

He nodded at her rather curtly and set off. After a few moments, Sam followed, already nibbling her chocolate. He was moving quite quickly but she didn't doubt her ability to overtake him. Bleeding townie, probably doesn't feel safe being more than a few yards from his car, she thought.

But as the track steepened and she came up close behind him, she detected a slight unevenness in his gait. Mrs. Appledore said he'd been ill and the poor bastard was definitely favoring his left leg. Her own bruised hip gave a twinge as if in sympathy. She saw him switch the briefcase, which looked quite heavy, from one hand to the other as if to adjust his balance. All at once her plan to move smoothly by him, offering a nod as curt as his own, seemed pretty mean-spirited.

She fell into step alongside him and said, "Great to see the sun, isn't it?"

"Yes, it is," he said.

He spoke evenly but she thought she detected an effort not to let her see he was breathing hard.

She said, "Like a bit of choc?"

He glanced at the bar and said, "You did not get enough toast for breakfast?"

"Yeah, plenty. You were counting?"

"I tried but I lost count," he said gravely.

The bastard was taking the piss! At least it meant he was human.

As if regretting the lapse, he went on quickly, "But thank you, no. It looks too dark for me. I prefer milk, English style."

"You do? I'd have guessed you'd have gone for black and bitter."

"Why so?"

"I don't know. The car. The gear you wear."

"I see. By the same token you should perhaps be eating a half-ripe lemon."

Another joke?

Before she could pick her response he went on, "I'm sorry. I did not mean to imply your garments are anything other than attractive. Perhaps however we both err toward the episematic."

"Sorry, you've lost me."

"A zoological term referring to the use of color or markings to enable recognition within a species."

"Like I'm telling the world I'm Australian? Why not? And what are you telling the world? That you run errands for God?"

She's been talking to our landlady, he guessed.

"There are worse jobs. I understand you are trying to track down some ancestor here in Illthwaite, Miss Flood. That must be fascinating, discovering your origins."

Letting her know that he'd been brought up to speed too.

"More frustrating than fascinating so far," she said.

"Things not going well? Will it trouble you a lot if your quest comes to nothing?"

"No chance of that," she declared.

"You're very confident. It's not given to us to know everything."

"You reckon?" she said, detecting a sermonizing note in his voice. "Why not? *There's no such word as unknowable. We must know, we shall know.*"

"That sounds suspiciously like a quotation."

"You're right. David Hilbert, German mathematician."

"Interesting. I prefer, *for now we know in part, but then we shall know even as we are known.* St. Paul."

"How was his math?"

"Better than mine, I suspect," he said. "He did say, *Prove all things. Hold fast that which is good.* How's that for a mathematician?"

She considered then said, "I like it. And there was a mathematical Paul who said that God's got a special book in which He records all the most elegant proofs."

"There you are then," he said, with a pleased smile. "It's good to know our two Pauls had God in common."

"Not so sure about that," she said. "Mine was a Hungarian called Erdos. He usually called God SF, which stood for the Supreme Fascist."

That wiped the smile from his face.

"You don't sound as if you approve of God, Miss Flood," he said.

"I approve of mine. Don't have a lot of time for yours," she said.

He looked taken aback by her frankness.

He said, "What form does your God take, if you don't mind my asking?"

"Why should I mind? If you really want to know something, asking's the only way to find out. So let's see. I'd say my God is the last prime number."

He did not respond to her definition, perhaps because he was pondering it, more likely she thought complacently because he didn't want to reveal he didn't know what she was talking about. Or maybe, she thought with a bit more compassion, it was merely because he needed all his breath to maintain an even pace up the hill whose steepening gradient was testing her bruises. But she didn't have far to go. A long low white-washed house had come into view. At right angles to it stood a taller building, unpainted and windowless, with a broad chimney at the furthermost end from which issued the column of smoke Sam had observed earlier. Presumably this was the forge or smithy which gave the house its name.

A rough driveway to the house curved off the road. There was no formal gateway but the entrance was marked by a huge slab of sandstone on which was carved THE FORGE with underneath it in smaller letters *Lasciate ogni ricchezza voi ch'entrate.*

"What's that all about?" wondered Sam.

"Its English version is usually 'all hope abandon ye who enter here,'" said Madero. "In Dante's *Inferno* it's part of the inscription above the entrance to the Underworld. But here *ricchezza,* wealth, has been substituted for *speranza,* hope. I don't know why."

He sounded like a schoolteacher passing on information to a pupil.

"I'll ask," said Sam. "This is where I get off. You going much further?"

"Up to the Hall, which cannot be all that far."

Sam glanced dubiously at the road ahead which looked to get even steeper.

"Why not rest your bones here a couple of minutes? I'm sure Mr. Winander will be good for a cup of tea."

He looked at her blankly for a moment, then said again with the polite formality of an adult explaining the grown-up world to a child, "Thank you, but I must go on. I have an appointment, you see."

She opened her mouth, probably to say something rude, but

was saved from herself by the sound of an engine. A Range Rover came bowling up the hill. It drew up alongside them. The driver was Gerry Woollass. Beside him sat a woman in a nun's headdress. There was another woman in the back but Sam couldn't see her properly.

Woollass got out and came toward them.

"Señor Madero, is it?" he asked, getting the pronunciation right.

"Mr. Madero in England," corrected Sam's walking companion.

"You're on your hour, I'll give you that. I'm Gerald Woollass."

They shook hands, then Woollass's gaze moved to Sam.

"Miss Flood, good morning," he said. "And how are you this morning?"

"Fit as a butcher's dog," she said.

"You and Mr. Madero are acquainted?"

Odd question, she thought. Maybe he's worried I'm on my way to the Hall too, and doesn't like the idea of an awkward Colonial falling over his priceless antiques.

"Nah, we just met," she said. "I'm on my way to see Mr. Winander, and Mr. Madero was kind enough to translate this inscription for me, but I still don't get it."

Woollass smiled. This was a first. He looked a bit more like the kind, well-meaning man that Edie Appledore had described.

He said, "It means that if you're so foolhardy as to step into Mr. Winander's workshop, you will be lucky to emerge with any money left in your pocket. Mr. Madero, why don't you climb in? You might as well join us for the last bit of your journey."

"Or if you prefer to walk, I'll be glad to stretch my legs and join you," said the nun, stepping nimbly out of the car. She was lean and athletic, in her thirties, with a narrow intelligent face. The headdress apart, she was conventionally dressed.

"Sister Angelica," she said, holding out her hand.

Madero shook it. Sam was amused to see how he dealt with

this dilemma. She guessed he'd much prefer to accept the lift, but the nun had put him on the spot.

Then she was faced with a dilemma of her own as the nun turned from Madero to herself and thrust out her hand again and tried another friendly smile. It didn't fade as Sam let her own fingertips barely brush the nun's and said shortly, "Sam Flood. G'day."

She caught Madero regarding her with disapproval and thought, what's with him? Just because she's a nun doesn't mean I've got to give her the kiss of peace.

Sister Angelica's smile didn't even flicker and her voice was warm as she said, "It's good to meet you, Miss Flood. Mr. Madero, on second thoughts I think maybe we should ride, if you don't mind. I just felt a small twinge of my rheumatism."

Liar, thought Sam. You've sussed out that the poor bastard's knackered and this is your good deed for the day.

"As you wish," said Madero.

He held the door to let the nun back into the front passenger seat, then opened the rear door and put his briefcase inside. The woman sitting there leaned over to pull it further in and Sam got a good view of her for the first time.

She was in her late twenties, with a long fine-boned face, beautiful if you liked that sort of thing. She had straight jet-black hair falling sheer below her shoulders. She was wearing shorts and a sun-top, but the flesh exposed showed little sign of the onslaught of weather. Her face had an almost lilial pallor which against her black hair could easily have produced a vampirical effect, yet far from being cadaverous, she somehow seemed to shimmer with life. She had a full well-rounded figure and the kind of long legs which would have graced a fashion house catwalk. Her eyes moved over Sam with the measured indifference of a security scan. They were a bluey gray that was familiar—like the driver's, that was it, but unlike his showing neither the potential for benevolence nor the presence of trouble. Her gaze held Sam's for a moment, a smile which had something of mockery in it and something of inquiry too, touched her mouth briefly, then she sat back as Madero hauled himself in beside her.

"My daughter, Frek," said Woollass. "That's idiot-speak for Frederika."

Madero shook her hand. At the same time a thunderous voice echoed out:

"Morning, Gerry. Window shopping, are we? Why not bring your friends in? You never know, you might see something that takes your fancy."

She turned to see that Thor Winander had appeared round the end of his house. Stripped to the waist and with a long-handled hammer resting on one shoulder, he looked more like the god of the Wolf-Head Cross than ever.

"Morning, Thor. Another time," called Woollass. "If you're ready, Mr. Madero . . ."

As Madero pulled his door shut, he frowned at Sam as if she were an attendant footman he was wondering if he should tip. Then the car drew away.

You're really making new friends this morning, girl, Sam mocked herself as she watched it go.

"You waiting for a red carpet or something?" called Winander.

He didn't wait for an answer but disappeared toward the smithy.

Sam looked up at the sandstone block once more and jostled the few coins she had in the pocket of her shorts.

"Wonder if he takes credit cards?" she said to a passing raven.

Caw! replied the raven.

Or, as this was Illthwaite where they crucified boys and ghosts searched your room, it might have been, *Cash!*

2

Inquisition

Mig Madero was more relieved than he cared to admit to be in the car. Physiotherapy routines got you mobile, but the last half-hour had proved yet again the old hiking adage that the only thing that gets you fit for walking steeply uphill is walking steeply uphill.

The drive to the Hall took less than a minute and the woman next to him showed no inclination to talk. The wide rear seat removed any risk of physical contact, but he found her closeness vaguely disturbing. Despite her icy pallor, warmth came off her and with it a scent composed of whatever perfume she used underpinned by faint traces from her own skin and flesh. She was beautiful, no argument about that, with a fine delicate bone structure that reminded him of the angels in the murals in the seminary chapel, but with flesh enough on her to turn the careless mind from the sacred to the profane.

Frek. The English loved their diminutives. It was his mother who started calling him Mig. Frederika was a lovely name, but Frek had intimacy.

The car came to a halt, rather to his relief, and he turned his attention to the less troublesome attractions of Illthwaite Hall.

His first impression was of an extremely appealing house

with little sign of that self-consciousness which comes from a desire to impress one's neighbors. The tall twisting chimneys belonged to the architecture of fairy tales, and the timbering too he had seen often in the children's books in his mother's house.

He stared up at an ornately carved stone set above the lintel of the brass-studded oak front door. On its left side was a coat of arms with three roses: one red, one white, one golden. On the right stood an angel with a sword, its robes white, its weapon silver with a smear of scarlet along its edge. Between, picked out in red and green, were some words, crushed so close together that reading them wasn't easy but he'd had plenty of practice at deciphering ornate and obscure scripts.

Edwin Woollass Esquire and Alice
His Wife made this house to be built
in the Year of Our Lord 1535
Cruce Fido

"'I trust in the cross,'" Madero translated.

"Our dog's a crook," said Frek Woollass as she went by him and opened the door.

"Family joke," said Woollass. "Usually left behind with childhood. Come in."

A good three inches shorter than his daughter, he moved with the determined gait of a man who anticipates obstacles but doesn't intend walking round them.

"It's a lovely spot, isn't it?" said Sister Angelica. Her voice was gruff without being masculine, and it had a fairly broad accent which Madero, who had early recognized the importance of the way you talked in his maternal milieu, identified as Lancastrian. "Very welcoming. Pity about the knocker, though."

The cast-iron door knocker, shaped like a wolf's head with

mouth agape and teeth bared, looked as if it were keen to bite the hand that raised it.

They followed Woollass into a broad entrance hall, so dimly lit that Madero got little impression of it other than lots of wood paneling and a few wall-mounted animal heads as they passed quickly along, down a little corridor and through another door which wouldn't have looked out of place in a dungeon.

The room it opened into had a flagged floor with at its center a vaguely oriental-looking circular carpet whose yellow-and-umber design stood out boldly against the gray granite. On it stood four wooden armchairs around a low oak table. The effect was rather theatrical, as though a single spot were lighting up the action area of an open stage. A huge fireplace almost filled one wall. No fire was needed today, but a tall vase full of multicolored dahlias burnt on the hearth and above the fireplace was the same coat of arms he'd seen over the entrance door.

As he took the chair Woollass indicated, Madero began to feel the past crowding in and sense other shadowy presences in the room which if he relaxed and admitted them might let themselves become more visible. But for the moment, he wanted to concentrate on his host and this unexpected nun who'd sat down on his left.

As if he'd asked for an explanation out loud, Woollass said, "I invited Sister Angelica along this morning because she is an old friend of the family as well as being something of an expert on matters historical, procedural and legal."

"You're overselling me as usual, Gerry," said the nun, smiling at Madero.

Woollass took the chair opposite Madero and leaned forward slightly.

"So let me look at you," he said, fixing him with his keen gray-blue eyes. "Your letter was interesting, but letters tell us only what their writer wants us to know. Forgive my directness, but I've never been a round-the-houses man. If you want to know something, ask it, that's the best way for simple uncomplicated souls like me."

Was that a faint sigh of disbelief from his left? Madero didn't look but fixed his attention wholly on Woollass.

"I quite understand, Mr. Woollass," he said. "It's no small thing to open up family records to a stranger. I'm happy to answer any questions and, of course, you have probably already contacted my referees, Dr. Max Coldstream of Southampton University, and Father Dominic Terrega of the San Antonio Seminary in Seville."

"Indeed. Let's have some coffee while we're talking."

On cue, the door opened and his daughter came in carrying a tray. It was a delight simply to see her walk across the room and set the tray down.

She took the remaining seat to his right and began to pour the coffee.

Woollass said, "The floor is yours, Mr. Madero."

So Mrs. Appledore's word had been apt. He wasn't going to get near the Woollass papers without an inquisition. The nun was here to cast a properly religious eye over him. And the daughter . . . ?

He glanced at her as she raised her coffee to her lips and he had to force his gaze away as he found himself transfixed by the gentle tremor of the upper visible portion of her pallid breasts as the hot liquor slid down her throat. He had a sudden vision of her stretched naked, her bush burning like black fire against the snow of her body. It was his first truly erotic fancy since the illness that had marked the change of his life direction, which meant the first since sixteen that didn't crash up against a vocational imperative. Perhaps that was her function, to see how easily distracted he was! Well, they'd be disappointed. Old habits die hard and the mental screen slid easily into place. The troublesome image was still there behind the screen, but he was back in control and with luck a little dry conversation could prove as effective as prayer and cold showers.

He fixed his gaze on the man and said, "As I explained in my letter, I'm doing a doctorate thesis on the Reformation, but I do not want to retread the old ground of power struggle, of political intrigue, of wars and treaties, of saints and martyrs. I want to approach it through the personal experience of ordinary men and women here in England who lived through—or in some cases died because of—these changes. I want . . ."

"Why England?" interrupted Woollass.

"I'm half English. Through my maternal family history I became aware that not too long ago there were still laws which discriminated against Catholicism in public life. The more I learned of English history the more fascinated I became by the survival of such a strong Catholic presence, especially here in the north, despite long periods of highly organized and legally imposed repression. Eventually I formalized my interest into a thesis proposal in which I stressed that I wanted to base my researches not on the great families who figure in the public records, but on ordinary families like my own."

Woollass nodded and said, "That answers, why England? Now, why Woollass?"

"A simple reductive technique, I fear," said Madero. "I wrote to all the surviving families who figured in Walsingham's record of recusants."

"Hmm. So it was little more than a disguised circular we got," said Woollass. "I usually dump those straight in the waste bin. So you're saying your interest in my family is purely because I replied affirmatively, Mr. Madero? If I hadn't bothered, or if my reply had been negative, you would have crossed us off your list?"

"I'm afraid so," he said. "A disappointment, but one of many."

Woollass looked at him doubtfully, then glanced at the nun, who leaned forward so that she could look directly into Madero's face and said, "But it would surely have been an especially big disappointment, considering the family had a close relative who was a Jesuit priest working on the English Mission?"

Damn, thought Madero. Here it was. They were concerned that his real interest might be Father Simeon. He hadn't anticipated such sensitivity. Too late now for explanation. Mention of his stop-off in Kendal would simply confirm Woollass's doubts.

But for a serious historical researcher to claim complete ignorance of the man would also look very suspicious.

He said, "Certainly, knowing that the family's problems must have been compounded by such a relative added a little to my interest. But the Woollasses were far from unique in this. And, had the priest been a son rather than just a nephew . . ."

He gave a Latin shrug. Make them feel superior, remind them you're a foreigner.

Sister Angelica nodded in agreement, then in a brusque matter-of-fact tone she said, "I gather you were yourself studying for the priesthood, Mr. Madero. Would it distress you too much to tell us what made you change your mind?"

Her source was Father Dominic, he guessed. Perhaps others also. The great Catholic world could sometimes be very small.

"No, it doesn't distress me. I discovered that my sense of vocation had vanished."

"And that didn't distress you?" she asked on a rising note of concern.

"I said my sense of vocation had vanished, not my faith," said Madero. "I thought it was God's will that I should be a priest, then I realized it was His will that I should do something else. Why should that trouble me?"

"But you have been distressed, I understand, physically if not mentally?"

Edie Appledore's knowledge of his background had prepared him for this.

He said, "I had a climbing accident. I damaged my skull, my left leg and my spine. Happily after many months' convalescence I am completely recovered."

His left knee gave him an admonitory twinge and, feeling Sister Angelica's keen eye upon him, he added, "Except for my knee, which will take a little longer."

The nun smiled and said, "So you're untroubled by doubts, Mr. Madero?"

"Completely," he said. "Though occasionally by certainties."

She let out a snort of amusement and nodded again, this time at Woollass, who said, "Thank you, Mr. Madero. If you'd give us a few moments . . . ? Perhaps you might care to see some more of the house? My daughter would be pleased to give you a short tour."

"That would be delightful," said Madero.

He stood up and followed Frek out of the room.

"So," he said. "You pour the coffee but you don't actually get a vote."

She said, "What makes you think I haven't voted already, Mr. Madero?"

His name in her mouth was like being caressed by her tongue . . .

He said hastily, "It would be, let me see, Henry the Eighth on the throne when the Hall was built?"

"That's right," she said with a faint knowing smile as if well aware of the subject he was changing. "But I'm afraid that unlike most houses of such antiquity, no one of royal blood or indeed of any particular distinction has slept here."

"Not even Father Simeon," he said.

"Why do you say that?"

"Because the home of close relatives of acknowledged Catholic sympathies must have seemed very attractive in times of need."

"By the same token, when the hunt was up for him, it must have been one of the places most likely to be searched."

"No doubt a hiding place had been prepared. Is there a priest-hole?"

She said, "If there is, who better than an expert like yourself to discover it?"

She spoke seriously, but he thought he could detect mischief in her eyes.

She led him back into the main hall. By now his eyes had adjusted to the dim light and he was able to take in more detail.

"This is the original Tudor hall, somewhat modified," said Frek. "Purists would probably say it's been ruined, but my ancestors were rather selfishly more concerned with their own convenience than Heritage. When something wore out, they replaced it."

"Like the staircase," said Madero.

At the far end of the hall, an ornate staircase of a design he didn't recognize but which certainly wasn't Tudor curved up to the first-floor landing.

"You noticed. Just as well, or I might have started thinking you were a fake, Mr. Madero. Yes, originally there was a stone spiral, great for sword fights but a little perilous for the old or infirm. Some eighteenth-century Woollass doing the Grand Tour spotted this one in France and brought it back with him. If you're interested you can see the old stone treads out in the garden. They were used in the construction of a summer house. Waste not, want not, is the Woollass motto."

"I thought it was *our dog's a crook*."

"Hardly in the house two minutes and already quoting our jokes," interrupted a high, rather nasal voice. "The mark of a true researcher or an investigative journalist. Good morning, my dear."

A tall, slender man was coming down the staircase. Clad in a long silk dressing gown of cardinal red, he might indeed have been an old Prince of the Church, come to give audience. He certainly had the features for it—wide brow, deep-set eyes, high cheeks, aquiline nose, and a mane of white hair so fine it gave the impression of an aureole.

"Good morning, Granpa," said Frek, standing on tiptoe to kiss his inclined cheek as he paused on the penultimate step. "How are you today?"

Madero could see a resemblance here, much more than he could detect between either of them and Gerald Woollass. Perhaps the short plump genes and the long slender ones leap-frogged each other down the generations.

"I am well, surprisingly so, for which I give due thanks. And you I take it are Mr. Madero. I'm Dunstan Woollass," said the old man, offering his hand which had a large ruby ring on the index finger. "Welcome to Illthwaite Hall."

Resisting the Spanish half of his blood which tempted him to kiss the ring, Madero shook hands. Dunstan Woollass didn't release his hand but kept a hold of it as he completed his descent, and now Madero had to resist his more frivolous English blood which tempted him to break into "Hello, Dolly!"

To restore the balance of sobriety he said, "I believe you are a historian yourself, Mr. Woollass. My supervisor, Max Coldstream, edits *Catholic History* and he recalled with pleasure several excellent articles you had submitted to the journal."

What Max had said was, "Woollass . . . There was a Dunstan Woollass. Don't know if he's still alive, but he was a man of some influence in northern Church circles. In fact, I'm pretty sure he got one of those decorations the Vatican dishes out from time to time. Used to write a bit in Catholic journals, more a polemicist than a historian, though he did submit the occasional article to *CH*. Euphuistic in style and rather fanciful in content, I recall. But occasionally there were shafts of light and wit."

There was light and wit in the old man's eyes now. The same bright blue-gray eyes as his granddaughter. And the same faintly mocking expression.

"Indeed? I wish I could recall his frequent rejection slips with equal pleasure," he said. "Yes, I have dabbled a little, but I have never been more than a dilettante. It is a pleasure to welcome a real scholar to Illthwaite. Not that I am dressed to suit the occasion. You must forgive my dishabille. These days I emerge by slow degrees from the pupal state of sleep. I need nourishment to give me the strength to dress, yet I have never been able to master the complex geometry of breakfast in bed which inevitably leaves me sticky with marmalade, itchy with crumbs and scalded by coffee. So I descend to the kitchen where no doubt the divine Pepi is even now pouring my orange juice and creaming my eggs. Ah, speak of angels and they shall materialize before our eyes."

The woman who'd appeared in a doorway at the left end of the hall was handsome enough but hardly angelic. In her forties with dark brown hair pulled tight in a bun above a wide forehead, big gray-blue eyes and a generous mouth, she wore a nylon housecoat which strained across her large breasts and broad hips.

"Pepi, this is Mr. Madero, the famous scholar. Madero, this is Mistress Collipepper, our invaluable housekeeper, the third of that name to have taken care of us poor feckless Woollasses. We're terribly hierarchical in Illthwaite."

The eyes registered Madero without any interest then moved on to the old man.

"Come on, Mr. Dunny, afore you catch your death standing there in the draft," she commanded.

"*Audio, obsequor*. Good luck to you, Madero. Incidentally, my grandfather, Anthony Woollass, wrote a short history of the parish. Like me he was very much an amateur—the book was privately printed—but you'll find a copy in the study bookcase if you care to spare it a glance. *À bientôt*, or should I say *hasta luego*?"

He released Madero's hand and followed the housekeeper through the doorway.

"He is . . . remarkable," said Madero. "And I noticed he seems to anticipate the Star Chamber will find in my favor. Does he, like yourself, cast a vote in absentia?"

"You mustn't probe our secrets before you have clearance, Mr. Madero," she said. "Now, what next? Are you interested in pargetting?"

"I don't know. I've never pargetted," he replied, his English blood still in ascendancy.

Before she could respond to his frivolity, Gerald Woollass appeared.

"There you are, Mr. Madero. I'm pleased to tell you that I've decided that your application to be allowed access to some of our early family records should be approved."

Frek clapped her hands together once, not so much a gesture of spontaneous joy as a formal signal of accord.

Madero said, "I'm honored and grateful. Thank you very much, sir."

"Yes yes," said Woollass, flapping his hand as if to dislodge a persistent fly. "A condition is that you sign a note of agreement giving me the right to see, emend or veto any passage in your thesis which refers to my family. I have had such a note made out in anticipation of a successful outcome to your interview. Is this agreeable to you?"

Just in case I do try to sneak in something he doesn't like about Father Simeon! thought Madero as he said, "Naturally, sir."

"Good. I presume you'd like to start right away? You will find the note of agreement on the desk in the study. Be so good as to sign it and give it to Frek. Lunch is at one. No documents to be removed. No photography. Presumably you'd like this. Its weight suggests you have come well prepared, but not, I hope, with cameras."

He handed over the briefcase which Madero had left by the side of his chair.

"No, sir," said Madero, opening the case. "Just a laptop, plus pen and paper as a failsafe. Oh, and there's this, which I hope you will accept as a token of my gratitude."

He produced a bottle of what an expert eye would have recognized instantly as the rarest and most expensive fino in the Madero Bastardo range.

Woollass took it and said, "Ah yes. Sherry. Thank you," then walked away, swinging the bottle by his side.

"Sorry," said Frek. "We're not really a sherry family."

"De gustibus non est disputandum," murmured Madero.

"Oh, I wouldn't say that," said Frek. "This way."

She set off up the stairs, her hair flowing down her back like a black torrent into which he felt an almost irresistible impulse to plunge his hands.

On the landing she paused and said, "The study's that way but you might like a quick glance first at our Long Gallery which gets a para to itself in Pevsner."

"By all means," said Madero.

In fact the Long Gallery wasn't all that long but it had some interesting stonework and a fretted ceiling in need of restoration. A line of round arched windows admitted the morning sunlight to illumine the row of family portraits on the opposing wall. He paused before one of a handsome young man, looking very dashing in modern military uniform.

"My grandfather," said Frek.

"I thought it might be. He has medals."

"Indeed. One of them is the Military Cross. He was just old enough for the last couple of years of the war, but typically he seems to have made up for lost time. Afterward, I think he wanted to forget it. He says it was his father's idea to have him painted in uniform. It can be an uncomfortable thing, trying to keep a proud father happy."

"Indeed it can," said Madero rather sadly. "But a good man will always try."

He walked slowly down the gallery, feeling himself watched by all those slatey eyes, living and dead, till he came to the portrait which had caught his attention as soon as he entered, partly because it had pride of place on the cross wall at the end of the room, partly because it was the only one to show two people.

As he had guessed, they were Edwin and Alice Woollass, depicted full length, almost life size, when they were both into middle age. She was a sturdy woman with lively intelligent features, he much taller with a serious ascetic face.

"Interesting," he said.

"Indeed," said Frek. "If only because she was the first and the last woman the Woollasses thought it worthwhile having a portrait of."

"Perhaps you will change their minds," said Madero with an effort at gallantry.

"I think I may change more than that," murmured Frek. "Have you seen enough?"

Something in her voice made him look more closely, then he said, "Ah. The priest-hole."

"You've spotted it then?"

"Now I look more closely," he said, "I see there's a certain asymmetry about the room. There should be another meter of wall after this end window."

She stepped forward and ran her hand down behind the portrait. There was a click and the whole picture swung out of the wall to reveal an opening.

"Clever," he said. "Clearly constructed as an afterthought, hence the asymmetry."

"There was no need of priest-holes in 1535."

"Of course not," he said, stepping through the aperture.

He'd seen far worse hiding places. A man could stand upright in here. There was a faintly musty smell. With the picture back in place it would of course be pitch-black. He stretched out his hands and leaned with his palms against the wall. Then he closed his eyes and stood stock-still for a good half-minute before stepping back out.

"Was that a prayer you were saying?" she asked.

"No. I was just trying to get a sense of what it must have been like."

"And did you?"

"Oddly, no."

"Why oddly?"

He hesitated then said, "I'm usually quite sensitive to . . . that sort of thing."

"Perhaps terror, hunger, thirst, angry voices, metal-shod feet tramping, mailed fists banging, are necessary for a true appreciation of *that sort of thing*," she said.

"True," he said. "So is it recorded that Father Simeon ever took refuge here?"

"It's recorded that the house was searched at least twice, including this chamber, and no trace of him was found," she said. "Why so interested in Father Simeon?"

"I'm not really. But your father seemed a little sensitive on the subject."

"Not without cause. A priest in a Catholic family is often as much a cause for concern as pride, as perhaps your own family discovered."

She was sharp.

"But you must be impatient to get a start," she went on. "Follow me, please."

She walked away with an effortless almost gliding motion he found so much more effective than any seductive hip-waggling could have been.

The study was on the same floor as the gallery, a broad high room though with only one window. Against the side walls stood a pair of matching bookcases in dark oak. From the window he could see the plume of smoke still rising above the Forge, and further below, across the river, the stubby chimneys of the Stranger House. But Madero only spared the view a passing glance. His main attention was focused on the desk.

Here was God's plenty. Half a dozen octavo volumes, cased

in leather. Three folio ledgers. An abundance of loose sheets of varying sizes in two open box files.

For a moment he felt disturbed by such liberal cooperation, as perhaps a bright mouse might scenting the ripe cheese so generously scattered over the floor of the trap.

But in some things mice and men, bright or not, have no choice.

"Here's the letter of agreement," said Frek. "Sorry."

"No need to be. Your father's a wise man," he said, scribbling his signature.

"Have you read it properly?" she asked doubtfully.

"I heard what your father said it contained. To study it would be both redundant and offensive," he said, handing her the paper.

Their fingers touched. To prolong the contact, he did not let go immediately.

"I'm grateful for your help," he said.

"How do you know you've had it?" she said, pulling the paper from his hand. "If you turn left out of here then left again into a short corridor, you'll find a bathroom first on the right. I think that's all, unless you have any questions?"

"No. You have given me all that I want. I shall have no excuse for not getting down to some good productive work, unless I let myself be distracted by the view."

It was not consciously intended as a clumsy compliment but he realized that was how it sounded even before her eyebrows arched. He felt himself flushing under that amused gaze and turned to look out of the window at the panorama of valley and hills which was what he had consciously been referring to anyway.

"Yes, it is lovely countryside, beautiful and brutal by turns," said Frek, as if she valued both qualities equally.

The window was slightly open and he heard voices below. Looking down, he saw directly below him the Range Rover parked outside the front door. Gerald and Sister Angelica were getting into it. A moment later, the engine started and the car pulled away.

"Now that's interesting," said Madero.

Where the car had been standing was a mosaic in the form of an eight-pointed star with at its center a circle of gold infilled with white. There were letters printed both in the white and on the gold margin.

"You recognize it, of course?"

A test? He closed his eyes, remembered what Max had told him, ran his mental eye over the possibilities and said, "The Order of Pius IX. *Virtuti et Merito.*"

"Well done. My grandfather received it years ago, long before I was born. My great-grandfather, the one who insisted on the portrait in uniform, again wanted to mark the distinction with another painting. Grandfather refused, but finally compromised on a permanent reproduction of the award itself. Even here he insisted that the commemorative design should be set at ground level where people would tread on it and only see it if humble enough to lower their gaze. In fact this room gives the best view. It's a pebble mosaic, using stones from local Irish Sea beaches. You saw the designer briefly when we first met. Thor Winander, down at the Forge."

"A talented man."

"Oh yes. Thor has many talents," she said with her secretive little smile. "Now I'll leave you to get down to work or admire the view as you please. Till lunch, then."

She left. It would have been easy to indulge his fantasies a little longer, but at the seminary he'd been famous for his concentration. Before the door closed, he was riffling through the loose sheets. Builder's plans, household accounts, letters in various hands.

He put them to one side and opened the first of the leather-bound volumes. The page before him was covered in a minuscule scrawl. He took a powerful magnifying glass out of his briefcase and began to read.

Within a very few minutes all residual thought of Frek and her lily-white flesh had vanished from his mind.

3

Wolf head, angel face

Sam stood at the open end of the smithy and removed her Ray-Bans to let her eyes adjust to the change of light.

The scene before her was like an old painting, all heavy shadow and lurid glow. Winander was shoveling coals on to a forge. The air was heavy with the pungent smell of fire and hot metal.

"There you are," said Winander. "Just as well that wanked-out priest got a lift. He looked fit to collapse."

He dropped the shovel with a clatter that made Sam start. She tried to conceal the movement but he grinned to let her know he'd noticed, then went to a cool-box on a trestle at the back of the smithy and took out a can of beer.

"Need to keep your liquor level up in here," he said. "Catch."

He tossed her the can which she caught with one-handed ease. It was ice cold and the label boasted it was the strongest Australian lager you could buy.

"You trying to stereotype me, Mr. Winander?" she said.

"No. I'm not that subtle. The stuff was on offer last time I got into a supermarket. Never pass up on a bargain, Miss Flood."

He raised his eyebrows comically as he spoke. His eyes had a distinctly flirtatious twinkle. How did he get it there? she asked herself. With an eyedropper?

"Bit hard on Mr. Madero, aren't you? Calling him a 'wanked-out priest?'" she said.

"Did I say wanked-out? I meant dropped-out," he said. "Decided there were better ways of spending his life than wearing a skirt and pretending he never got horny. Perhaps I did mean wanked-out."

He ripped the ring-pull off a can, raised it high and let the beer arc into his mouth. Some of it ran down his cheeks and jaw on to his body. He was sucking his belly in, she noticed. Did he really think he was impressing her?

As if sensing a challenge, he set down his can and moved back to the forge where he put his right foot on a set of foot-bellows and began to pump the dull red coals to a white-hot heat.

It was a pretty effective performance, she had to admit. His skin was almost as brown as her own, his torso still slab muscled despite the waistline sag. His plentiful body hair was rejuvenated from gray to ruddy gold by the reflected fire. With each bend of the knee she could see the contours of his huge thigh muscle outlined against his trousers before he drove his foot down in a rhythmic movement which a susceptible woman might find erotically mesmeric.

And where, she wondered, sucking at her lager, did these mesmerized women pay the price of their susceptibilities? Did he take them here in the heat of the forge, creating Thor-like thunder by beating his hammer against the huge anvil as he grappled them close, then mocking their ecstatic cries as he entered by plunging a length of glowing metal into the cooling trough? Or did the great god carry them up to his god-size bed?

Or was he past all that and just enjoying talking the talk even though he could no longer walk the walk? Geriatric sexuality wasn't an area she had much experience of. Unlike Martie, she hadn't had to fight the dirty old dons off. Sometimes basilisk eyes came in useful.

She yawned widely, then said, "Is that good for your heart with the extra weight you're carrying? I'd really like to hear what you can tell me about my namesake before you drop dead."

He stopped straightaway. To do him justice he didn't seem out of breath. Also he smiled as if acknowledging a telling stroke and let his belly bulge over his waistband.

"Let's get to it then," he said. "You look ready for a refill."

He tossed her another can. Rather to her surprise she realized he was right and the first one was empty. He led her out of a door at the back of the smithy into a cobbled courtyard. Here she could see the rear of the main house and alongside it what had probably been a barn but which now had wide plate-glass windows to admit light into what looked like an artist's workshop.

The yard itself was scattered with the materials of his trade, or rather his trades. Lumps of wood, chunks of rock, a tubful of seashells, another of polished stones, some wrought-iron garden tables and chairs, and a small menagerie of delicate and detailed wildlife in various metals. But the thing which caught the eye was a tree stump standing upright on the cobbles and leaning back against the smithy wall.

The barkless and sun-bleached surface of the bole curved and twisted with a kind of monumental muscularity, as if some huge beast were trying to escape from the confining wood, an impression confirmed by the topmost section which was in the process of being carved into a gaping-jawed wolf's head. It was both repellent and compulsively attractive.

Sam went close and ran her hands over the sinuous undulations, feeling the grain against her skin.

"Irresistible, isn't it? Not a gender thing either. Men and women both the same," said Winander close behind her.

"It's the Wolf-Head Cross, isn't it? The other one I read about in Peter K.'s *Guide*."

"Now why should you think that?"

She peered at the residual branches which formed an irregular stubby crossbar.

"The nail holes are a bit of a giveaway," she said. "Did you put them there?"

"Nail holes? What an imagination you have! A few beetle holes perhaps. It's exactly as it was when we dragged it out of the Moss, except a bit drier."

"The Moss? Mecklin Moss, would that be?"

"You're remarkably well informed for a stranger," said Winander. "If you stay another couple of days, we'll have to elect you queen. Yes, it was Mecklin. I was helping a neighbor haul out a beast of his that had got bogged down when we chanced upon this. Something in that bit of bog must have preserved it, I don't know how. I hauled it out, cleaned it up and left it standing here till it told me what it wanted to be."

"And it told you, wolf?"

"Not really. In fact it was Frek Woollass who came up with that idea. She saw something lupine in the twist of the grain. She offered to commission me. I said I didn't want her money just her body so we shook hands on that. As many hours modeling for me as I took on the wolf head."

"So you've been dragging your feet," suggested Sam.

"Perish the unprofessional thought!" said Winander, twinkling. "I've had to prepare a site too. She wants her grandfather to have a view of it from his window. Gerry, her dad, isn't keen on having a view of it from anywhere. Too pagan for his taste. But like most young women of my acquaintance, it's Frek who calls the tune. So it will be in place as promised before she goes back to Cambridge which is this coming weekend."

"Cambridge? You mean the university?"

"That's the one. Our Frek is a real-life don. Eddas and sagas and Nordic mythology's her thing, hence maybe her fancy for the wolf. You don't seem impressed?"

"Seems a waste of good money teaching that stuff at university," she said.

"An opinion I'd keep to yourself if Frek's around," he said. "Anyway, this is promised, but if anything else takes your fancy, we'll see if we can work out a deal."

Another twinkle. He was irrepressible, she thought, as he flung open the double barn door and led her into the workshop. This was relatively tidy after the yard. Bang in the middle, lit by the rectangle of light falling in through the open door was a wide-eyed marble angel brooding over a headstone. Sam stood before it, struck by a sense of familiarity stopping short of recognition. She lowered her gaze to read the inscription:

BILLY KNIPP
taken in his 17th year
sadly missed by his grieving mother
"Think what a present thou to God hast sent"

"This the boy they buried yesterday?" she said.

"Yes. Almost done. I'll be setting it up later."

"Nice inscription," she said.

"Milton. If you knew Billy, you might think it a touch ironical."

He gave her a twinkle as if expecting curiosity about the boy.

Instead she asked, "So what are you, Mr. Winander—international artist or village jobbing craftsman, like your ancestors, according to Peter K.?"

He was hard to put down.

"From the stuff I see winning the Turner Prize year after year, the latter is the nobler designation. I am proud of the fact that once upon a time round here the Winanders did everything that needed to be done with hammer and chisel and saw and adze. First Winander son was the blacksmith, second the mason, third the carpenter."

"What did they do with daughters? Stake them out on a hillside?"

"You've definitely been reading up on us," he laughed.

"So what number son are you?"

"I was unique," he said. "So I had to do it all."

"Including the wild pranks I read about in the *Guide*?"

"Especially the pranks. Seen enough?"

"I reckon."

As she turned from the memorial she noticed something on the floor concealed by a piece of sacking. She pulled it aside and found herself looking at a reclining nude, half life-size, in some kind of creamy, almost white wood. It was a piece full of energy with the violent chisel marks clearly visible and nothing classical in the pose. It was blatantly sexual, legs splayed, vulva boldly gouged. Yet it had the same pensive features as the marble angel. And suddenly she knew whose they were.

"Miss Woollass certainly keeps her side of a bargain," she said.

If she hoped to surprise him, she failed.

"Yes, you know where you are with Frek," he said.

"You can even see where you've been," she said ironically. To her surprise her response made him roar with far more laughter than it deserved.

He led her from the workshop now into the house.

"Find yourself a seat in there if you can," he said. "Won't be a second."

Chaos resumed in the room he left her in. The only chair with space enough to sit on looked as if it had been cleared by natural slippage and her feet rested on a slew of books. The floor was littered with artifacts ranging from a Valkyrie bust in sandstone to a giant wrought-iron corkscrew twisted into a granite cork. The main ceiling beam was covered with hooks from which depended a row of grotesque and sexually explicit corn-dollies which dangled there like Execution Dock on a bad day.

The only conventional piece on show was a portrait enjoying sole occupancy of the broad chimney breast. Its subject was a smiling young man with tousled blond hair standing beside an apple tree just beginning to blossom. He was leaning forward with his outstretched hands cupping a nest in which half a dozen chicks had just broken out of sky-blue eggs. Around his feet were primroses, cowslips, wood anemones, all the flowers of spring, while the hills behind were bright with the yellow of gorse. Yet nothing in this exuberance of vernal color reduced the brightness radiating from the youth. On the contrary, he seemed its center if not its source.

"Ready for another?" said Winander.

He'd pulled on a T-shirt with the inscription *Love is an extra.* She checked the can in her hand, found once more it was empty. Beer and toast just vanished in Illthwaite.

She caught the new can he sent flying toward her, crushed the old one in her hand and looked for somewhere to deposit it.

"Chuck it in the corner," he said. "I'll probably be able to sell it to some rich Yank. Now, Miss Flood, as you've made it pretty clear you're not interested in either my art or my body, what is it you've come for?"

"I told you before. I want to hear about my namesake. Look, let's not pussyfoot, you saw me find the inscription on the church wall. You were up the tower, right?"

It was a guess but he didn't even argue.

"Yes, I went up the ladder, partly because I don't attend religious ceremonies, also to check to see if there were any evidence of your claim to have heard someone up there."

"Why didn't you just ask your Neanderthal chum? I was convinced I'd just made a mistake till I realized in the pub there were two of them."

"I did wonder. But you don't get far asking Laal questions he doesn't want to answer."

"Laal? That's what you called the one digging the grave, wasn't it? It can't have been him up there, must have been the other. What's his name?"

Winander took a suck of lager and said, "Laal."

"They've got the same name? Isn't it hard enough telling them apart anyway?"

"Impossible. That's the point. But here in Skaddale we find a way of dealing with impossibilities. So the rule is, whichever one you're talking to is Laal, which incidentally means little. The other one's Girt, meaning big. But as you never talk to him, to all intent and purposes, he doesn't exist."

He cocked his head on one side as if expecting bewilderment, or at least dissent.

Instead, after a moment's thought, she nodded vigorously.

"I like it," she said. "It's algebraic. And, paradoxically, even though it's a device to counter the problem of differentiation, I presume they go along with it because to object would be to allow themselves to be differentiated?"

He shook his head and said, "Too subtle for me, Miss Flood. I'm just a simple Cumbrian marra."

"Don't know what that means exactly, but I know it's a load of bull. You saw me read your inscription, Mr. Winander—"

"*My* inscription?" he interrupted.

"Come on!" she said. "I recognized the style. It looks like half the inscriptions in the graveyard, and that fancy Italian stuff on your gatepost was the clincher. You saw me, and you decided you'd better check me out, to see if I was going to kick up a blue about it or go quietly. Well, now you know. I'm not going anywhere, and the only reason I'm going to be quiet is so you can tell me what the hell this is all about. So start talking, Mr. Thor Winander, or I start yelling!"

4

Alice's journal

Miguel Madero was deep in the past.

He was a fast worker and within a very short time he'd seen enough to make him feel enormously privileged to be allowed access to this material. There was stuff here which a lot of TV historians would have given their research assistant's right hand for.

The octavo volumes were a combination of day-book and journal written over many years by that Alice Woollass whose name appeared on the date stone over the door. They required careful handling, the sheets having been sewn together, perhaps by Alice herself, and in many cases already either the thread had snapped or turned the hole in the dry paper to a tear. The leather cases were simply that, rectangles of animal skin cut to the size of the octavo sheets and folded round them for protection. Over the centuries the creases had become permanent. Part of Madero's mind deplored that nobody had ever thought to have the books properly bound, but another part was thrilled to be in contact with material exactly as its creator had left it. As he brushed his fingers over the sheets, he felt that his spirit was brushing against the spirit of the woman who'd written them.

And it soon became clear she was a woman worth knowing.

The journal element was not continuous, for there were many periods of their life, such as childbirth (frequent), sickness (her own or a child's, also frequent), and other emergencies or periods of intense activity when the opportunity and/or energy for writing was not available. Often it consisted of little more than an *aide-mémoire* account of domestic events. But from time to time Alice found leisure to indulge in longer, more reflective passages which allowed insight into her thoughts and concerns and personality.

She was, Madero worked out, only eighteen when the house was built and she lived another sixty-two years, during which time she saw first her son, then her grandson become master of Illthwaite Hall, on each occasion relinquishing just sufficient of her domestic responsibilities to her daughter-in-law and grand-daughter-in-law to affirm their status without noticeably diluting her own overall authority.

The first journal started with the arrival of the Woollasses in their new house. From what Alice wrote it was clear that, her youth notwithstanding, she'd been determined that her wishes and opinions about the layout of the building should be heard. In the journal she expressed her pleasure when she felt her desires had been met, but where they'd been ignored, she was vehement in complaint which she did not hesitate to pass on to her husband.

Yet she was no termagant bride, such as might make a man regret his folly in ever marrying. She was clearly proud of Edwin's standing in the community, she admired the way he managed his affairs and his estate, she praised and joined in his many acts of charity, and, though this was no confessional diary, recording and analyzing the intimate details of a physical relationship, an early entry—*to our chamber betimes Jub. Deo*—suggested that she took as much pleasure as she gave in the marriage bed. *Jub. Deo,* which Madero read as a reference to the hundredth psalm which begins *Make a joyful noise unto the Lord,* was subsequently shortened to *JD* in its frequent appearances, the last of which was dated only a couple of days before Edwin's death in April 1588.

This and other details he noted with a scholar's eye as he did a rapid preliminary scan through the books. There was much material here for his thesis in the form of a vivid contemporary response, sometimes at a distance, sometimes uncomfortably close up, to the see-saw rise and fall of Catholic fortunes in the sixteenth century. Alice's delight in taking possession of her new home was clouded by news of the destruction of the county's monastic centers. The Priory at Illthwaite, like Calder Abbey to the west, was an offshoot of the great Cistercian Abbey of Furness. Its main claim to distinction was that it had in its keeping certain alleged relics of St. Ylf which were associated with several instances of miraculous healing. When news of Calder's destruction reached the Hall, Alice prayed that Illthwaite, being much smaller, might be overlooked, but a few weeks later she recorded that Thomas Cromwell's men had appeared, the Priory had been pillaged, its treasures destroyed or stolen, and its buildings razed to the ground save for the Stranger House, which the dissolvers had used as their lodging and stables.

Nor was there better news elsewhere. The dismantling of the great and powerful Abbey of Furness stone by stone was recorded with horror. A small cause for rejoicing was the news that the prayers of the locals in Cartmel had been answered and the church of the priory there was to be spared though the rest of the site was leveled. But generally it was a tale of woe and destruction.

He skipped over the early pages which recorded the Woollass men's participation in the 1536 Pilgrimage of Grace which had nearly cost Alice's brother-in-law, young Will, his head. She gave thanks to God when Mary came to the throne in 1553, but it said much for her humanity that she reacted to news of Protestants being burned at the stake with the same revulsion she had shown at assaults on her coreligionists.

Then in 1558, Elizabeth inherited the crown and the screws began to turn again. The anti-recusancy laws, first introduced during the brief reign of Edward, were reinforced and much more rigorously applied. And soon there began that great priest-hunt which was eventually to have such significance for the Woollass family.

Alice had few illusions about her wild young brother-in-law, describing him at the time of her marriage as *a railing, mery rogue, fit for little save drinking and laiking; yet I cannot find it in my heart to dislike him!*

Her delight in his marriage to Margaret Millgrove was unreserved. Her husband, however, had mixed feelings. It was in his eyes a low and unsuitable connection for a Woollass. Cloth merchants, he proclaimed, were little more than plebeian leeches feeding off the real work done by shepherds, shearers, landowners. On the other hand to get Will settled was much, and Edwin allowed his wife to persuade him into acceptance.

However, as the Millgroves prospered and rose in social status, their enthusiastic embracing of the Protestant faith soon provided another source of contention. The story he'd heard from Southwell was all here, but from a much more personal perspective.

Alice deplored the growing rift between her husband and Will, and was active in encouraging the friendship between Simeon and her own sons, till Will accused the Illthwaite Woollasses of filling his boy's head with treasonable matter and forbade the visits. Simeon obeyed, and Will eventually added distance to duty by sending his son as the firm's agent first to Portsmouth, then to Spain.

Alice's journals now took Madero where Southwell's researches had not been able to go.

When Will finally severed relations with Simeon, he commanded his wife to have no more correspondence with her son. Dutifully, she obeyed. But she had not been formally forbidden from communicating with her Illthwaite in-laws and through Alice she obtained news of Simeon, who had kept in close touch with his cousins.

Alice was very careful never to record anything in terms which could incriminate herself or her family if read by a third party. Indeed, as Madero did his first rapid scan through all of the volumes which continued until just a day before Alice's death in 1597, he had a sense of gaps which closer examination confirmed, with sentences half-finished at the foot of one sheet not resuming at the top of the next. Perhaps the dilapidation of the primitive binding had allowed some pages to be lost over the centuries. Or perhaps Alice herself on a rereading had decided that some entries were potentially too revealing.

Nevertheless, with Mr. Southwell's neat record in his hand, Madero was able to reconstruct various events.

The search of Will's house in Kendal had taken place on a December morning in 1587. On the same day, Alice had noted that a traveler from Kendal en route for the port of Ravenglass had stopped at the hall briefly for refreshment.

Her next entry recorded, almost casually, that an officer of the North Lancashire Yeomanry, a gentleman of a family known to her husband, had called with a small troop of soldiers and asked permission to search the house and outbuildings for a fugitive priest. The search proving fruitless, the officer had apologized for disturbing them, then accepted their invitation to sit down with them and take supper.

It was clear to Madero what had happened. As the searchers departed from Will's house, Margaret had guessed that they were now heading for Illthwaite. She had then revealed to Will that she knew Simeon was in regular communication with his Illthwaite relations. Will would have flown into a fury but Margaret's fears for her son were far stronger than her fear of her husband. Again and again she would have protested, "But think! What if our son is at the Hall and they discover him?"

Finally Will's anger had faded as he contemplated the likely result of his son's capture. He had probably seen a heretic's execution. Memory of those brutalities would be enough to drive even the strongest anger out of a father's head. A trusted messenger must have been despatched to Illthwaite with orders not to spare his mount in his efforts to overtake the soldiers and warn his brother of the imminent search.

Then he and his wife sat silent to endure the long hours till the messenger returned.

Miguel Madero sat back from his work and let his creative imagination loose to roam this ancient house. He heard the soldiers arrive, registered Edwin and Alice's indignant reaction, watched the men trample through the chambers in their vain search. The officer sounded like a man who would direct the searchers conscientiously but without fervor. As for his men, probably most of them were indifferent as to whether they were ruled by a Catholic monarch or a Protestant so long as they got paid. So poke about, make a bit of noise, goose the maidservants, but don't do anything that might really piss off the family and make them chintzy with the victuals.

Had Simeon been here? he wondered. Alice was too wise to give even a hint in her journals.

The house had been searched at least once more after 1587. The second search in February 1589, conducted by the Yorkshire pursuivant Francis Tyrwhitt, seemed to have been a much more thorough job. Alice saw no reason to let discretion get in the way of setting down her typically forthright reaction to Tyrwhitt, describing him as having *the fawning maner of a Welsh dealer trying to sel a spavind nag at a horse-fayre.*

It was during this search that the concealed room in the Long Gallery had been discovered.

Typically Alice made no written admission that it was a priest-hole, saying only that *They made grate commotion when they chanced on that privy closet which my late husband had caused to be created for the more secure storage of our precious goods in the event, which Godde forbid, that Civill Strife or foreign invasion disturb the peace of our beloved countrie.*

Clever old Alice to have a good cover story ready in case the authorities ever found the hiding place, though, of course, like a trout in the milk, a priest in the hole would be more difficult to explain away.

You have e-mail.

It was the voice of his laptop, dragging him forward four centuries.

It was from Max Coldstream.

Hi, Mig

Glad to hear Southwell was a help. Nothing useful from Yorkshire yet. Tim Lilleywhite says he's unearthed a fair-sized portfolio of Tyrwhitt's personal records, but nothing on Simeon other than a bare reference to his admission to Jolley.

I passed your query about Molloy on to our library IT wiz who dug up some stuff. First name Liam. Seems to have been a competent freelance journalist who from time to time cobbled together books on topics he thought might titillate the debased palate of hoi polloi. Topcliffe and torture sounds very much his style. Our wiz came across a ref to a website which presumably went defunct with its creator, but evidently these things can have a kind of immortality of their own which may assist the Recording Angel in his work. The lad in the library seemed keen to try to track it down, so I said go ahead.

Good luck at Illthwaite. Be careful. Not sure how far the laws of God or man apply in those remote places!

Best, Max

Mig smiled. Coldstream was very much an urban animal, a small cuddly hamster of a man who loved the cozy nest he'd created for himself in Southampton but had somehow contrived to have connections and influence all over the world. In Max all that the view out of the study window would have provoked was a shudder.

Perhaps he was right. Perhaps other laws than those of God or man applied in this place.

He dismissed the speculation and turned to another, almost as troublesome. Had Father Simeon visited the Hall during those turbulent years of his work on the English Mission? Madero felt sure he must have done. Yet it was strange, that lack of vibration he had experienced as he stood in the hiding place in the Long Gallery. He had been a touch disingenuous when he told Frek he had a certain sensitivity to that sort of thing. It went a little further than that. If he closed his eyes now and emptied his mind of all distractive thought, he could get a sense of . . .

A strong human presence!

"I'm sorry you find our family records so soporific, Mr. Madero."

He opened his eyes and sat upright. Frek was standing behind him.

He reached forward and removed Max's message from the laptop screen. Had she had time to read it? Did it matter?

"Sorry, I was just . . ."

". . . communing with the spirits?" she completed. "Of course. Well, I'm sorry to drag your mind from the spirit to the flesh, but it's time for lunch."

If only you knew how easily you can drag my mind from the spirit to the flesh, he thought.

He stood up.

"Lead on," he said. "I have built up quite an appetite."

5

An amicable pair

Sam Flood and Thor Winander sat facing each other. He had picked up a wooden chair, tipped its contents on to the floor and set it down a couple of feet in front of her so that their knees almost touched.

He leaned forward. At this distance the whites of his eyes were bloodshot and she could see a network of tiny veins on his strong nose.

He said, "Let's get one thing out of the way so you don't build up too many expectations. You say it was the spring of 1960 your grandmother sailed?"

"That's right."

He said, "Our Sam Flood didn't come to live here till the summer of 1960. A year later he was dead. So that seems to cut out any possible connection with your gran."

His tone was brusque, his expression blank, as if he were merely stating facts too abstract to be involving. But the stillness of his body gave this the lie. It was the stillness not of relaxation but of control.

Sam said, "You said you'd tell me about him anyway."

"Did I? So I did. But I'm not always to be relied on, Miss Flood. I said I'd take care of Sam too, and look what happened to him."

He was trying to maintain a calm tone but she detected an undercurrent of savage self-reproach. For the first time it occurred to her that maybe people might be reluctant to talk about her mysterious namesake, not because there was something to hide but because there was something to hide from.

But she'd come too far to back off now.

"Look, I'm sorry if this is painful . . ."

"Are you?" he said savagely. "Know about pain, do you?"

"A bit."

"Yeah, yeah. The young know a bit about everything. OK. Let's get this done."

He sat back and his gaze focused away from her.

"Sam Flood," he said softly. "Like I say, I don't see any way you can be connected to Sam, but if you had been, then you'd have been very lucky. He was the best person I ever met. Absolutely. In every respect. The very best."

Suddenly he smiled directly at her. Or was it the other Sam Flood he was smiling at in his memory?

"So how did a notorious reprobate like me meet up with such a paragon? By blind chance, as I would put it. Or by the grace of God, as Sam would have put it. For he wasn't only naturally good, he was good by profession and vocation."

He paused while Sam worked this out.

"You mean he was some kind of priest?" she said.

"Indeed. You don't look impressed by the information. Not your favorite people, perhaps? Mine neither, but that's what Sam was, curate of this parish, no less, back in the days when the C of E could afford curates. Nowadays it's only the fact that Pete Swinebank is virtually self-supporting that means Illthwaite still has a vicar of its own. Of course, in Pete's case, the hereditary principle applies too, but he looks set to be last of his line, unless he's been ploughing fields and scattering the good seed in places we don't know about."

"Tell me about Sam Flood," insisted Sam, sensing evasion.

"That's what I'm doing," he said. "I met Sam when I was

doing my art course in Leeds. That surprises you? Me with qualifications, not just a natural genius. My father saw there wasn't much future in shoeing horses so he started to diversify. Even traveled abroad, which no self-respecting Illthwaitean did, met a Norwegian girl and married her. That's how I got to be Thor. Fitted somehow, as Winander is a Viking name anyway. Windermere means the lake belonging to Vinandr. I sometimes think I'll put in a claim."

For some reason this information put Sam in mind of her visit to the churchyard, but she brushed the irrelevancy aside.

"So you met this guy when you were a student," she prompted.

"That's right. He was at some vicars' training college close by. There was this chap making some interesting furniture in the same neck of the woods. I rode out there on my motorbike one day to take a look round his workshop. The bike spluttered a bit when I set off back to town and I was just passing the college gate when it gave up the ghost. Also it started to rain. In a few minutes it was a deluge. A bus stopped close by and some young guys, students from the college, got out. Most of them sprinted through the gates, but one of them came over. He said, 'Having trouble?' I answered something like, 'Who the fuck are you? The Good Samaritan?' You know, really gracious."

"Nothing's changed then," said Sam.

Winander grinned. He had a nice grin when it was spontaneous.

He said, "Wrong. Nowadays I'd recognize this guy was my best chance of getting out of the wet and come over all pathetic. Fortunately, as you've guessed, this was Sam Flood, and ill-mannered crap like mine just bounced off him."

He paused, then repeated, "Bounced off him. When I said that to Frek Woollass, she said he sounded like Balder. You ever heard of Balder?"

Sam shook her head.

"Me neither, till then. Seems he was one of the Norse gods,

the loveliest of them all both in appearance and in personality. He was goodness personified and everybody loved him so much that his mother Frigg had no problem getting everything that existed, animal, vegetable and mineral, to swear an oath that they would never cause Balder any harm. Eventually it became a favorite after-dinner game of the gods to hurl plates and spears and furniture and boiling oil at him, just for the fun of seeing it bounce off while he sat there laughing at them."

"Sounds more like the Pom upper classes than gods. I guess they didn't have any videos to watch in those days. We're drifting away from the story again."

"Not really. The only thing Frigg didn't get a promise from was the mistletoe, which she reckoned was too young and slight to pose any danger. Another god called Loki, who got his kicks out of making mischief, took a sprig of mistletoe, sharpened it into a dart and gave it to Balder's brother, Hod, who happened to be blind. Joining in the fun, Hod, guided by Loki, hurled the mistletoe and it pierced Balder right through the heart."

He fell silent. Sam had a feeling there was stuff here it might be dangerous to stir up. But all she wanted at this time were the straight facts.

"So Sam the Samaritan helped you," she prompted.

"That's right. Invited me to come and shelter inside. I did. We drank coffee and talked till the rain stopped. Then we went back out to the bike and got it to start. I said thanks to Sam. He was a genuine Christian with a real faith in human goodness. Not many around. Also he was a trainee parson, a Bible puncher, an idiot who felt called by God to waste his life standing around a drafty church, preaching to six old ladies on a good Sunday. Too many of them around. But Sam was different. I really liked the guy. He said he enjoyed football, so I gave him my address in Leeds and invited him to drop in next time he came to see United play. In fact I said if he came before the match, we could go together, and if there's anything I hate more than religion, it's football!"

"He sounds a real winning character," said Sam.

"Indeed. And before your brutish antipodean mind starts getting the wrong end of the stick, let me emphasize the attraction was queer only in the sense of odd. I had no desire to fondle his bum. I'll admit to enjoying the sight of him when we swam together in the buff, but it was an artist's enjoyment in beauty, the same that I might possibly get if you were to strip off, my dear, but without any of the concomitant carnal stirrings."

He leered at her unconvincingly.

She said with some irritation, "OK, you weren't after his body. What was it he was after? Your soul?"

"Certainly not my arse'ole," said Winander. "He was so straight you could have drawn lines with him. No, we just got on somehow, despite all the obvious oppositions. An elective affinity, I think the scientists call it."

"Or an amicable pair," said Sam.

"Sorry?"

"In math, that's what we call two numbers each of which is equal to the sum of the divisors of the other. The smallest ones, 220 and 284, were regarded by the Pythagoreans as symbols of true friendship."

"Well now, for a plain-speaking wysiwyg Aussie, you're full of surprises. Anyway, whatever the cause, we became good friends. I invited him to stay with me in the hols. He loved Illthwaite and of course Illthwaite loved him. Naturally he went to St. Ylf's during his visits. Surprisingly he and old Paul—that's Rev. Pete's father—seemed to get on well. Paul was old school, hellfire and damnation. Perhaps what he saw in Sam was all those parts of Christianity like compassion and forgiveness which his own leathery heart couldn't reach. Also that same leathery heart had been diagnosed as dodgy and he probably wanted someone he could rely on to keep the place ticking over till his own boy, our Rev. Pete, was old enough to follow the family tradition and rule at St. Ylf's. When he twisted his superiors' arms into providing him with a curate, and made sure Sam got appointed, even the ranks of infamy could scarce forbear to cheer."

"And Sam jumped at the chance to come here, did he?"

Winander shook his head.

"In fact, no. He agonized over it."

"But why, if he liked the place so much?"

"That was the trouble. He really felt it was too easy coming somewhere like this, to work in an area he adored among people he knew and liked. He thought he would be more needed elsewhere. He even asked what I thought. Big mistake."

"Why's that?"

"It was a bit like Eve asking the serpent whether he thought apples or pears were better for her teeth. I was at my subtle best. I didn't take the piss out of his desire for poverty and adversity. Instead I told him he could find that here if he cared to look. And I said maybe this yearning to fight the good fight in some godforsaken hole where everyone would know he was a hero was in itself a form of indulgence. Oh, I was persuasive because I was sincere. I wanted him to come here. And in the end I prevailed."

He fell silent for a moment then said flatly, "I sometimes think it was the worst day's work I've done in my life."

"Why do you say that?" asked Sam.

"Because if he hadn't come here, he might still be alive today."

Then he laughed without much humor and said, "On the other hand, if he were, he'd probably be a broken-down old nag like me."

"Comes to us all, I guess," said Sam. "But even avoiding that fate's not much consolation for dying at . . . how old would he be? Early twenties?"

"Yes."

"So how'd he die?"

And when he didn't reply she went on, "Killed himself, did he? Is that why he doesn't have a proper headstone?"

"You're a real little detective, aren't you?" he said. "Wondered why you seemed to get on so well with Noddy Melton."

She put that aside for future consideration and said, "So why did your friend who was such a great guy that everybody loved him, a guy who was so religious he became a parson, why did someone like that top himself?"

"Despair," he said shortly.

"Despair? What the hell's that mean?"

"God, you are young, aren't you? How can you be expected to get your head round the notion of grim-visag'd comfortless Despair?"

"From the sound of it your chum was just my age when he died, so try me."

He shook his head.

"No details. They're nothing to do with you. All I'll say is that the very essence of Sam Flood, the source of all his strength and the basis of his faith, was a belief in human goodness. Confronted by something that seemed to give the lie to this in a direct incontrovertible and personal way, he lost his whole *raison d'être*."

That his grief was genuine and deep was beyond all doubt. His body seemed to fold in on itself, and with the light of mischief and mockery switched off, his face became the face of despair, of a man condemned as much as of a man mourning.

Then he took a deep breath as if consciously reinflating himself and stood up so abruptly he knocked his chair over.

"End of stories, his and mine," he proclaimed. "And that's it, my young friend. I'm sorry if the sad coincidence of your name has caused you inconvenience or distress, but I'm sure it will quickly pass. For us who live here it's different. We had a young god living with us for a while, but we weren't good enough to keep him. If we don't talk about him, it's simply because nobody wants to talk about their shame. Please excuse me now. I have a headstone to finish and move down to the church."

"Couple more questions," Sam said peremptorily. "Tell me about the inscription."

He said, "Back in 1961 suicide was still a criminal offense and very much the unforgivable sin in the eyes of church traditionalists, and they didn't come any more traditional than old Paul Swinebank. Church burial was out of the question, so Sam was cremated, and you couldn't get near the crem. chapel for mourners. Then some of us scattered the ashes at St. Ylf's, around the Wolf-Head Cross. Someone said, "The cross will have to do for his memorial. Pity we can't carve his name, though." And I thought, right, we'll see about that. And I went into the churchyard one Sunday morning and carved my little tribute on the wall."

He grinned and said, "They could hear the sound of my chisel during the quiet moments in the service. Chip chip chip. I thought old Paul might try to get the inscription erased, but to his credit he didn't. He just let the nettles and briar grow over it. I didn't mind about that. Everyone who mattered knew it was there. They still do."

"And still keep their mouths shut more than four decades later."

"We're close and private people, us Cumbrians. We go to bed with gags on in case we talk in our sleep. And we don't trust strangers till they show us they can be trusted."

"No? Well, that works both ways, mister," said Sam, growing angry. "First time we met, I'd just been knocked off a ladder, remember? And I'm still not sure it was an accident. And last night in the bar when I asked for help, all I got was some crap about a guy who won a competition for pulling faces. So why should I trust you? What kind of place is it anyway where you get prizes for looking ugly? I'm not surprised that your chum couldn't take it."

She was ashamed of the crack even as it came out. It was a bad habit, going over the top. It made it that much harder to drive home your legitimate grievance.

But Winander was looking at her as if he understood, or at least as if he didn't resent what she'd said. It began to dawn on her that there was a pain here which nothing she might say could add to. Time for truce.

"Look, I'm sorry," she said. "That was out of order. I'm just disappointed. Your friend sounds like he was real special."

"Oh yes, he was," said Winander.

He was standing looking away from her with a faint reminiscent smile.

She followed his gaze. It took her to the painting on the wall.

"That's him, isn't it?" she said.

It was obvious. Now she looked again she could see the affection which had gone into creating the portrait. She studied it closely—the smiling mouth, the tousled blond hair, the bright blue eyes—looking for any resemblance with herself or her father.

There was none.

"He looks a nice guy," she said. "A real spunk. I'm sorry for your loss."

"And I'm sorry for your disappointment. But with your evident detective talent, I'm sure you'll track your family origins down in the end."

Her mind went back to his earlier comment and, glad now to move away from the dead curate, she said, "What did you mean about me getting on with old Mr. Melton?"

"Noddy? You don't know? He was a policeman. Started as the village bobby here years ago when I was just a kid. Moved on, but came back when he retired."

"Must have missed the place," said Sam, recalling the old man's reaction to the name Illthwaite.

"Funny way of showing it if he does," said Winander. "He's a nosy old sod, always stirring it."

"Why do you call him Noddy?"

"Enid Blyton. Gets a bad press these days but used to be

like a set text way back. We called him PC Plod to start with, but that didn't really fit till one of us kids said he looked more like Noddy the Elf, and that stuck. Like another beer?"

"No thanks. Time to go. Thanks for being so open with me."

"I'm sorry we gave you the runaround," he said. "I'll see you out. Sure there's nothing you want to buy?"

"Not on my budget," she said, laughing.

"You never said what you're doing here in the UK. Holiday, is it? The grand tour, backpacking round the world?"

They'd reached the front door and she was saved from answering by the appearance of an old pickup which came bumping down the driveway. In it were the Gowder twins. As it moved slowly by, Sam felt their eyes hold her in their sights.

"My helpers," said Winander.

"They work for you?"

"And for anyone who'll employ them," said Winander. "The Gowders used to be important people round here, but even with the slow rate of progress we admit in these parts, they still managed to get left behind. Jim, the twins' father, after his wife died he spent more time and money pissing up against walls than mending them. By the time the twins came into the farm there wasn't enough stock or land left to make it a going concern. They'd have lost the house too if Dunstan Woollass hadn't stepped in."

"The squire?"

"The same. And old Dunny takes his squirely responsibilities seriously. When Foulgate, that's the Gowder house, came on the market to settle their debts, he bought it and let them stay on at a peppercorn rent and saw to it that they can make a fair living odd-jobbing."

"Very community-hearted of him. I gather Gerry takes after him."

"Outdoes him in general do-gooding, but when it comes to the Gowders they're miles apart. He hates their guts. I think they must have bullied him at primary school."

"But you like them?"

"Good Lord, no," he laughed. "But they're part of Skaddale, like the rocks and the moss. And if you need brute force, send for a Gowder. Got to watch them, though. Because they can carry a tup under either arm, they think nothing's beyond them. Block and tackle's for wimps. We're taking Billy's angel down to the church later. Left to themselves they'd try to pick it up bodily and toss it into the back of the pickup. Eternal vigilance is the price of employing a Gowder."

"I'll leave you to it then," said Sam. "See you later, maybe."

At the gateless gateway she glanced back. Winander waved. The Gowders had halted their vehicle by the smithy and got out. She felt the intensity of their gaze like a gun leveled at her. And she knew with a certainty beyond the scope of mathematical logic that this was the same gaze she'd felt in that split second before the trap slammed shut on the church tower.

Suddenly her heart ached with a longing for home.

And I've eaten my last Cherry Ripe, too! she thought.

6

Ejection

Mig Madero sat in the kitchen of Illthwaite Hall and felt happy.

He and Frek Woollass were to eat alone. On the landing they'd met Mrs. Collipepper, carrying a tray. Dunstan, Frek explained, usually returned to his bed after the exertion of descending for breakfast. He lunched off a tray, then reemerged for tea.

The housekeeper passed without a word. Madero smiled at her but she didn't return the smile. He wasn't bothered. He had other things on his mind. Frek had set off down the stairs and as he followed, despite all his efforts at diversion, he found his gaze and his fancy focused on the point, occasionally visible as her T-shirt rode up from her hipster shorts, where that arrow-straight spine split the apple of her buttocks.

In the kitchen she completed his happiness by apologizing for the absence of her father who along with Sister Angelica had gone to a meeting of an educational charity whose committee they both sat on.

He'd expected something like the room in the Stranger House where he'd drunk cognac with Mrs. Appledore the previous night, but this was completely different. Contemporary wall units and electrical apparatus all looked perfectly at home against a background of golden-tiled walls. The broad windows let in plenty of light and looked out on a rising bank of grass and heather out of which some kind of platform seemed to have been carved about ten feet up. In the middle of the kitchen was a pine table of generous dimensions but a mere dwarf by comparison with that in the Stranger. On it stood a cheese board, a fresh cottage loaf and a bowl of fruit.

Frek shook her head when Madero pushed the bread toward her. Instead she took an apple and cut it in two. As the demiorbs fell apart, Madero's thoughts went back to his lubricious imaginings as he descended the stairs. Apple was wrong with its golds and reds. Frek would be white, two smooth scoops of ice cream with the promise of hot plum sauce hidden somewhere beneath . . .

"Are you all right, Mr. Madero? Not off with the spirits again?"

He realized he was sitting completely still with the cheese knife raised in his hand.

"I'm fine. But I wonder if I might have some water? It's a bit warm in here."

"Sorry. It's the Aga. Pepi always keeps the temperature up high for Grandfather's sake. Would you like a glass of wine? There should be a bottle . . . yes, there we are . . ."

She glanced around as she spoke. Like a sky-watcher who has found a new star, he kept his eyes fixed on her, and he saw discovery turn to recognition then to dismay.

He let his gaze drift along the line of her sight till it reached the looked-for bottle. It was his gift of El Bastardo standing already open next to a large crystal bowl through whose sides it was possible to see a layer of red topped by a layer of yellow.

"I think," said Madero carefully, "your housekeeper is preparing a sherry trifle."

"Yes. I'm sorry . . . Mrs. Collipepper must have picked it up by accident."

"Of course. Perhaps we should lead her out of temptation . . ."

She rose and brought the bottle to the table. It was three-quarters full.

"Would you prefer something else? It hardly seems right, offering you your own drink . . . and I don't even know if it goes with bread and cheese."

"We will call them *tapas*, in which case the fino is the perfect accompaniment. Your father will not mind us sampling the wine without him?"

He asked the question gravely, saw her seeking a polite way of saying Gerry wouldn't give a damn if they poured it down the sink, then smiled broadly and said, "Good. Glasses, if you please. Two. It is not polite to drink El Bastardo alone."

She went to a cupboard and produced two wineglasses, not *copitas*—that would have been expecting too much—but medium-sized goblets which he half filled.

"*Salud!*" he said.

"*Skaal*," she replied.

"What do you think?" he asked after they'd drunk.

"It's different from what I expected," she said.

"Not what you look for at the bottom of a trifle, you mean?"

"I have drunk sherry before, Mr. Madero," she said. "Sometimes it's unavoidable . . . Sorry, that sounds rude. I mean, sometimes . . ."

"Please, I understand," he interrupted. "In Hampshire, too, where my mother lives, the famous English sherry party is sometimes unavoidable. Usually served at the wrong temperature in the wrong glasses."

"I'm sorry if I've got it wrong . . ."

He said, "A bastard has to be robust enough to stand a little abuse. Which is not to say it lacks the refinement you would expect in a wine of such expense."

"I didn't imagine you'd brought Daddy a cheap bottle," she murmured. "But it does seem a strange name to give to an expensive wine."

"It dates back to a time when the Madero line looked as if

it might be cut short," he said. "Our family have always been merchants. Our business records go back to the conquest of Granada. We were prosperous, and well respected. Then in 1588, for reasons best known to himself, the third Miguel Madero of our records—first sons were always called Miguel—went off to fight the English with the Great Armada, taking with him his only son and heir. They both perished. His widow was a capable and determined woman, but ability and determination were of little use then without a man to channel them through. Happily, just as it seemed that the Madero line and business were doomed, it emerged that her lost son had contrived to impregnate his affianced bride before sailing. The boy was only sixteen and the girl fourteen, but the marriage had been arranged for almost a decade, and it suited the honor of her family and the fortunes of ours to acknowledge and accept the resultant bastard. Indeed, they even contrived to legitimize him by getting papal sanction for a retrospective marriage."

"They could do that?" said Frek.

"If you knew the right strings to pull. I think perhaps someone like your grandfather might have managed it, or do I read him wrong?"

She smiled and said, "No, you're right. But finish your story."

"Until the boy came of age, his grandmother kept the business afloat, quite literally. And he turned out to be a man of such energy that during the eighty-nine years of his life, he laid the foundations of the business as it exists today. Despite his papal legitimization, he was always known as the Bastard, and this name began to be given to the best of the wine he produced and shipped. Much later in the nineteenth century when the true refinement of sherry began, the very best of our finos were accorded the title alone. So I give you the toast. *El Bastardo*!"

Frek said, "A fine if lengthy story. Here's to bastards."

They raised their glasses and drank. He poured a refill and

helped himself to some brie. She took a wedge of cheddar and began to eat it with her apple. Watching the golden cheese and the red-and-white apple go into her mouth made him feel dizzy and he took another sip at his wine.

She said, "How is your work going, Mr. Madero?"

"I would like it if you would call me Mig."

"Like the Russian aeroplane?"

"I do not fly so fast nor am I so deadly."

"Surely nowadays it's regarded as rather slow and old-fashioned?"

"Then it fits me very well."

She smiled. They drank and refilled.

"And may I call you Frek? I like Frek. It sounds Nordic somehow. Like the old goddesses. Freyja, Fulla, Frigg. Yes, it fits you well."

A nicely turned compliment, he thought complacently.

She laughed and said, "I see you know your Norse myths a little."

"More than a little, I hope," he said, slightly piqued.

"But not enough to know that the nearest thing to Frek you'll find in them is Freki, who wasn't a goddess but one of Odin's wolves," she said. "Thank you all the same. It's good to know that even in Spain there's an interest in the Northern myths."

"I had a tutor who said the first duty of a good priest is to know the opposition."

"And he considered the Northern pantheon who haven't been around for a thousand years as opposition? That's a bit paranoid, isn't it?"

"Men have always invented the gods they need. Understand the gods and you'll understand the men. A priest should be able to understand men, shouldn't he?"

"It would be nice to think he might even be able to understand women," said Frek dryly. "I take it you don't include Christian deities in this pragmatic category? There we get into eternal verities, right? All the rest can be demolished euhemeristically."

"I wasn't trying to demolish, I was merely suggesting that an understanding of pagan belief systems is an essential sociological tool," said Madero, wondering how the hell his clever compliment had got him here. "I'm a historian, remember, not a priest."

"So you say. But to adapt a modern cliché, you can take the man out of the seminary, but can you ever take the seminary out of the man?"

"I don't know." He looked at her over the rim of his glass. "How about you? You come from a family willing to take great risks for the Catholic religion. I'd guess you went to a convent school. Your father clearly still adheres closely to the faith he was brought up in. Yet in you I detect at least a separation if not a distinct skepticism."

She said, "I bet you got full marks on your Father Confessor courses."

He felt himself flushing and said, "I'm sorry. I didn't mean to sound . . ."

"Priestly?" she concluded. "I'll be charitable and put it down to the historical researcher in you. You're right. If I have to pick a mythology, I find I much prefer that of the old Norsemen. That's why I've been teaching it at university for the past eight years."

He adjusted her age upward a little. Her looks were timeless.

"But you're not saying that you subscribe to their faith system?" he pressed.

"I can understand it. It was a religion for its times. Aren't they all? I sometimes think Christianity's time is passing. And just as Christianity cannibalized paganism, so the Next Big Thing will help itself to whatever it fancies from Christianity. It's already started, hasn't it? The music, the art. You can get a kick out of Bach's St. Matthew Passion without giving a toss about the story. And watch the tourists pouring into York Minster, how many of them sit down and say a prayer?"

"And will this Next Big Thing be another divine intervention? Or totally secular?"

"God knows. Or maybe not."

They both laughed. A shared moment. Then Madero said, "At least in a place like this you're not likely to be confronted by extreme manifestations of novelty."

"Don't be too sure," said Frek. "It's in places like Illthwaite, which no one in high authority pays much attention to, that changes begin."

"I think you'll find that Rome pays more attention than you realize to even its remotest outposts," said Madero rather smugly.

"I'm not talking about Rome," she said irritably. "Catholics are completely peripheral here. In the sticks, the C of E rules, OK? Oddly enough it was the Church of England that got me interested in paganism. I used to go to Sunday School at St. Ylf's. We were ecumenical in Illthwaite before they knew how to spell it in Rome or Canterbury. And in the summer Rev. Pete—that's Peter Swinebank, the vicar—used to sit us all down in the churchyard around the Wolf-Head Cross. Have you seen it yet?"

"No, but Mrs. Appledore mentioned it."

"You must let me show it to you if we can find time. It's a Viking cross full of reference to Nordic myths, all adapted to the Christian message of course. Rev. Pete used to explain it all, never realizing he was proselytizing for paganism! The Christian stuff I found pretty tedious, but that other world of gods and heroes and monsters and magic really turned me on. St. Ylf himself struck me as a boring do-gooder till I discovered his name meant wolf, and in some versions of his legend he took a wolf's shape when he appeared to lost travelers, and he only led those to safety who showed no fear, the others he drove over a cliff and ate. This stuff doesn't half make you talk!"

She held up her glass to be refilled. He topped up his own at the same time. The level in the bottle had sunk very low.

"It is one of its many beneficent effects," he said. "But you sided with your father when your parents separated; not, I presume, on religious grounds?"

For a second he thought this was a familiarity too far, but after a sobering appraisal from those cold blue eyes, she said, "He needed me more. But enough of me. Now it's your turn in the confessional."

"What can a man who has led such a sheltered life as me have to confess?"

"You can tell me for a start why you don't reckon Father Simeon spent much time in the priest-hole. You can tell me why you're so interested in Simeon, not to mention Liam Molloy and Francis Tyrwhitt. In fact, you might like to give a rather fuller account of yourself than the carefully weighted and meticulously filleted version you offered in your letter and your interview."

Wow. While he'd been fantasizing about this young woman's body, she'd been taking notes and doing close analysis.

"I see," he said, keeping it light. "You want full confession. And in return . . . ?"

"You get absolution, of course."

He sipped his sherry thoughtfully. It was tempting. There was an intimacy in the confessional which could lead to . . . what?

He opened his mouth to speak, not yet knowing what he was going to say.

He was prevented from finding out by the sound of footsteps approaching on the flagged floor outside, then the door burst open.

"There you are, Mr. Madero," said Gerald Woollass. "Enjoying your lunch?"

He sounded angry, and it occurred to Madero that somehow his lustful thoughts about Frek were visible, and he felt himself flushing even as his rational mind told him this was absurd. But there was definitely something bothering the man.

"Yes, very much," he said.

"Good. And your researches, how are they going?"

"I've made a good start."

"Yes, I know that. A very good start. But you made that yesterday in Kendal, didn't you, Mr. Madero?"

"Father, what's going on?" inquired Frek.

"You may well ask. I've just attended a committee meeting in Kendal, Mr. Madero. It's a Catholic educational charity aimed at helping disadvantaged youngsters and inculcating the virtues of piety, application, and a love of the truth. Worthy aims which I had assumed you would approve of, Mr. Madero. Until I got to chatting with our chairman after the meeting. His name is Joe Tenderley. Ring a bell? Tenderley, Gray, Groyne and Southwell. And you know what he told me? He said that his junior partner had turned up late for a meeting yesterday with the excuse he'd been detained by a visiting historian desperate to learn everything that could be dug up about Father Simeon Woollass. Now I knew it couldn't be you, Mr. Madero, having been assured only a couple of hours earlier that you knew next to nothing about Father Simeon and had only the most peripheral of interests in him. But it's a strange coincidence, isn't it?"

The savage sarcasm left no room for denial.

"Mr. Woollass, I'm sorry," said Madero, conscious of Frek's speculative gaze. "I should have mentioned I'd spoken with Southwell, but believe me, my interest in Father Simeon is incidental rather than central to my interest in your family. Let me explain . . ."

"Explain?" exploded Woollass. "You mean you have a backup story ready? What is it, I wonder? I know! You're really a *promotor iustitiae* specially appointed by the Holy Father himself to investigate the case of Father Simeon!"

"Of course not. What I'm trying to do . . ."

"Save your breath. I opened my family's records to you, Madero. I had doubts from the start, and I was right. Please collect your things from the study and leave. My daughter will accompany you to make sure you remove only what you arrived with."

"Father!" protested Frek.

"Just do it," commanded Woollass.

He turned on his heel and strode out of the kitchen.

Madero looked at the woman and waited for her to speak.

She said, "I suppose technically you ought to take the trifle."

"I can explain . . ."

"I'm sure you can. But *never complain, never explain* is a wise saying. Come."

She rose and made for the door. Together they went up the stairs and into the study. Here he carefully sorted out his notes, laying them to one side of the desk with the journals and household records. On the other side he set his laptop and briefcase.

"Perhaps you would like to check," he said.

"Don't be silly," she said.

"I doubt if your father would think it silly," he said. "Besides, if I may, I should like to use your bathroom before I go."

"Of course. Corridor on the left, the second door on the right."

He went out. Would she check that he wasn't taking anything he shouldn't? Her decision, and at least he had given her the chance.

The left turn took him into a short corridor with two doors on either side.

Just as he made the turn he froze in mid-stride as the second door on the right opened and a figure draped in cardinal red came out. He recognized Dunstan Woollass's dressing gown but it wasn't the old man wearing it.

It was Mrs. Collipepper.

She turned down the corridor without glancing in his direction. He watched her move away, registering the oil-pump shift of her heavy buttocks beneath the scarlet silk.

His mind was trying to sort out unvenereal reasons why she should be wearing the garment as she pushed open a door at the end of the corridor and slipped out of sight.

The door clicked shut and he resumed his advance to the bathroom. But he'd only taken a couple of steps when he saw the tail of red silk caught in the bedroom door. The dressing gown, made for a much taller figure than the woman's, had become trapped. Even as he looked, the door opened again, releasing a blast of warm air. Mrs. Collipepper, stark naked now, stooped to pull the rest of the gown inside. Over her shoulders, Madero glimpsed a four-poster bed with a venerable white-haired head resting on the pillow. The source of the heat was a deep fireplace in which a dome of coals and logs glowed red.

As the housekeeper straightened up, her gaze rose to meet his own. Her face showed no reaction. He lowered his eyes in confusion. She had breasts to match her buttocks with dark nipple-aureoles the size of saucers. He raised his eyes again and mouthed, "Sorry." Gently she closed the door.

In the bathroom he found his penis slightly engorged and had to wait a moment before he could pee.

As he stood there, a line flashed into his mind from Shakespeare whose works his mother had insisted he should read to balance Cervantes and Calderón.

Who'd have thought the old man to have so much blood in him?

Frek was waiting on the landing. Silently she handed him his briefcase. As they went downstairs, he wondered if she knew about her grandfather and the housekeeper. Of course she must know! Indeed, probably the whole village knew. It was well said that in the countryside a secret is something everyone knows but no one talks about.

Was it an active relationship? he wondered. Or was Mrs. Collipepper merely an Abishag to old King David?

Mig put the prurient speculation out of his mind as Frek opened the front door.

He stood there a moment, taking in the view. The sky was cloudless, the sun warm, the air so clear that he could pick out detail of rock and stream on the hills rising on the far side of the valley. The range of color was tremendous—vegetation all shades of green shot with patches of umber verging on orange where some plant was dying off; rocks black, gray and ochrous; water white falling, dark blue standing; and the land itself, pieced and plotted in the valley, rising to the horizon in pleats and folds like some rich material painted by one of the Old Masters.

"'The world lay all before them, where to choose their dwelling place, and Providence their guide,'" he said.

His mother's poetic patriotism had even overcome her religious prejudices.

"That's more or less what the Norsemen thought when they set out. Many of them chose Cumbria," said Frek. "Where will Providence guide you now, Mr. Madero?"

"Only as far as the Stranger House initially," he said.

He stepped across the threshold and turned to face her. His left leg took this opportunity to remind him it wasn't yet ready for complex maneuvers. He staggered a little and winced as he forced himself to put his full weight on it.

She didn't seem to notice, but miraculously she said, "Tell you what, I have to go to the village and I promised to show you the Wolf-Head Cross. Let me give you a lift."

"I doubt if your father would approve."

"I got over my Elektra complex several years ago," she said. "Come on."

She closed the door behind her and went to the parked Range Rover.

Madero headed round to the passenger door. His knee felt fine. He sent it heartfelt thanks for having done its job of getting him the lift.

"What are you smiling at?" she asked.

"At the thought that it's not so bad being ejected from Paradise so long as Eve goes with you."

It was by his standards boldly flirtatious, but it didn't fare much better than his previous attempt.

She said to him rather sadly, "I fear you really are going to find that you and I inhabit different myth systems."

And then they were speeding down the hill toward Illthwaite.

7

The tale of Noddy

"This used to be the police house," said Noddy Melton. "I came here back in 1949 I think it was. It was pretty primitive then, but it was my own. I loved it, ghost and all."

The old man was sitting upright in a tall-backed armchair which dwarfed him. Sam sat in a matching chair on the other side of the fireplace. We must look like a couple of kids who've strayed into a giant's house, she thought.

"You've got a ghost of your own?" said Sam.

"Hasn't everyone? Specially in Illthwaite," said Melton. "They took great delight in telling me the tale down at the Stranger when I first came. Long time ago the cottage was occupied by a widow who made a living out of making candles, hence the name. Seems one winter night when it was blowing a blizzard she opened the door to an old woman begging for shelter. She brought the visitor in, set her by the fire, and shared her supper with her. As she did so she got more and more worried by various things such as the size of the old woman's feet, her gruff voice, the hair on the back of her hands.

"But her worry became terror when, after they'd eaten, lulled by the warmth of the fire, the old woman dozed off with her head tipped back, revealing an unmistakable Adam's Apple. It was a man! Worse still, with the blizzard piling snow up against the windows, the candle maker was trapped, her and her young child sleeping in the corner."

"So what did she do?" said Sam, eager to short-circuit the story.

"She was desperate at the thought of what he might have in mind for her and her child when he woke. In the hearth there, by the fire, stood the tub of tallow into which she dipped the wicks to form the candles. The man opened his mouth wide to let out a tremendous snore. And without any more ado, the widow picked up the tub and poured the bubbling tallow down his open maw."

"Jesus," said Sam, shocked despite herself. "I guess that killed him."

"Oh yes. Worse, it was three days before a thaw allowed her to get out of the house and call help. Child in arms, she ran across to the church and got the vicar. It was probably a Swinebank. He came with a couple of other men, and one of these recognized the poor devil sitting here with his belly full of candle wax.

"Seems he was a harmless idiot out of Dunnerdale who, since the death of his mother, had taken to traveling around from church to church, dressed in his mother's shawl and gown, and begging alms."

"The poor bastard!" exclaimed Sam. "So what did they do when they realized what had happened?"

"That's what I asked when I first heard the story in the bar of the Stranger. There was a long pause, then Joe Appledore, the landlord, said, 'The way I heard it was, they took him into St. Ylf's, someone put a wick in his mouth, they lit it, and he burned lovely for the best part of a year.' Then they all fell about laughing."

"You mean it was all a gag?" said Sam indignantly.

"No. Seems likely it's a true story, except for the last bit. That's just their way of dealing with things. Now I don't believe in ghosts, but I learned two lessons from that tale. One was not to jump to conclusions. The other was, if ever I find myself dozing off in front of this fireplace, I get up and go to bed!"

"Wise man," she said. "So, despite the story, you liked the place so much you asked if you could stay on here after you retired. That's really nice."

She heard in her voice the reassuring note she used on small children and nervous dogs. She guessed he heard it too for he smiled and said, "I didn't spend all my career here. The cottage came on the market just as I was coming up to retirement. Change of policy, village bobbies out, two townies in a Land Rover driving by three times a week in. Progress! So they sold all the old police houses off. I pulled a few strings and got first refusal. Even then it cost more than I made on my place in Penrith."

"Penrith?" The only Penrith Sam knew was back home in New South Wales.

"Where County Police Headquarters is," said Melton.

Careful now, Sam said, "So you worked at HQ? That meant promotion?"

"Oh yes. Gradual. Sergeant . . . Inspector . . . Super . . . Chief Super . . . I ended up as the County's Head of CID."

He eyed her mischievously as he slowly went through the ranks.

Oh shit, she thought.

"That's great," she enthused. "You must have loved it here to want to come back."

He frowned and said, "Loved it? Illthwaite?"

He spat the word out with the same force he'd used twenty-four hours earlier.

Illthwaite. An ill name for an ill place.

So what was going on here? wondered Sam, as she sipped the tea he'd made and nibbled a biscuit. He'd offered her bread and cheese as it was getting on for lunchtime, and she'd said no, though if he had anything chocolate, the darker the better . . . and he'd come up with half-coated milk digestives.

Well, beggars couldn't be choosers of chocolate, but they could certainly pick their pitch, and she was starting to think this could be a complete waste of time.

Melton said casually, "They've probably told you I'm a bit cracked."

"Something like that," she said. "But I make up my own mind."

"That's the impression I get," he said. "Which makes me think it might be better if before we get on to your story, I tell you mine."

"I like a good story," she said.

He laughed, a high-pitched whinny.

"That's a perfect cue," he said. "*Do you like a good story?* was what my first caller said back in 1949. Farmer called Dick Croft. Big man in these parts, family had been farming here since the Dark Ages. I said, yes I did. He nodded and said, 'Then get yourself signed up with the traveling library next Monday, because you'll have plenty of time for reading.' I asked him what he meant and he said, 'The law's here already, son. There's God's Law and there's Sod's Law, and they take care of most things, and what they don't cover, we like to take care of ourselves.' And then he shook my hand and went."

"Weird," said Sam. "And was he right?"

"Mostly he was. I certainly did a lot of reading. But a young man can't live on books alone, and after three or four years when I began to feel I'd got accepted as one of the community, I picked myself a girl. A local lass. Her name was Mary. Mary Croft."

"Like in Dick Croft? His daughter?"

"The same. We didn't make a big public show of things. Not that you needed to in Illthwaite. Break wind in the church and they'll get a whiff in the Stranger thirty seconds later, that's what they say. Anyway, I was smitten. I asked her to marry me. Imagine that. I asked Dick Croft's daughter to marry me, and her only eighteen."

"So?" said Sam, puzzled.

"Still a minor back in those days. Needed her father's consent. Her mother had died when Mary was a lass. There was a stepmother, far too young to be a second mother to Mary. Anyway, her father had things worked out for her future. A neighbor's son. Bring the two landholdings together. But Mary dug her heels in. She and her dad didn't get on. He was a right hard bastard, but she had a mind of her own too."

He paused. The sharpness of his eye was misted. It was hard to imagine this aged elf as a young romantic but Sam made the effort.

"So what happened?"

"She vanished," he said.

He spoke the word flatly, leaving her to grasp at its meaning.

"Vanished? Like . . . what? She took off? Got abducted? Died . . . ?"

He said, as if she hadn't spoken, "We used to meet behind St. Ylf's, by the Wolf-Head Cross. Popular place for courting couples. Well hidden—at least, that's the theory."

He rose from his chair and went to stand by the window from which the stumpy church tower was visible over a clump of blood-pearled rowan trees.

"I wanted to talk to her father, but she said it was pointless, he'd rather see her die an old maid than get mixed up with a thick copper. I could see only one way to get Croft to agree to a wedding. That was to get Mary pregnant."

He turned to face Sam.

"You know what young men are like. I'd have been at it already, but Mary always said she didn't want to take the risk. But now risk was our best hope. At first she looked at me like I was daft. When she saw I was serious, she said she'd think about it and we arranged to meet three nights later. I said, 'Come to Candle Cottage if you decide yes. I don't want our first time to be in a cold and drafty churchyard.' She kissed me then. A real passionate kiss. It felt like a promise."

He looked around the room, as if searching for something he had misplaced.

After a while Sam prompted, "So what happened?"

"You can imagine the state I was in for the next couple of days. I kept thinking of that kiss. God, how the time dragged. Then the night came. I couldn't sit still. I must have walked twenty miles up and down this room. It's a wonder I didn't put my hand through the window the number of times I rubbed the pane to see if I could spot her coming."

Abruptly he sat down once more.

"But she never came. I sat up waiting till I fell asleep in my chair. Early next morning I was woken by knocking. It was Dick Croft, demanding to know where Mary was. He burst in and started searching the cottage. It was the start of a very confusing period. I didn't know if I was on my arse or my elbow. By the time things got official, the story had settled down to this: Mary had told her stepmother that I'd given her an ultimatum, either we had sex or it was all off between us. She was going to say no and wanted to do it to my face but was a bit scared. And then she'd vanished."

"I thought you said she didn't get on with her stepmother?"

"I said she couldn't be a proper mother to her. Anyway, we've only her word for what was said. But the upshot was, suddenly I found myself sitting in front of a DCI hitting me with questions about whether she'd come to the cottage to break things off and I'd got angry and there'd been a fight and maybe there'd been an accident . . . He thought he was offering me an easy way out. I told him to sod off. God knows how it would have finished, but then things changed. Mary's stepmother found some clothes were missing. And the following day she took a phone call from Mary. *I'm OK. I'll be in touch when I'm settled.* Nothing more. There was no technology in those days to check where the call came from. Or even if it came at all. But it was enough for the CID. Now it was simply another runaway case. No crime, so I was no longer a suspect.

Which was ironic, as I was the only policeman in the county who didn't believe she'd done a runner."

He shook his head and fell silent for almost a minute, rapt in his memories, till Sam, who had never been long on patience, rattled her teacup.

"Sorry," he said. "I'm talking too much about me. This should be about you."

"No, no," said Sam. "I need to know what happened next."

"That's simple. I left Illthwaite. It's funny, if we'd got married I'd have happily spent the rest of my days as the village bobby. As it was, Mary's disappearance was the making of my career. A year later I transferred to CID. I was a natural. The trick-cyclists say a good detective will always have at least one case he keeps open in his mind long after it's been closed in the files. I brought mine to the job with me."

"And you've kept it open ever since."

Sam tried to sound sympathetic but prevarication wasn't her strong suit.

"You're thinking that makes me a sad bastard, aren't you?" he said, smiling. "I could have been, but I met a lass in Penrith. We got married, me and Alison. I never forgot Illthwaite, but it didn't get in the way of having a life. If we'd had kids, or Alison had survived to share my retirement, I doubt if I'd ever have come back here. But we didn't, and she didn't. Cancer. God rest her."

"I'm sorry," said Sam.

"So am I, every day. She left a gap I filled with work. And when the work stopped, I had to find something else to fill that gap. When I saw the Authority was selling off Candle Cottage, it seemed like a message. So I bought the cottage, and came back here. Me versus Illthwaite, round two. First round Illthwaite won hands down. This time, I thought, it's going to be different. If that's sad, I'm sorry. But it's kept me alive."

"What about Mary?" asked Sam. "You get any nearer to finding out the truth?"

He smiled rather slyly and said, "Hard to say. Dick Croft died a few years later and the stepmother sold up and moved away. But I'm still here where everyone can see me. There's two histories of Illthwaite, the official one, the kind that gets printed in books like Peter K.'s *Guide*. And the true history that only gets written in people's minds. To read that you need to be around a long time. Passing through, you've got no chance."

"Which is why you asked me here, right? To improve my chances?"

"I don't know if I can, my dear, but if I can, I will. First you must tell me what it is you are truly seeking for."

He settled back in his chair, fixed her with a keen unblinking gaze, and said quietly, "In your own time, my dear."

8

A bag of stones

Nothing had changed, at least nothing you could factorize. But somehow it felt to Sam as if Melton had switched elderly eccentricity off and an interrogation tape on. She was beginning to think this wasn't a guy to mess with. On the other hand, unless he started after her with a rubber truncheon, she saw no reason to give more detail than she'd already put on public record.

She said, "Like I said in the pub last night, I'm looking for information about my paternal grandmother. All I know is she was called Sam Flood, she came from England to Australia in spring 1960, and she might have some connection with Illthwaite."

Melton took a notebook out of his jacket pocket and made a note.

He said, "Did she sail with other members of her family?"

"No. She was part of that Child Migrant Scheme there was all that fuss about when the details came out a few years back."

"I remember," he said. "Isn't there a Trust that gives advice and help?"

"Tried them. Nothing positive."

Not directly anyway, and it seemed best to keep things direct.

"Have you found anything to support this possible connection since you got here?"

"Only the name Sam Flood carved on the churchyard wall."

He showed no reaction, which must mean he'd known about it too.

"It struck me as odd that no one made any reference to it," she went on. "But I've just been talking to that guy Thor Winander and he filled me in on the story and now I guess I can see why people don't want to talk about it."

"Yes, he tells a good tale, Mr. Winander," murmured Melton. "So now you're happy it's just coincidence? Mission accomplished? No link?"

She thought about this then said, "Almost. But once you write stuff on the board you can't just scrub it off."

He looked puzzled then said, "Are we talking mathematics here?"

"That's right. Sometimes you do a calculation on a blackboard. Blackboards are good because it means you can see the whole thing at once. Most calculations aren't aimed at finding something out but at arriving somewhere you want to be. But you don't always get there. Maybe you've gone wrong. Maybe you started in the wrong place. But even if you wipe the board clean, all that stuff's still in your mind to go over again and again, maybe for years, maybe forever. Sorry, does that sound crazy?"

"Sounds like good detective work to me," he said, going to a tall mahogany bureau that occupied almost the whole of one wall. From his pocket he took a bunch of keys attached to his belt by a chain. He used three of the keys to unlock the bureau cupboard doors which swung open to reveal lines of files and a stack of cardboard boxes.

"My blackboards," he said. "Nowadays it would be disks, but I'm a paper man."

He removed one of the files then dragged out a box which seemed too heavy to lift. He sat down and opened the file on his knee.

"Samuel Joseph Flood. Appointed curate of St. Ylf's in August 1960. Found drowned in Mecklin Moss in March 1961. Inquest held in April . . . Here we are."

He took out a folder which held some typewritten A4 sheets stapled together.

"What is that stuff?" demanded Sam, impressed.

"Record of the inquest."

Jesus, when he said he had connections, he meant connections.

"How'd you get a hold of that?"

He said, "I told you. I was Head of CID for fifteen years. All cases of sudden death came under my remit. Any linked to Illthwaite I took a personal interest in."

She was starting to think there was something just a bit scary about Noddy Melton. Not the scariness of insanity, maybe, though it might have something to do with its near cousin, obsession. But if it prompted him to help her, why knock it?

"Now, what do we have?" he asked, studying the report. "Canceled Bible class that afternoon. It was a Sunday. At two o'clock the vicar, Mr. Swinebank, took Sunday School with the younger kids in church while at three Flood held a Bible class for the eleven-pluses in the church room attached to the vicarage. That day the kids found a notice on the door saying the class was canceled . . . no one much bothered till he failed to turn up for evensong . . . the vicar might have got worried a bit sooner but he was distracted by a family emergency . . . checked Mr. Flood's room in the vicarage after the evening service . . . no sign . . . reported his concern to PC Greenwood circa 7.30 P.M. . . . Greenwood mounted a search but soon had to call it off because of darkness and foul weather . . ."

"PC Greenwood? Your successor?"

"Next but one. The one that followed me didn't take, so they got him moved."

"Who's 'they'?"

"The power brokers—Woollasses, the vicar, Joe Appledore at the Stranger—"

"You mentioned him before. What's his relationship to Mrs. Appledore?"

"Joe was her father."

"Then why's she called Mrs.?"

"It seems she went off to catering college in Lancashire. Did her course, fell for one of her tutors, they got wed and set up in business down there. When her dad died she and her man—Buckle was his name—came and took over the Stranger. I gather Buckle didn't like it round here. He wanted to sell up and move back south. That can't have gone down well. There's been Appledores running the Stranger for centuries and they don't like change in Illthwaite. But, to general relief, he died before anything was decided. Heart attack. They said. So Edie stayed put. Pretty soon folk were back to calling her Appledore, with the Mrs. tagged on in acknowledgment she was a widow."

"Weird," said Sam. "What about her mother?"

"Died when Edie was fourteen. After that she ran the house and helped out in the pub."

"With all that hands-on experience, why did she need to go to catering college?"

"Good question," said Melton approvingly. "Story is she had a disappointment. Round here that can mean anything from cut out of a will to crossed in love. Anyway, same result, she almost got away, but the tendrils snaked out and pulled her back in."

Like you, thought Sam.

"You were telling me about the local power brokers?" she prompted him.

"Oh yes. A lot of voices, but ultimately it's the Woollasses who really make things happen. Local power's nothing unless you've a line to the big power sources outside. Committees, dinners, charities, old-boy networks, that sort of thing. Upshot was that in the end they got the kind of policeman they wanted.

Sandy Greenwood. Stayed here for nigh on twenty years till they pulled the plug on village bobbies."

"So he'd know the patch pretty well?"

"He'd know which farm would dish up the best tatie-pot and how many free pints he could sup after hours at the Stranger and still be able to cycle home," said Melton scornfully. "Likely if they'd told him not to worry about the curate going missing he'd have done nothing. But people were worried. The missing man was very popular. It was established that there'd been three sightings. One as he came out of the vicarage gate, the next along the main road through the village, the third and last on Stanebank, the track that leads up by the Forge and the Hall. If you keep going where the track bends round to Foulgate, you get to Mecklin Moss. First thing next morning the search was concentrated up there, and about nine o'clock a cross belonging to Flood was found. They kept on looking and the body was recovered at quarter to eleven."

"Poor bastard," said Sam. "And he'd definitely drowned himself?"

"Didn't seem any doubt. No note, but they found that Flood's pockets were filled with stones. I've got them here."

Out of the box he pulled a Hessian sack which he opened to let Sam see inside. It was filled with smooth rounded stones, black and white and gold and ruddy brown.

Jesus! she thought. What else had he got in there? Skulls and body parts?

"About four kilos, I'd say," said Melton. "Enough to counter the natural buoyancy of his clothes. No point hanging about when you've made up your mind. No marks of violence on the body, evidence of an agitated state of mind . . . Hard to make it accidental death, so the coroner reluctantly brought in a suicide verdict."

"Why was he reluctant?" said Sam, dragging her gaze away from the sack.

"Serious business in those days, suicide. You could go to jail for it."

An old police joke, she guessed. Maybe it had once been funny.

He went on, "In addition, Flood was a Man of the Cloth. Farmers can top themselves in droves and it's regarded as a risk of the job, but vicars are expected to show a better example. Also everyone who gave evidence went out of their way to say what a splendid young man he was . . . beloved by everyone . . . a picture of perfection . . ."

"Balder," said Sam, recalling Winander's story.

"Sorry?"

"Nothing. Any explanation of this agitation?"

"None offered formally. Law says all relevant information has got to be supplied to the coroner. What's relevant is up to the investigating officer. In this case it was an old boss of mine, DI Jackson. Good man, Jacko. Not much got past his beady gaze. Dead now. His missus told me after the funeral, take anything you want, Noddy. As a souvenir. I had a ratch around. Jacko was a bit of a trophy man. Liked something positive to remind him of his cases. His wife was going to junk it. Don't blame her. Some of the stuff . . ."

He shuddered. Pot calling the kettle black, thought Sam.

"That's where you got the stones?" she said.

"That's right. The Illthwaite connection. But what I really wanted was this—"

He delved in the box again and produced a battered notebook which he opened.

"You can learn a lot from a good cop's notebook. Jacko might have had his little quirks, but he was good. Now, let's see. The vicar, Mr. Paul Swinebank, that's Rev. Pete's dad, gave a glowing testimonial. His explanation was that maybe his curate felt the woes of others too intensely. In some ways—his words—he was too good for his own good."

"Much good it did him," said Sam.

"Eh? Oh yes. The inscription. The anticlerical Mr. Winander. Took a nonbeliever to get really indignant that they wouldn't give him a church burial."

"What did the vicar say about the way Flood was acting the day he died?"

"He appeared quite normal during the morning services and at lunch. The vicar left shortly before two o'clock to go to the church in preparation for the Sunday School. He was accompanied by his housekeeper, Mrs. Thomson. He was a widower, by the way. Mrs. Thomson's duties included acting as monitor at Sunday School. I gather some of the kids used to get restless during his analysis of the Church's Thirty-Nine Articles."

He uttered his ironies deadpan in a neutral monotone.

"Any suggestion he was screwing her?" asked Sam.

The old man looked at her blankly for a moment, then grinned.

"Jacko did write *Query jig-a-jig* alongside their names, which I wasn't going to mention out of delicacy but I see I needn't have bothered. Who knows what goes on under a cassock? But I doubt it. Rev. Paul was old school. St. Ylf's didn't need central heating. His description of hell could get you sweating on the coldest winter day."

"You knew him?"

"Oh yes. He was in charge when I arrived. Not a comfortable man. To him pastoral care meant getting your Sunday roast carved before the gravy went cold. His son's a different kettle of fish, like he's trying to compensate. Real helpful to everybody."

Not to Aussie visitors asking awkward questions, thought Sam.

"To continue," said Melton. "On their return shortly after three, he and Mrs. Thomson were surprised to find a note canceling the Bible class pinned to the vicarage door. About fifteen minutes earlier, the curate had been seen coming through the vicarage gate by two boys on their way to Bible class. Silas and Ephraim Gowder."

"The Gowder twins?" exclaimed Sam. "Jeez, no wonder they don't bother with names. Which is which?"

"How would I tell you?" said Melton. "You've obviously met them."

"I saw one of them digging a grave when I visited the church yesterday. And I've got a feeling the other was up on the church tower."

"Before your accident? Which I heard was caused by the wind blowing the trap shut. But you suspect a human agency?"

"I'm probably wrong. Why should a Gowder want to harm me?"

"The thought processes of the Gowders are mazy and hazy," said Melton. "They strike me as a throwback to some race which preceded man. They are not brutes, they are not malevolent, but they act and react instinctively, which means that sometimes their actions can appear both brutish and malevolent. I shouldn't care to provoke them."

"Which I did by climbing up the ladder?" said Sam incredulously.

"Hard to credit, but not impossible for a Gowder. I doubt he meant to harm you."

"Then he shinned down the ladder and left me for dead? Sounds like harm to me."

"All he would see was trouble for himself if he tried to help you or summoned aid. But to return to their evidence: they declared that Mr. Flood stopped when he saw them and told them the class was canceled. They didn't notice anything odd."

"Would they, being the Gowders?" said Sam.

He said, "Oh, they're sharp enough, believe me. Next witness was Miss Clegg, district nurse. At five past three she passed Flood walking down the main road. They spoke briefly, a conventional exchange, she said, but he seemed rather agitated."

"That's two down," said Sam. "Who was it who saw him going up Stanebank?"

"That was Dunstan Woollass from the Hall. He was driving down the Bank about three-thirty when he spotted Flood. He wound down the window to say hello. The curate just nodded and went on by. He looked very pale, the squire thought. On his return that evening when he learned that Flood was missing, Mr. Woollass contacted the police and that's why they concentrated the search on Mecklin Moss."

Sam ran her eye along a mental blackboard, checking the equations so far and trying to compute where they might lead.

She said, "And the verdict was suicide, so something happened early that afternoon to push him off his trolley."

"True. Though as I once heard the police trick-cyclist say, we shouldn't forget that an event can take place in the mind with no apparent external cause."

"Nothing happens without cause," said Sam with the certainty of one to whom the concept of infinity was a working tool. "Any lunch guests? Any visitors after lunch?"

"No guest. No visitors that came forward."

"What about the son, Pete? He'd just be a boy then. Was he at home?"

Melton smiled approval, and said, "Jacko asked that too. Yes, he was there."

"And did Jacko interview the boy?"

"Ultimately. This was the emergency I mentioned before. Pete was eleven. When he found Bible class was canceled, he bunked off before his dad got back and headed up the valley with the Gowder lads. They were in the same class at school and quite matey. They were scrambling around on some rocks when he slipped. Only fell about six feet or so, but he managed to bruise himself badly, twist an ankle and break his wrist."

"Poor kid. No wonder his dad was distracted!"

"Distracted . . . yes. And probably hopping mad his son had been breaking the Sabbath. The boy had to go to hospital, of course. They kept him in for observation. The Rev. Paul got back just before evening service was due to start. He expected that his curate would have shown up by now and have everything in train, so I daresay he wasn't best pleased to find he had to head straight into church himself and do the business."

"So when Jacko got to see the kid, what did he say?"

"Nothing helpful. Yes, he'd spoken briefly with Sam after lunch—he called him Sam, Jacko noted. He said he'd been in his bedroom getting ready for Bible class when the curate called up the stairs that it was canceled. Then he went out."

Sam thought for a while, then said, "So what it's all down to is a crisis of faith. Suddenly starts wondering if there really is a God, so kills himself to find out. Is that it?"

"*Balance of mind disturbed*, it says here. I think your version sums it up better."

"What about DI Jackson? What did he think? You said he had his own ideas."

"Maybe. But nothing to bother the coroner with."

"I don't reckon you've kept hold of his notebook out of sentiment, Mr. Melton."

"You're right there," said Melton. "Get sentimental about the past, you stop seeing it properly. OK. Jacko did have a working hypothesis, nothing he could prove, so it stayed in his head with a few hints in his notebook. It ran something like this. Sam Flood got on well with kids. Both sexes. Maybe too well. When pressed, Greenwood admitted he'd heard a rumor about the curate and some underage kid, but no names and nothing substantial enough to make him dust his magnifying glass off. Mind you, Jack the Ripper would have been on his sixth victim before Greenwood began to get suspicious."

"But your Jacko found nothing to confirm this?"

"Not a jot. The more questions he asked, the more they clammed up. Pride themselves on taking care of their own here in Illthwaite. So all Jacko could do was speculate. Suppose Mr.

Flood found he had a taste for young flesh? Suppose he even found himself fancying young Pete Swinebank? Jacko got a sense the boy was holding something back. Maybe something happened after lunch when they were alone."

"Like?"

"Like he went to the boy's room and saw him naked and was horrified to realize just how much he fancied him. Or maybe it had nothing to do with the boy. Maybe he got a phone call. Or made a call and heard something that really threw him . . ."

Sam shifted in her chair. It was time to go. As an exercise in mathematical logic all this might be of some interest, but from a personal point of view all Melton had done was confirm what Winander had told her. But the old cop had been very kind.

She said, "Thanks for going to all this bother."

"No bother. It's always good to entertain a pretty young stranger. Sorry I've not been able to help much, but maybe that's not a bad thing."

"How do you work that out?" asked Sam.

"Your gran left England in spring 1960, the Reverend Sam Flood didn't arrive here till summer 1960. Conclusion, there's no connection, which has to be good news because, believe me, Illthwaite's the last place on earth you want to be looking for something the locals don't want you to find. Ask them the time of day and they'll likely say they'll let you know as soon as their sundial comes back from the menders."

Sam laughed and said, "Does that include everybody? I mean, when the vicar said I couldn't look at the parish records because they'd been stolen in a recent burglary at the church, was he telling the truth or just trying to stop me spotting Sam Flood's name?"

Melton went to his bureau and produced another folder.

"Silver chalice, paten, two collection plates, candlesticks, poor box—nothing about records. Would surprise me. Billy was no

Einstein, but in his own line of business he knew enough never to steal anything he couldn't sell."

"Billy? You mean the police know who did the break-in? Has he been arrested?"

"Not by the police," said Melton. "Didn't even figure on their list of suspects till I told them. Even then they could find no evidence. But everyone round here knew it was Billy, like they knew it was him did the Stranger last summer, and the Post Office too just before it closed down. He probably got fair warning. But kids like Billy don't listen."

"He must be really scary if the locals let him get away with robbing their own church," said Sam.

"I think most of them felt they could leave it to God to take care of his own business. Which, it would appear, He did. Billy had a motorbike. There was an accident. His full name was William Knipp. Illthwaite's teenage tearaway. They buried him yesterday."

9

Interpretations

Mig Madero stood before the Wolf-Head Cross. He felt no impulse to kneel.

"I've seen a lot of Christian antiquities," he said slowly. "But never one that felt as *alien* as this."

"You feel that too?" said Frek. "Usually Viking crosses are interpreted as showing how the new religion took over from the old. This one makes me look at things the other way round, as if the old religion were getting a burst of energy from the new."

"So let my lesson begin," said Madero. "Tell me what I'm looking at."

"If you like. Right, let's start at the bottom panel here at the front," said Frek.

She took him through the cross's Viking elements, speaking quickly and not dwelling overlong on any one feature, but this was no mere tour guide's rote recitation. Everything she said was shot through with real enthusiasm.

"And this panel here is really interesting," she said finally. "As you can see, it's badly eroded. In fact I think there's more damage here than even ten centuries of Cumbrian weather can account for. I'd say at some point someone took a hammer to it."

Madero stared at the panel on which he could scarcely make out anything.

"Christian orthodox backlash, you mean?" he said. "Some pagan linkup that went too far for even the Illthwaiteans to stomach?"

"Maybe. I've looked at it very closely over the years. Made rubbings, taken photographs. I think it's something to do with Balder. You know the Balder legend?"

"Yes. Killed by a dart of mistletoe. But why should he attract special attention?"

"Think about it. The legend is clearly a version of the same nature regeneration myth we see in the cults of figures like Adonis and Thamuz and Attis. Balder, son of Odin, is slain. Later he rises from the dead to take his place in the reconstituted creation that emerges from Ragnarok, the Nordic version of apocalypse. Remind you of anyone?"

"Yes, yes," he said impatiently. "I have read a little."

She seemed amused rather than annoyed by his sharpness.

"Sorry to be teaching my grandmother," she murmured. "Then you'll have no problem seeing that using Balder as an unsophisticated prefiguration of Christ was a pretty obvious move for the clever old priests reworking the ancient myths. But suppose a mason somehow managed to insinuate that Christ was merely a pale imitation of Balder who is the real regenerative spirit?"

A movement caught Madero's attention and to his annoyance he saw a figure coming round the corner of the church. It was the strange Australian child, her mane of red hair awash with sunlight. Not child. Woman, he corrected himself. But with a childish indifference to interrupting the adult intimacy he hoped was springing up between himself and Frek.

She made straight for them, responding to his discouraging glance with a mouthed *Hi.*

Frek, showing no sign of having noticed Sam's arrival, went on, "In addition, some scholars have detected the presence of two figures on the defaced panel. The other could be Hod, Balder's blind brother, who was tricked into throwing the fatal dart. Hod too rises after Ragnarok and takes his place alongside Balder in the new pantheon. That would be like elevating Judas alongside Jesus in Christian terms. You can see how this might be too much for some true believers to swallow, hence the defacement."

Sam said, "Everyone round here seems pretty taken with this Balder guy."

Frek looked at her as if one of the attendant sheep had spoken.

"Everyone?" she said with polite incredulity.

"Thor Winander anyway," said Sam. "Said you thought my namesake, the guy who topped himself, sounded a bit like him."

Mig understood none of this but it seemed to make some sense to Frek, who was regarding Sam with rather more interest.

"So I did. It was well before I was born, of course, but some stories enter into local legend. In the poor fellow's reputation for goodness, charisma and beauty, I felt there was a parallel with Balder. Is there a possible link with your family, Miss Flood?"

She made it sound as if she hardly thought it likely.

"Doesn't seem to be anything I can find and the dates don't check," said Sam.

"A pity. Or perhaps not. Now here's something which is really interesting, Mig."

She stooped to indicate the inscription on the lowest step of the cross's base, obliging Madero to stoop also, physically reinforcing her verbal exclusion of the Australian. He felt quite sorry for the girl.

Frek continued, "The carving is clear, but the meaning is completely obscure. Could be Runic with a bit of Ogam, maybe. One more than usually nutty Oxford professor claims to have proved it was a version of the ancient Cypriotic syllabary. It's been variously interpreted as a prayer, an epitaph, and a biblical quotation. Take your pick."

"How about the maker's name?" said that by now unmistakable voice.

Frek turned her head this way and that with the faint puzzlement of a saint hearing voices in the bells. Then she rose to her full height, at the same time lowering her gaze to take in the little Australian.

"I'm sorry?"

"Sort of a label," said Sam. "I wondered about it when I saw it yesterday. I had this hunch the symbols could be semagrams maybe forming a rebus. And the crossed lines could be a date. Thought I'd like another look."

"You are an expert on archaeological decipherment?" said Frek incredulously.

Sam laughed.

"Hell, no. But I did go out with this guy who thought that encryption/decryption was the be-all and end-all of mathematics and I read some of his books so we'd have something to talk about. There was a lot of language stuff in there, the Rosetta Stone, Linear B and so on. I guess you need to be a mathematician as well as a linguist to really get to grips with that gobbledegook."

"Is that so?" said Frek, in a voice so coolly polite you could have served caviar on it. "And has this strangely acquired wisdom produced any positive interpretation you care to share with us? The date perhaps?"

The Australian frowned slightly as if for the first time detecting antagonism, but replied relatively mildly, "Let's see. If it's a simple pentadic system, it would be 1589. Yeah, that would be it."

Frek laughed out loud.

"Only five or six centuries out," she said. "Or the mason couldn't count?"

Sam removed her sunglasses and turned her unblinking

slatey gaze on Frek who, rather to Madero's surprise, let herself be faced down.

"Sorry," said Sam. "I should have said. I didn't mean the original maker's name but the repairer's. It came to me when I was talking to Thor Winander this morning and he told me his name was the same as some old Viking who got a lake named after him."

"Thor's been playing that little game with you, has he? My ancestor who owned Windermere," said Frek, smiling. "But it's true that it figures on old maps as Winandermere, meaning the lake of a man called Vinandr."

"There we go then," said Sam. "This oval here with the wavy line in it, that's this Winander lake."

"And these earlier symbols, you're saying they're semagrams too?" said Frek, clearly still doubtful but now, Madero observed, genuinely interested.

"Yeah. Difference is they form a rebus. This one here, the triangle like a roof, I think that's a barn. And this one with the little cross on top, I reckon that's an abbey. All the other stuff is just a bit of ornamentation to confuse matters."

"And this gives you . . . ?"

"Barn abbey Winandermere," said Sam slowly. "Barnaby Winander who, according to Peter K.'s *Guide*, restored the cross in 1589. And from what I've read about the family and seen of this Thor guy, that's exactly the kind of daft trick he'd get up to!"

"Well, well," said Frek softly. "You are a surprisingly clever little thing."

Madero could see that the Australian didn't care to be patronized.

"Nice of you to say so," she said, looking up at Frek as if seeing her for the first time.

Then her eyes widened in what looked to Madero like a parody of recognition and she exclaimed, "Hey, I thought you looked familiar."

"I saw you briefly this morning outside the Forge," admitted Frek grudgingly.

"No. Not outside the Forge. Inside. You must have been the model for that carving Mr. Winander did. It's a real close likeness."

She let her gaze slide down the other woman's body and grinned as she added, "So far as I can see, that is."

A tiny smudge of color touched Frek's cheeks.

Madero, intrigued, said, "What's this then?"

Sam said, "Hang around and I daresay you'll get the chance to check it out for yourself."

She paused long enough to see the smudge spread into an angry flush before adding, "Yeah, Mr. Winander said he'd be bringing it down here this afternoon. It's the headstone for Billy Knipp's grave. Miss Woollass modeled the angel. Right?"

Their gazes locked. The flush subsided. Then surprisingly there was the suspicion of a smile and Frek said, "I may have provided the features, the form was Thor's idea. It's been nice to meet you again, Miss Flood. You've given me food for thought."

She offered her hand to Sam who took it, surprised rather than reluctant.

Frek brought her other hand up and held Sam's enclosed in both her own as she continued, "I hope you enjoy the rest of your holiday. You too, Mr. Madero. I need to be off now. No need for you to rush. You must be dying to see the inside of the church. Perhaps Miss Flood, who knows so much, can give you the tour. Unless you don't feel up to walking and really need a lift back to the Stranger . . . ?"

Nice twist, thought Sam approvingly. She had spotted that the woman had taken Madero by surprise. Would he play the poor invalid or take it on the chin like a hero?

He said, "I'm fine."

"Then I'll say goodbye. I'm sorry things didn't work out."

She gave Sam's hand one last squeeze, let go, turned and walked swiftly away.

Together they watched her out of sight round the side of the church.

"Lovely mover," said Sam. "Things didn't go so well then?"

He didn't try to deny it.

"No," he said. "Does your fund of arcane knowledge in fact extend to showing me round the church?"

"I'd rather not," she said. "Someone in there doesn't like me. Anyway, I need to get my gear together. I'm moving on today. See you around maybe."

She moved forward past the cross to the churchyard wall and stooped down to push aside the veiling weeds.

"Well, Sam Flood," she murmured softly. "What are you? Mr. Perfect, or Mr. Pervert? And have you got anything at all to do with me? God knows, and maybe it's best I stop trying to get in on the secret."

She released the vegetation, stood up and turned round to find herself face to face, or rather face to neck, with Madero whose curiosity had made him follow her.

"Talk about creeping Jesus!" she said angrily.

"I'm sorry," he said. "But that name on the wall, isn't it yours? Sam Flood?"

"That's right. So what?"

"I've no idea. Is this what you and Miss Woollass were referring to just now?"

"Why don't you ask her? No, sorry, I forgot. It doesn't sound like you two will be getting much chance of talking again."

"Doesn't it?" he said, slightly taken aback by the sharpness of her riposte. "Well, they say fortitude is the virtue of adversity, don't they?"

"Not where I come from. Kick against the pricks till the pricks stop kicking back, that's what my pa says."

He surprised her by laughing out loud, knocking a decade off his age.

"A natural philosopher by the sound of him. But my morning hasn't been altogether wasted. As for meeting Miss Woollass again, I daresay God will provide an excuse, such as, for instance, my need to retrieve my briefcase from the back of her car."

He smiled at her, and she found herself smiling back. When he smiled you could almost forget he was a wanked-out priest.

They walked together round the side of the church. She noticed that he was moving much more easily than when last she'd seen him laboring up Stanebank.

As they came in sight of the churchyard gate, they saw it was wedged fully open and Pete Swinebank was helping the driver of a pickup to reverse in. On the back was Billy Knipp's memorial stone. Supporting it on either side, like a pair of pet apes positioned to emphasize the angel's brooding beauty, stood the Gowders.

Safely through the gate, the vehicle came to a halt as near as it could get to the young man's grave. As Sam and Madero approached, Rev. Pete turned and saw them. He looked distinctly uneasy.

Not without cause, thought Sam grimly. Not mentioning my name being carved on his wall and all that crap about stolen records. I could probably get him defrocked!

She had a flash image of ripping off his cassock and seeing him standing there in frilly undies. This, plus the almost comically abject guilt of his expression, softened her heart toward him a little and when he said uncertainly, "Hello again, Miss Flood. How are you today?" all she replied was, "What do you think, Vicar?"

Madero gave her the same look he'd given when she'd chilled out the nun, then said with a compensatory if not quite natural heartiness, "Vicar, I'm pleased to meet you. Michael Madero. I've just been looking at your splendid cross."

They shook hands. Thor Winander got out of the cab. Sam walked toward him. As she passed Swinebank he gave her an appealing glance. She ignored it, fixing her gaze on one of the Gowders at random and saying, "Lovely day, Laal."

He studied the statement and her face for a menacing moment before replying ponderously, "Not si bad, eh?"

It works! she thought.

Winander smiled at her as if appreciating her experiment and said, "Nice to see you again. And in clerical company once more. He seems quite taken with my angel."

Madero was standing by the pickup, staring up at the angel, rapt, while Swinebank was hurrying toward the church, probably to try a quick prayer for my rapid disappearance, thought Sam.

Winander called, "Good day, Madero. Thor Winander. We met briefly last night."

The Spaniard wrenched his gaze from the memorial.

"Mr. Winander, pleased to meet you again," he said.

He advanced to shake hands then glanced back at the statue.

"It's a fine likeness," he said.

"You recognize my model then? The lovely Frek is an artist's dream, her essence redolent through all materials. Wood you can smooth and polish till you can hardly get a grip on it, yet gouge a cut with your chisel and there's always the risk of a splinter."

He glanced at Sam as he spoke and did his eyebrow thing.

"As for marble, that's perfect too." He reached up and laid his hand on the angel's breast. "Always cool, even in the sunlight. Oh, by the way, talking of Frek . . ."

He returned to the cab, reached in and pulled out a briefcase.

". . . I met her getting into her car just now and she asked me to give you this—"

What God gives he can take away, even excuses, thought Sam.

Madero accepted the case with grave thanks, took a last rather sad look at the angel, nodded at Sam and said, "If you'll excuse me . . ."

As he walked away Sam saw that his limp had returned.

"I gather he's been banned from the Hall," said Winander. "I asked Frek why. She said something about sherry trifle, but I never could get much sense out of her. Or indeed anything else. Don't suppose our divine dropout gave you a confessional hint?"

"Wouldn't recognize one of them if it peed against my leg," said Sam, finding herself surprisingly defensive. "Don't see that it's anyone's business but Mr. Madero's."

"Good Lord," said Winander, looking at her closely. "Is this why you spurned me? Muscular athleticism is *démodé*. Mediterranean injured boy look is in! Well, my dear, in case you're dejected at the thought of competition, perhaps I can reassure you there—"

Sam interrupted what sounded like more tedious innuendo by saying sweetly, "Excuse me, but I think your angel could be about to lose one of her wings."

Winander turned to follow her gaze. The Gowders, impatient of delay, were maneuvering the statue off the truck by main force. One twin was standing at the tailgate with his arms wrapped round the angel, which looked ready for flight. Only the presence of his brother on the flatbed hanging on to one of the wings stopped the whole weight of the marble from crushing him into the ground.

"Jesus wept!" screamed Winander. "How many times do I have to tell you stupid bastards to wait till I set up the block and tackle!"

They had themselves a real problem, she thought with a certain not very becoming satisfaction. But one which could be solved by a bit of simple math involving critical angles, friction resistance, and dead weight.

She wished all her problems were as easily solved.

10

Knock knock, who's there?

Once again, as on Stanebank that morning, it didn't take Sam long to catch up with the Spaniard. As she drew alongside he gave her a not very welcoming glance. Up yours too, she thought, thrusting the Illthwaite *Guide* at him.

"You might as well have this," she said. "I'm out of here soon as I get paid up and packed."

She would have accelerated by him, if he hadn't snapped out of miserable mode, flashing that rejuvenating smile as he said, "No chocolate on offer this time?"

"I'm right out. Thought you didn't like it anyway."

"I feel I could do with an injection of energy from any source. But that's life. We never want what's on offer till the offer is no longer there."

"That from the Bible?" she inquired.

"Oh no. The Bible says *Ask and it shall be given you.*"

"Handy. So why's it not raining chocolate?"

"I think the offer predates the product."

"Pity. Your mob could have done themselves a bit of good if you'd been able to break squares off a choc bar instead of handing out those tasteless little wafer things."

"You have a problem with religion, I think," he said gravely.

"Why should I? You don't have a problem with me, do you?"

He thought about this and then smiled again and said, "No, I don't think I do. You seem to have made a friend of the famous forger back there."

"Sorry?" said Sam, puzzled by the shift.

"Mr. Winander. From the Forge. Hence, forger."

A joke. But a hit too. She had the impression that Winander would get as much pleasure from fooling you with a forged masterpiece as from producing a real one. Maybe the Spaniard felt this too. More probable, she thought, he's taken against Winander because he's had Miss Icicle as a model. In which case, he should thank his anti-choc god he didn't get to see the wood carving!

They walked the rest of the way to the pub in a silence which, surprisingly, was more companionable than combative. In fact, with the sun shining bright and Madero by her side, the distance seemed only half of what it had been the day before.

When they reached the Stranger, they found it locked, and several loud bangs at the door failed to rouse Mrs. Appledore.

"Not to worry," said Sam. "I've got a key."

She unlocked the door and they stepped inside.

On the landing, Madero said, "I hope you find what you're looking for, Miss Flood."

"You too," she said.

He offered his hand which she took. Rather gingerly, but he didn't hold on half as long as the Woollass woman.

In her room Sam found an envelope on the pillow. In it were her bill and a note.

Dear Miss Flood
Dead quiet this lunchtime so I thought I'd shut up early and head off to do some shopping. If you've decided to move on, please leave money or check on kitchen table. No credit cards. Sorry. Hope you enjoy the rest of your visit to England.
Best wishes
Edie Appledore

Sam felt some regret that she might not see Edie Appledore again before she went. There was something very likeable about the woman. But there was no reason to hang around. While it seemed a large coincidence that there'd been a bloke here called Sam Flood who'd topped himself, her study of probability theory had taught her to be unimpressed with coincidence. Flood was a common enough name, the dates didn't fit, and the curate's sad end explained why the locals wanted to draw a decent veil over the event. So best to ship out. The fact that her appointment in Newcastle wasn't till the following afternoon gave her the chance to drive at her leisure and enjoy the scenery.

She checked her bill which was fine except that Mrs. Appledore clearly had a problem with VAT at 17.5 percent and had settled for something like 12.3 recurring. Sam adjusted it, wrote a check and put it in the envelope. Then she went down to the kitchen. She pushed the door open, stepped inside and did a little jump as she saw a dark figure standing at the end of the huge table.

It was Madero.

"Jesus!" she exclaimed, annoyed at showing her shock. "How the hell do you get down those stairs without them creaking? That something you learned at the seminary?"

She regretted her rudeness instantly but Madero didn't show any sign of reacting. Indeed he hardly seemed to have noticed her entrance. He was leaning forward with both hands on the table, his head bowed, like a man about to say grace before dinner.

"You OK, Mr. Madero?" she said, moving toward him.

Now he raised his head slowly. The pupils of his eyes seemed huge, as though expanded in a desperate search for light.

He said, "I felt something in here last night . . . It was what I expected to feel up at the Hall . . . but something more . . . yes, something stronger . . ."

He started moving down the side of the table, running his fingers along its edge.

Sam went to prop her bill up against the telephone. She noticed the phone was unplugged. The reason for Madero's presence was made clear by the sight of a laptop connected to the point. Her gaze drifted to the screen. There was an e-mail displayed plus the *Download Complete* box. She didn't mean to read it, but even a brief accidental glance was enough to print words and images on her mind.

> *Hi! Just to say my tec wiz unearthed the old Molloy website. Nothing on it but a self-promoting CV plus a selection of articles he'd written, presumably the best—if so, God help us! But interestingly one of the pieces (which I attach) demonstrates that he'd actually been to Jolley Castle and dug into the archive there. Tim Lilleywhite's been back on this morning. He's 99% sure he's trawled up all the Tyrwhitt stuff now and definitely nothing more on Simeon. Sorry, but this Simeon thing is really a bit of a red herring, isn't it? The main thing is your recusancy research. Hope that's going well. Try not to fall into any priest-holes!*
> *Cheers*
> *Max*

As she turned away, she found herself thinking, with slightly malicious amusement, old Max isn't going to be pleased when he hears how his Holiness has cocked things up!

She set off toward the door. Madero was now sitting at the bottom end of the table, his face still rapt. As she passed him his hand snaked out, seized her wrist and forced her hand between his legs.

"Feel this," he said. "What do you think this is?"

She bunched her other fist preparatory to punching him in the throat, then realized he was pushing her fingers along the table's under-edge.

About nine inches from the corner there was a groove about

two inches long, ending in a deep hollow. When her no longer resisting hand was moved along, she found another one the same distance from the other corner.

"They mean something," he said. "I feel it as strongly as I didn't feel it at the Hall."

"Feel what?" she demanded.

"There was this so-called priest-hole," he said impatiently, as if expecting her to understand him without explanation. "But I got nothing there. Whereas here . . ."

So Max, the e-mailer, hadn't been joking. He really was looking for priest-holes! Which, he might be surprised to discover, she knew a great deal about. Well, a little deal.

One of her teachers used to read her class books she'd enjoyed in her own English childhood. OK, they'd been a bit old-fashioned, but Sam had loved these tales of tomboy girls in remote manor houses and boarding schools who were forever stumbling on secret passages and hidden chambers. Priest-holes were ten a penny in the UK, it seemed to the young Sam, and the land must be so honeycombed with subterranean passages that it was a wonder it didn't just crumble underfoot.

Madero, like a good failed priest, was looking upward in search of inspiration. Sam looked up in search of clues. Right above her were the cured hams dangling from the hooks beneath the crossbeam. She recalled her reaction when she first noticed the pulley system the previous day.

She said, "What's a ham weigh? Ten kilos? Wouldn't have thought you needed such a high-geared ratchet for that."

Madero's gaze came slowly back into focus.

"Maybe they had bigger hams back then," he said.

"Maybe."

She went to the spindle on the left-hand wall and examined it closely. After a moment she pulled out the brake chock and began to lower the ham.

"Come on!" she said impatiently, looking across at Madero.

He took her meaning instantly and went to the other wall.

For a few moments the only sound was the clacking of the ratchets as the hams descended. Hers landed first and, as she started to unhook it, she glanced his way again but this time did not need to speak. Funny how well their thought processes seemed to slot in together when they got beyond their instinctive antagonism. Together they bent down to fit the free hooks into the grooves and hollows beneath the table, then returned to the winding gear and in unison began to turn the handles.

Even with the gearing cogs, it took a good effort to lift the solid table, but slowly the massive legs rose. The hams began to slide down the slope and Sam paused, but Madero kept winding, so she resumed, wincing as the hams crashed to the floor.

When the table reached an angle of about forty degrees, Madero commanded, "Enough," which was just like a guy. You have the idea, he's not happy till he's taken over. Now he dropped to his knees to examine the granite slabs of the floor, in particular the two which bore the circular print left by five centuries of pressure from the table legs. They were both a couple of feet square.

"There is some movement here, I think," said Madero excitedly.

"So what?" said Sam. "Even if it does lift out, unless all your priests were my build, you'd never get one of them through a hole that size."

"But it must signify something," he insisted.

"Maybe. Look, if these old monks were clever enough to devise that lifting gear, they'd probably have something a bit more complicated than a simple trap."

"Like what?"

"Well, like a counterweight system. Yeah, that could be it. How about if these two small flags are counterweights and when the table legs are resting on them the trap entrance is completely locked. Let's see . . ."

She looked around, and finally her gaze came to rest on the greenish rectangular slab with the carving on it.

"This looks a possible. What the hell does this stuff say?"

"It's from the Bible. Matthew 7:7. Curiously, I quoted part of it as we walked along the road. *Ask, and it shall be given you. Seek, and ye shall find. Knock, and it shall be opened unto you.*"

"Knock, and it shall be opened," she echoed. "OK, let's try."

She knelt down and gently tapped the end of the slab.

Nothing happened.

She tapped again, harder.

Still nothing.

He said with a patience worse than mockery, "I think unless there is somebody down there to answer, your knocking theory is a non-starter."

"Don't be a smart-ass," she retorted. "If these guys were as bright as I think, they'd know to the last gram just how much pressure you needed to move the counterweights, and it wouldn't be much, else what's the point? You'd want something like this to be swift and smooth and pretty quiet. Know what I think?"

"Not yet," he said.

"I think it's got gunged up. Jeez, could be centuries since it's been used."

She stood up, reached one foot forward and drove it down on the slab.

Nothing moved.

She did it again.

"Think I felt something there," she said.

"Sam, be careful," said Madero.

It was the first time he'd used her given name but it didn't feel like a step to intimacy, more like a parent admonishing a naughty child.

So her natural adult reaction was to act like one.

She fixed him with her slatey gaze and said, "Knock, knock; who's there?"

Then, jumping as high as she could into the air, she came down with all her slight weight on the end of the slab.

It was enough. It was more than enough.

With a smooth swiftness which gave her no time at all to react, the slab pivoted away beneath her feet to reveal a black hole into which she vanished like an insect picked out of the air by the tongue of a lizard.

11

Trapped

Sam lay on her back looking up.

It took a lot to frighten her. Snakes and spiders she could react to with clinical efficiency. Heights didn't faze her and she had been able to swim like a fish since the age of two. But dark confined places found all of her panic buttons.

In one sense, she knew exactly why. She could recite the math of increased blood pressure, diminution of oxygen supply, failure of motor functions and so on in great detail.

But what really pressed these buttons, she didn't have the faintest idea.

It was a relief therefore to be able to fix her gaze on the distant square of luminosity that marked the heaven of the kitchen. The silhouette of Madero's head which now appeared should also have been a comfort, but all she could think was that the stupid bastard was blocking the light!

"Sam!" he called. "Are you hurt?"

She didn't rush to judgment but put things to the test before she replied.

"Don't think so," she called back. "Can you get a ladder or a rope or something and get me out of here?"

"Wait," he called. "I'm coming down."

"Don't be so fucking stupid!" she began to yell. Then she

realized he didn't mean he was going to jump down into the pit alongside her, thus trapping them both. Instead he was descending a near vertical set of stairs, really no more than a series of protuberant stones in the cross wall that marked this end of the hidden chamber. If she hadn't been too frightened to notice them, she could easily have clambered out herself.

He knelt beside her and she had to admit it was a comfort to feel his presence.

"Are you sure you haven't broken anything?" he asked anxiously.

"Absolutely," she snapped. In fact her body was sending signals suggesting there'd be new bruises to add to those sustained when she fell off the ladder at St. Ylf's, but she wasn't about to invite him to run his priestly hands over her in search of fractures.

"Good," he said.

"So now can we get out of here?"

"Of course. But don't you want to take a look round first?"

No, she bloody didn't, was the true absolute answer, but his arrival having raised her from the depths of utter panic, she found she did not care to let him know just how scared she'd been, so she settled for the conditional.

"Oh yes? And how are we supposed to do that when it's pitch-black?"

This wasn't quite true as the light from the kitchen, though not itself very strong, was already diluting what had seemed like an overflow from the Black Lagoon.

Now Madero again proved another of her pa's maxims, never say *maybe* when you mean *no bloody way!*

He reached into his pocket and produced a pencil torch.

"*Lux fiat*," he said smugly, sending the thin but strong beam probing the darkness.

She could still have exited, of course, but now that would really be drawing attention to her wimpishness.

She followed the line of light with attempted aplomb. Though little more than five feet wide, in length the chamber seemed in Sam's prejudiced view to stretch forever.

As usual, she sought refuge in inductive logic.

"There must be cellars," she said. "Real cellars, one at the front, one at the back, seemingly with a common wall. But in fact there are two walls with this chamber between them. But if this was built at the same time as that priory place that got knocked down, why would they need a priest-hole when you lot were ruling the roost anyway?"

Over his shoulder—the idiot was moving off toward the furthermost still dark area—Madero said, "No, it wouldn't be built as a priest-hole. I would guess that it was constructed as a safe house for the priory's valuables in times of strife. But it must have seemed an ideal place to hide Father Simeon later."

"Who?"

"Sorry, of course, you don't know anything about him, do you? One of the Woollass family who got persecuted during the sixteenth century. The legend of the Dark Man at the Stranger House must have helped too!"

And I bet it was Alice Woollass's idea to hide him here, he thought. What an ingenious woman, building a red herring priest-hole at the Hall, which they claimed was a secret storage place for valuables, while all the time using a real secret storage place for valuables to hide Simeon!

"Well, that's really fascinating," said Sam brightly. "Look, shouldn't we report this to someone . . ."

"You want to get out?" A gent wouldn't have said it so bluntly, but she made no effort to deny it, and he went on, "OK. Just hang on a minute. Now this is amazing . . ."

He was just a darker shape against the darkness now. She heard him moving stuff around, what kind of stuff she couldn't imagine and didn't want to.

Then his voice changed and he muttered something low and fast in what sounded to her to be Latin or maybe Spanish. A prayer perhaps? That was another trouble with priests. They confused praying for things and actually doing the things they were praying for. God looked after those who looked after themselves—one of Pa's ripostes to any attempt at religious argument. It was time to give God a hand.

"I'm out of here," she said negligently. "I'm moving on and I need to throw my things together."

She hadn't meant to offer a justification which, though true, sounded pretty feeble even in her own ears.

She turned to the stone ladder. Above in the kitchen there was a noise. An indeterminate hard-to-identify kind of noise, not all that loud but to her straining ears as sinister as a leper's bell.

Silence for a moment, then a kind of scraping, crescendoing to a great crash!

And with a suddenness like death the entrance slab flew back upward, lay flat against the ceiling, and the light was gone.

Now Sam let out the shriek which had been spiraling around inside her head ever since her fall.

Madero was back by her side in a couple of seconds. He caught her with one arm and pulled her close, holding the torch up between them so that it lit both their faces.

"It's OK," he said soothingly. "Nothing to worry about. It's OK."

"That's what you think, is it?" She sought solace in anger. "That's the best that shaven skull of yours can come up with? We're trapped down here in a dark hole, and you think that it's OK?"

He seemed to take her question seriously and, after a moment's thought, nodded and said, "Yes, actually, I do think it's OK. We can work out what's happened, which I suspect is that one of the pulleys gave way and the other couldn't hold the table up alone. And we can work out what's going to happen, which is that Mrs. Appledore will eventually return and, finding her kitchen in a bit of a mess with knocking sounds coming from beneath the floor, she'll get help to lift the table and pull us out. Meanwhile we have light, and the air down here is far from fetid, which suggests there is an inlet. So all we need is a little patience."

She forced herself to track his reasoning and could find no flaw in it, and what made it particularly soothing was the absence of any reference to divine providence.

She took a deep breath and moved away from him but not too far. It seemed a good time to come clean. After that scream, what was there to hide?

She said, "Yeah. Sorry. The thing is, I'm slightly claustrophobic. No, hang about, let me qualify that. No point being coy, not in a situation like this. I'm completely fucking claustrophobic. Put me in a dark place that I can't get out of and pretty soon I start running around and screaming and tearing my fingernails out on the walls till eventually I hyperventilate and collapse in a fetal ball and die. This I know because I've been through the whole process, except the last bit obviously."

"I'm glad to hear that," said Madero. "Anything else I should know about you?"

"Jesus, isn't that enough?" she said. "How long will your torch battery last? Soon as that light goes, you'd better look for cover else I'm likely to tear your eyes out."

"That would in the circumstances be taking coals to Newcastle, isn't that the phrase? It's a fresh battery so we should be all right. Mrs. Appledore can't be too long. I am sure the drinkers of Illthwaite expect their pub to open on time. Why don't we sit down and wait till we hear something from above."

"OK. As long as you mean in the kitchen."

This amused him. They sat side by side, the torch between them, leaning against one of the walls. After a while he said, "Tell me about yourself, Sam."

"What's this? Occupational therapy, or the confessional?"

"Whatever you want it to be. I just thought talking might pass the time."

"And stop me throwing another wobbly, you mean?"

"That would be a good result," he agreed. "But it would help me as well. Darkness holds terrors for me too sometimes. Not the same as yours, but real and devastating nonetheless."

"That's supposed to comfort me?" she said. "Look, if we're going to talk, I need something to call you. What was it Dracula's daughter from the Hall called you? Mick?"

"Not Mick. Mig. That's what my friends call me."

"Then that will have to do, though it doesn't mean we're friends."

"And I shall continue to call you Sam, with the same qualification."

"I thought you men of God had to be friends with everyone," she said.

"Indeed," he said. "But with some people it's harder than others."

She knew what he was trying to do. Get her angry, get her talking, get her doing anything that might keep the darkness from finding its way into the heart of her being.

She said, "I remember my pa sitting with some of his mates having a drink one night and one of them had the toothache real bad. And Pa said to him, 'Have you tried shoving a banana up your arse?' And he said, 'Will that work?' And Pa said, 'No, but it'll give your friends a laugh.'"

Madero laughed and said, "Stoicism Australasian style. You love your father, I think, Sam."

"Yeah. Don't you?"

"Yes, I did. I miss him greatly."

"He's dead? I'm sorry."

"Me too. My religion says I shouldn't be, but I am."

"How come you still go on about your religion even after you gave it up?"

"You've been talking about me? I'm flattered. But you are

misinformed. It would be truer to say it gave me up, or rather it directed me to another path. But I still need it to tell me who I am. What about you, Sam? Perhaps you are one of the lucky ones who are so sure who they are that external help isn't necessary. So who are you, Sam? Why don't you tell me who you are, so I'll know whether I can like you or not?"

She fixed her eyes on the torch and thought, why not? Might as well talk about herself before that self became reduced to a single unit of terror as small as that point of light.

"Why not?" she said. "Seeing I don't have anything better to do."

She took a deep breath and began.

12

Sam

Tell you who I am? That's hard.

You grow up and no one ever tells you who you are. Not even math, which tells you most things, can do that. You've got to find out for yourself. Mostly you do it piecemeal, one small new thing following another till, with luck, you get a picture.

Sometimes you get a big piece and don't recognize it. Not till much later. I got one when I was eleven, but I managed to ignore it for the next ten years.

I was at university by then and I reckoned I was pretty cool. I knew how the world ticked. Life was a game of chance, if you got dealt a decent hand, you'd be mad not to play it. Me, I was good, I'd drawn four to a running flush: I had a loving home, good health, no financial worries, and I was doing a course I loved.

Mathematics.

At school it was dead easy. I've got one of those memories, I can scan a page and recall every word of it, even if I don't understand half of what it means. It wasn't till I got to university that I began to feel even slightly stretched, and I loved it.

I had great tutors, one in particular, Andy Jamieson, a Pom

from Cambridge UK on sabbatical. In my finals year, AJ asked me if I fancied coming to his old college to do my doctorate. My best friend Martie who was at Melbourne with me was sure he wanted to get into my pants. But I knew the truth was both better and worse. AJ hadn't got the slightest interest in my body. He just knew I was a better mathematician than he was.

That's not vain, by the way. In math you know these things.

I said yes, why not? It was only later the thought of traveling right across the world began to get to me. When I was eleven I'd seen this TV play about these kids who got shoved on a boat without a by-your-leave and ferried out to Oz to start a new life. It really got to me then, but I hadn't thought about it for years. Now I recalled those poor kids in the play who'd made the journey the other way, not knowing what awaited them, and I felt really ashamed of feeling scared.

I got my First then came home to work for Pa to earn some bucks to help finance the trip. He'd have coughed up the lot, no problem, but I could see he was pleased. My mate Martie was getting married to some jock with a Greek-god profile whose old man owned half of Victoria. She asked me to join her on a pre-wedding shopping spree, and Pa told me to go and kit myself out with some wet weather gear for Cambridge.

We'd been away three days, having a great time, when my mobile rang. It was Ma, telling me that Gramma Ada, that's my pa's ma who lived with us, had collapsed. It was her heart, it was bad.

I headed home straightaway. Gramma had been part of my life for so long that I couldn't imagine how things could be without her.

Maybe I'd get home and find it had all been a false alarm, I told myself. But when I saw the priest's car parked outside the house, I knew things must be bad. Your money or your life, that's all those bastards ever want from you, that's what my pa used to say.

Sorry.

Gramma was a Catholic. Pa never got in the way of that, but he didn't even pay lip service. I didn't know why he took against your lot so much, but I let him set my agenda because he was my pa and knew everything.

When I got to know what he knew, I was glad.

Sometimes Gramma would talk to me about the Church in her easygoing loving way, usually after the priest had paid a visit. I think he must have gone on at her about me. I don't know if he ever had a go at Pa, but if he did, I'd guess he only tried once.

When I went up to Gramma's room, I thought I was too late. She lay there like a corpse and for the first time it struck me how very old she was. I knew Pa was only just turned forty. And I knew Gramma was eighty-five. But it wasn't till I saw her lying there that it occurred to me that she must have been well into her forties when she had Pa.

So much for my mathematical mind.

Ma said, "Here's Sammy to see you."

I went and sat down by the bed. On the other side sat the priest, playing with those beads you lot lug around. I once asked Pa about them. He said they were like a holy abacus to help reckon up how much the Church was going to get from someone's will.

Gramma's priest looked like he was minded to stay but Ma said, "Let's go downstairs and brew a pot of tea, Father." She could be pretty firm herself, Ma.

I took Gramma's hand and she opened her eyes, recognized me and said, "Sammy, you're here. That's OK then," and closed her eyes again.

For a second I thought that she'd just held on till I got home then decided to give up the ghost. But now she spoke again, so low I had to strain to hear her.

What she said didn't make much sense.

She said, "I thought not having kids of my own was a curse,

but it turned out a blessing. Soon as I saw him I knew your pa was the one, even before I heard his name. And then he gave us you with your lovely red hair. That's the color I'd have chosen for myself, and now I'd got it in you, and that was even better 'cos I'd got you with it."

She reached up to touch my hair, but she didn't have the strength, so I bent over her and let it fall over her hand and her face and when I drew back she was gone.

I didn't say anything to anyone till after the funeral.

That was a real bash. She'd been well loved. Afterward everyone came back to the house even though it was a hell of a drive for most of them. The priest was there too. He'd given Gramma a good send-off in the church, so I reckon he deserved his throat-easer, and you had to admire the way he downed the stuff like mother's milk.

When he came to take his leave, he offered Pa his hand, which Pa took like it was a copperhead.

"I'll be off now, Sam," he said, real hearty, like they were best mates. "I know how much you'll miss your ma. I promised her I'd keep an eye on you all and I'll be back very soon to see how you're getting on."

"No, you won't," said Pa.

You could have heard a pin drop.

"I'm sorry?" said the priest.

"You heard," said Pa.

I said he didn't waste words.

And to give the priest his due, he had the sense not to keep pressing.

He went out of the door. Pa turned to the remaining guests and said, "All this talking makes a man thirsty. Who's empty?"

It was later that same night after all our visitors had gone and me and Ma and Pa were sitting together nursing mugs of tea that I spoke.

I told them what Gramma had said and asked what it meant.

Pa didn't hesitate. He said, "They adopted me."

I said, "Is that it?"

He said, "I'm adopted. You're not. What's your problem?"

I could see his point. I mean he was the one who'd found out his ma and pa weren't his real ma and pa, not me. But I'd still felt my life had taken a little lurch.

I said, "I've just seen someone I thought was my grandmother put in the ground, now I find she wasn't really related to me at all."

"So you're going to miss her less?"

"No, of course not!"

"Well then."

He stood up and ran his fingers through my hair.

"Your ma knows the tale, such as it is. I've got some things I need to check."

I sometimes think Pa will live forever, 'cos whenever death comes for him, he'll always have something he needs to check.

When he'd gone out, I turned to Ma and said, "Well?"

And she told me what she knew from talking to Gramma over the years and what she'd managed to extract from Pa.

Gramma Flood's tale was one of sorrow turned to joy.

She'd wanted children and so had Granpa. When she reached her forties and they hadn't come, their thoughts turned to adoption.

Technically they were a bit old, but they were in good with their priest, who gave them such a red-hot intro to a Catholic adoption agency, they checked out fine.

No shortage, it seemed. Odd thing that about you Catholics; even those ready to risk the sin of fornication still draw the line at contraception.

Gramma loved to tell Ma the tale. Seems Granpa was taken by a strapping boy with lung power to match his physique. Then Gramma spotted this smaller kid, with a stubble of red hair. He lay very quiet, though when you got close you could see his eyes were alert and watchful. When the nun in charge saw her interest, she smiled and said, "Now I think there may be a message here for you, Mrs. Flood. You take this one, you won't have to change his name because he's called Flood already. Sam Flood."

That clinched matters. How could this be simple coincidence? asked Gramma. In her eyes, this baby was gift-wrapped from God. And Sam, my pa, seemed to confirm her judgment by growing up a loving son and taking to wine making like it was in his blood.

In himself he stayed as he was when first she saw him: quiet, watchful, self-contained. Granpa saw no reason to tell him he'd been adopted, but Gramma thought different and when he got to sixteen, she decided it was time to tell him the truth.

Not that there was much to tell. All she knew was that his mother had been a young woman who'd got into trouble, turned to the nuns for help, and died in childbirth. No details known about her origins or the baby's father.

I can see Pa taking in this news. I bet he said next to nothing, asked a couple of brief questions maybe, showed no emotion. But a couple of days later he vanished.

He was away for a week. He'd gone in search of more information about his real mother. What he discovered seems little enough, but for a boy of sixteen to discover anything was remarkable. Don't know who's better at walling up a secret, the government bureaucrats or you Catholic bastards.

Sorry. Maybe things are better now, but this was a decade before that English woman who finally got all this murky stuff out in the open started chipping away. Don't expect her book was on the curriculum at your seminary, but if you ever get to read it, you'll see what a hell of a job she had to make progress.

What he discovered was that his mother, Samantha Flood, far from being a young woman who'd got into trouble and sought the help of the nuns, had been little more than a child herself and already in the nuns' care when she got pregnant.

And she was English, an orphan brought out here for resettlement.

When Ma told me this my mind went hurtling back ten years.

"You mean she was like those kids in that play?" I asked incredulously.

"Looks like it," said Ma. "Back then no one knew how many of them there were, of course. Somehow your pa got to see her death certificate. It gave her address as St. Rumbald's Orphanage."

"This wasn't where Gramma went to choose Pa then?" I interrupted.

"No, that was the baby unit of the Catholic Hospital. They don't have facilities for taking care of infants out at St. Rumbald's. Or anyone, from the sound of it. Your pa hitched a lift out there and asked to see the records but they told him there weren't any. He got real frustrated. That's why he decked the priest."

Told you you wouldn't like this.

"Pa hit a priest?" I said, surprised without being amazed. "Why?"

"I asked him that," she said with a bit of a smile. "He said, hitting a nun wouldn't have looked so good. But when I pressed him, he said he reckoned the tight rein those nuns kept their girls on, the only bastards who'd get close enough to dip their wicks would have to be priests."

I took this in. My grandmother the child. My grandfather the priest.

The police had got involved, but the decked priest had shown Christian charity, or maybe just didn't want publicity, and no charges were brought. Pa came home as if nothing had happened, except that from then on in he'd have nothing to do with the Church.

This must have been a trouble to Granpa and Gramma, but even at sixteen I guess they knew where they were with Pa. If they'd made it a stay-or-go issue, he'd have gone.

He doesn't say much, but Pa never has any trouble getting his message across.

The same when he met Ma four years later. Within a fortnight he'd asked her to marry him. Ma didn't go into details but I doubt if it involved making flowery speeches from a kneeling position. They were married in another fortnight.

I asked Ma if he ever did anything more about finding out about his real mother.

She said no. After watching that play, Gramma had been very upset and had said to Ma that she hoped Sam's mother hadn't been one of those poor kids. This was the first Ma heard anything about Pa being adopted and naturally she hadn't rested till she got the whole story, such as it was.

"I asked your pa why he hadn't told me and he said, would it have made a difference? And of course I said no, and he said, well then. I reminded him of all the stuff we'd read about these child migrants and all, and asked if it didn't bother him. He said he could see why anyone who'd grown up here, not knowing the truth about themselves, would want to dig. But he'd been born here, been brought up by good people, he'd got his own family he loved, what was in the past for him but pain, and wasn't there enough of that waiting to jump out on you without going looking for it?"

As I listened to Ma I felt all that indignation I'd experienced in front of the telly aged eleven welling up again, only this time it was personal. I had a grandmother who'd been brought over here against her will when she was just a kid. What had happened to her then I didn't know, but from the stuff that had come out, it wasn't likely to be good. What was certain was that she'd been placed in some orphanage run by nuns who'd taken so little care of her she'd got pregnant and they'd let her die giving birth to my father.

I went out and found Pa and blazed away at him for ten minutes or more, asking him how he could sleep easy in his bed knowing all this and not trying to find out who his real father was.

He listened in that way he has, not saying anything till he's quite sure you've run out of steam, then he said, "I know who my real pa is. I've just buried your gramma alongside him. As for that other bastard, last time I went out looking for answers, I decked a priest. This time, all the stuff that's come out about those poor migrant kids, I could end up decking the Pope. You going to cancel your career and take care of things here while your pa's in jail?"

This was a long speech for Pa and, like most of what he said, there was a lot more in it than just the words he used, a lot of stuff about love and responsibilities and options. If Pa précis'd the Bible, he'd get it down to a slim pamphlet.

I simmered down, told myself it was Pa's call, and I put it to him straight. Was he certain he didn't want to know the truth? And he said, "Truth's like a dingo, girl. It'll run till you get it cornered. Then watch out!"

So I made the rational objective decision and decided to let it be.

Or, put it another way, I made the emotional personal decision that my work came first. Selfish? I admit it. My work means everything to me. Whether it will ever mean anything to anyone else, I'm not sure, but probably even Newton had no idea he was going to change the way folk looked at the universe when he set out. Not that he saw it that way. He ended up saying he felt like he'd been a boy playing on the seashore, occasionally finding a smoother stone or a prettier shell, while the great ocean of truth lay undiscovered all around him.

I guess I'll be lucky if I can get close to picking up even one pretty shell on the beach. But in going to Cambridge I feel like I'm striking out into that great ocean. Maybe if I can hold my breath long enough, I might even get down to some new coral reef.

If I'd said that to Pa, he'd have asked if I'd been on the turps. But that's how it feels. You said you needed religion to define who you are. I guess I need mathematics.

So I made my decision to let things be.

Then something happened. A way-out coincidence. Maybe you'd call it a divine message. No need to bring God into it. Me, I know that mathematically chance can be illusory. Often if you analyze what seems amazing coincidence, you find it was just as likely to happen as not to happen. Sometimes more likely.

Years before, Martie had upstaged my indignation after I saw that TV play by remarking her family knew all about it as her Aunt Gracie was one of those kids.

I'd completely forgotten that and when I met Gracie at the wedding it didn't ring a bell. She was in gray. It suited her, she was that kind of woman: wispy gray hair, wide gray eyes that never quite focused in a tiny pale gray face. If the weather had been misty she'd have disappeared. But unfocused or not, I felt those gray eyes scan my face closely. And from time to time during the celebration, I caught her gaze following me.

Later as I was helping Martie get ready for her grand departure, she said, "You made a great impression on Gracie. She said you reminded her of someone. The name too. She asked a lot of questions about your family. Especially dear old Ada. I'm real sorry she's not still around, Sam. She was a lovely lady."

"Yeah, she was."

I hadn't told Martie about the revelations which had followed Gramma Ada's death. Some time in the future maybe, not in the run-up to her wedding. But suddenly it came back to me.

"Wasn't it Gracie you said was one of those migrant kids all the fuss was about?"

"That's right. Doesn't like to talk about it though. Just turns vague if it's mentioned. And when Gracie turns vague, she doesn't have far to go!"

We laughed, but my mind was racing.

Later, after we'd seen the happy couple off, I went looking for Gracie. Saw no point messing around. Compared with Pa, I'm a pussy-footer, but I can be pretty direct.

I said, "Martie tells me you thought you recognized me."

She looked embarrassed.

"It was the hair mainly. And the name. But I knew it was just a coincidence when Martie told me about your grandmother. I was sorry to hear she'd died. She sounds like a nice woman. You must miss her."

"I do," I said. "Only she wasn't my real gran. Pa was adopted. His ma was like you. A child migrant from the UK."

I reckon Pa would have been hard put to be more direct. I thought I'd overdone it. I wouldn't have thought she could have got any grayer, but she did.

"And her name . . . ?" she sort of croaked.

"Same as mine. And Pa's. Sam Flood."

She began to cry. I felt a heel. I was so keen to check out what looked like a real lead that I'd gone plowing in without the least consideration for poor old Gracie.

But I wasn't going to turn back now. And she proved to be tougher than she looked. I reckon you had to be to survive what those bastards put those kids through.

We sat down together and drank whiskey and she told me what she knew about my grandmother.

To start with it was a huge disappointment, like one of those calculations which starts great then suddenly fizzles out. All Gracie could tell me about little Sam Flood with the flame-red hair was that she'd been on the same boat as her from Liverpool.

I asked her when that was, expecting her to be vague. But this was one thing she was certain of. It was 1960, the year Kennedy became president. She'd looked it up. Seems Kennedy was the first Catholic president and the nuns thought it was like the Second Coming and they made the kids watch it on television, which they didn't mind as it was about the only television they ever got to see in those days. So, definitely 1960. And Elvis singing "Are You Lonesome Tonight?" was top of the pops. That was the other thing she remembered. I think she thought it was dead appropriate.

On that boat, there'd been three main bunches of kids from different orphanages in the Liverpool area, but Sam Flood didn't seem to belong to any group.

"I don't know where she came from and, when we landed, we all got sent off to different places and I never saw her again. It was all confused. It was spring when we left and autumn when we got here. They took the summer from us. They took everything. I couldn't make sense of it. It was very confused . . ."

Confused. That sums up what life had done to Gracie. I suppose everyone finds a different way to cope with shit. Gracie's way had been to walk away from it when she got to be old enough to take care of herself. But when there was all that publicity in the nineties, her husband persuaded her to get in touch with the new Child Migrants Trust. Turned out Gracie was right. There was nothing in it for her, she really was an orphan, so no happy reunions there. But one good thing came out of it from my point of view.

There was this other girl from the same orphanage as Gracie. Betty Stanton. Sounds like the kind of kid who gets by taking lame dogs under her wing.

Sorry, that doesn't sound right, you know what I mean.

Well, Gracie must have been a natural candidate. And Sam Flood was another.

Betty kept an eye on her, Gracie told me. And she thought they got taken off to the same place on arrival. It sounds as if this Betty was one of the Trust's success stories. They'd tracked down her mother who was still alive in the UK and the two of them had been reunited. And when they realized Gracie was from the same Liverpool orphanage and had been part of the same consignment, they put them in touch.

At least they put Betty, who lived over in Perth, in touch

with Gracie. Gracie really didn't want to know. The past was outback to her. You could get lost there. So after a few letters, Betty gave up and settled for being on Gracie's Christmas card list.

And Gracie gave me her address. Betty McKillop her married name is.

I dropped her a line, told her who I was, asked if we could meet and talk. I got a letter back from her daughter saying Betty was in the UK, place called Newcastle, where her own mother was very ill. But the daughter said she'd spoken on the phone and Betty remembered my gran very well and would love to talk with me when she got back. Naturally I said I was on the way to England myself very shortly and maybe we could meet up there. And she came back to me with a phone number to ring when I got here.

I rang a few days ago but it was a bad time. The old lady had just died. The funeral's today and Betty's flying home tomorrow night. I said I was sorry and maybe we could just fix a time to talk on the phone, but she said no, she'd rather see me. She said she'd be through by lunchtime tomorrow, so if I could get up to see her early afternoon before she set off for the airport, that would be fine. When I checked the map, I saw that it wasn't that far over from Cumbria. And I recalled the last thing Gracie had said to me.

She'd gone into a kind of trance, and I was feeling real shitty for making her go back somewhere she didn't want to be. So I got up to leave. Then she looked up at me and said, "I've been racking my brains for anything else I can recall. Most of us had these labels to start with, like we were bits of luggage, with our names and the address of the orphanage we came from. Sam didn't have one of these, just a bit of paper which she kept folded up in her pocket. If anyone spoke to her, she was so shy she'd just bring out this bit of paper. That's how we knew her name. But there was an address on it too."

"An address?" I said. "Gracie, can you remember what it was?"

She shook her head and said, "I'm sorry. I only ever saw it once and it was all creased and hard to read. I think the place was *Ill* something. Maybe *Illthwaite*, but I can't be sure. I'm sorry, the harder I try to remember, the vaguer it becomes."

She was almost in tears. I calmed her down and told her she'd been great, which she had. And when I got home, I dug out my old world atlas and looked in the index.

The only thing which came close in the whole world was where we are now, Illthwaite in Cumbria, England.

Of course Aunt Gracie might have got it completely wrong. In fact, if you met Gracie, you'd put odds on it. Betty sounds a much safer bet.

But I was impatient to be doing something. I'd spent a few nights in London, crashing out on the couch of some Melbourne Uni mates in Earl's Court, getting over the jet lag. Now I was ready to be off. I thought, I've got to go to Newcastle to talk with Betty McKillop, why not check out this Illthwaite place en route?

So I rented a car and set out.

And here I am. It's been a complete waste of time. Not only that, it's got me sitting in a hole in the ground, which terrifies me, making my confession to a priest.

OK, I know you're not, but that's what it feels like. Pa would have a fit!

And you were right about one thing at least.

I think it has made me feel a bit better.

Anyway, that's me done and dusted. Now it's your turn in the box.

13

Mig

My full name is Miguel Ramos Elkington Madero, though in England I am known as Michael Madero. In both countries my friends call me Mig.

So I have two names. And two passports.

Sometimes I think that in fact I am divided into two people, except that when you put the halves together you do not get a whole.

I am the elder son of Christine, née Elkington, of Hampshire, England, and Miguel Madero of Jerez de la Frontera, Andalusia, Spain. Jerez is where the English word sherry derives from. For five centuries the Maderos have been in the wine business, a little longer than the Floods, I think. You may have encountered our rarest fino, El Bastardo? No? Ah well. Australasia has never been one of our strongest markets.

There is little you need to know about my childhood except that from time to time, usually in the spring, I felt a certain discomfort in my hands and feet which in my teens became unmistakably, so I thought, the stigmata, which as I'm sure you know means the appearance of wounds equivalent to those inflicted by crucifixion. Not quickly, but perhaps inevitably, I decided that their message was that I should enter the priesthood.

Oh, and there's something else which I am reluctant to mention in our present circumstances, but it is relevant to my story.

I seem to be able to conjure ghosts, a talent incidentally which I was surprised to find not much valued in would-be priests.

Be reassured. I shall try to keep it in check.

Anyway, after overcoming many doubts, internal and external, I began my formal studies for the priesthood. I was still troubled by ghosts, and by girls too, but that's a problem shared by most ordinands. And whenever my doubts returned, I reassured myself by thinking of my stigmatic experience. What else could it mean?

Then, for me as for you, a family loss proved a turning point. On New Year's Day last year my father died unexpectedly.

After the funeral I sat alone in the twilight on the veranda of our family house and let memories of Father sweep over me. His kindness and his care, also his strong discipline. His old-fashioned courtesy toward women, mocked by some advanced feminist thinkers of his acquaintance, but nothing they ever said could provoke him into behavior he would have felt unbecoming in an *hidalgo*. His pride in the family business and his narration of episodes from family history which were the fairy tales of my childhood. His delight when I grew to share his passion for exploring remote regions and for mountain climbing. His love for my mother and for all things English, except their ignorance of the true glories of sherry wine.

And I also recalled his unconcealable disappointment when I told him I definitely wanted to enter the priesthood. I felt I had let him down and nothing I told myself of God's will could bring consolation.

I felt my father so close, it seemed easy to bring him before me visibly. But at the seminary I had come to accept that such traffickings with the afterworld were perilous, so I rose and went downstairs and found company and broke the spell.

The head of my seminary, Father Dominic, a good man and a good friend, told me to take time off to come to terms with my loss. I went into the Sierra Nevada, to an area where I spent many happy holidays climbing with my father. Solo climbing is dangerous sport at the best of times, but now it was the middle of winter and the weather was foul. Yet one morning I found myself attempting a climb we had once done together, not a difficult ascent for two experienced climbers in decent conditions, but folly for a man alone in a disturbed mental condition.

I should have turned back as the weather worsened, but something drove me on. The wind grew stronger, driving flurries of snow into my face and seemingly trying to rip me off the cliff face which was covered in ice. I could see no way to advance. But going down wasn't going to be easy either.

Needs must when the devil drives, and I began to descend. I had only managed a few feet when I slipped. Desperately I scrabbled for foot- and finger-holds. Somehow I managed to arrest my descent, but every single point of contact with the cliff face was minimal and temporary and deteriorating. A few more seconds and I would fall.

I was too terrified even to pray.

Then I saw another climber, a snow-spattered figure on a broad ledge a little above me and to my right. I called to him. He turned and reached out a hand. All I had to do was grab it and lunge sideways and upward, and his strength and my momentum should see me safely on to the ledge. I took my hand off the cliff and reached out. At the same time I saw his face.

It was my father who had taught me all I knew about climbing.

Can you catch the hand of a ghost?

I believe you can. I think that if our hands had met, he would have taken the weight of his foolish son on his arm and borne me up to safety.

But in the second before contact I felt the pain of the stigmata shoot through my palms and my ankles, worse than I had ever known it before.

And I fell.

You see the significance of this? This stigmata which I had taken to be a sign of vocation had prevented me from accepting help from my father's spirit, which surely could not have been offered without the grace of God.

I did not of course reach this conclusion then. I was too busy being terrified.

Down I went through the snow-filled air. For what seemed an eternity, I could still see my father above me, his hand outstretched. Then he was absorbed in the whiteness of the blizzard and I hit the side of the mountain for the first time. The first of several times. I broke both legs, one arm, most of my ribs, punctured a lung, and fractured my skull, though in what order I cannot be sure.

Finally the whiteness turned to blackness. When I opened my eyes again, I was in the hospital. Fortunately the people I was staying with had been more concerned about my safety than I myself.

There was none of that mnemonic vagueness which often seems to follow accidents. My mind was as clear as a bell. I remembered everything up to the last impact.

I gave thanks to God for my rescue.

And I knew with absolute certainty that my sense of vocation was fallacious, the foolish misinterpretation of a vain and immature mind. Whatever message was being sent to me all these years via the stigmata, it had nothing to do with becoming a priest.

I informed Father Dominic of my change of heart when he came to see me. He said, "No hurry. As you recover, you will have plenty of time to think and pray."

I tried to explain to him that this was no simple intrusion of doubt, no mere stage fright as the moment of commitment got nearer. This was knowledge so positive it made my previous sense of vocation seem a whim. It had nothing to do with loss of faith.

He simply smiled as if he had heard all this before. In the end I saw that just as he believed time would make all clear to me, so must I leave time to do its work on him.

Well, it has done its work, and I am glad to say that, despite my defection, Father Dominic and I have remained good friends. In a way it is because of him that I am here now. He brought me reading matter in the hospital, not the usual magazines and paperbacks, but material which he hoped might rekindle my vocational fires. Because of my English connections, he thought the stories of the Forty Martyrs of England and Wales might be particularly inspirational, and wherever possible he supplied me with photocopies of original documents, handwritten and usually in Latin.

There were harrowing stories of the fate of priests who worked undercover in England during the period of proscription and persecution when capture meant long torture and painful death. The more I read these accounts, often written by the priests themselves, the more aware I became how unfit I was to join the company of such men.

When I said this to Father Dominic, he told me that no man could know what he might endure for his faith until put to the test. I could not argue with this, but I knew I was right in my decision.

Among the reading matter Father Dominic brought me were several sheets scrawled over by the wavering hand of someone clearly greatly distressed both in body and mind as he wrote. These turned out to be the scribblings of a Jesuit who had suffered at the hands of one of Elizabeth's pursuivants, the officers who tracked down and extracted confessions from Catholic priests.

His name was Father Simeon Woollass.

That's right. The same name as the family in Illthwaite Hall, though at the time it meant nothing to me. Like yourself, I had never heard of Illthwaite.

There were some notes attached to these scribblings which indicated that they had been subjected to official Church examination. I subsequently learned that the family had at various times inquired why he had never been given the formal acknowledgment received by so many of the priests in the English Mission. The trouble was that, almost uniquely, after his interrogation he had been released and allowed to return to the Continent. No formal accusation of collaboration was ever made, and the Church's stance was that he didn't figure among the two hundred Blesseds from whom Pope Paul chose the Forty British Martyrs for canonization in 1970 for the simple reason that he died more or less peacefully in his bed at the English College in Seville.

I do not know the truth of what happened, but much that I read in his scribblings suggested a man racked with guilt and regret. Composed in a strange mix of Latin, Spanish and English, and written in an almost illegible hand, they rambled on, repetitively and incoherently, trembling on the edge of that despair which is the ultimate sin, but always clinging to that trust in God's mercy which is the ultimate salvation.

I suspected that Father Dominic's hope was that my own spiritual troubles would pall to insignificance alongside the writhings of this lacerated soul, but repetition can make even the cries of a man in torment tedious, and I was about to give them up when I saw something which reached out and caught my attention with hooks of steel.

Miguel Madero. My own name.

Nothing else, unless the phrase that followed (scored so deep into the paper that at one point the quill had penetrated to the next sheet) was in some way connected:

Padre me perdona . . .

Father forgive me . . .

Seeing my name like this felt like receiving a message from another world.

And as I read it, I suddenly had a memory of an early ghostly experience I'd had in the great Gothic cathedral of Seville when I'd been approached by a mad old man, babbling incoherently. I felt certain now that this manifestation had been Father Simeon.

There was a message here, but it wasn't very clear and, having already shown such a talent for supernatural misinterpretation, I was not about to rush to any conclusion.

I recalled my father telling me, frequently, how two of my forebears, father and son, both called Miguel, had perished in the tragic defeat of the Great Armada in 1588.

Could it be one of these two Miguels the scrawl referred to? It was a possibility, but to my historian mind, it seemed somewhat unlikely. Had either survived to be taken by the English, it would have been apparent to their captors that here was a wealthy member of the *hidalgo* class worth ransoming. My rationality told me Madero was a not uncommon name. Perhaps after all this was simple coincidence.

I was distracted from further examination of my family history by a more immediate problem. Or rather two problems.

Cristóbal, my brother, was now head of the firm, a job which my defection to the religious life had dropped into his grateful lap. While he is the most loving of brothers, I could see his concern growing that I might now wish to claim my birthright as the elder son.

Matters were not improved by our mother, Christine. After Father's death, she had decided to return permanently to her family home near Winchester and resume the life of a quiet well-bred English lady. But my brush with death had brought her back to Spain. As Donna Cristina she had always taken a lively interest in the business. But when Cristo took over, I suspect he was not displeased when she decided to move to England.

Now she was back. At first she was entirely preoccupied with my state of health. But as I moved off the critical list, she began to take notice of certain changes Cristo was making in the organization of the firm, and was temperamentally incapable of keeping her objections to herself. Sparks began to fly.

My solution to both problems was simple and elegant enough to please a mathematician. As soon as I could move on crutches, I told my mother it would please me to have a complete change of scenery and continue my convalescence in England.

The prospect of being totally in control of me delighted her, and the prospect of getting both me and Cristina out of his hair delighted Cristo.

Healthwise it turned out to be a good move for me also.

Eventually, feeling the need for intellectual stimulation as well as, I admit, a desire to get out of my mother's control, I decided to resume my historical studies. I had been reading about the English Reformation and decided, some might say was guided, to focus my attention there. Father Dominic, with whom I kept in touch, was delighted to hear of this. He still has hopes for me. No mean historian himself, he put me in touch with an old friend of his in the History Department at Southampton University, Dr. Max Coldstream, one of the foremost Catholic scholars of our time. We met, liked each other, and soon I was formally signed up as a research student.

As I studied the Reformation, I found my interest shifting from the experience of priests to that of ordinary people. I was particularly intrigued by the problems of recusancy, the refusal by many ordinary Catholics to attend Church of England services. It was a dangerous path to tread. The penalties could be severe, ranging from fines through confiscation of land to imprisonment and even death. Much depended on which part of the country they lived in, what kind of influence they had . . .

But I suspect I have passed the point where I have even the smallest hold on your interest. Let me press on.

During Elizabeth's reign, security was overseen by her Secretary of State, Francis Walsingham, whose network of agents and informants was a potent weapon against Catholic conspiracies, both real and imagined. One of his lieutenants collated details of every recusant family in the country and, through the good offices of Dr. Coldstream and Father Dominic, I obtained access to these papers.

There was much fascinating information and the more I read, the more I resolved that here was my most rewarding line of research. The great noble families mentioned had doubtless been well trawled over during the last couple of centuries, but there could still be a treasure trove of journals and records lying undisturbed in those of the lesser houses which were still occupied by the same families four centuries on.

I set about discovering which fell into this category, approaching my task alphabetically so it was almost done when I came across a name which rang familiarly.

Woollass.

I had quite forgotten Father Simeon Woollass and the odd coincidence of my own scrawled name in his papers. Now I quickly established that the Woollass family still occupied Illthwaite Hall. A little further digging confirmed that Father Simeon was indeed a member of the family, the son of a cadet branch then residing in Kendal, now defunct. Walsingham's records of the pursuit and capture of priests on the English Mission told me only that his presence was known from the 1580s and he was taken up in 1589 by Francis Tyrwhitt, a lieutenant of the notorious pursuivant, Richard Topcliffe.

Do you know of Topcliffe? No? Why should you? He was Elizabeth's chief priest-hunter, a monster. His devotion to his work was such that he applied for a license to set up a torture chamber in his own home, which meant that he could pursue his interrogations with minimal disruption to his domestic life. When the dinner gong rang, he could toss another shovelful of coke on to the hotbed under the griddle on which his latest victim lay, then pop upstairs for his well-done sirloin.

By all accounts, Tyrwhitt was the right servant for such a master. He was a cousin of Sir Edward Jolley, a Protestant judge whose sentences, especially against Catholics, were infamous for their severity. He allowed Tyrwhitt to use the dungeons of Jolley Castle, near Leeds in Yorkshire, as his interrogation center and it is alleged that in those airless depths he matched Topcliffe in zeal, and outdid him in brutality.

It was into this monster's hands that God placed Father Simeon.

And it was this same monster who let him go.

So what happened?

As we know from the annals of World War II, officially sanctioned psychopaths are usually meticulous in their records, so I was fairly optimistic when I began to investigate, but all I could find was a reference in the Walsingham archive to Simeon's arrest, followed by a bald statement that he was put to the test, and subsequently released.

I shared my difficulty with my supervisor, Max Coldstream, who is hugely experienced in the complex detective work of research. He knew all about the Woollass family's obsession with proving Simeon innocent of crimes he'd never been formally accused of. This seemed to have been resolved about forty years ago when Dunstan Woollass received a papal honor. In the accompanying encomium listing his merits and those of his family, particular reference was made to the noble part played by Father Simeon in the English Mission of the sixteenth century.

So it seemed the slate was clean. Max warned me that the Woollasses might not take kindly to anyone trying to scribble on it once more, but as my interest was personal rather than scholarly, I asked him to see if he could dig anything up.

He immediately suggested it might be worth looking at the archives of the Jolley family. A few days later he rang me to say that we were in luck. Jolley Castle is now a National Trust property and the family's somewhat chaotic records are being cataloged. An archivist called Tim Lilleywhite, a former pupil of Max's, had undertaken the task, and he confirmed that there were references to Tyrwhitt and also some personal records the man made of his interrogations. He promised to look out for any mention of Simeon.

Meanwhile I put all this to the back of my mind and set about contacting the dozen families I hoped might be able to help with my researches. Within a week I had received three downright refusals and four expressions of regret that time, accident, or carelessness had destroyed any papers the family might have had.

I was beginning to think my bright idea might not have been so bright after all.

And then I got Woollass's reply.

I am not a fatalist but I heard the voice of fate in this.

I wrote back at once accepting his invitation to come for an interview.

My mother was pleased I had found an occupation, less pleased when she saw the car I bought myself for my trip up to Cumbria. She described my lovely Mercedes SLK as a teutonic sardine tin, totally unsuitable for bumpy mountain roads, and with internal dimensions that would put my recovery back by months every time I squeezed into it.

I retorted that I needed things to help me conquer my disability, not things to help me be comfortable with it. And I tried not to limp as I strode away into the house.

She apologized later and said of course I was quite right, it was my choice.

But as I slipped into the car to start my journey north a couple of days later, I noticed she had put my walking stick on to the passenger seat. I waited till I was out of sight of the house before I picked it up and hurled it into the hedge!

I did not know what lay ahead of me in this strange place

called Illthwaite but, whatever it was, I was determined to meet it standing erect on my own two feet.

Alas, I have to admit that, as usual, my mother was absolutely right!

Max Coldstream was right too in warning me to tread carefully as far as Father Simeon was concerned. I did some research into his family in Kendal on my way here, which I thought wise to keep under my hat, but Cumbria it seems is a very small world, and Gerry Woollass, Frek's father, got wind of it. My diplomacy must have looked like sheer deviousness. Which is why I was given my marching orders.

But *felix culpa*, had I not been summarily ejected from the Hall, I might never have found my way into this chamber where I feel so very strongly the presence of . . .

14

A real live woman

Whose spirit Madero felt the presence of Sam was saved from discovering.

At that moment the torch battery gave up its ghost and the light, already diminished to a pinprick, went out.

She screamed.

She didn't want to but she knew no way not to.

Then she felt his arms being wrapped around her and he drew her close, almost on to his lap.

"It's OK," he murmured. "It's OK. We'll soon be out of here. There, there. Be calm. Be calm."

He was talking to her like a child again, but she didn't mind it. Like a child, what she wanted in this predicament was adult comfort and reassurance.

Madero, on the other hand, as he hugged her close and felt the warmth of that lithe body reach him through the thin cloth of her skimpy T-shirt, found to his dismay that, however his eyes might have deceived him as to her age, after a few moments his own frail flesh was telling him he had a real live woman in his arms. He tried to twist away to conceal his arousal but if anything the movement only drew attention to it. He sent his mind in search of all the antaphrodisiac stratagems he'd developed in the seminary only to discover that, effective though they'd once been against the fancy's images, they had no potency against the physical reality.

"I'm sorry," he began to say, but Sam interrupted him.

"Listen!" she said.

He listened.

There was noise above them. A footfall. Then an exclamation.

With one accord they began to cry, "Help!"

It took another fifteen minutes for Edie Appledore to round up the three strong men necessary to raise the heavy table and release the entrance slab.

The three strong men in question turned out to be the Gowders and Thor Winander, whom she'd flagged down as they drove past from St. Ylf's.

Pushed from behind by Mig and pulled from above by Winander, Sam scrambled out into the light of the kitchen which fell on her like a glorious dawn.

"Nice to see you again, Miss Flood," boomed Thor. "Trying to find a shortcut home, were you?"

"Ignore him, dear," said Mrs. Appledore. "Drink this. You look a bit shook up."

She handed Sam a glass of brandy which she downed in one and did not resist when offered a refill.

The Gowders had propped the table up with cast-iron chairs brought in from the beer garden. Winander now offered his hand to Madero, who was standing with his head appearing through the gap in the kitchen floor.

"No. Thank you, all the same," he said with a formality that set Sam, still light-headed with relief, giggling. "Mrs. Appledore, do you have such a thing as a flashlight?"

Shaking her head at the stupidity of men, the landlady found one. Winander took it from her but instead of handing it down, he dropped into the underground chamber himself, provoking more head-shaking from Mrs. Appledore. Now the two men vanished, presumably to continue the exploration which the collapse of the slab had interrupted.

The reason why the table had fallen back to the floor was clear.

There must have been some dry rot in the crossbeam and under the weight of the table one of the pulleys had pulled loose. The sudden extra pressure on the other had snapped the rope, allowing the table to fall back on the counterweight slabs, bringing the entry slab crashing down.

"So what's been going on?" inquired Mrs. Appledore when she was satisfied that Sam had recovered sufficiently to be questioned.

Sam told her, finishing with an apology for her part in what had been effectively an act of trespass resulting in physical damage to the kitchen.

"Never mind that," said the landlady. "All these years I've spent sitting over yon hole, never knowing a thing about it. God knows what's down there. Could be anything!"

She shuddered at the thought, then her expression brightened.

"Or it could be valuable. Come on, you two! What have you found? And don't forget, whatever it is must belong to me!"

"Is that so, Edie?" came Winander's voice. "In that case, here's a down payment."

So saying, he reached his arm out of the aperture and placed a human skull and a couple of bones on the floor.

Mrs. Appledore let out a gasp of distaste without seeming too bothered by the grinning relic. Sam recalled Madero's muttered prayer. He'd known all the time they were sharing that dark chamber with a skeleton. But, probably wisely, he'd said nothing.

His voice came from the ground now.

"I really think we should leave the remains in place," he said sharply. "The police will want to look at them."

There was an anger in his words which went beyond mere procedural objection.

"This is archaeology, not crime," said Winander. "Let's have a look at the stuff before the experts get their grubby little hands on it."

The next thing to appear was a cross, about four feet in length. It seemed to have been bound round with sacking, the dusty remnants of which still clung to it. One of the Gowders picked it up and started to brush it off with his great red paw. As the detritus was cleared, the cross began to glow with the dullness of old gold and the brightness of polished gems. He set it down hastily, as though it were hot.

"Oh my God," said Mrs. Appledore.

More items were handed out of the hole, some chalices, a pair of candlesticks, a chrismatory and a pyx—but, much to Sam's relief, there were no more bones.

Finally the two men clambered out.

"Haven't you done well, Edie?" said Winander. "If you can claim this lot, they'll crown you Most Desirable Widow at the Skaddale Show. What do you think, Madero?"

Madero shrugged.

"I do not know the English law," he said. "My guess is that this was the place where the monks of the Priory stored their treasures in time of need. A good spot, belonging to the Priory without actually being in the Priory. When word of the king's men came, they must have decided the time had come to hide what they could. Not everything, because if they found the place stripped of all valuables, the destroyers wouldn't have rested till they got someone to tell where they had gone. I've no doubt they found a cross in place. But not one like this."

He regarded the jeweled crucifix with reverence.

"So who does it belong to?" said Winander. "The Church? Or finders keepers?"

"Ultimately it belongs to God," said Madero. "But then so does everything. Miss Flood, are you all right?"

"Fit as a butcher's dog," said Sam, glaring at Madero and

challenging him to make any further reference to her recent debility.

"Good. Perhaps you and I should clean up. We will need to make statements to the police."

Sam looked at him in surprise. Perhaps it was a Spanish convention that you looked your best when communicating with the police. True, he was a bit dusty, but not too bad. If anything, the way he was holding his jacket tight around his body as if the chill of the nether chamber had struck into his bones, what he really needed was some of Mrs. Appledore's brandy. But he was already at the door, where he paused.

"Mrs. Appledore, you'll phone the authorities?"

The landlady glanced at Winander who shrugged and said, "He's right. They like to know about bones, even ancient ones."

"Right then," said the woman.

Sam was now recovered sufficiently to glance down at her limbs. For some reason she seemed to have gathered twice as much dust as Madero. God knows what was in it!

She stood up and followed the Spaniard up the stairs.

As he opened the door of his room, she said, "Thanks."

"For what, Miss Flood?"

"For helping me get through that. And what's with this Miss Flood stuff? Or do you only use first names when you've got a girl up close and intimate?"

She gave him a grin to let him see she'd noticed, then went into her room.

A glance in the mirror stopped her grinning. As well as the dust, there were cobwebs in her hair, and her shorts looked as if she'd played rugby in them. She grabbed her spongebag and towel and headed out to the bathroom.

But first she tapped on Madero's door, which swung open.

"OK if I get first stab at the bathroom?" she said.

He looked up, startled, almost guilty.

He was sitting on the bed with some kind of book on his

lap. It was quarto size and looked very old and dusty. Dustier than he did. Suddenly she understood his eagerness to get out of the kitchen.

She said, "That's what you had under your jacket!"

She didn't mean to sound accusatory but he reacted as if to accusation.

"Why not? I think if anyone's entitled, it is I."

"Listen, mate, you do whatever you want, so long as you don't do it in the street and frighten the horses," said Sam, turning away.

He stood up and said, "No, wait. I'm sorry."

She halted and looked back at him.

He had that haunted look on his face again.

He said in a quick low tone, "It's just that, what I felt down there, I think Father Simeon hid in that chamber. But I think someone else was with him for part of the time."

He paused as if unable or at least reluctant to go on.

Sam said, "So? Maybe he had a traveling companion. Must have been a lonely business he was in. A little bit of comfort in the night would have come in handy."

She hadn't meant it to come out as a salacious innuendo, but Madero didn't react. He was still too concerned with his internal debate, which seemed to have less to do with what he was reluctant to tell her than with what he was unwilling to admit to himself.

"Spit it out," she advised. "Better than choking on it."

"Your father again?" he said, attempting a smile. "He really does sound like a man of good sense. All right, you already think me weird because of my beliefs. You might as well think I am crazy too. That sense of another presence I had down there in the chamber—a ghostly presence, I mean, in addition to Father Simeon's, but this one was stronger. It was almost as if I myself had been there five hundred years ago."

"Jeez, and here's me thinking you were still this side of fifty," said Sam. "And the book you lifted?"

"It felt so strongly connected to me that I had to take it," he said.

"So what's it say?"

"I don't know. I can't read a word of it."

He managed a rueful smile, then became serious again.

"But it has to mean something, doesn't it?" he appealed. "All of my life I have felt something trying to speak to me. It sent me down highways and byways, but in the end it's this place, Illthwaite in the Valley of the Shadow, that it was calling me to. And there's one more thing I'm starting to feel very strongly. You're part of it too, Sam. You're part of it too!"

15

God.com

If it hadn't been for his attempt to bring her into his crazy equation, Sam might have been more sympathetic. The guy had some good points and despite their obvious differences there was something about him which drew her to him. But trying to fit her up with a role in his superstitious shadow play was going too far.

"So what you're saying is you've been getting like e-mails from God dot com?" she mocked. "How do you know it's not just spam from the devil like your confessor tried to tell you?"

Her mockery came out rather more vehemently than she intended and she felt a pang of guilt, recognizing this as a reaction to the way her terror of the darkness had caused her to lay herself so bare. She also recalled that he'd done the same, not out of terror but partly in response to her openness and also to keep her mind occupied with matters other than her claustrophobia. Plus there'd been that moment at the end when the old Adam had taken over from the wannabe priest!

Calling truce isn't as easy as declaring war. He was regarding her coldly as he said, "I thought you claimed to be a mathematician."

"What's that mean? 'Claimed'?"

"Aren't mathematicians supposed to strive for cool objectivity in their observations? To withhold belief or disbelief until they've examined all offered proofs and attempted their own? Any mention of religion to you is like waving a *muleta* at a bull. Objectivity out, emotion in. It all becomes personal!"

That wasn't a *muleta*, that was a *banderilla*.

"Personal!" she exploded. "What else should it be but personal? But it's a gender thing as well. Show me a religion which doesn't rate men as superior and I might take a closer look at it. But that's not the end of it either. It's a philosophical thing and a volition thing too. I can't find any logical or scientific arguments that add up to God, and anyway I really don't want to believe in a god who could let all the shitty things happen that do happen. All this old stuff you're into about people torturing each other and ripping each other's guts out in the name of religion, it's not history, you know. It's still going on. The way I see it, women shouldn't be going down on their knees, begging to be given full rights in your religions, they should be giving thanks for their partial exclusion and taking steps to make it absolute!"

Where had all this stuff come from? she wondered. It was pointless and untimely, and she ought to get out now. But she didn't believe in turning away from a fight.

They stood glowering at each other for a long moment, but she wasn't much good at glowering and he wasn't in the mood for theological debate.

He sat back down on the bed and said rather wearily, "Some interesting points, but can we leave them for another time? Please, I'm not patronizing you. On the contrary, talking about things being personal, this is what this is to me, I freely admit it. What I'm hearing here isn't a message from God saying I'm especially holy, but the most powerful of voices from my family's past . . ."

"You don't think that skull belonged to this ancestor, do you?" interrupted Sam, looking to get back to concrete evidence, even old bones. "Or this guy Simeon maybe?"

"No. Neither. Though it felt very old, and very holy too somehow. I think it could be some sacred relict which the monks hid with the other treasure. There are experts who will be able to tell the skull's age and sex. And believe me, I want to find concrete evidence to support what I feel too. Perhaps it will be in this old book. I'm sure there will be experts who can interpret it. Meanwhile, however irrational it seems, I am stuck with this certainty that at some time there was a Madero hiding down in that chamber."

"But you said that you were the first of your family who ever got close to being a priest," she objected.

"I am," he agreed. "No, I don't think he was a fugitive priest like Father Simeon. The only possibility I can think of is he was one of the two Maderos I told you about, who were lost with the Great Armada. Probably—because the pain I feel is the pain of youth—it was the young man. It means that somehow he came to this part of the country, I do not know how. And while he was here, something terrible happened to him. I don't know what. But he was here, and he suffered here, in Illthwaite, of that I am sure."

He paused and looked at Sam as if anticipating another outpouring of scorn.

Instead she said, "Oh shit," as her instinctive skepticism was joined by something else . . . words, and an image . . .

"What?" he said, picking up that this wasn't a comment on what he'd just said.

"Look," said Sam. "Probably just coincidence, but there's something in that old guidebook of Mrs. Appledore's you maybe should read."

"Coincidence is the way God talks to us," said Madero. "Which bit?"

The book was lying on the bedside table. He handed it to her and she opened it at the section on the Other Wolf-Head Cross.

"Here," she said, handing it back.

He took it and started reading.

Curious to get his reaction, she didn't leave but glanced down at the collection of dusty pages he'd laid on the coverlet. They looked as if they'd been loosely bound together but the binding material had decayed and snapped. The leaves, however, were in a relatively good state of preservation. They were covered in tiny close-packed writing, not in any recognizable language but in symbols, some bearing a strong resemblance to letters of the Greek alphabet, others resembling numbers or simple geometric shapes.

Sam studied the first page, frowning with concentration.

Madero meanwhile had run his eyes over the story of Thomas Gowder's murder and the mysterious fate of his assailant.

After a while he said savagely, "This cannot be."

Then he got control of himself with a visible effort and said, "These are merely the scribblings of some amateur historian based on little more than local folklore. The truth needs more scholarly sifting than this."

What was it he found so hard to take in? wondered Sam. That his ancestor suffered a terrible fate? Or that he might have been a cold-blooded killer?

"And you've got one of your funny feelings you could find the truth in this book you stole, right?" she said.

"I haven't stolen anything," he said wearily. "It will be replaced with all the other material from the chamber before the police arrive. I wouldn't like to feel I'll be a trouble to your conscience when you come to make your statement."

His sarcasm struck her as both uncalled for and unjust.

"Maybe it's your own conscience that's bothering you," she retorted. "As for these pages, could be you're right to hang on to them. After all, they've got your name in them."

It took him a moment to work out what she was saying.

"You can read them?" he burst out incredulously.

"No problem," she said airily and made as if to move through the door.

"Wait!" he commanded.

This got him one of her slate-eye looks and he quickly added, "Please. You must explain . . . I mean, I would appreciate it if . . ."

"Glad to see you've not forgotten your manners," she said briskly. "Yes, I can read it. First bit at least, then it goes a bit weird. I recognize the code. Strictly speaking it's a nomenclator—that's a combination of cipher and code using a symbolic alphabet indicating letters and also some common words. Like I said in the churchyard, I had this boyfriend who was into encryption in a big way. The math end of it's quite interesting actually, but I read something about the history of encryption too which is where I came across these symbols. Surprised you didn't recognize them yourself."

She regarded him with mocking challenge.

He said, "There is something familiar . . . but I do not know how . . ."

"Perhaps you came across it when you were reading about that guy Walsingham, Elizabeth's spook-master. That's right. This is the cipher used by Mary Queen of Scots and the Catholic conspirators when they were plotting to assassinate Elizabeth. They were the good guys in your book, I'd guess."

Madero said doubtfully, "And how can you be sure this is the same code?"

"I told you, dummy. Because I can read some of it. I suppose these undercover priests liked to use some kind of secret writing in case they got caught. Good thinking, but this Father Simeon can't have been all that bright, using a code that must have been broken to get the evidence to convict Mary. When did she get the chop?"

"In 1587," said Madero.

"And the Armada?"

"1588."

"Like I say, not very bright, even for a priest."

He said, "So what does it say?"

She picked up the page and studied it then said, "*After three days the fever has broken for which be thanks. His wounds though I keep them clean as I am able are yet livid and pustular. He woke and was in great fear till I calmed him, telling him what I was, and where we lay, and hearing me speak in his own tongue he grew calm and fell into a deep sleep, though not before telling me his name was Miguel Madero.*"

Sam stopped and looked up at the Spaniard who said impatiently, "Go on!"

"I think he jumps a few hours then he says that the young man is awake once more and is keen to tell his story which he wishes Father Simeon to take down so that he may let his family know his fate if, as he fears, he does not return to Spain, but Simeon does. There's a hell of a lot more but you'll need to sort that out for yourself."

"Please, I beg you. You must go on," he said desperately.

"I'm not playing hard to get," she said patiently. "It's just that after this it gets into some lingo I don't speak. If this is your boy, it could be Spanish, yeah?"

"Which Father Simeon spoke fluently," said Madero.

He opened his dressing-table drawer and took out a writing pad and a ballpoint.

"I'll need you to write out the code. Please."

The tone was peremptory, the *please* again an afterthought.

He's still talking to me like some schoolmaster to a kid, thought Sam. But I felt you getting a hard-on, you bastard!

"Glad to," she said, smiling sweetly. "But first I'm going to get cleaned up. I won't be long, then you can have the bathroom. The cops will be here soon, I expect."

She turned and went out. He'd waited over four hundred years for this, he could wait a few minutes longer!

Madero glared after her in frustration then turned his gaze back on the book. That he'd been led here to uncover the mystery of his ancestor's fate he could not doubt. That he had come by such a roundabout route was his own fault, caused by his hubristic misinterpretation of the message.

And here he was being prevented from God's purpose by the mocking whim of this Australian child! Who of course wasn't a child, he admonished himself. Which was just as well, else the way his body had reacted as he held her close in the chamber would be cause for serious concern. No, she was a bright intelligent adult woman only a few years younger than himself, and it was time he started treating her like one.

He looked at himself in the dressing-table mirror. Those years in the seminary had left their mark, not so much outwardly as on the man inside. Preparation for the most serious job a man could undertake, a job in which people twice your age would call you Father, made you strive for a maturity beyond your years. At the same time the turning away from worldly things and in particular that control and denial of the sexual impulse which in his case had begun years earlier had left him a mere boy in his relationship with women. He was still in his twenties. He had to learn again what it was to be a young man. Then perhaps he would be able to engage with Frek Woollass on level terms.

As for Sam, his arousal there had been a mere coincidence of proximity and long frustration. There was something about her which, despite all the negatives between them, formed a positive bond. But its roots, he assured himself, had nothing to do with sexual attraction. Rather it was a correspondence of purpose. She was on a quest too. Like his, it seemed to have been delayed by misinterpretation and misunderstanding, with her visit to Illthwaite turning out to be what the English called a red herring.

Yet, if she hadn't come here, it was doubtful if he would be trembling on the brink of solving his family mystery. This made him think that perhaps her error was part of God's purpose too . . .

"Mr. Madero! Are you there?"

Mrs. Appledore's voice from the foot of the stairs broke in on his meditation.

He went out to the landing and said, "Yes?"

"Police are here."

He was surprised. He'd expected a gap of at least half an hour, probably longer.

He said, "I'm coming," then returned to his room, and tucked the purloined papers gently under his pillow.

Downstairs he solved the mystery of the rapid police response. This was no high-powered investigatory team but a single constable who had got the call in the Powderham Arms where he'd been checking security, which everyone knew was a euphemism for chatting up one of the waitresses. A comfortably built young man, he seemed both excited to be first cop on the scene and uncertain what he actually ought to do. But he was soon helped by the arrival of a strange little man in a garish waistcoat who spoke in his ear, and rapidly thereafter everyone was ushered out of the kitchen into the bar.

When Mrs. Appledore protested at being ordered around in her own home, the constable said in the stilted tone of a newly conned part, "We need to keep the crime scene uncontaminated till SOCO get here, ma'am."

The mystery of this new authority was solved when Madero asked Winander, "Who is that old man? Is he too a policeman?"

"Was. Noddy Melton, Head of CID, retired. At least he knows the ropes, which is just as well as this bugger doesn't seem to know his whistle from his whatsit."

Now there was a further diversion as a handful of early drinkers came into the bar only to be told the pub wasn't open and probably wouldn't be for some time.

During the debate which ensued, Madero noticed the old man slip out. He followed and found him in the kitchen, examining the skull.

"What are you doing?" asked Madero. "I thought this place was to be kept clear."

"Not of me," said the old man mildly. "Nice to meet you, Mr. Madero. I would say this is pretty old, wouldn't you? A man. Pre-dentist, by the look of it. There is a story that some relicts of St. Ylf were kept at the Priory. Didn't find a silver bullet, did you?"

"I am sorry?"

"The legend says he turned into a wolf to show travelers the way, which makes him a werewolf, and the best way to kill them was a silver bullet."

"Mr. Melton, are you OK?"

Sam Flood, smelling of scented soap and changed into low-cut jeans and a sweatshirt, came in. She shot Madero what he felt was a quite undeserved admonitory glance.

"Hello again, Miss Flood," said the old man. "Yes, I'm fine. I happened to have my radio tuned to the police frequency and when I heard them put this shout out . . ."

"And they mentioned bones, did they?" said Sam anxiously. "But I think you'll find these are pretty old, isn't that right, Mr. Madero?"

"I think we've established that," said Mig, wondering why she felt it necessary to reassure the old man who looked perfectly in control of himself and the situation.

"Great," said Sam, taking the skull out of Melton's hands and laying it on the table. "Why don't we head outside and see if Mrs. Appledore can rustle you up a drink?"

She led the old man into the hallway where they saw the landlady coming out of the barroom, which still sounded a scene of lively protest. She looked hot and flustered.

"There you are, Noddy," she said. "I'd appreciate it if you could have another word with young Starsky back there before he starts a riot."

"Mr. Melton was looking at the bones we found under the kitchen," said Sam significantly. "I think a drink might help."

"Do you now? All right, but not before you get that lot sorted. They see you getting a drink, they'll all want one."

"I'll see what I can do," said Melton. Then to Sam he added, "You have been most kind. I hope I can return the favor."

There was a surge of noise from the bar. He smiled and went through the door.

"I think he thought they might be his Mary's," said Sam.

"Told you about that, did he?" said Mrs. Appledore. "Looks spry enough to me. See what a hornet's nest you two have stirred up! And I'm losing money because of it."

Sam realized that Madero had made another of his silent sorties and was standing beside her. He looked ready to be contrite in the face of the landlady's remonstrance, but Sam retorted, "Tell you what, Mrs. Appledore. I'll give you a night's takings for your share of whatever the loot back there brings in. Could be nothing, of course . . ."

A slow grin spread across Mrs. Appledore's face.

"Think I'll take my chances, dear. Sounds like things are quietening down."

She turned and reentered the bar.

"So what was that all about with the old man?" asked Madero.

Quickly Sam filled him in on Melton's background.

"You seem to have learned a great deal about the locals in a short time," he said.

"A trick I picked up at uni," said Sam. "It's called listening. You should try it."

They stood in the shady hallway and looked at each other.

He thought, when she is being kind and thoughtful instead of brash and boisterous, she is not unattractive.

She thought, when he is being natural and unguarded instead of pompous and priestly, he's a bit of a spunk.

Then the bar door opened and the thwarted drinkers spilled out, still protesting in colorful terms about this breach of their native rights, and the moment was past.

PART FOUR

TRUTH

Don't clam up, prophetess, I've questions to ask
and I won't stop asking until I know all;
who are those young women? and why are they weeping?

"Balder's Dreams" *Poetic Edda*

1

Into the light

Early next morning Sam finally left Illthwaite.

There'd been no question of her leaving the previous evening. It took nearly an hour for the first CID officer to turn up. Unimpressed by assertions that the bones were too ancient for this to be a crime scene, he called in a forensic team to do a full appraisal.

By the time they'd finished and Sam had given her statement for the third time, it was too late to contemplate driving to Newcastle.

Somehow she and Madero hadn't bumped into each other again that night. From the fact that she didn't see him being led away by men in white coats, she assumed he'd omitted from his statement any reference to communion with the spirits. Before she went to bed she'd scribbled out the key to the Mary Queen of Scots cipher and pushed it under his door.

The following morning as she started up her car he came out of the pub with a long black sweater pulled hastily over his pajamas, which she was entertained to see weren't black but striped red and yellow. She bet his mother had bought them.

"You were going without saying goodbye," he said accusingly.

"Don't expect we'll ever meet again," she said.

"All the more reason to say goodbye," he protested.

"Nah," she said with the certainty of one who understands the difference between real and apparent logic. "All the less."

He shook his head slightly as though to clear his mind and said, "Thank you for writing out the code."

"Nomenclator," she said. "No problem."

She put the car in gear and began to pull away.

"Good luck in your quest," he called.

"And you. Love the jarmies. If you're going to buzz around like a bee, you might as well look like one. Ciao!"

And that had been that. Last sight of Madero, followed very shortly by last sight of Illthwaite.

No reason why she should be troubled by either the place or the man again.

The journey to Newcastle took her through lovely countryside, but she was driving eastward into the morning sunlight and, even with her Ray-Bans on, she needed to keep all her attention on the road. On the fringes of the city, she stopped at a service area, bought a street map and checked out the address Betty McKillop had given her in a northern suburb called Gosforth. It was her mother's flat, the woman had said, sheltered accommodation which was why she had to vacate it so soon after the funeral.

It took another forty minutes to reach what turned out to be a cul-de-sac consisting of four two-story blocks of flats, purpose built for the elderly. They could have looked barrack-like, but the use of a warm red brick with a variety of pastel colors for doors and windows gave them an attractive air, and the lawned areas between them were generously planted with ornamental shrubs. On the whole, not too bad a place to attend death.

She was well ahead of her appointed time so she drove on till she reached the edge of the urban area and found a pub with a beer garden. Here she sat, letting the autumn sun fill her hair with colors to match the changing trees. On impulse she took out her mobile and rang home. It would be late evening there, her parents if not already in bed would be thinking about it, but the desire to hear their familiar voices was strong.

Lu answered.

"Hi, Ma."

"Sammy! Hi, hon. How're you doing? Everything OK?"

"Fine. Just felt like a chat. Sorry it's so late."

"It's not late. What do you think we are? Pair of clapped-out geriatrics? So how's it going? You in Cambridge yet, or are you still rubbernecking?"

"Still touring around, getting the feel of the country."

She felt uncomfortable not being straight with her mother. Eventually she'd come clean with her, but not before hearing what Betty McKillop had to say. Then and only then would she take a decision about what, if anything, to tell her father. Or more likely she'd off-load the decision on to Lu.

"Yeah? And how does it feel?"

"Fine, but not like home."

"Hope it never feels like that, hon, but give it time and I'm sure you'll find plenty to like. Hang on. Here's your pa."

A pause, then that quiet voice which packed more authority into monosyllables than most politicos and preachers got into a sixty-minute harangue.

"How's tricks, girl?"

"Fine, Pa. I'm doing fine."

"Not ready for home yet?"

"Pa, I just got here last week!"

"Yeah? Seems longer. Missing you, girl. Here's your ma."

Missing you, girl. The simple statement provoked a longing for home more powerful than any she'd experienced since her departure.

She spoke with her mother a few minutes more, keeping it

light and chatty. When they said goodbye and she'd switched off her phone, for a few moments the autumn sun seemed to have lost all its heat and the trees and buildings and people around her faded to a ghostly tableau into which she had somehow strayed.

Then a girl appeared with the sandwich she'd ordered and as she set it down she said, "Hope you don't mind me asking, but is that hair color natural, 'cos if it's not, I want to know where I can buy some!"

"Sorry," said Sam, laughing. "That's the way it came."

"Oh well. Just have to get a wig then, won't I?"

In fact the girl's hair was a pleasant shade of brown and so fine that the light breeze drifted it across her face in a manner Sam guessed young men would not find unattractive. But she knew from experience that persuading yourself that what you had was in fact OK was not the easiest task a young woman faced.

But the exchange had served to bring her back to where she functioned best, in the here and now. She ate her sandwich, followed it up with a coffee, then killed time strolling along a nearby riverbank and making conversation with the anglers before she headed south once more to Gosforth.

The flat was on the ground floor. She rang the bell and waited. After a moment she saw a figure behind the frosted-glass panel. Then the door was opened by a woman in her fifties, broad in the bust and beam, with henna'd hair and a full fleshy face fraught with enough makeup to launch an amateur production of *The Mikado*. She looked at Sam, nodded, and said in a strong Australian accent, "I'm Betty McKillop. No need to ask who you are. You got the build, and of course the hair. Lucky girl. Come on in."

"It's good of you to see me at a time like this, Mrs. McKillop," said Sam, following the woman into a sitting room still containing a three-piece suite and a low table but denuded of pictures and ornaments. "I'm sorry about your mother."

"Call me Betty. Yeah, well at least I knew her for a few years. Those bastards told me she was dead, you know. If it hadn't been for the Trust . . . angels them people are, angels. I'm surprised they haven't been able to help you more."

"To tell the truth, I haven't really bothered them, Betty," said Sam, sitting down. "It was just the coincidence of Gracie being the aunt of a friend of mine that got me wondering. And when she mentioned you, and I was coming over here anyway . . ."

"To Cambridge Uni, you say? Bright girl. Good onya. World needs bright girls. Sorry I can't offer you a cuppa. Everything's packed up or junked. Just the furniture to go, and someone's coming round to clear that out later on. So let's enjoy the comfort while we can. It's your show, Sam. What do you want to ask me?"

"That's easy," said Sam. "What I want to hear is anything you can tell me about my grandmother, that's Sam Flood, who sailed to Australia with you. Gracie said you and her were pretty friendly."

"Yeah, we got that way, as far as it was possible with little Sam." She hesitated then went on, "You want the lot? Some of it won't be pleasant, you appreciate that?"

"From what little I know, I'll be surprised if any of it is," said Sam.

"Then you won't be very surprised. OK, where shall I start? The beginning, why not? The journey out."

She settled back on the sofa, lit a cigarette and began to talk.

2

Betty

All told, the voyage out wasn't so bad, though there were plenty of bad times. Like being sick. And realizing after a while that we'd gone too far ever to turn round and go back.

But I made new friends, and most of the sailors were kind. And, looking back, and knowing now what was waiting for us after we arrived, those days seem like a pleasure cruise.

For years I could never remember much of this stuff, you know, not even the voyage. Not because I'd properly forgotten but because I reckon I made myself forget. It was like looking back into a dark pit you were trying to climb out of. There were faces in there and little hands clutching and voices calling out in fear and pain, and all that any looking back did was start you sliding down into the pit, and you knew it had no bottom because wherever you'd been before or whoever you'd been before was out of your reach forever . . .

Sorry. I'll be all right in a minute. But it's been hard. I brought up a daughter and she was always asking questions about the way things were when I was a little girl, the way kids do, and that got me looking back into the pit even when I was laughing with her and telling my made-up stories. Then she grew up and got married and gave me a granddaughter and I thought it's going to be the same again, her curious, me telling stories, but always skirting round the truth because I couldn't talk about it, not even to my husband, not even to my own child . . .

I think if I thought anything I thought I must have done something really terrible to deserve such punishment. Yes, that's it, I felt guilty. Makes you laugh, doesn't it? I felt guilty! Makes you cry.

Then one day I read in the paper about this Migrant Trust thing that this English woman had started. It was funny. I'd got so used to trying not to think about it because there was no point that it was real hard to start thinking about it again. Suppose it turned out I was right and I deserved what happened to me? But in the end I had to write to the English lady and I got this reply inviting me to go and see her next time she was in Australia, so I went.

There were a lot of other people there waiting and one of them kept looking at me and finally she came over and said, "Aren't you Betty?" And then I remembered, we'd been on the boat together, and we started crying. Jesus, we must have cried a whole bucketload of tears, and it was like they started washing stuff away, and the more we cried and the more we talked, the more I remembered . . .

Not being alone was better and it was worse. When I realized just how many of us there'd been—not just one boatload but whole convoys over whole decades—for the first time I began to think maybe I wasn't so specially bad after all. But then you start to ask, if we weren't so specially bad, what in the name of God were we doing on those boats? Who decided we should be on them? Where did we all come from?

But you know all about this. There's been newspaper articles, there's been books, there's been commissions of inquiry. You want to know about your gran, the little sick girl. I keep calling her little. She wasn't all that big but she was two years older than me. I was ten. Can you imagine that? Ten, and they put me on a boat and sent me so far away from home, if we'd gone any further we'd have been coming back! But the girl, Sammy—that's what we called her because when you asked her about herself, she never spoke but just pulled this piece of paper out of her pocket and when you unfolded it you could just about read this name. Sam Flood. One of the girls thought it must be short for Samantha, which sounded a real fancy name back then. The sick girl didn't say anything, so we called her Sammy anyway.

There was some kind of address on the paper too, but it had all got so scrunched up it was hard to read. Didn't seem important, anyway. What did addresses in England have to do with us anymore? Names were different. You had to be called something. Everyone needs a name. Once you let the bastards just call you a number, they've really won, haven't they?

What was I saying? Oh yes, her age. That was the first word she ever spoke to me. I kept asking her how old she was, just for the sake of making her think someone was interested in her, I suppose. Really I reckon I was more interested in myself. When you're heading down, one way to stop yourself hitting bottom is to find someone worse off than yourself and take care of them. I see that now. I'm not saying I wasn't really sorry for the girl—I was—but I was really sorry for myself too and this helped.

Twelve. She said she was twelve. Two years older than me. But that didn't stop me thinking of her as some kind of helpless kid sister I had to look after. Maybe they thought we really were sisters or something, because when we got off the boat, me and Sammy got sent off together with three others, none of them girls I knew well. The ones I did know, like Gracie, got sent off somewhere else. There was no time to say goodbye to her or any of the others. Off we were pushed in different directions, like sheep at a market.

The woman who took us away with her was a nun. I knew about nuns. I'd been brought up a Catholic. It was with the nuns in Liverpool my mother left me when she couldn't manage anymore, and when she came back to get me, I was gone . . . but that's my story. All of the other kids on that boat were Catholic too from what I remember. I doubt if many of them are now. I lost any faith I had a long time ago, but sometimes I hope I'm wrong and they're right. I'll tell you why. Because if they're right, there's a whole bunch of them burning in hell this very minute for the way they treated us. Oh yes, this minute, and every minute from now till the end of time if there's justice in heaven, which there certainly didn't seem to be down below.

But little Sammy wasn't a Catholic. I don't think she'd ever seen a nun. What I think she had seen somewhere was a picture with Death in it, wearing a hood and a cowl, so she thought it was Death was taking us away. Maybe she was right.

When we got to this place, I knew what it was straightaway. It was a kids' home run by the nuns, like the one I'd been in back in Liverpool. I remember thinking, why have they brought me all these thousands of miles across the sea to stick me in the same kind of place I'd been in back home? But I soon found I was wrong. There were differences. That one back in Liverpool was a five-star hotel compared with this place.

It was called St. Rumbald's. We had to learn all about St. Rumbald. Seems he got born, said, "I'm a Christian," got baptized, took Holy Communion, preached a sermon, arranged his own burial, then died, all in three days. We used to joke that the poor little sod knew if he'd lived any longer he'd have been sent to somewhere like St. Rumbald's, so he took the easy way out. Even in hell, you try to joke.

That first day when we arrived, they lined us up to take our details, meaning our names and ages—what else did we have? None of us had any papers or photos or anything. It was like the people who sent us hadn't wanted us to have anything that could be traced back to them. Only Sammy had her pathetic little scrap of paper. She was in front of me. When the nun at the desk asked her name, she just stood there. Another nun standing beside us started to shake her. I piped up that her name was Samantha and she was twelve and this nun just lashed out with her hand and caught me such a blow across the mouth, I fell over. "Speak when you're spoken to," she said. I lay there with my mouth bleeding and watched poor little Sammy pull her piece of paper out. The nun at the desk took it, read it, and said, "Sam Flood. What sort of name is that for a Christian girl? Samantha, is it? I think that's a kind of Jewish name. We'll be keeping an eye on you, girl."

She wrote something down in her ledger, then scrumpled up the piece of paper and dropped it into a wastebasket. I saw little Sammy's gaze follow it like it was her life she saw being dumped. Then she was pushed away and I was dragged to my feet and made to give my details through my bleeding mouth.

One thing about them nuns, they kept their promises. They said they'd keep an eye on Sammy and they did. Her not being a Catholic meant she was always drawing attention to herself anyway. All that crossing yourself stuff, and knowing when to stand and when to kneel, and singing the responses, none of it meant anything to her. Jesus, I saw her take blows that would have felled a prize steer. But that wasn't the worst of it, not by a long way.

I tried to help her, I know I did. But soon it became hard to think of anything but getting myself through to the end of every dreadful day. And, like I said before, each day I got through became part of that stinking pit I was trying to get out of and if you looked back at all, you just saw stuff to make you despair, so I parceled it up as I went along and left it behind me and willed myself never ever to remember.

But all that changed after I went to that first meeting. Now at last there was a reason for remembering. Now someone was trying to do something about it. That English woman, she's a saint. At least if I still believed in saints, she'd top my list. After I got in touch with the Trust, nearly every day I recalled something new. And the Trust found things out for me that I thought I'd never know. About my mother. I was one of the lucky ones. She was still alive and I got to know her, and I've been able to spend these last few weeks with her. My mother. And the bastards told me she was dead.

But you don't want to know about that . . . No, it's all right, don't apologize. It's not selfish, it's focused. I know what it's like tracking back this stuff, remember?

So, Sammy, the little sick girl, my kid sister who was two years older. We've all got personal, individual horrors that we've stored up, but what happened to her is a horror shared by every one of us that saw it. I managed to put a lid on most of what happened to me, but that was something I could never blot out. It was the same for the others, I've discovered. We all remember that day . . .

Like I say, Sammy never looked well. After a while we didn't pay much heed. None of us were all that well, what with the food we had to eat, the work we had to do, the conditions we had to live in. To us, being unwell was normal. But in the end it was bad enough with Sammy for the nuns to take notice. They got their doctor to take a look at her, not so much out of any sense of care, I'd guess, as to check she wasn't swinging the lead.

Next thing we know is we're all called into assembly and there's little Sammy standing in front of us with the nuns behind her, and Mother Posterior (that's what we called the boss nun who was a big fat cow) stood up and went into this rant which was all about mortal sin and eternal damnation and such, the kind of stuff we got by the bucketload, so normally we tried to look pious and switched off. But this time we listened 'cos gradually we realized she was telling us something completely incredible.

She was telling us, though she couldn't bring herself to say the word, that little Sammy was pregnant!

And when she finished, you know what those bitches did?

They cut off Sammy's hair.

She had this lovely red hair, just like yours. That's how I knew you soon as I saw you. On the boat it had been almost as long as yours. At St. Rum's we all had our hair cut shorter, but Sammy's was still a sight worth seeing. Now they set about her, two or three of them with garden shears, and they hacked and hacked till you could see the white skin among the stubble, only in places it wasn't white but red 'cos they'd stabbed right through and drawn blood.

Sammy just stood there, tears and blood streaming down her face, but she didn't utter a sound, till finally they were done. Then they marched her out and that was the last any of us saw or heard of Sammy.

So what happened to her? She didn't look in any state to make it through to the next day, but you being here means she must have done. I still see her in my nightmares after all these years, standing there quietly weeping while her red locks drifted to the floor like autumn leaves around her.

What happened to her, Sam? What happened?

3

Scary stranger

Betty McKillop had chain-smoked as she talked, lighting one cigarette from another and throwing the butts into the grate. Now she threw the last one, followed by the empty packet, and leaned forward to look Sam right in the face.

"I don't know," said Sam. "I don't know what happened, except she died having my father. He got adopted, grew up, got married, had me."

She spoke quickly, plainly. That was her story, that was all she had to tell. She looked at the older woman and saw her eyes were brimming with tears. Then her arms reached out offering to embrace her, but fell back as Sam sat stiff and upright, her face stony. There would be a time for grief, for anger. But for the moment she needed to keep her wits about her. There were things here that didn't add up. What she wanted was information not consolation.

"How long did all this take?" she said. "I mean, how long had you been at St. Rumbald's before they assaulted my grandmother?"

"I can't be exact. Time didn't mean much there. Sometimes an hour could seem like a week."

"You must have some idea," said Sam impatiently. "A year? Longer? It had to be a year at least, didn't it?"

Betty looked at her in surprise.

"Hell no," she said. "Nothing like that. This all happened in the first few months we were there."

The statement was so self-evidently wrong that for a shocked second it brought everything else Betty had told her into doubt. But why invent a story like that? No, this had to be a simple misunderstanding.

"But that doesn't compute," said Sam, shaking her head. "My pa was born in September the year after you arrived. Why should those bastard nuns lie about that? So Sammy got pregnant a few months after she arrived. Pa reckons it was a priest. I bet those nuns didn't let any other men get close to you. I bet they kept you closer than a duck's arse."

"You're right there, dear," said the woman, drying her eyes and blowing her nose. "Getting knocked up at St. Rum's, you'd have had to do it on the wing, like a swallow. Some of the nuns had roving hands and some of the priests too, from what I heard. But I never heard of anyone going the full hog. Anyway, I'm sorry, but you've got things mixed up. Like I said, we'd only been there a few months when they savaged little Sammy's head, may they spend hell with red-hot skewers up their backsides. No, she must have been pregnant already when I met her on the boat. That's why she was so sick, I see that now."

Sam shook her head again, this time as much in desperation as denial.

"No, it's you who's getting mixed up," she insisted. "Pa was born in September 1961, I've seen the certificate. And your ship sailed from Liverpool in the spring of 1960—"

"Spring 1960?" Betty McKillop laughed. "Who told you that? Gracie, was it? I bet it was Gracie!"

"Yes. And she was so positive about it. Elvis was top of the charts with 'Are You Lonesome Tonight?', and Kennedy became president that year. She remembers seeing it on television, and that was definitely 1960, I checked it out."

"Now just hold on there," interrupted Betty. "This is my life you're trying to tell me about, remember . . ."

Then she paused, let out an exasperated laugh and said, "Hang about, I think I see what's happened. Kennedy, you say? Yeah, it was 1960 when he got elected. November 1960. But what Gracie would have seen was his inauguration in January 1961. We all did, at the orphanage in Liverpool. Generally those nuns kept the telly to themselves but this was special, a good Roman Catholic taking the oath as president, next best thing to getting a new Pope. So we were all wheeled in to watch and give thanks. As for Elvis, I bet if you check that song, it came out in '61, not '60."

"But she was so sure," said Sam, thoroughly bewildered. "She said she was born in 1950 and she was ten when she came to Australia."

"She was ten when she got on the boat, all right," said Betty. "But she'd turned eleven by the time we landed. Not that we had birthday parties, anything like that. No, it was hard for any of us to keep track, even if you had a mind for it. We lost a whole summer on that trip. But it was definitely 1961. Poor Gracie. Don't be too hard on her. We all need to find our own way to deal with things, and from the sound of it Gracie's way was just to get even vaguer about things than she was when I knew her."

"She wasn't so vague she didn't remember about Sammy," protested Sam, still reluctant to accept this radical rearrangement of all her timings.

"No, but then the combination of your hair and your name is a pretty strong nudge! Look, dear, I don't know if it matters, but one thing you can be sure of is that poor little Sammy was definitely already knocked up when she got on the boat. Them nuns at St. Rum's didn't do a lot for us, but they certainly kept us virtuous."

Sam's face registered shock and bewilderment as she tried to take in this new information. Betty regarded her with shrewd compassion and leaned forward to pat her knee.

"Don't take it so hard, dear," she said. "Does it really matter? It was a long time ago and little Sammy's dead. At least it means your grandfather wasn't one of them bastard priests. As to who the bastard really was, some things you're better off not knowing. What my mum told me about my father didn't make me want to rush off and find the rotten bugger even if he is still alive, which don't seem likely."

She watched Sam as she spoke and she could see her words were falling on deaf ears.

She leaned forward again and said, "Listen, Sam, if you're really determined to find out more about her, you should talk to the people at the Trust. They know the ropes. They'll keep you straight. And even if they can't help you find out any more, they understand how important it is to help you let go."

With a great effort Sam got herself together. Now it was more important than ever that she asked the right questions, set out the right equations.

"Yes, thank you very much. I'll remember that," she said. "Just one thing more, Betty. That bit of paper with her name on it—Gracie thought there was an address on it too. She tried to remember but all she could come up with was that the town name ended in *thwaite*, and she wasn't too sure about that."

"No?" Betty laughed. "Well, for once, Gracie got it right. Nowhere I'd ever heard of. Illthwaite, that was it. In Cumberland."

"Cumberland? That's the same as Cumbria, right? Was that on the paper too?"

"I don't recollect. I don't think so. Sam Flood, the Vicarage, Illthwaite, is what I remember."

"The vicarage?" said Sam through dry lips. "Gracie didn't say that."

"Not surprising. I've just recalled it myself. Yeah, it definitely said the vicarage."

"But not Cumberland? So why did you say Cumberland?"

"Because that's where Sam said she came from," said Betty.

"You talked with her about her background?" said Sam eagerly. "What else did she tell you?"

"Not much. You've got to understand that talking to Sam was a bit like talking to a frightened kitten. If you kept at it, you might get it to give a little purr, but it sure as hell wasn't going to start talking back. So it was me who did most of the talking when we got a chance to talk, which wasn't all that often. If them nuns could have cut our tongues out and sewn on extra ears to pour their talk of hellfire into, that's what they'd have done."

"But she did tell you something about her background?" pressed Sam, desperate for every scrap.

"Nothing much, apart from living in Cumberland. Nothing about parents, but that wasn't surprising. Lot of the kids knew next to nothing about where they came from. Like I say, she didn't say much and what she did didn't make much sense. Sometimes it was hard to make out if she was talking about herself or someone else called Sam. She'd say something about Sam being warm in bed, Sam taking care of her. She answered to Sam, but that could have been because none of us ever called her anything else. For all I know, this name Sam Flood on her piece of paper referred to someone else entirely. It's just a possibility, but worth keeping in mind if you are going to carry on looking."

It's strange, thought Sam. People could say things that changed the shape of your universe without them ever realizing it.

She stood up abruptly. She needed to be away and by herself.

"Yes, I'll definitely keep it in mind. Thank you. You've been very helpful," she said formally.

Betty was looking surprised. And concerned.

"Don't rush off," she said. "I've got to hang on here till they come for the furniture. Let's just sit and yack, OK? Tell me about your family. And Gracie—tell me about old Gracie."

"My family's fine, Gracie's fine, I'm fine. But I've got to go. I've got things to do. Thanks a lot. Really. Thanks."

She headed for the door. She knew she was being rude. There was nothing but sympathy and kindness on offer here.

She stopped and turned back and said, "Betty, thanks a million. It's been really kind of you to take time to see me, especially with your ma just dying. I'm real sorry about that."

Betty's arms came round her and drew her into her ample bosom. Feeling that strength, that warmth, hearing soothing words being murmured in that home-evoking accent, it would have been easy to let go, relax, let the tears come.

But beneath her pain there was anger and hate. She didn't want them to be assuaged, she didn't want their edge to be blunted.

Still dry-eyed, she began to disengage.

Betty said, "Now you take care of yourself. Keep in touch, won't you? I'd really like to get to know you better. Maybe your pa would like to talk to me . . ."

Sam kissed her and broke loose.

"Yes, I will. Thanks again. 'Bye."

As she walked from the door, she didn't look back till she was in her car with the engine started. Then she waved and drove away.

She didn't feel she could drive far. Round the corner there was a parade of shops with parking spaces in front of them. She brought the car to a halt. She felt something, but didn't know what it was. She'd felt like this as a kid when she'd run around too long hatless in the midday sun. She didn't know whether she was going to be sick or faint.

Finally she leaned forward with her head against the steering wheel and, without forewarning, tears came.

After a couple of minutes she sat upright and wiped her eyes. She looked around, half expecting to be a focus of attention, but there weren't many people about and those that were didn't show any interest in her.

That was OK. That was how she wanted it. Take care of your own business. That was the way of the world. She certainly planned to take care of hers.

One of the shops in the parade was a hardware store. She got out of the car, went inside and bought a pair of kitchen scissors. Then she returned to the car and drove away and kept on driving till buildings thinned out and were replaced by fields and trees.

She turned up a quiet side road then parked close against a hawthorn hedge. She pulled down the sun visor and looked at herself in the small vanity mirror. The slate blue eyes that stared back were like a stranger's.

Finally she took hold of a tress of her rich red hair, stretched it out to its full length, laid it over the saltire of the scissors, hesitated for a long moment, then brought the blades together with a savage click, and let the long tress fall to the floor.

The first cut was the hardest. Wasn't it always? After that it was as if the scissors controlled her hand, dancing a mad cancan over her head, blades kicking high and closing hard, hair flying to left and right like sparks from a raging bonfire. From time to time the sharp metal grazed her scalp but she never paused till not a lock of hair longer than half an inch remained to be seen.

Now the woman in the mirror really was a stranger to her. A scary stranger.

Scary was OK.

That's what she wanted to be, scary.

Back in Illthwaite they prided themselves that they didn't scare easy.

"We'll just have to see about that," said the woman in the mirror.

PART FIVE

LOSS OF INNOCENCE

She calls on her strength to stand straight by the column;
flame darts from her eyes, her lips drip with venom.

"The First Lay of Gudrun" *Poetic Edda*

1

Jolley jinks

Miguel Madero had been surprised by his sense of loss as he watched Sam drive away.

He had only known her for a single day, there was a fundamental antagonism between them, yet somehow it felt like losing an ally. Even though he had seen the last of her, he still felt as though they were united by more than just the common drawing together of strangers meeting on unfamiliar territory. But if God had purposed that they should be here together, then He had also decided that it shouldn't be for long.

At all levels, her work in Illthwaite was done.

On her own behalf she'd followed a false trail laid by coincidence she now regarded as meaningless. He prayed she would find some sort of closure in her conversation with this woman in Newcastle.

But there had also been what he thought of as the real purpose of her visit to Illthwaite. Without her he might not have raised the table and found the hiding place. And certainly without her he wouldn't be reading the terrible story written in the cramped hand of Simeon Woollass from the fevered ramblings of his own distant ancestor and namesake.

Strictly the journal belonged to the Woollass family. Or the

Catholic Church. Or perhaps to the Crown as treasure trove. That was for lawyers to sort out. But not before he had translated and copied out what was written here.

Using Sam's key, he started transcribing the words, at first slowly and awkwardly, but then, as he grew familiar with both the cipher and the cryptographer's own abbreviations, with increasing confidence, till finally he was keying the words into his laptop at full speed. By halfway through the morning he had finished.

He sat there till the screensaver appeared and wiped away the words. Then he went and lay on his bed, looking up at the low-beamed ceiling, as if by will alone he could force his gaze through the stained and cracked plaster up through the roof tiles and after that through the vaulting cerulean itself in search of answers to that oldest of questions—how can such things be?

Part of him felt the need to go and seek out a priest to share his feelings with. But he didn't even know where the nearest Catholic church was. And what would a priest say anyway? He shuddered at the recollection of his arrogance in thinking for a while that he himself might have been called to act as God's interpreter and man's comforter in matters as complex as this.

In the end, like his mother at times of confrontation with the inexplicable, all he had to fall back on was a line from one of her favorite poems: *Oh, God He knows! And, God He knows! And, surely God Almighty knows!* Which was usually followed by another more prosaic line, probably passed down from some seafaring ancestor—*lying around in your hammock's not going to get you to China.*

He rose from his bed and set about translating the script once more, this time from Spanish to English. Others would want to read this, in particular Max Coldstream.

The English translation finished, he wrote an explanatory e-mail to Coldstream and attached the file. He went downstairs. Mrs. Appledore was hoovering the barroom. When he asked about access to her phone point she said, "Go ahead. Them daft bloody policemen wanted to call it a crime scene, but I told them I had a pub to run and a one-eyed idiot could see those bones were far too old to be of any interest to CID. When they checked with their lab they said much the same, the bones were clearly several centuries old and they'd passed them on to the museum services so they could do their own analysis. Do you really think they might be St. Ylf's like old Noddy was saying? I could do with a miracle the way custom's fallen off these past few years."

"We could all do with a few miracles," said Madero.

He went into the kitchen, connected his laptop and got online.

A message asked him if he wished to locate the download he'd made from Coldstream's e-mail the previous day. In the excitement of what had transpired thereafter, he'd completely forgotten about it. Now he brought it up.

It was an article by Liam Molloy that had appeared in one of the tabloid supplements. He winced as he read its title:

JOLLEY JINKS!

Jolley Castle. It sounds like something you hire for a kids' party. In fact you probably could, if you had enough money.

Jolley Castle, 15 miles southwest of Leeds, is a National Trust property now. The posters say You can have a really jolly time at Jolley Castle.

Not if you were a Roman Catholic priest in the sixteenth century, you couldn't.

Then the family head, Sir Edward Jolley, was a Protestant judge, famous for the swingeing sentences he laid on anyone found guilty under the anti-Catholic Recusancy Laws. But his treatment of Catholics was as nothing compared with that meted out by his cousin, Francis Tyrwhitt. He was a colleague of the infamous Richard Topcliffe, the Queen's chief pursuivant, or persecutor of those still clinging to Catholicism. Topcliffe was given special permission to build his own torture chamber in his house at Westminster. Tyrwhitt, who worked mainly in the North, did not need to build. The dungeons of Jolley Castle were already equipped with all the basic necessities. Here, by permission of his cousin, Tyrwhitt brought his prisoners, usually priests sent from the Continent on what was known as the English Mission, to bring succor and the Holy Office to beleaguered Catholics.

He kept meticulous records of his interrogation sessions. What is clear from these is that, while he is Topcliffe's match in brutality, he outguns his master in subtlety. He understood not only the application of pain, but the psychology of torture also.

Let's take a look at a few examples.

There followed a selection of what Molloy obviously regarded as juicy samples of Tyrwhitt's torturing technique, with explanatory notes to ensure the reader knew what was going on. Names were mentioned, but nowhere did Father Simeon's name appear.

The piece ended with an enjoinder to readers on their next family outing to Jolley Castle to remember as they ate their cream teas in the café what had once gone on not very far beneath their feet, the implication being that it would put an edge on their appetites.

A final note gave the information that Liam Molloy was currently working on a book called *Topcliffe and Friends, An Illustrated History of Torture in the Age of Elizabeth*, with a tentative publication date the following year.

Man proposes, God disposes, thought Madero with more satisfaction than piety, for which he reproved himself.

He deleted the article, brought up the e-mail he'd already written to Max and added a postscript:

Thanks for yours. You'll see how wrong you were about Simeon when you read my attachment! By the way, could you get Tim L. to check if there's any record of anyone from the Woollass family accessing the archive?

Best,

Mig

Back upstairs in his room he leaned on the low sill and peered out through the tiny window. Above the sun-gilt fells he could see a sky as blue as any he'd seen in Andalusia. He lowered his gaze till he picked out the twisted chimney pots of Illthwaite Hall. Frek was up there. And maybe the answer to his questions was up there too, but getting close to either wasn't going to be easy.

He turned to look down at the fragile sheets containing the neat ciphers of Simeon Woollass, so very different from the crazed and crazy scribblings through which he'd first encountered the man.

The longer he kept quiet about his removal of the coded journal, the harder it was going to be to reestablish relations with the Woollasses.

It was no good telling himself he'd only done what any other scholar worth his salt would have done.

This wasn't just a question of scholarly standards and historical research. This was personal, this was where God had been directing him for months, years, perhaps all his life. Max had called it a red herring. He was wrong. Mig felt he knew all about red herrings. Hadn't he spent many years of his life following one?

And no matter what the cost, he wasn't about to risk going astray a second time.

He sat on the bed with his laptop and settled down once more to read what he feared were the last words of his namesake and distant ancestor.

2

Miguel Madero

My name is Miguel Madero son and heir of Miguel Madero of . . . no, not heir, for he is dead . . . I saw him die, most foully slain . . . oh my father, my father.

On my sixteenth birthday my father (whose soul now flies high over the treacherous oceans with the angels) let me sail with him in our lovely ship, La Gaviota, *for the first time. To Cyprus we voyaged and Crete and beyond. Our trade went well, our fine wine was much appreciated and highly valued, we took payment in gold and goods, and the sky was blue, the wind fair, the hold richly laden, and dolphins danced beneath our bow as* La Gaviota *flew homeward across that friendly sea. Everyone said I had quitted myself well and I could hardly wait for landfall so that I could show my mother and my sisters that I was a boy no longer. Never in my short life had I felt so perfectly happy. The world lay before me, a sunlit happy place. I sang a joyous hymn of thanks to the Blessed Virgin for the goodness and mercy she had poured upon me with such a generous and unstinting hand. There was nowhere in the most hidden corner of my being for even the shadow of a dream of such a terrible place as this northern wilderness, with its cold rain, its biting gales, its vile customs and its cruel and savage people . . .*

Father, I know I should forgive—I pray you, show me how.

When we landed at our home port of Cadiz, there were soldiers waiting for us on the quay under the command of a boy not much older than myself, who waved a scented handkerchief to keep the smell of unwashed sailors from his nostrils and told my father he was Bernardo de Bellvis, nephew of the Duke of Medina Sidonia, commander by His Majesty's command of the great fleet which was soon to set sail for England and bring that errant nation back to the fold of the True Church. Merchant ships were being commandeered for service in the Armada. My father had thought himself lucky in the spring of the previous year when La Gaviota *had put to sea only days before the foul pirate Drake so treacherously attacked Cadiz, sinking many vessels and making off with much good wine. But now he felt he was paying for his luck when de Bellvis produced papers giving him authority to take over the ship and sail her to Lisbon to join the others.*

He seemed to think he could step aboard instantly and be on his way in a minute, but happily there were more seasoned officers in his force who listened to my father when he protested that the ship would need to be refitted and provisioned before they could think of sailing. These same officers, though obliged to acknowledge this Bernardo as their military chief, had no desire to put their lives in his hands as navigator, and were pleased when my father volunteered to retain sailing command of La Gaviota. *I begged to be allowed to accompany him. My mother, however, was loud in opposition, too loud, for if she had worked at my father in private he might have agreed with her, but he could not let himself be seen to be ruled by his wife, and so I was admitted to the crew.*

My friends were all envious, but my mother wept, and so did Maria, my affianced bride, the daughter of Benito Perez Montalvo. We had been pledged in marriage when she was five and I was seven, and so used were her chaperones to seeing us together as children that even though we were now no longer children, they saw no harm to let us roam alone out of their sight. And when I saw how she wept, I comforted her and she lay soft in my arms, and, Father forgive me, I scarce know how it happened, but I took her, meaning no harm as our wedding was planned within a twelvemonth anyway. Yet I know that it is the devil's voice which urges us to sin because we mean no harm.

God spare Maria that no evil has come out of my ill-using, for I fear that I may never see her again in this life.

No, my friend, my namesake, thought Madero. No evil came of it. Only *El Bastardo* who preserved our line and on whom all our family fortunes are based. It was God at work when you took your fiancée in your arms, not the devil's. But you do not need me to tell you that now.

We sailed to Lisbon, where there was further fitting of armament, then at the end of May the command was given for the Great Armada to set forth to destroy the infidel queen.

Our first port of call was Corunna to take on fresh provision. It was an ill-omened voyage from the start with storms blowing up to scatter us far and wide before the expedition was yet properly begun. But Gaviota *came to no harm, no thanks to de Bellvis who, if he had his way, would have run us aground on the Galician coast, so fearful was he of the tempest and eager to be back on land.*

Toward the end of July we were all gathered together once more and sailed for England. I know not what our Commander planned. Perhaps it was to lure all the English ships into one place; if so, his plan worked too well, for soon after a battle in which we lost the Rosario *and the* San Salvador *we were pursued along the foot of England toward the narrow straits of Calais where more of the enemy lay in wait.*

Here we anchored, all men disputing what course to follow. And while we argued, our foes acted, putting fire to some of their own ships in the night and sending them drifting among us.

There was no time even to raise anchor. We took axes to our cables and scattered.

This was not how I had imagined a sea battle. I had thought of ships grappling close, brave men fighting hand to hand, driving each other from deck to deck till one party gave way. Instead we seemed to drift aimlessly, till suddenly we came in range of an enemy ship and for a short while the air would burn with ball and shot. Men died, ships foundered, but no one knew who was winning, who losing. Many times my father's commands took us out of danger, though usually de Bellvis was screaming opposite orders. Happily the men ignored him. Finally a ball took him through the chest and he fell over the side, still ranting, which was the only good sight I saw all day.

Now a storm blew up, driving us first toward the Flemish sandbanks, then, as the wind changed, north with the enemy in pursuit. Soon they abandoned the chase, perhaps deciding we were no longer a danger, in which they were right for when our depleted forces once more came together, orders were received from the Commander to continue north and make our return to Spain by sailing right round the head of the isle of Britain.

The season was summer, yet the further north we went, the wilder grew the seas. With my father in command we still had hope and when at last we turned south with a strong wind at our backs, our hearts rose. Alas for our hopes. Soon the wind became a gale before which we sped with little control. Then the wind shifted from the north to the west and the coast which had till now been but a thin line of darkness far to port began to loom large till at last we could see the waves crashing on the shore.

And then we struck. Water came pouring into poor Gaviota *from beneath as well as above. What boats we had were long since carried away. My father gave the order, "Save yourself who can!" Then, seizing a barrel with one hand and me with the other, he leapt into the arms of the ocean which flung us around at her own sweet will. I felt darkness descending on me and scarce had time to say a prayer before I lost all sense.*

When I opened my eyes again, all was calm. I lay on my back. My body felt cold and wet but above the sky was blue and there was sunlight on my face.

I moved my head and saw I was lying in a shallow rock pool on a broad beach close to where a narrow river found its way into the sea.

Giving thanks to God, I turned my head further, and the thanks choked in my throat.

About twenty yards away I saw my father. He lay on his back. Over him stooped two men, not offering succor, but trying to drag the jeweled rings off his finger. My father awoke. I doubt if he knew what was happening to him but he raised his head and spoke. And without hesitation or thought, one of the men took a broad dagger from his waist and slit his throat, and then started chopping at his fingers with the same weapon.

I must have cried out in anguish and protest, for they both looked my way.

The ruffian with the dagger straightened up, freed the ring from my father's severed finger, wiped the blood negligently against his breeches, then came toward me.

His intent was clear. I tried to rise and flee but had no strength. He did not trouble to hurry, so certain was he of my defenselessness. Now he towered over me, now he stooped to bring the knife to my throat. I felt the steel against my skin and tried to gabble some prayer commending my soul to my maker.

But it was not yet my appointed time. Suddenly I saw him seized from behind by a woman who dragged him backward, screaming words I could not understand.

He hit her with the back of his hand. She fell to the ground but still kept yelling at him. He looked from her to me as if assessing what she was saying. Then he shrugged, snarled at her and, pausing only to remove from my person what small ornament I carried, he returned to plundering my father's corpse.

This was my first view of the man I came to know as Thomas Gowder. The woman was his wife, Jenny. And the other man was Gowder's brother, Andrew, as like to him as grapes on a vine, and equal also in evil.

They took me with them from the beach to which they had come, I learned later, in search of freshwater pearls at the mouth of the river. They had a small cart pulled by a skinny pony in which the two men traveled while the woman walked behind, which was shame to them but life to me, for without her help I would surely have stumbled and fallen, upon which I do not doubt they would have murdered me without compunction.

We came eventually after some hours of travel to the house I now know as Foulgate Farm. Here I was thrust into a byre with two cows and the door was locked. Later the woman came to me with some bread and water and spoke to me in a low voice. I did not understand her words but guessed from the way she spoke and some fearful glances she sent to the door that she was here without knowledge or consent of the men.

With food in my stomach, my young body soon regained its strength, but my mind and spirit, thrown down by my father's death and the dreadful manner of it, were not so easily salved. Here too without the aid of Mistress Jenny I might have given myself over so completely to despair that either I would have choked my heart with grief or damned my soul with self-destruction. But she held me to her like a mother and whispered words which, though I did not understand them, contained messages of comfort.

She was not much older than me, but had already been married to Gowder for some years, and not yet had any children who might have been a solace to her, for there was little else in her life to take pleasure from. So it was as a child that she saw me and saved me, though I think it was the prospect of having a young body around the farm to do all the most toilsome tasks that tipped the balance in Gowder's mind. From the start I was made to work harder than I'd ever known, and when my best efforts did not satisfy the brothers, which was often, I was urged on with kicks and blows.

At first they used to hobble my ankles with thick rope and lock me in at night, but after a while they did not bother with the hobble. Without it, I could work harder, and where could I run to? The countryside here is wild and terrible, the harshness of winter tightened its grip on the land with each passing day, and they knew that every hand would be against a runaway, particularly one foreign in speech and appearance.

Besides, though I was daily at the mercy of the two men I had cause to hate worst in the world, here also was my only friend. Without Jenny I think they would have let me starve to death. But she was constant in her care, providing food and warm clothing, and when she was found out, as was inevitable, despite threats and blows, she stood up to the Gowder men and told them that if not out of Christian charity, then out of simple self-interest they ought to be glad someone was taking care of such a good and strong slave. I think they saw the sense of this for thereafter her visits to me were more open.

I know all this because within a few weeks I was able to speak and understand many basic words, and when she saw this she set about teaching me more.

Things changed gradually between me and Jenny. At first she saw me as a child and when the season of our Lord's birth arrived, which even these heathen men celebrated, I wept like a child at the memory of my family's feasts and worship the previous year. Then she took me in her arms and comforted me as a child.

But I was no child, and the more she saw me every day, the clearer this must have become. As snow melted and trees began to shoot, my body seemed to share the returning warmth and I found myself beset by lewd dreams in which sometimes I sported with my affianced bride Maria and sometimes, God forgive my weak flesh, with Jenny.

I did not dare believe that she might have any such thoughts of me, not knowing what I learned later of her revulsion at finding herself bound to a man little better than a beast, and who rutted with her like a beast, not as a man should with his married wife.

One night in the barn I awoke from one of my dreams. In my agitation I had pushed to one side the sacking which acted as my bed linen and I lay there feeling the drafts of cold night air playing over my fevered flesh.

Then, as my eyes unraveled the gloom, I was aware of a figure kneeling by me.

It was Jenny, looking upon my naked arousal. I reached out to her. And she did not turn away.

That was the first time.

It was sinful I know, Father, but even as we took pleasure in it, we gave comfort too, and with each successive time, the comfort felt as strong as the pleasure, and surely that makes it not altogether sinful?

Soon I began to feel almost happy. Perhaps that is why I deserve punishment, not for taking pleasure with another man's wife, but for finding happiness in the house of the man who had murdered my father.

So God punished me. We grew careless. Gowder and his brother went off to market. We thought they would be away all the day, staying late to drink with their cronies. Jenny took me into the house. It is a comfortless place compared to my father's villa, but after the barn, it felt luxurious. We made love in the morning. Then I went to do my chores. Late in the afternoon I went back into the house and we made love again.

And Gowder came into the room and caught us.

His rage was terrible to behold. He drew his knife, the same with which he had slit my father's throat, and hurled himself at me. Naked and supine, it was all I could do to grasp his arm and prevent him from plunging the blade deep into my chest. But his strength was so much greater that within a very brief space he must have prevailed and skewered me to the floor had not Jenny flung herself upon him, her fingers tearing at his eyes. He responded by swinging his elbow at her head with such force it drove all sense from her and she slumped backward on the floor, but her intervention gave me space to thrust Gowder off my body and roll aside into the fireplace. He came after me. As I pushed myself upright, my right hand rested on a heavy fuel log. He drove the knife at my throat. I ducked aside. And I swung the log at his temple.

He fell like a tree. I went to help Jenny who still lay with eyes closed though I could see she was breathing. But before I reached her, I heard a cry from the doorway and turned to see the other Gowder, Andrew, standing there. For a moment he seemed so astounded by what he saw that he could not move. And in that same moment I rushed to the narrow window and forced my naked body through it.

I feel shame now to think I left Jenny, but I knew beyond doubt that Andrew would finish what his brother had begun and I had no strength to resist a second onslaught.

So I fled, I knew not where. Naked and afoot in strange and rough terrain, I had no hope of escape but flew on the wings of fear. But when eventually I heard, distantly at first but getting ever closer, the mingled hubbub of angry voices and excited barking which warned me of pursuit, terror clipped the wings it had given me. Finally I collapsed in the midst of a small wood and prayed the trees would hide me from my pursuers.

Vain hope. The dogs found me first and might have finished me if their owners had not beaten them off. Perhaps this was done out of charity, yet I cannot thank them, for what Andrew

Gowder purposed for me was far worse than the rip of a dog's fangs.

They raised me to a tree and bound me there. I could not understand all they said but they called me murderer, which I did understand and then my heart sank at the thought that my blow had killed Thomas Gowder. For his foul murder of my father he deserved to die and I had the right to be his executioner. But having killed one of their own number, now I knew I should not look for even the doubtful succor of judgment by whatever law these savages observed.

Even then I had no anticipation of what was to happen next.

In the fitful light cast by the torches that they bore, I had observed Andrew Gowder standing aside hacking at billets of wood with his dagger. Now he came toward me. Still I did not understand. But when I felt the splintered point of the wood against the palm of my hand, then I understood.

I screamed before he struck. With each blow I screamed more. My hands, my feet. I did not think such pain could be, and a man still live. And finally, just when I thought that at least the worst was over, he took his dagger and sawed through the rope that bound me to the tree, so that in a trice all the weight of my body fell forward and I was held by those dreadful wooden nails alone.

I think even some of my tormentors were shocked by what they had done, for through my agony I was aware of a sudden silence. Even the dogs ceased their yapping.

Then Gowder, as if he too felt the terror of his own deed, cried, "Away! Leave the murderer to the foxes and the crows. Away!"

And they all fled, leaving me hanging, praying that death would come quickly.

How long I hung I do not know. If you want experience of eternity in this life, Father, let yourself be hung from a cross. Perhaps this is one of the meanings of our Savior's Passion.

It grew so dark I felt that death must be near. Then I heard a noise, and felt the touch of a hand against my body, and thought Gowder had returned to torment me further.

But the voice that now spoke was not Gowder's. It was Jenny's.

How she got me down from the tree I do not know. I had no strength to help her and as each of my limbs was freed the pain of being supported by the others alone was beyond bearing and several times I fainted, till finally I came back to my senses and found I was lying on the ground.

She had brought a blanket for my naked body and a bladder full of water with which she washed my wounds. She cried piteously as she saw the state of me, and all the time she declared, "I cannot stay. He will kill me too if I am found here. I cannot stay."

But still she stayed till a glimmer in the sky warned that day drew near.

Jenny told me that Thomas was dead and Andrew believed, or affected to believe, I had foully murdered his brother when he caught me trying to ravish her, having first struck her on the head to render her defenseless.

I knew I must move from this spot and I knew also that I could not let Jenny stay with me. For her own safety she had to agree with the story that I was her ravisher, which would be hard to maintain were she found by my side. I asked for her help in getting upright. She fetched a pair of stout branches to lend my crippled feet support. And now I urged her to go, pretending my strength was greater than it was.

Before she went, she kissed me. I knew it was our last kiss. It was as bitter as our first had been sweet.

I began to move also, not caring where I went as long as I was away from that accursed place, and also knowing that wherever it was I halted for rest, there would I lie till either death or my enemies took me up.

I may have kept going for an hour, perhaps more. The sky was bright with spring sunshine when I finally collapsed among some gorse bushes. I closed my eyes.

When I opened them again I was being nuzzled by a horse. I saw its rider dismount. Convinced that my end must be nigh, I closed my eyes once more and began to recite a prayer to commit my soul to heaven.

I felt an arm around me. Then I was raised in the air and laid across the horse's saddle and my senses fled once more.

The next time I awoke I felt sure I must have died and gone to heaven, for I was lying on a soft couch and a woman with gray hair and a kind face was washing my wounds. But soon from what she said and what I was able to see I became aware that God in his mercy had led me to the only place of safety I was like to find in this barbarous place. It was the lady's son who had found me. Recognizing from my dying prayer that we were of the same true faith, he had brought me to his house rather than to the authorities. I had no strength then to tell my story as I am telling it to you, Father, but my fevered ramblings must have persuaded them that I was innocent of the desperate crimes Andrew Gowder was accusing me of.

After a time, I know not whether it was long or short, they said that they must move me, it was no longer safe for me to remain in their house, and I was taken at dead of night to another place. Half-conscious though I was, my fears all returned when I saw that I was being lowered into a dark pit beneath an upraised slab of stone. Did they believe that I had passed away and was I being consigned to the tomb? I tried to struggle and cry to warn them of their mistake but still they lowered me into the darkness.

But just as I was ready to abandon all hope, I saw a glimmer of light, and in that glimmer I saw your face, Father, and heard you speaking words of comfort to me in my own tongue, and I was able to close my eyes in peace once more.

3

The deluding of Mig

"Mr. Madero!"

His name was accompanied by a banging at his door.

When he opened it, he found Mrs. Appledore standing there, looking out of breath and irritated.

"Siesta time, is it?" she said. "I've been shouting up the stairs for two minutes. There's a phone call for you. A Mr. Coldcream, I think he said."

"Thank you, Mrs. Appledore. Sorry," said Mig.

He ran down the stairs and into the kitchen. The receiver lay on the windowsill. He picked it up and said, "Hello, Max."

"Mig, my boy! How are you after your adventures? I've not heard anything like it since I stopped reading the Famous Five."

"I'm fine," said Mig. "You've looked at the document?"

"Indeed yes. This is a fascinating find. You've got no doubt about authenticity?"

"None. In my hand it feels right."

"Good enough for me, but we can easily get some tests done for the sake of those who don't appreciate your special talents as I do."

"Fine," said Mig. "But as I said, there may be a problem about ownership."

"Yes. It's a pity you had to fall out with the Woollasses,"

said Coldstream. "On the other hand, there's nothing that redounds to their discredit here. In fact, the reaction of Alice and her son was both charitable and noble. And Father Simeon comes out of it well too. Despite his own peril, he clearly took care of the boy, physically and spiritually. And even if the lad didn't survive, he proposed making the effort to contact the family with news of his fate if he himself made it safe back to Spain."

"Which he did. But he didn't contact the family," said Mig. "At least, there's no record of it, which I'm sure there would have been."

"Yes. That is odd. I keep forgetting it's actually your family we're talking about here. Sorry. This must be hard for you."

"It certainly makes me more appreciative of the Woollasses' sensibilities," he said. "Gerald is convinced that my sole motive in coming here was to dig up dirt on Simeon. I suppose I could tell him everything, but I'm not sure if even that would convince him I'm not after producing one of those titillating historical pop-biographies."

"Which of course you're not," said Max. "Are you? Sorry! Look, if the worst comes to the worst, I can always publish your translation in next week's issue of *CH* and get it in the public domain that way, but then everyone would have access. Much better if you put on the Hispanic charm and mend a few fences. I gave Tim Lilleywhite a ring, by the way, and asked him to check out that thing you asked about Jolley. I think I see what you're getting at. Bit of an ace in the hole if it comes up, perhaps. But let's not jump our guns. Meanwhile, just start groveling! *Adios*!"

Madero replaced the receiver. Grovel before the Woollasses, he thought. He doubted if it would do him much good, though there was one member of the family he wouldn't mind subjugating himself to.

He turned round and found himself looking at Frek.

She was standing just inside the kitchen. There was no way

of telling how long she'd been there, but she was smiling in a friendly enough fashion.

"There you are," she said mockingly. "A true historian. You come to our little village and within twenty-four hours you reveal to us what's been lying beneath our eyes, or at least our feet, for centuries."

He returned her smile and said, "More luck than judgment, I fear."

"Luck? The same kind of luck that made you turn up your nose at our so-called priest-hole? I think there is something of the truffle-dog in you, Señor Madero. You sniff out what lies beyond the detection of mere human noses."

She strolled around the kitchen, looking at the pulleys, running her hands underneath the table edge to feel the holes.

"Was it Mrs. Appledore you wanted to see?" he asked, reluctant to make the assumption that he was the object of her visit. "I think she went into the bar."

"No. Just idle curiosity. We didn't hear anything at the Hall about the excitement here last night, but this morning I happened to be talking to a friend on the County Museum staff and she was full of the find. You could be rich if it turns out you're entitled to a share of the value once they work out who owns what."

Was that a pointed comment? Had she overheard his conversation? Looking at her, he didn't think so, she seemed so relaxed and friendly.

"I would guess the Church has the best claim," said Mig.

"Indeed. But which church?" said Frek. "If the cross is worth as much as my friend guesses, I can't see the holy accountants of either Rome or Canterbury letting it go without a fight. The bones are another matter. The Anglicans probably won't compete there, even if they are confirmed as the lost relicts of St. Ylf. What did your ghostly antennae signal, Mr. Madero?"

He said, "I only know for certain they don't belong to any member of my family."

Faintly surprised, she said, "But why on earth should you think they might?"

He felt himself flushing under her coolly assessing gaze that seemed capable of cutting through to the innermost chambers of his mind and discovering Father Simeon's journal hidden there.

"It's a lovely day," he said, ignoring her question. "I thought I might take a walk and enjoy it while it lasts."

It was as near as he dared come to an open invitation.

She said, "That's a very English view of weather. Your mother's influence, I would guess, and therefore preeminently reasonable. May I join you?"

"Of course."

"So where shall we walk? A quiet stroll along the river, or did you have in mind something a little more adventurous?"

She smiled as she spoke the last word. Could he read anything into that?

He said, "The river sounds fine, though I'm not averse to a bit of adventure."

"We must see what we can do then," she said.

Outside, the autumn sun kept its promise, falling as pleasantly on Mig's skin as it had on his eye through the window.

As they strolled across the humpback bridge, Mig said, "If it were always like this, your Lake District would truly be a landscape without equal."

"Nonsense," she said briskly. "It would be very dull. The best landscapes remain beautiful whatever the weather. Flood, drought, frost, blizzard, it makes no difference here. Why, it's even beautiful in mist when you can hardly see it at all."

"You don't hanker after those icy lands where your northern gods live, then?"

"But they live here too, didn't you realize that? This is why the Vikings settled here. Rivers and lakes filled with salmon and trout, forests full of wild beasts and deer, broad fertile meadows and steep mountains running down to the great western sea. It must have seemed a land fit for the gods, and if you can't be a god yourself, the next best thing is to choose to live where they would surely have chosen to live. The Wolf-Head Cross was the flag those settlers planted here to establish possession. I sometimes think they're still here."

"Really? I haven't noticed a lot of horned helmets hanging up in the Stranger."

"Why would you? The Vikings had a culture of heroism but a mythology of deceit. A large proportion of the stories in the *Poetic Edda* are based on deception and mischief, and the first part of Snorri's Edda is called 'Gylfaginning'—the Deluding of Gylfi. But you're looking blank. I thought you had a nodding acquaintance with the Norse myths."

"The kind of acquaintance where you half recognize a face but can never recall a name," he said jokingly. "When I see an edda approaching, I cross the street to avoid embarrassment."

Frek didn't look amused.

"Edda is semantically obscure and variously interpreted as a poetic anthology or random jottings," she said in a school-marmish voice. "The *Poetic Edda* consists of a collection of mythological and heroic poems. The *Prose Edda* is a combination of historical analysis, anthology and treatise on poetics, written by Snorri Sturluson. Dare I hope you've heard of Snorri?"

"Sorry. No," he said. "Though I'm glad to see you're on first-name terms with him."

Again his attempt at lightness fell like a snowflake on to a griddle.

"Sturluson isn't a surname, it's a patronymic. In Iceland first names have always been used for identification. As for Snorri, he was a thirteenth-century Icelander. He was a top politician, legislator, historian, poet, and activist. He makes most of the so-called Renaissance men you probably do know about look like kids with a hatful of GCSEs and attitude."

"I apologize for my ignorance, which I shall begin to rectify as soon as I get within striking distance of a library," he said, taking care to keep any hint of levity out of his voice.

She nodded approval, then smiled a smile which was worth a bit of pain.

"Good," she said. "I'll test you later. And you should know that us Vikings are pretty hot stuff when it comes to tricky questions."

On the far side of the bridge they had turned to walk upstream, following a sun-dappled path sometimes on the riverbank, sometimes curving away beneath close-crowding trees, mostly alders and willows, with here and there a rowan on which the berries were already turning bright red, and silver-columned birches with bark flaked like gimcrack, and now a pair of ancient oaks whose roots exposed by the crumbling bank bent over the water like a mountain troll's knees. Though they still looked massively solid, there was little sign of living growth on these two trees, and most of what there was belonged to a narrow tortuous plant which held the oak in a close embrace.

"Mistletoe," said Frek, following his gaze. "Balder's bane."

"Which the English now use as an excuse for kissing," he said daringly.

"Kissing, killing, it's all connected," she mocked. "Hod, who threw the fatal dart, is blind. As is the Roman Cupid, a wayward child who fires his arrows off indiscriminately. Where they strike, they may not kill, but they can render men who had felt themselves invulnerable slaves of a destructive passion."

Was she warning him off or egging him on?

Whichever, she now led him away from the temptation of the oak trees. A little beyond them, the path divided, one branch turning away from the river and mounting the steepening fell-side.

"Where does that go?" he asked.

"Up to Foulgate, the Gowders' farmhouse. Beyond that, it

turns into Stanebank, which curves round the edge of Mecklin Moor and drops down past the Hall. Do you feel up to such a physical challenge?"

Again the mocking ambivalence.

He said, "I'm in your hands."

"Let's take things easy then," she said. "In fact, why don't we take a rest?"

Just past the bifurcation, a rough bench had been created by setting a length of wood onto two logs beneath a tall tree whose elegant leaves were freaked with crimson and amber. Across the river they could see the stumpy tower of St. Ylf's. Something moved on it, then vanished. A big bird, perhaps. Maybe a raven.

She sat down. There was scarcely room for two and Mig remained standing, but she looked up at him with a smile and said, "Don't just stand there like Alexander, blocking the sun. Come on, there's plenty of room."

He squatted down beside her, their flanks pressed close. He could feel her warmth through her thin dress and his light cotton trousers. He even imagined he could feel the pulse of her blood through the veins of her thigh. He sought for words to break the silence which seemed to be wrapping itself around them, pressing them ever closer.

"It's an ash," he said, looking up. "Like Yggdrasil—isn't that what the Norsemen called the tree which holds up the world?"

"Well, well," she said, turning his way so that her breast brushed against his ribcage. "Such expertise. I see that I am the one who has been deluded, Mr. Madero."

"Yesterday we agreed on Mig," he said.

"That was before you were expelled from the garden," she said.

"No. I think that you were still Migging me in the churchyard. I was certainly Freking you."

"Well, I shouldn't like to be thought of as the sort of woman who would let herself be Freked without Migging in return," she said, with a mockery of coquetry which was still coquettish. "So, Mig, I've let you see what's important to me. Now I'll shut up and give you a turn. What is it that makes your life worth living?"

He recalled her warning—never complain, never explain—but he felt a strong impulse to tell her everything about himself. Why not, when he'd unburdened himself so comprehensively to Sam Flood?

He began to talk. She was a good listener. He recalled from his Shakespeare how Desdemona with a greedy ear devoured Othello's discourse, and while Frek showed no sign of weeping, or offering for his pains a world of kisses, she did sigh sympathetically from time to time, and looked deep into his eyes, and once—it was as he described his fall from the mountain—she put her hand on his knee and dug her fingers in deep.

Even if in the beginning he'd purposed any restraint, by the time he reached the latest end of his tale, all thought of keeping anything back had fled. He told her about the journal, his translation of it, and even gave the gist of Max's information and advice.

When he finished speaking, he felt that they were in such a state of emotional intimacy, its physical counterpart could only be a gauzy thickness away.

He shifted slightly on the bench and put his arm along her shoulders as if to steady himself. She turned her head toward him. Her mouth was slightly open, he could see the glimmer of her small white teeth, the pink moistness of her parted lips.

He moved his head toward her.

She said, "Now that was really fascinating. I'm almost sorry I have to go."

And stood up.

He looked up at her, bewildered and frustrated. Was this some part of the courting ritual he'd simply never reached? So far as jousting with the opposite sex went, he might look like a mature man of the world, but his learning curve had stuttered to a halt at the age of sixteen.

He heard himself saying foolishly, "But you can't go yet."

"Can't I?" She spoke the words as if this were some proposition in logic she needed to examine. "Why?"

"Because . . . because there are things I need to discuss. About what I've told you . . . what I should do next."

"I'm not clear," she said. "Are you asking for a general comment, or a specific recommendation as to how you should proceed?"

"Both. Neither. I don't know." He was speaking wildly, like an inarticulate teenager. He pulled himself together. "Your family and mine are both concerned here. Your father is at least entitled to see the words that Father Simeon wrote. But I suspect that if I made a direct approach, he would set the dogs on me."

"No worry there, then. Our dog is not only a crook, but a very old Labrador who might attempt to lick you to death, but no more."

The light tone should have been reassuring, but it wasn't. If anything it was slightly condescending.

He stood up, his bad knee stiff as an old oak root, and he looked her straight in the face.

"Perhaps in that case I should go to the Hall now and explain what has happened."

"No point. Daddy's out and I expect my grandfather's taking his morning nap."

"His nap? Oh, we mustn't disturb old Mr. Dunny's morning nap, must we!" he said savagely. "I can guess how much he looks forward to it."

She looked at him with a faint smile and said, "If you're referring to his dalliance with Mrs. Collipepper, yes, I believe he does look forward to it. In any case, it's practically a family duty. Her mother and her grandmother were housekeepers at the Hall too. It's one Woollass tradition I don't think Daddy's concerned himself with, but in these matters Grandfather's an absolute stickler."

More shocked than he cared to show at this frankness, Mig said, "I'm sorry, it's none of my business. But I too have a strong sense of family which he might understand. I want to do the right thing about Simeon's journal and I'm sure if I could just sit down and talk with your father or grandfather, we could come to some accord."

She thought about this then nodded. "You may be right. I'll see what I can do."

"And what about you?" he asked, unable to let her go without having their own relationship spelled out clearly. "I thought we were reaching some accord, too."

"I think we did," she said. "I certainly found your story interesting, if a touch sad."

"Sad?"

"Yes. It seems to me that a vivid imagination, a rather unfocused religiosity, and a hysterical medical condition have combined to make you interpret a couple of simple coincidences as a message from God. Which is indeed sad in a man of intellect and education. You're not put out, I hope? I know my directness can sometimes offend."

"No, no," he said, trying for control. "I suppose I had hoped for something a little more empathic from someone as immersed in an ancient myth system as you seem to be."

"You shouldn't confuse immersion with absorption," she smiled. "I am a scholar. My interest is primarily academic. Yours should be also. Personal involvement may add a spice to research, but it should never be allowed to get in the way of objective truth."

"Truth," he echoed. "A young man who was one of my ancestors was shipwrecked on these shores and treated monstrously—you'll admit that as true, I suppose?"

"You forget, I haven't studied the document myself," she said. "But, accepting your interpretation as accurate, you shouldn't ignore the fact that he was also treated with more kindness and compassion than an enemy of the state might have expected in those troubled times. The Gowder woman saved his life and offered him all the comforts a woman can offer a man. His life was saved a second time by my own ancestors, at no inconsiderable risk to themselves. Would an English sailor shipwrecked in Spain have received the same treatment, I wonder?"

"I don't think there's much point in comparing brutalities," he said.

"Of course not. In any case, behavior must always be judged in the social context in which it occurs. I see you have the Swinebank *Guide* with you. His take on the events at Foulgate makes interesting reading, don't you think? There are two sides to everything. Now I must be off. I'll talk to my father and grandfather and ring you later. I can't offer you more than that, Mig, believe me. Good day. I'll be in touch."

She walked away, upright, unhurried, a column of pure white light in a world of shifting colors. He sank back down on the rough bench and watched her go. Into his mind, uninvited, dropped Winander's comment yesterday about the marble angel.

Cool even in the sunlight.

The sun dappling his bare arms did not seem so warm now. A winged insect settled on the back of his hand. It was a pale green and translucent white, a lacy fragile thing.

But when he brushed it off, it left a red mark on his skin.

4

Mecklin Moss

For several minutes after Frek's departure, Mig sat, staring sightlessly at the river's sparkling surface. He felt unhappy, he felt frustrated, above all he felt foolish.

He had observed the cycle of desire and rejection often enough during his school and university days, and sometimes when he wasn't too busy struggling to subdue his own body, he had felt rather smugly that an intelligent observer probably knew more about the game than many players.

Wrong! And the result? Here he was, a twenty-seven-year-old adolescent, feeling sorry for himself!

To divert his mind from these painful speculations, he opened the Illthwaite *Guide* and read again the passage describing the fate of the waif boy.

It was an ill-judged attempt at diversion. Emotional and sexual frustration was a mere cat's-paw compared to the tempest stirred up by the measured terms of the Reverend Peter K. He felt again what he had felt that first night as he approached the Stranger House—the mist swirling around his head; the fear coating his tongue; the desperate pumping of his lungs inflating the chambers of his heart to bursting point.

He leapt up to escape it, but he bore it with him. And when

he reached the fork in the path which led to Foulgate Farm, his feet seemed to turn uphill of their own accord.

But the ghost of an experience four hundred years old could not serve to strengthen living limbs, and certainly not to lend grip to a pair of casual shoes which were fine for a gentle stroll but ill suited to this increasingly rough and rugged track.

Soon he was back wholly in the world of here and now. His bad leg was aching and he was breathing so hard it must have sounded like the approach of a traction engine to the inmates of Foulgate.

The Gowders certainly looked as if they'd anticipated his coming, he thought with a shiver. They were standing in their cobbled farmyard, one holding a plane in his hands, the other a bradawl. Between them on a trestle lay a half-assembled coffin.

This, he thought with a shock of recognition like a blow, this was the house in which that other Miguel had fought with Thomas Gowder. There was the barn in which he had first lain with Jenny Gowder. Across these cobbles and up that track ahead he must have fled, almost naked, from the fury of the younger brother.

And these two men standing looking at him with eyes that were neither surprised nor welcoming, these were the descendants of that Andrew who had driven the wooden spites into Miguel's hands and feet, and left him hanging from the blasted oak tree.

One of them spoke.

Laal, he thought, recalling what Sam had said about identifying them.

"Can we help you, mister?"

"I'm going to Mecklin Moss," he said.

"Then you're going right," said the other. Who must therefore also be Laal.

It was very confusing. It was hard enough separating the living from the dead without the separation of the living from the living being a problem too.

He made his way carefully around them and out of the other end of the yard. He was sure they would stand and watch him out of sight, but after only a couple of steps he heard the rasp of the plane.

Their indifference felt more of a trouble than their interest.

The track here was wider and rutted by wheels. It wove upward through tummocky drumlins, and soon the buildings of the farm were out of sight.

Beyond the drumlins this main track began to bear to the left, following the contour of the fell. Eventually it must curve downhill and become Stanebank and descend to the Hall. But at the highest point of the curve, his feet chose a narrower path, scarce more than a sheep-trod, which led straight on.

He knew with a certainty beyond need of proof that this was the way his young terrified ancestor had fled.

The main track had been worn to the visible bedrock but now, as the ground leveled off into a relatively flat expanse of moorland, he felt the path beneath his feet become increasingly soft and damp, as though here the earth's bones lay too deep to reach. Yet strewn across this marshy moorland were huge boulders, deposited there by God knows what glacial drift or subterranean tremor.

He paused to examine two massive slabs, or perhaps the halves of one even vaster rock, leaning drunkenly against each other to form a lofty tent. The dark recess looked uninviting now, but in a storm with no other choice it must look almost welcoming. That someone had found it so was suggested by a circle of scorched earth at its mouth. Fire, the fourth element, which might help a man survive the perils of the other three, when earth became treacherous and air surged with invisible violence. As for water, no longer content simply to seep up around his shoes, it now gleamed darkly in sinister pools amidst the coarse grass, and soon he found even apparently solid patches of bright green turf dissolving beneath his feet to sink him deep in clinging mud.

He glanced at the sketch map in the *Guide*. While not detailed enough for precise navigation, it confirmed that he was on the edge of Mecklin Moss. Mecklin Shaw must be somewhere over to his left. Or rather, must have been. Even in the Reverend Peter K.'s day, it had almost disappeared. Now, a century on, what could remain? But to that other Miguel, as he glimpsed the darkness of the trees swaying against the lighter darkness of the sky, it must have looked to offer some slight hope of refuge.

Ahead, now as then, there seemed nothing but the certainty of getting irretrievably bogged down in the space of a couple of dozen meters.

His thoughts turned to Sam Flood's namesake who had drowned himself up here in the Moss. Self-destruction, a fearful choice for any man, for a priest far worse. And what a place to choose! No simple plunge into deep drowning waters was on offer here, but a long struggle out through quag and bog till at last the mud held you fast and you must prostrate yourself as though in worship to bring the longed-for end.

He shuddered and said an intercessory prayer for the poor lost soul. A man who by all accounts was informed by an overwhelming desire to do good.

Much good it did him.

A bitter tribute to futility.

He arrived at the place where the wood must have been.

All traces of it had vanished, at least on the surface. Perhaps deep below there still lay ancient roots. But for too long now there had been no thirsty trees and, left undrained, inevitably the ground had been taken over by the relentless slough. He had no way of knowing for certain this was the right location. So far he had experienced nothing more up here than the natural reaction of any sensitive being to such a dreary place.

It could be that, having brought him so close to the end of his voyage of discovery, his otherworld guides were leaving him to his own devices. If so, he should feel glad. They had often been uncomfortable traveling companions, and dealing with this world on this world's terms looked likely to present enough problems to occupy him fully.

But no man who has for so long felt different is ever completely grateful to lose the feeling.

He turned his back on the Moss. Another thin trod ran away downhill to rejoin the curve of Stanebank. It was in this direction that the other Miguel, bleeding and lame, must have staggered after Jenny Gowder had released him. Knowing what her own fate must be were she caught in his company, she had not dared to help him further, yet what she had already done was an act of great courage.

And so the injured youth had limped and crawled downhill till he was too weak to move further, then lain exposed to the savagery of the elements till by the grace of God the young Woollass had chanced upon him.

He had much to thank the Woollasses for, thought Mig. It had been that sense of obligation, as well as his sense of desire, that had made him unburden himself so comprehensively to Frek. Now it was up to them.

He set off down the trod and within a few minutes found himself rejoining the relatively broad track of Stanebank.

Left would take him back to Foulgate, right must lead downhill past the Hall.

That was his quickest and easiest way, though he found himself unhappy at the prospect of meeting any of the Hall's inmates in his present befouled condition. It wasn't just his shoes that were ruined. The mud had managed to reach his knees, though he had no memory of ever sinking so deep.

He set off down the grassy track. Walking downhill on a firm surface was a pleasure after the Moss. He felt as strong as he'd been before his accident. Soon the Hall came in sight. He paused where a natural terrace on the fellside gave a fine oversight. The ground dropped steeply then began to level off toward the kitchen end of the house. A flat area scooped out of the slope and leveled with gravel caught his eye. It looked like a niche prepared to receive some piece of garden statuary. Maybe Dunstan had picked up a marble Venus on his last trip to Rome! He worked out that one of the first-floor windows he could see was probably the old man's bedroom. Perhaps even now he and the statuesque but very non-marmoreal Pepi were enjoying themselves up there. With an example like that, no need for a late starter like himself to worry. He still had half a century to learn the game!

The thought stayed with him as he strode past the Hall and as he approached that other reminder of the possibilities of age, the Forge, it returned to make him smile again.

"Dear God! It doesn't take much to make you monks happy," said a mocking voice. "Why didn't you roll in the mud and really enjoy yourself!"

Thor Winander was standing in his driveway.

"Good morning, Mr. Winander," said Mig.

"And good morning to you. What the hell have you been up to?"

"I went for a walk and found the ground wasn't as hard as I'm used to."

"Edie Appledore isn't going to thank you for tracking that clart into her house, and you must be in her black books already for messing up her kitchen. Come in and clean up. No, I insist. We didn't really get a chance to talk about last night, did we?"

Not too reluctantly, Mig let himself be drawn into the house. Winander took him upstairs and opened a door which led into a bedroom.

"Bathroom in there," he said, pointing to another door. "I'll leave some clean things on the bed for you. I'll be downstairs with a hot drink when you're ready."

Five minutes later, Mig descended the stairs wearing trainers and chinos, both a touch too large but not unmanageably so.

"In here," called Winander.

He tracked the voice into a basic but well-ordered kitchen.

"Sit yourself down," the big man commanded. "Won't take you into the parlor. Had the little Aussie in there yesterday and she was a bit satirical about the mess. Doesn't mince her words, does she? So, how do you like your coffee? With or without?"

"Just a very little milk, thank you."

"I wasn't talking about milk," said Winander, holding up a bottle of rum. "This stuff will put the color back in your cheeks. It did wonders for the British Navy's cheeks, so they say—above and below."

He poured a generous dollop into a mug, topped it with coffee and passed it over.

"There we go. *Salud!*"

"Cheers," said Mig.

"So," said Winander, back into a chair. "And how are you after last night's adventures? And the marvelous midget, how's she bearing up?"

"Miss Flood, you mean? She's gone. Drove off first thing."

"With never a goodbye? After all I did for her. There's Aussie manners for you."

"What exactly did you do for her, Mr. Winander?" said Mig.

"Call me Thor. Well, now I come to think of it, not a lot. But I'm sorry to have missed her. Sort of grew on you, didn't she? Which was just as well as she seems to have stopped growing on herself!"

Mig surprised in himself a pang of resentment which came close to being jealousy. Changing the subject, he said, "I didn't thank you properly for your prompt action last night. I gather it was you who worked things out so quickly."

"Not difficult. Pulley ropes broken, hooks under the table, voices from the ground. Scratch the patina of artistic sophistication and you will find us Winanders are still basically jobbing craftsmen."

"Us Winanders? Are there many of you?"

Thor frowned and said, "No. In fact there's only me. I am the end, there is no more, there's an apple up my arse and you can have the core, as the poet said."

Under the coarse flippancy Mig detected that this was a source of genuine pain.

"You never married?" he said.

"No. When I was younger I never saw the need for it; later I was past my sell-by date. But all things good and bad come to an end, eh? Must be something in the scriptures to cover that, Father. Sorry. Miguel."

"Mig," said Mig. "On the contrary, I think the scriptures are more about infinity than the finite. What is good is forever."

"That's what you think, is it? Well, no one minds the smell of their own crap. Sorry, I didn't ask you in to be offensive. It's just that old Illthwaite is dying on its feet. The school's gone, the post office is gone, even the bloody Herdwicks look like going with hill-farmers feeling the pinch and selling up or trying to make a living out of cream teas and tourists. No more Winanders after me, no more Appledores after Edie, not much chance of there being any more Woollasses. Even the bloody Gowders have ground to a halt unless they've got a couple of mad wives locked in their attic, which wouldn't surprise me as you'd have to be mad to marry a Gowder."

"They seem a not very prepossessing family," said Mig with careful neutrality.

"You've noticed? Brutes and bandits, that's what they've always been. Seems only fitting that they should end up putting their neighbors under the ground, which is more or less what they've been doing for the past five centuries! But you've probably had it with Illthwaite. In fact, I'm surprised you're still here. Someone should have warned you how sensitive the Woollasses are about their precious Father Simeon. Even Frek."

"Frek did not strike me as being much concerned about such matters," said Mig.

"Not on the surface, maybe. But you'll soon see red Woollass blood coming through if you scratch Frek's fair white skin. Not that there's much chance of you doing that."

Mig found himself flushing, partly with embarrassment, partly with annoyance.

Was it so obvious that he'd been stricken by the woman?

And was it common knowledge already that she'd turned him down?

Winander was looking at him curiously.

"Forgive me for asking, old chum, but you get on well with the fair Frek, do you?"

"I think so," Mig replied, trying not to sound too brusque.

He downed the rest of his coffee. The rum gave it a darkly decadent flavor.

"Now I must get back," he said. "Thank you very much for your kindness."

"But you haven't bought anything! Come to think of it, neither did young Sam. I can't have two tourists in succession getting out of here with their wallets as full as when they arrived. Let me show you my workshop."

Reluctantly Mig let himself be led into a high airy room full of light from three huge plate-glass windows.

"Have a look around," said Winander. "If you see anything you fancy, just shout."

Mig wandered round the workshop, counting the minutes till the demands of politeness would have been satisfied and he could go.

"This might interest you," said Winander. "A kind of companion piece to the angel."

He drew a piece of sacking away from the reclining nude.

Mig recognized the face instantly, and as he took in the blatant sexuality of the splayed legs, he felt a knot of anger form in his chest at what seemed a deliberate and malicious provocation on Winander's part.

But the man was chattering on, unconcerned.

"After I'd done the angel, I tentatively suggested a nude. The pose was Frek's choice. Always been a bit of a game between us ever since she told me she was gay, her still trying to get me going, me demonstrating my indifference. It's intellectual with her, I think. The theater of the absurd, she calls it, watching men jump through hoops in the hope of earning a treat. Daren't let Gerry see it, of course. He's old-fashioned enough to come after me with a horse whip!"

It took Mig several moments to let the meaning of what he was hearing penetrate his anger. First came disbelief, then shock, and then a slow unraveling of the knot in his chest as he took in not only what Winander was saying but his motives in saying it. And his methods. He was letting him know that Frek was a lesbian, but doing it as if assuming that Mig had recognized this all along and hadn't let himself be made a fool of.

No. He corrected that. He'd made a fool of himself. All that Frek had done was . . . nothing. Why should she? And she'd brought matters to a halt when it must have been clear he was on the point of taking direct action.

Father Dominic, talking of the vow of chastity, had said that it had nothing to do with morality as many supposed, and everything to do with the power of sex to cloud judgment, squander energy, divert the will.

"That's why among your list of things coming to an end in Skaddale, you included the Woollasses," he said, trying for a man-of-the-world tone. "But surely nowadays it is almost a commonplace for lesbian women to start families."

"Not Frek," said Winander. "I asked her and she said that happily the maternal impulse hadn't been tossed into her cradle by a malicious fairy godmother. When I said that old Dunny must be distressed to foresee the end of his line, she laughed and said not as distressed as he'd be at the thought of a Woollass coming out of a test tube. Funny world we live in, ain't it?"

Mig did not respond. He'd turned away from the disturbing wood carving and was staring out of a window into the yard where his gaze had been drawn to something which gave him a shock less definable than the news of Frek's sexuality, but for some reason even more powerful.

"What is *that*?" he demanded.

"What? My wolf head, you mean? Or perhaps I should say Frek's wolf head."

"Frek's?"

"Yes," said Thor. "She commissioned it, so to speak. That's how she came to be my model. Come and have a closer look if you want."

As they crossed the yard, he told the story of his deal with Frek, but Mig wasn't listening. His gaze was riveted on the huge wood sculpture. There was something truly menacing about it. He came to a halt a couple of feet away, then took a further step back.

Winander said, "Interesting. Most people can't resist touching it. Little Sam almost wrapped herself around it. But you look like you're scared it would bite."

"Do I?" said Madero. Then added, more to himself than Thor, "It feels alive."

"Thank you kindly, sir," said Winander, taking this as a comment on his carving.

Mig didn't correct him. He didn't care to share the sense he got that this towering lump of wood was vibrant with intent, and it wasn't good.

"Where did it actually come from?" he asked. He felt he knew the answer.

"Didn't I say? It came out of Mecklin Moss," replied Winander. "You'd have expected anything in that acidy bog would rot away in no time. But this is absolutely solid." He gave it a slap and laughed. "Reminds me of an Eskdale lass I once knew. Finest Cumberland wrestler I ever met, only the rules wouldn't let her enter at the shows, so she had to make do with best of three falls in the hayfields with the likes of me!"

His laughter gave Mig strength to turn away from the Wolf Head and make his farewells. Common sense told him Winander was right. There was no way this could have any connection with the ordeal of that other Miguel four hundred years before.

But as he walked away down the hill he was both glad and ashamed that he hadn't found the courage to touch that smooth and sensuously curved slab of old wood.

5

Shoot-out

That same evening at six o'clock prompt, Miguel Madero entered the bar of the Stranger House.

As he pushed open the door, a memory from childhood of the old Western films he'd loved (and still did) flashed into his mind. The hero enters, the chatter of conversation dies away, the piano tinkles to silence, the bartender freezes in the act of pouring a drink, and the man he's pouring it for turns slowly to face the door, smiling a welcome at the newcomer even as his hand adjusts the Colt in his holster.

It was a ludicrous memory and the fact that the room was empty made it even more so. But still he felt like a Western hero, come for the showdown.

Back at the Stranger, he had headed straight up to his room but only been there a couple of minutes when there was a tap at his door.

He opened it to find Mrs. Appledore standing there, holding a plate with a sandwich on it.

"Thought you might fancy a nibble after your exertions," she said with that discomforting Illthwaite assumption of knowing exactly how he'd spent his morning, but her warm smile more than redressed the balance.

She must have been a very attractive woman in her younger

days, he thought, as he took the sandwich with a smile of thanks. In fact even now it would be very easy for a man to stop thinking of her as comfortably motherly and start thinking . . .

Oh God! Stop this! he commanded himself angrily. Just because he was no longer committed by formal vows to the celibate life didn't mean that lustful thoughts were any less sinful. But he knew he was reacting less to the idea of sin than the memory of the way his adolescent fancies had made him such an easy target for Frek Woollass.

As if the thought had nudged Mrs. Appledore's memory, she said, "By the way, Frek Woollass just called. She said to tell you she's passed on your message and are you going to be here in the pub tonight? If you are, fine. No need to ring back."

Meaning presumably that Gerry didn't care to have him back in the Hall but, having listened to his daughter's report, was willing to talk on neutral ground.

"No time was mentioned?"

"Round here, tonight's a time," she said, laughing.

She was an easy woman to make laugh. That was one of her many attractions . . .

¡Mierda! There he went again with that knee-jerk prurience.

"You'll be wanting some grub, if you're staying in," she suggested.

"That would be good," he said. He certainly did not intend to sit in his room, waiting anxiously.

"Sausage or ham?" she asked. "And what time?"

"Let's make it early, before you get too busy," he said. "Six? And sausage."

"Six and sausage it is," she said.

And now six it was, and the sausage wasn't far behind.

"Evening, Mr. Madero," said Edie Appledore from the bar. "I've reserved the table in the nook for you. Let me get you a drink, then I'll see to your grub. Will it be a sherry to whet your appetite?"

It was a kind thought but he did not care to think how long a bottle of sherry in this bar might have been standing open.

"No thanks," he said. "A half of bitter, please."

"When in Rome, eh?"

She drew a half-pint, looked at it critically, and poured it and another three away before she was satisfied.

"First of the night," she said. "You don't want stuff that's been lying in the pipes."

If only they took care of their wine as they took care of their beer, he thought.

He carried his glass to the table in the corner by the fireplace and chose the chair with its back to the wall.

A good shootist never sat with his back to the entrance door.

Would Frek come with her father? he wondered. Knowing what he knew now, how would he react to her? Down by the river she'd played him like a fish, hooked him, landed him, then left him floundering on the bank. He had told her everything. She had told him nothing. Unlike his exchange in the kitchen chamber with Sam, there had been no sense of sharing, of giving and taking comfort. Theirs had been an enforced intimacy, but it had been an intimacy for all that. Yet he couldn't accuse Frek of being deceitful. She hadn't created an illusion, simply allowed him to create one for himself.

His life so far had been defined by phantasms. Perhaps it was time to move on. But not without putting to rest the ghost of that other Miguel.

His thoughts were interrupted by the arrival of Mrs. Appledore with a plate fully occupied by a monstrous coil of sausage and a small mountain of chips.

He began to eat. It was really excellent this sausage. He wondered how well it held its flavor, cold. Chopped into small slices, he could envisage it taking its place among its more highly spiced cousins on a *tapas* tray.

The door opened and Thor Winander came in. He gave

Madero a friendly nod but made no effort to join him, taking a stool at the bar. A little later the old ex-policeman they called Noddy Melton appeared. He came straight to the table and shook Mig's hand.

"Good evening, Mr. Madero," he said. "I hope I find you well. It was good to meet you last night. My sources tell me we were right about the bones' antiquity, so I may have touched the head of a saint. I do believe my rheumatics were a little better this morning. Will your friend, Miss Flood, be joining us this evening?"

"No, she's gone, I'm afraid."

"Really? Then I look forward to seeing her on her return."

"I don't think she plans to come back," said Mig.

"Ah yes, but there's plans and there's life, Mr. Madero."

With this faintly enigmatic comment the little man went to the bar, nodded at Winander, paid for the pint which the landlady had already drawn for him, and took a seat just inside the door.

Others arrived over the next fifteen minutes or so. Some he recognized, like the Gowder twins, who ignored him completely. Others he thought he recollected from the crowd protesting at being shut out of the bar the previous night. Certainly all were local. And no one showed the slightest inclination to come near his table, not even Pete Swinebank, the vicar, who did however give him a friendly wave before settling down alongside a couple of farmers who looked more baffled than blessed.

Mig's sense of being in a movie returned. Probably all that had happened was that Mrs. Appledore had mentioned to each new arrival that his table was out of bounds as he was expecting company from the Hall. Yet he couldn't see why the imminent arrival of Gerry Woollass should cause such a tension of anticipation. A man of influence, certainly, but hardly a charismatic figure.

He finished his meal and pushed the plate away. It was the

perfect moment a good director would choose for the bar door to swing open to reveal the Man With No Name.

Dead on cue, the door opened. The figure that stood there wasn't Clint Eastwood, but his presence was almost as surprising.

It was Dunstan Woollass, resplendent in an immaculately cut cream-colored linen suit, with a silver-knobbed cane in his hand, a silk cravat at his throat, and a pale pink rose in his buttonhole.

He should have looked slightly absurd. He didn't.

He wasn't alone. Behind him Mig could see the grim-faced figure of Gerry with Frek on his left side and Sister Angelica on his right.

For a moment the new arrivals just stood there. The room fell silent. Then Dunstan said, "Good evening. I believe a man can get drink here."

There was a burst of laughter and a chorus of greeting.

Dunstan advanced, using the cane for support but with a grace that reminded you of Astaire rather than his age. Tables and chairs were pulled aside to allow him a direct course toward Mig's table. He nodded acknowledgment and bestowed gracious smiles on most people. Only to the Gowders did he speak direct, saying, "Silas, Ephraim, how are you?" Does he really know which is which? wondered Mig.

The twins muttered an inaudible reply, at the same time touching what would have been their cap-peaks or their forelocks, if they'd sported either. Sister Angelica smiled approvingly on this display of feudal hierarchy, but Gerry scowled as if he'd prefer to exercise his seigniorial power by having the Gowders flogged behind a cart.

Frek meanwhile diverted to the bar and slid elegantly on to a stool next to Thor Winander.

Mig stood up as the trio reached him and pulled out a chair for the nun, another for the old man. Gerry had to borrow a chair from a neighboring table.

Sister Angelica said, "Ta," as she sat down and Dunstan said, "Good evening, Madero. I trust I find you well?"

In the same instant Mrs. Appledore materialized with a tray bearing four well-filled brandy balloons which she set on the table.

"Evening, Mr. Dunstan," she said, clearing away Madero's dishes. "Nice to see you back in the Stranger. It's been a while."

"I lead a busy life, Edie," he said.

"So they say. Just shout when you want a refill. You'll not be disturbed."

"Well, here's to us," said Sister Angelica, taking a sip of her drink.

"Good health," said Madero, following suit.

It was, as he'd anticipated, the same excellent cognac Mrs. Appledore had given him in the kitchen on the night of his arrival.

Gerry Woollass seemed disinclined to join the toast, but under the nun's calm expectant gaze he took a token taste.

"Mr. Madero," said Dunstan. "Frek has passed on what you told her this morning."

He paused. Mig glanced toward the woman at the bar. She had a small wineglass in her hand which she raised in mock salute when their eyes met.

He didn't speak. It was up to Woollass to set the terms of this encounter.

The man continued. "It explains a lot. I can see how you might feel you've been treated unjustly. On the other hand, you were not as open with us as you might have been, so you must take your share of the blame."

Madero nodded.

"I do. My defense is it was a sin of omission. My principal motive in contacting your family was as stated, to pursue my researches into recusancy. If you had not replied positively, I wouldn't have come anywhere near Illthwaite."

"Fair enough," said Dunstan.

The expression on his son's face suggested he wasn't inclined to be so understanding, but Angelica was smiling at him encouragingly.

It was time to move things on. He picked up his briefcase which was resting against the table leg and opened it.

"Mr. Woollass, I have something to show you. As Frek will have told you, I found a document in the hidden chamber last night. It was in code. This is a translation."

He set his laptop on the table, brought up the translation and turned the screen toward the old man.

Dunstan read it with nothing in his expression beyond polite curiosity. Sister Angelica read also and from time to time scrolled the document down. Gerry didn't even look at the screen but said angrily, "And where's the original document that you stole?"

His father glanced at him long-sufferingly, then murmured, "Very interesting, Madero. And I gather that you are persuaded this fugitive with your name is in fact a direct ancestor of yours?"

"All the evidence supports such a belief."

"Including your own—how shall I put it?—metaphysical experience?"

"Frek clearly told you everything about me," he said, trying not to sound aggrieved.

"Which would make you, in some degree, an agent of God's purpose," said Dunstan with a faint twitch of the lips as though he found the concept amusing.

"Aren't we all His agents, Mr. Woollass? In some degree," said Madero.

Gerry looked as if he was going to break out again, but Sister Angelica gave him a warning glance and Mig an encouraging smile. He was beginning to understand her presence, both here and at the initial interview. She wasn't Gerry's spiritual so much as his worldly advisor! The man, despite his down-to-earth manner and appearance, lacked any real shrewdness in his dealings with others. To his father, who Madero judged wouldn't have been out of place in the super-subtle political world of the Curia, he must have been a great disappointment. Possibly the nun also reported directly, or rather indirectly, to the old man, who clearly had a certain way with women.

Mig said, "Putting aside any dispute as to final ownership of the journal, what it establishes beyond all doubt is that my family has as real and personal an interest in Father Simeon as yours."

"Beyond all doubt?" said Dunstan, raising his eyebrows. "I think we might need expert advice on that."

"Seek it by all means. But I need neither written words nor expert opinion to tell me that my ancestor once hid in that chamber. Nor I suspect do you."

"What do you mean by that?" demanded Gerry indignantly. "You've no right to judge others by your own shifty standards."

The nun made a wry face as if to apologize for a teenager's outburst.

Mig regarded Gerry thoughtfully. Unless he was a very good actor, he clearly knew nothing about Simeon's encounter with Miguel. Unlike Dunstan, who he guessed had already known a great deal even before he saw the transcript.

As for Sister Angelica, how much does she know? he wondered.

In fact, what was there to know?

It was pretty clear that the secret of the Stranger's hidden chamber hadn't been known by anyone in the family, or surely it would have been explored years ago. Probably it was passed on by word of mouth alone during those dangerous years. It hadn't been till much later, as late as the middle of the eighteenth century perhaps, that such a revelation would have ceased to have its attendant dangers. But by then the fragile word-of-mouth chain could so easily have been broken by early death, or the onset of senile memory loss and, once broken, there was no way of repairing it.

But even given the care Alice Woollass had taken in the way she recorded events in her journal, a subtle-minded scholar with more time to scan the document than a single morning might have been able to guess at much.

And indeed, given that the same scholar had had all the time in the world to study the journal, who knows what portions of it may have been removed before anyone else was allowed near it? He recalled his sense of breaks and jumps in the narrative.

Dunstan said, "You say the original is in code? Not a very complex code if you managed to break it so quickly."

"I had help," said Madero.

"Indeed? Would that perhaps have been from the young Australian woman who seems to have been causing a stir in the village? I gather she has some expertise in the field of ciphering."

Frek really did keep him informed, thought Madero. Perhaps this was her way of compensating for the huge disappointment she must have caused Dunstan by bringing the Woollass line to a full stop.

"Yes, it was Sam," he said.

"An interesting woman by the sound of it. I should like to meet her."

"I'm afraid that's not possible. She decided there was nothing for her here and moved on this morning," said Mig.

He was beginning to feel maneuvered away from the main theme of this encounter. He looked for a way to get things back on course, but he was preempted by Gerry, who clearly agreed with him that things were being allowed to drift.

"I've got better things to do than sit around listening to idle chitchat," he declared impatiently. "If you've got anything to say about our family, Madero, why don't you spit it out? Otherwise, just hand over our property, which you illegally removed from the chamber, and we can bring this meeting to an end!"

His voice rose as he spoke, drawing attention from the rest of the room. Not, Mig suspected, that attention hadn't already been focused on the nook, but hidden beneath a surface of normal barroom sociability. Now heads were unambiguously turning their way.

Across his mind ran the silly irrelevance that this was the point at which a good movie director would factor in a dramatic interruption.

And once more it was as if he'd put a megaphone to his lips and cried, *Action!*

The door burst open and into the bar erupted a small slight figure like a creature escaped from fairyland under the hill. Its eyes looked huge in a death-pale face and its skull was spattered with tufts of bright red hair between which patches of white skin gleamed like traces of snow in a poppy field. For a moment no one recognized her, not even Mig.

Then she opened her mouth and her identity was unmistakable.

"Now listen in, you lying Pommy bastards!" she cried. "Two nights ago I stood here and asked if anyone knew anything about my gran, Sam Flood. You all said no, the name meant nothing to you. I knew you were lying then, but I was still stupid enough to be persuaded your Sam Flood had nothing to do with me. All of you bastards knew different. Now I know different too. My gran came from here, and she left here in 1961, and all she took with her was a piece of paper with Sam sodding Flood's name and address on it. No, I'm forgetting—not quite all. There's something else I know which some of you had to know too. She was twelve years old when she left and she took a little bit of Illthwaite with her. She was pregnant. So come on, you bastards. Which of you's my grandfather so I can say a proper hello? Or is he in hell where he belongs? Was screwing my gran the reason your precious perfect bloody curate topped himself? *Well, was it?*"

6

Wasn't that fun?

Silence.

Mig Madero tried to take in everything.

Thor Winander slumped on his bar stool and seemed to put on ten years. Next to him Frek Woollass was unmoved except perhaps by her usual secret amusement. The Gowder twins looked at each other as if seeing each other for the first time. Pete Swinebank closed his eyes while his lips moved. In prayer? Noddy Melton's sharp gaze darted hither and thither around the room. Edie Appledore stood frozen for a moment then turned and vanished from behind the bar.

Closer to, Dunstan's eyebrows arched in mild surprise, then he slowly turned his head to give himself a view of this interesting newcomer. Sister Angelica's lean good-natured face registered shock and compassion, while Gerry looked like a spacewalker whose safety line has just broken and who finds himself falling away from the security of his ship into the unfathomable depths of deep space.

But it was back to Sam Flood that Mig felt his gaze irresistibly drawn.

The little Australian stood with her back to the bar, those huge eyes glaring defiantly, but now it was defiance shading into despair as the rage which had carried her this far began to drain away and with it her strength. She tried not to let it show, leaning against the bar for support. But Mig saw it and began to rise, wincing as his left knee gave notice that the exertions of the morning still had to be paid for.

Even without the knee, he probably wouldn't have been as quick as Sister Angelica, who was moving swiftly forward, her face creased with sympathy.

"Let's find you somewhere to sit down and talk this over, dear," she said, reaching out toward Sam.

The response was shocking.

"Don't you dare touch me, you fucking cow!" said Sam in a voice so low and vibrant with hate that it sounded as if it came from another world.

It stopped Angelica in her tracks. Then before she could make the possibly fatal decision to move forward again, Edie Appledore came into the bar, pushed past the nun, put an arm round Sam's shoulders and, without speaking a word, led her unresistingly out of the room.

As the door closed behind them, talk resumed in the bar, hesitant at first, a word here, a phrase there, but quickly building up to a buzz. There were some who didn't talk. The Gowders had vanished almost immediately, leaving undrunk beer in their glasses. And the vicar had slipped out in the wake of Sam and Mrs. Appledore.

Sister Angelica, visibly shaken, returned to the table where Gerry Woollass was draining his brandy glass with a greed suggesting that if it had been full to the brim he would still have emptied it.

"Sit down, Sister," said Mig. "Are you all right?"

"Yes, don't worry about me," said the nun, pulling herself together. "I've been called worse, and that was in the convent. It's that young lass we should be worrying about. Clearly something pretty awful's happened to her."

"She's not a lass, she's in her twenties and highly intelligent," Mig heard himself saying defensively. "She has a First in math from Melbourne University and she's here to carry on her studies at Cambridge."

"That makes it worse," said Angelica. "For a mature woman to react like that means . . . I can't think what it might mean."

"Extraordinary," murmured Dunstan. "Whatever it means, I think it marks a convenient point to terminate our meeting. I was already feeling a little fatigued. I don't get out very often, Madero, and when I do, I rarely encounter such excitements as these. Now I feel I could not give these weighty matters we were discussing my full attention. Would it be possible for you to join us up at the Hall in the morning? About eleven o'clock, no point in being uncivilized."

"That would suit me very well," said Mig.

"That's settled then," said Sister Angelica. "Come on, Woollasses. Let's get you home. Then it's up the wooden hill to Bedfordshire for both of you by the look of it."

She escorted the two men across the room. At the door Frek joined them, but made no move to take over the nun's comforting role. She glanced toward Mig, raised her eyebrows as if to say *wasn't that fun?*, then followed the others out of the bar.

All eyes watched them go but no one called goodnight.

Mig finished his brandy, taking his time. Then he too rose and made for the door.

En route he let his gaze touch everyone he knew, but no one was catching his eye.

Out in the dark hall, he could see a chink of light under the kitchen door.

What was going on in there?

Should he knock and ask how Sam was?

He thought about it.

The answer was no. Whatever balm Edie Appledore was pouring on to the little Australian's troubled spirit, he didn't want to risk disturbing the process.

He made his usual silent way up the stairs to his bedroom.

7

A slice of cake

It wasn't till she'd been talking to Edie Appledore for ten minutes that it struck Sam that in fact this woman wasn't part of the solution but part of the problem.

By then she'd drunk an ounce of the landlady's excellent cognac and was now drinking her second mug of coffee and, not having eaten since the pub at lunchtime, feeling a strong inclination to get her teeth into a second slice of the scrumptious chocolate cake which had been set on a plate before her.

Another woman in face of these goodies might have felt inhibited from suddenly diverting from confidence to accusation, but such social niceties had never troubled Sam.

"You lied to me as well," she broke out. "Soon as I got here, the way I looked, and my name, they all meant something to you but you said nothing."

The woman made no attempt at denial.

"I'm sorry," she said. "But round here you don't tell folk what you don't need to tell them, not until you've got some idea exactly what it is they're after."

This philosophy was close enough to her pa's to quieten Sam for a moment. But rapidly she resumed: "It was more than just keeping quiet, wasn't it? You did things too. OK, nothing as extreme as knocking me off a ladder like the Gowders. But you spread the word about me, didn't you?"

"I rang Thor, yes. But that was it. If what you say about the Gowders is right, I'm sorry, but I'm not responsible for what they get up to, am I?"

"I suppose not," said Sam, beginning to feel frustrated. "But you searched my room, right?"

"I did not!" declared the landlady indignantly. "I never laid a hand on your things."

"Someone did."

"Then I apologize. In my house! I've been meaning to get proper locks on those bedroom doors. Anyone could have crept up the stairs and got in. You believe me?"

Sam nodded. Why shouldn't she believe her? This was truth time.

She finished her story, telling all that she'd discovered in Newcastle, and then she settled to wait for the payback.

They were seated at an angle of the big table, chairs skewed so they faced each other. Mrs. Appledore stretched out her right hand, laid it on Sam's left and squeezed hard. It was a gesture too natural to be intimidating.

Then she said, "I bet you've hardly had a thing to eat since you left here this morning, right? Get stuck into that cake. It's all right, you know. We don't do the dead any good by starving ourselves."

She wasn't being evasive, Sam recognized, just practical. And she was right.

She carved another slice of cake and took a large bite.

"Grand," approved Mrs. Appledore. "Now, where were we? Oh yes. You're dead right, of course. Soon as I set eyes on you I thought of little Pam. It was the hair. Not so much the face, though I do see a resemblance, except in the eyes. And of course she was a little elf of a thing like you."

"And you said nothing!" accused Sam.

"What was I to say? You said your name was Sam Flood. It was all I could do not to slap your face! I thought someone's playing a dreadful joke on me. Then I saw your passport.

I've never asked to see a passport in my life, but I needed to see yours. When I saw your name really was Sam Flood, I began to think it was maybe just an unfortunate coincidence. Or more truthful, I began to hope it was. And when you said your gran had left in 1960, I heaved a sigh of relief. It was still very odd, but you were so definite. And one thing I knew for certain was that it was 1961 when little Pam left Illthwaite."

"Tell me about her. It's Pam you're calling her, not Sam, right? Did she have a second name?"

"Galley. Like the ship. Pamela Galley. But we all called her Pam."

"So it would have been easy for her to answer to Sam?"

"Oh yes. Though the truth is little Pam wasn't much for answering to anything. She was the quietest kid you could imagine, and afterward she was even quieter if that was possible."

"Afterward? After what?"

The woman shrugged, not indifferently but with a suppressed anger.

"Who knows?" she said. "But now we can guess. We just thought it was the shock of her seeing Madge Gowder die. Maybe that's what we wanted to think. After what you've found out, though, it's pretty clear . . . God help us!"

Sam felt that great wave of anger which had exploded in the bar welling up in her again but she forced it down. Its time would come; now what she wanted was information.

"This Madge Gowder, she related to the twins?"

"Their ma."

"So the Galleys lived in Illthwaite too?"

"No," said Mrs. Appledore. "In Eskdale, not far away as the crow flies. But they were kin of the Gowders."

"The Gowders? You mean I could be related to the Gowders?" exclaimed Sam, not trying to conceal her horror.

"Aye. Well, like they say, you can choose your friends but you can't choose your relatives. I shouldn't worry too much though. Cousins they called each other for convenience, but the family connection was a lot further back than makes true cousins in my book. For all that, round here even thin blood's still thicker than water. The Galleys never amounted to much, while the Gowders used to be one of the important families in Illthwaite. But they always took care of the Galleys in their way, if you call tossing the odd bone to a starving hound taking care of it. So when little Pam were orphaned, it seemed natural she should be brought over from Eskdale and left at Foulgate."

"Natural to leave a little girl with the Gowders!"

"You're a bit quick to judge, if you don't mind me saying so," said Mrs. Appledore, regarding her critically. "Is that an Aussie thing?"

"Quick to judge? Were you listening when I told you what happened to my grandmother?" demanded Sam.

"OK, keep your hair on. Sorry, not trying to be funny. You've made a right mess of yourself, you know that? God, when I was young, I'd have given my right arm for hair like yours and Pam's. Anyway, Madge Gowder, the twins' mother, were still alive then, though ailing. It was her being sick and then dying that set Jim Gowder, her man, drinking away what was left of the farm. Sad really, when you think what they once were. Employed a dozen men, didn't tip their hats to the squire, and had their own pew in the church. Madge would have seen little Pam right but, like I say, she was sick. For a while the doctor was never away, then the vicar was there as often as the doctor and we knew it couldn't be long."

"The vicar? Mr. Swinebank's father, you mean?"

"Yes. And Sam, the curate. In fact, Sam was probably there more often. Madge preferred Sam. Everyone did. Old Paul was hot on hell, but Sam had the knack of making religion sound a lot more attractive somehow."

"I bet!" said Sam harshly. In her eyes, this saintly fucking curate was still number one suspect. "So Madge Gowder died, right?"

"Yes, she died. It was little Pam who was with her, or found her, no one knows which. Someone went to Madge's room, and there she was, dead, with Pam sitting at the bedside, holding Madge's hand. She was in a state, but not the kind of state that drew attention, if you follow me. Just even quieter and more withdrawn than ever. You could forget she was there. I suppose eventually someone would have thought to ask what was to become of Pamela, left up there with the two lads and their drunken father. But Sam Flood didn't hang around to ask. He took her out of Foulgate straight off. Gave her a bed up at the vicarage. His own bed. The Rev. Paul didn't like it, nor old fish-face Thomson, his housekeeper. They reckoned that if God's house had so many mansions, He didn't need the vicarage, so they wanted her out. But they couldn't just chuck her into the street. By now she was a worry to us all, quiet as a ghost and looked like one too. Like I say, most of us put it down to losing her mam and dad and then losing Madge Gowder in quick succession. There were some ready to gossip, of course. In a village there always are and generally it's best not to listen . . ."

"Especially when the gossip's about the local saint!" Sam burst out.

Mrs. Appledore's hand, which had been resting lightly on hers, suddenly gripped it till it hurt.

"Listen," she said, and her voice which till now had been conciliatory and understanding was harsh and emphatic. "You make a big thing of liking things straight. Well, there's something we've got to get straight. I heard what you said in the bar and I hear what you're saying now. But you're wrong, absolutely wrong. What happened to Pamela Galley I don't know, but one thing I'm absolutely certain of is that she got nothing but love in the proper Christian sense from Sam Flood!"

In this mode, Edie Appledore was formidable, but Sam refused to be fazed.

"How can you be so sure? He was a man, wasn't he?" she

declared. "He had her to himself at the vicarage. OK, you all say he was a good man, a very good man, but good and bad doesn't come into it when their cocks start crowing. All it means is that afterward he must have known that what he'd done was unforgivably wrong, for anyone, let alone a priest, and he couldn't live with himself, so he committed suicide. How else can you compute the data?"

"Data? Is that the way you see things?" said Mrs. Appledore scornfully. "You come here from the other side of the world and within two minutes you're making judgments like it can be done by arithmetic."

"So point out my errors," said Sam. "I can only work with what I'm told and round here that's not a lot! Someone got my gran pregnant and then she was shipped to the other side of the world in some cockamamie scheme that charities, churches and the government dreamt up between them. And the only guy Pam seemed to trust and be close to is a curate, and he tops himself. Come on, Edie! You must have wondered if something was going on. For God's sake, it wasn't as if there weren't rumors flying around that he was having underage sex! What kind of community is it that can hear gossip like that and not do anything about it?"

She drew her hand away from the landlady's and stared defiantly into her face. But the woman's gaze was focused over her shoulder. Sam looked round to see Thor Winander standing in the doorway. His expression was untypically serious. He nodded, not at Sam but at Mrs. Appledore, then came into the room, closing the door behind him. He sat down at the far end of the table.

Edie Appledore's attention returned to Sam and she said in a still flat voice, "You've been talking to Noddy Melton, haven't you? For once, he's right, old Noddy. Yes, there were stories about Sam having a relationship with an underage girl."

"There you go then!" cried Sam triumphantly. "Do it with one, you get a taste for it, isn't that what they say?"

Then something in Edie Appledore's face made her add, "If it was true, of course. Was it true, Edie? Do you know it was true?"

The woman's gaze moved from Sam to Thor Winander and back.

Then she said, very quietly, "Oh yes, it was true, my dear. I know that for sure. You see, the girl was me."

8

Edie Appledore's story

For a second Sam was completely thrown.

Then her mind incorporated this new information and all she could see was that it confirmed her theory. A priest who could screw around with one kid wouldn't have too much difficulty screwing around with another! It was going to be hard to press this point without hurting the woman sitting before her, who looked to be hurting enough already, but she was getting too close to the truth now to hold back.

She said gently, "I'm sorry, Edie, but surely you can see that if Sam and you were—"

"No!" broke in the woman. "You're missing the point, which is that Sam and I weren't! And it wasn't because I didn't want to, believe me! What you need to get straight is we're not talking perversion here, we're talking love!"

This sounded like denial to Sam. She said, "Edie, you can't have been more than a kid back then . . ."

"That's right. A kid. In fact when he first came to Illthwaite on holiday to visit Thor, I was just thirteen. I remember he came into the pub and we looked at each other and that moment I grew up. I think he knew too that I was the one for him. And don't imagine that shows he had a thing about kids! I was an early developer. From twelve on I was a stunner, though

I say it myself, fit for any man's bed. I could see it in our customers' eyes every night of the week. You must have known girls like that."

"Yeah, my best friend's one of them," admitted Sam. "All the same, it doesn't make it right—"

"You're not listening! There wasn't anything to make right. We just looked. Sam must have got a real shock when he found out how young I was. He never caught my eye after that, not till he came to be our curate. I was fifteen by then. I make no bones about it, I went after him. Few months more and I would be sixteen and legal. I could be wedded with my dad's permission and bedded without it! Not that I wanted to wait. But Sam wasn't having any, even though once we started seeing each other, it was clear he fancied me as much as I fancied him. God, he must have had the willpower of a saint, the tices I put on him! But his beliefs made him hold out till I was legal. At least that's what I thought. No kid looking forward to Christmas found the days drag by as slowly as I did those last few weeks till my sixteenth.

"And at last it came. It was on a Saturday. My mates kept me busy all day, and that night Dad and the regulars put on a bit of a party for me here in the pub. Sam didn't come. I didn't mind. What he and I were going to do to celebrate didn't need a roomful of people. Next day, Sunday, I went to church in the morning. Sam was taking the service. He kept on looking toward me from the pulpit then looking away. God, I could hardly keep still in my seat, people must have thought I'd got worms! Sam and I usually met on a Sunday night after evensong but I couldn't wait. I helped Dad in the bar that lunchtime till it got toward closing—it was two o'clock on a Sunday back in them days—then I told Dad I'd do the clearing up when I got back—he liked to go fishing on a Sunday afternoon—and I set off up to the vicarage.

"I knew the vicar took the Sunday School in the church at two o'clock, and as I went by at about five to, I saw him and his housekeeper going in as usual with armfuls of books and such to get things ready. Sam had his Bible class in the vicarage at three. That gave us a good hour. Long enough, I thought. But no time to waste.

"I went at him like a . . . I don't know what. I kissed him, I caressed him, I felt him roused, and when he didn't move quick as I wanted, I even took his hand, God help me, and put it between my legs. It must have been like dipping it into a bowl of hot honey.

"And he pulled away.

"I didn't know what was happening. He was talking, saying that he couldn't, not till we were married, his conscience wouldn't let him, we had to wait, stuff like that. I wasn't listening. I was bewildered, ashamed, angry, humiliated. I opened my mouth to yell at him. Then there was a tap at his door.

"I straightened my clothes. All I wanted to do was get out of there. It was Pete Swinebank outside. He was only a kid then, just eleven. I'd forgotten he might still be around. It didn't matter now anyway. I pushed by him and headed back here to the pub.

"Dad had gone off fishing as usual, but there were still a few men in the bar, drinking up. He trusted his regulars, Dad. And it was true what they say about the old days, you didn't need to lock your front door, at least not in the countryside. Someone shouted at me as I went past the barroom door, but I didn't stop, I just headed straight up the back stairs to my bedroom. I flung myself on the bed and lay there crying.

"A bit later I heard the regulars leave. But not all of them. There was a knock at my door. Then it opened. And Thor looked in."

She paused and turned her gaze once more to the far end of the table. Sam turned her head. Rapt by Edie's narrative, she'd forgotten all about the presence of another listener. Somehow he didn't look like himself, but older, careworn. Even when their gazes met, he didn't smile.

Edie Appledore said, "Thor asked me if I was all right. He'd brought a tray up with tea and biscuits. I sat up and looked at myself in the mirror. I was a mess. But Thor didn't seem to notice. He poured the tea, took a flask out of his pocket and added a shot of Scotch. He said it would do me good, then he sat on the end of the bed and we smoked a couple of cigarettes and talked. He was always good for a laugh, Thor. One of my favorites in the bar. Easy to talk to. I found myself telling him what had happened. He said Sam must be mad . . . the loveliest lass in the valley . . . now, if it had been him—that kind of stuff, just what I wanted to hear. And somehow, it seemed inevitable that after a while he put the tray on the floor and lay down beside me, and suddenly my body was on the boil again, and our clothes were off and he was on top of me and I was yelling encouragement . . .

"And that was how Sam found us when he pushed open my door."

She stood up abruptly and started opening drawers.

"I gave up smoking twenty years ago, but I could do with one now," she said. But her voice suggested she was just looking for an excuse to turn her back and hide her tears.

Thor Winander spoke, simply and undramatically.

"So you see, young Sam, your namesake was the very best of men, and my dearest friend, and I killed him. By the time I got dressed and went after him, he had vanished. I didn't realize then it was for good. We were wrong to try and fob you off with evasions and half-truths, but it wasn't clear that any of this really had anything to do with you. Pain makes you selfish, and just about everyone in Illthwaite feels pain when they recall we had a man like Sam Flood in our midst and he chose to kill himself. What they don't know and what I've never had the courage to tell them is that that guilt isn't theirs. It's mine alone. I killed him."

"*We* killed him, Thor," said Mrs. Appledore gently. "Don't take it all on yourself. But I hope you can see now, lass, that whoever abused little Pam Galley, it wasn't Sam Flood. He never did a dishonorable thing in his life. He loved me. I offered myself to him, I put his hand between my legs and he had the willpower to turn away. You don't think a man like that could have abused a child, do you?"

Even if Sam had still thought it, in the face of such loss and grief, she would have found it hard to say so. But when she ran the equations across the blackboard in her mind, she found the conclusion proved beyond all doubt.

"No," she said, "I don't. I'm sorry. It must have been terrible for you . . ."

"Must have been? Still is. Time heals, you can forget most things. But you never forget your own birthday. And every one I've celebrated for forty-odd years now I've had to think, tomorrow will be the anniversary of the day the only man I ever really loved drowned himself because of me. You should take a look at the birthday cards I get. No one round here knows all the truth, but they saw what Sam's death did to me, and they've got long memories. I don't get many of them jokey cards, believe me."

"I'm really sorry," repeated Sam, rising. "Look, I'd better go."

"Go where? You got somewhere to stay?"

She hadn't. Nor had she thought about it. She hadn't thought about much but her grandmother for the past few hours.

"Thought not. You can't go rushing off into the night looking like that—you'd frighten the owls. Your room's not taken. Get yourself back in there for tonight at least."

Edie Appledore was right. The prospect of driving off and looking for a room somewhere was less than appealing.

"Is that OK? Thanks a lot. I'm really sorry for bringing all this pain back to you."

"At least I've not cut my hair off," said Mrs. Appledore. "You'd best start wearing a hat tomorrow, else folk will think you've escaped. We'll talk more in the morning, dear. You've likely still got questions to ask."

"One or two," said Sam, making her way to the door. "Just one more now. I take it my grandmother had been shipped off to Australia before this happened."

"Oh yes. Couple of weeks."

"And from what you say, I can't see that my namesake would have been all that keen on this. So how did it happen?"

"No, he wasn't too happy. He talked to me about it a lot. That was one of the things I loved about him. He talked to me about everything, like I was fifty rather than fifteen. It was only when it came to sex he remembered my age."

She laughed, with surprisingly little bitterness. It seemed to Sam that despite their feelings of guilt at their involvement in his death, Edie and Thor had memories of her namesake so delightful they transcended negative feelings.

"He was really concerned about little Pam. She trusted him more than anyone else in the world, I think. But even with Sam it was a silent trust. She never talked about what was going on inside. But Rev. Paul was pushing him all the time, saying something had to be done about the child. Clearly she couldn't go back to Foulgate. The only alternative seemed to be social services, though we called them something different back then. Once they got their hands on her, she'd just have vanished into some children's home, and Sam refused to countenance that. Then the vicar and Dunstan got their heads together. Dunny had lots of connections in the Catholic Church, of course, charities and orphanages, that sort of thing. It was just after the Pope had made him a knight or something, and the nuns all thought the sun shone out of his arse. He knew all about this scheme for sending orphans to Australia. The way him and Rev. Paul told it, most of them were snapped up for adoption by caring families as soon as they arrived. It seemed an ideal solution. Sam had doubts, but finally he was persuaded this was the best on offer for the kid. A new chance in a new land where the sun always shone and the rivers ran with milk and honey—how could he stand in the way of that?

But no one knew the lass was pregnant. You've got to believe that, dear. No one knew she was pregnant."

"I believe you," said Sam. She looked with some regret at the chocolate cake. Somehow in the circumstances it didn't seem right to ask if she could take a slice to bed with her.

"Yes, I believe you," she repeated. "But if you think that makes it any better, you couldn't be more wrong. I'll say goodnight."

9

Counting to fifteen

Seated on his rickety chair, staring at his laptop which was perched on the dressing table, Mig Madero heard the stairs creaking. No reason he should recognize the Australian girl's tread, but he knew it was her.

Her steps were on the landing now. As they reached his door, they hesitated. He found himself willing her to knock. But then the steps moved on.

He recalled words quoted in one of his seminary lectures—he couldn't recall their source but it didn't matter—*When God's response to prayer is silence, maybe He's telling you that you're praying for something you can do for yourself.*

He stood up, moved swiftly to the door and pulled it open.

Sam, her hand on the handle of her own door, looked round.

"Hi," she said.

"Hi. Are you OK?"

"I've been better. You?"

"OK. I translated that document. Would you like to see it?"

He had a feeling that any direct reference to what had brought her back would have sent her straight into her room.

"Yes, I would," she said.

He liked the way she didn't hesitate.

She came into the room and he sat her before the computer then brought up the translation on the screen.

As she read it he stood looking down at her cropped skull. She'd made a real mess of it. He could see cuts and scratches in the skin over which scabs had not yet had time to form.

She said, "Wow. This Miguel, he's that ancestor you were talking about?"

"Yes," he said. "My lost ancestor."

"And now you know what happened to him. That's amazing."

"I do not yet know everything, but I will know," he said.

"I saw you in the bar with Woollass, the one whose daughter you fancy . . ."

"Gerry," he said. "And no, I do not fancy Frek."

"Fallen out, have you?" she said indifferently. "Shouldn't worry. You fell out with her dad too, but now you're drinking buddies. There was an old guy there too."

"Dunstan Woollass. You took in a lot for someone who was so . . . upset."

"I suppose I hoped someone would jump up with guilt written all over them and make a break for it, like in the old black-and-whites. Life's not like the movies though."

He smiled as he thought of his own cinematic fantasy.

"Sometimes it gets close," he said.

"Does it? So what were you and the squires doing together?"

"I'll tell you about it. But first things first."

He went to his bag and took out a small medicine box.

"My mother insists I always travel with this," he said. "As usual, she is right."

He took out a small tube of ointment, squeezed some on to his index finger and gently began to rub it into one of the scratches on her skull. Instinctively she jerked away, then relaxed and did not flinch as his finger resumed contact. As he sought out and anointed her cuts, he gave her a quick sketch of what had happened to him that day, skipping over though not completely censoring his dealings with Frek.

When he finished he didn't invite comment but tapped his finger gently on her skull and said, "So, are you going to tell me what this is all about?"

"Why not?" she said. "It's been a good day for finding out about ancestors. Or maybe not so good."

He listened to her story without interruption.

When she finished, he said, "That is a truly terrible story. May God forgive all those concerned."

"And that will make it OK, will it?" she snapped. "Well, you can tell this forgiving God of yours he needn't expect any help from me. You not finished there yet?"

"Not quite."

In fact he'd dressed even the smallest grazes, but he found himself reluctant to give up this excuse for touching her ravaged head.

Her gaze met his in the mirror. She glowered. He smiled. After a moment, she smiled back.

He said, "So we have been treading parallel paths. Perhaps after all we may turn out to be—what was that phrase you used?—an amiable pair?"

"An amicable pair," she corrected. "Could be."

"Anyway," he went on brusquely, for fear his small diversion toward intimacy might drive her away, "we are both near the final answers now. I wonder if we will want to hear them?"

"I don't believe in final answers," she said. "In math, the best answers always ask new questions."

"Is that what you meant when you said God was the last prime number? If you get the final answer, then you must have found God?"

"Maybe," she said. "Or maybe I just meant that there is no last prime number. Euclid offered a proof two thousand years ago. Add one to the product of all known primes and you will have another prime, or a number one of whose factors is an unknown prime. It's so beautiful it's probably already in that book I told you about, but they should have put it in the Bible too."

He thought, I'll need to learn a new language if I'm to communicate with this woman.

He said, "That's an oversight I must point out next time I'm invited to speak to the Vatican Council."

She stood up and examined her head in the mirror.

"That should do the trick. You anoint me any more, you'll have to make me a queen or something."

"Queen Sam the First," he said. "It has a ring to it."

"You reckon? Thanks anyway. For the treatment. And the talk."

"I was glad to talk too."

"You were? I almost knocked on your door as I passed, then I thought that I'd disturbed you enough over the past couple of days."

"Maybe more than you know," he said. "I heard you hesitate outside. I'm glad I helped you make up your mind. Talking is always good."

"Depends who it's with," she said. She looked at her watch. "Jeez, it's still early."

"Yes, it is. You sound disappointed."

"It makes for a long night. I wasn't looking forward to it anyway, not with everything that's been going on. Now it'll feel like forever. That's another reason I almost knocked. I didn't feel like being on my own."

He loved her directness. It was rare to meet honesty with no hint of calculation.

"So stay then. By all means," he said.

"Stay? Is that a proposition?"

He felt himself flushing.

"No! I mean, to talk, if you want. Or if you want to sleep, please, use my bed. I'll be fine here."

He indicated the rickety chair.

Sam laughed.

"Not if you want to sleep. Anyway, it's your bed. You deserve a share of it."

She must be suggesting he should sit on the end of it. What else could she mean?

He looked at the bed doubtfully.

"It's very narrow," he said.

"Me too," she said. "See. I take up next to no room."

She moved her hands and stood before him naked. He wouldn't have believed clothes could be removed so quickly. Nor would he have believed that the sight of a body so skinny with more straight lines than curves and breasts that would vanish in the palms of his hands could have such a devastating effect on him. His mouth went dry, his body burned, his knees buckled with a weakness that had nothing to do with his mountain fall. His now tremulous sight registered that she was a deep golden brown all over except for the fiery red of her pubic hair, then she was sliding out of sight beneath the duvet.

"Acres," she said. "You could hold that meeting of the Vatican Council in here."

Perhaps the religious reference should have had a cooling effect. Instead somehow it merely turned up the heat. He may not have matched her speed of undress, but at least he gave it his best shot.

That was his last contact with rational thought for a little while.

A very little while.

After the first time, Sam said, "You've not done a lot of this, have you? Here's a tip. A gent usually tries to count up to at least twenty before he gives his all. You can count up to twenty, can't you? Fifteen would do at a pinch."

After the second time, she said, "You're a fast learner. With the right training you could be a contender."

And after the third time, she said, "That was great. Now, if you don't mind, I'd like to try a bit of sleep."

For his part, he thought he would never sleep again but just lie there savoring the endless joy of her presence alongside him. But sleep came all the same, and when it came it was full of sweet dreams and peace and quiet breathing.

10

Keep practicing

Miguel Madero awoke.

He was alone.

His first thought was: It's all been a dream.

His second: But can a dream leave the sweet odor of her in my nostrils?

Agitated, he jumped out of bed, forgot to duck to avoid the low crossbeam, and cracked his brow so hard that tears came to his eyes.

When they cleared, Sam was standing in the doorway, fully dressed, with a broad-brimmed floppy white sun hat pulled over her ravaged skull.

"Hi," she said. "Bathroom's all yours. Shall I tell Mrs. A. you'd like a cooked breakfast? Or have you had enough of the big sausage for now?"

Her gaze slid slowly down his body. His hands came round to cover himself and she turned away and ran down the stairs, laughing. It was the loveliest sound he could recall hearing.

I must be careful, he told himself. I am the tyro here. She is the experienced woman. She was lonely, distraught. She took comfort in me as a woman of an earlier age might have taken a sleeping draft. I must not read more into this than an experienced man of my age would read.

But nothing he could tell himself, and nothing he could tell God either as he recited his morning office, did anything to staunch the spring of sheer joy bubbling up inside him, and instead of his usual soft-footed descent of the stairs, he took them at a run, three at a time.

In the kitchen, Edie Appledore heard the noise, wrinkled her brow for a moment, then a slow smile spread across her face as she turned the sausage in the pan.

In the bar Sam was finishing a bowl of cereal. She still had her hat on and when she leaned forward over the bowl, the brim hid her face.

He sat opposite her and said, unthinking, "So what shall we do today?"

She raised her head slowly. There was milk on her lower lip. He wanted to kiss it away, but her expression didn't invite such familiarity.

She looked at him blankly then said, "You've got an appointment at the Hall, haven't you?"

"So I have. You know, I'd forgotten. But I needn't get up there for another hour or so."

She said, "I suppose not," and the concealing brim came down again as she took another spoonful of cornflakes.

Mrs. Appledore came in with a plate of sausage and mushrooms which she placed before him. She then transferred his breakfast cutlery from the neighboring table without comment and went back to the kitchen.

"You decided I would be hungry?" said Mig.

"I'd have taken bets on it."

He thought about this, smiled, and began eating.

She poured herself some coffee from the jug and watched him gravely.

He didn't speak, fearful of not finding the right thing to say.

After a while she said, "I was thinking . . ."

"What?"

"Your ancestor. Do you think he killed Thomas Gowder?"

"Good Lord. I don't know. I could hardly blame him if he did. Does it matter?"

"Truth matters," she said with absolute certainty. "In your translation Miguel says, *He came after me. As I pushed myself upright, my right hand rested on a heavy fuel log. He drove the knife at my throat. I ducked aside. And I swung the log at his temple. He fell like a tree.* But the account in Swinebank's *Guide* says: *After some months of living at Foulgate and being nursed back to health, the youth repaid their kindness one night by assaulting Jenny. On being interrupted by her husband, he wrestled the man to the ground and slit his throat from ear to ear, almost severing the head from the neck.*"

The way she spoke the words convinced him this was verbatim not a paraphrase.

"I'm impressed," he said.

"Why?" she said. "It's a quirk, not a talent. Like a digital camera, only the images are harder to delete."

"A useful quirk," he said.

"Not always. I mean, what earthly use is it for me to know that you have a small hairy mole, ovoid in shape, approximately one square centimeter in area, situated seven centimeters on a fifteen-degree diagonal to the left of your belly button?"

He took a larger bite of his sausage than he'd intended and, after a lot of chewing, managed to say, "It might come in handy if you had to identify my body."

"No," she said. "There are other things I'd look for. You haven't answered my question."

"Are you worried because it could turn out you're related to the Gowders?" he asked, laughing.

She didn't laugh back.

"Only if it turns out the connection's any closer than a couple of centuries," she said flatly.

He took her meaning and said, "But the twins would only have been young boys themselves then . . ."

"There was their father. He sounds to have been a piece of work. Look, Mig, someone got Pam pregnant and it certainly wasn't the Angel of the Lord."

Before he could reply, Edie Appledore's voice floated through the doorway.

"Sam, telephone!"

"Excuse me," said Sam.

In the kitchen Mrs. Appledore said rather disapprovingly, "It's Noddy Melton."

Sam picked up the phone. Behind her she could hear the landlady working at the sink. Fair enough, it was her kitchen, but if this got private, Sam would have no compunction in asking her to leave.

She said, "Hi, Mr. Melton. Sam Flood here."

"Good morning, Miss Flood," said the little man's precise voice. "How are you this morning?"

"I'm fine. How about you?"

"I'm well. It occurred to me after listening to you last evening that in some important respects the case has altered, as they say."

"Which case would that be, Mr. Melton?"

"Which indeed? You ask such good questions, Miss Flood. If you have a moment this morning, perhaps I can help you find answers to match. Any time. Good day."

Sam replaced the receiver.

"Thanks, Edie," she said.

"My pleasure. Listen, I know you're desperate for answers, but be careful when you're dealing with Noddy."

"That's more or less what you said to me that first day in the bar," said Sam.

"The difference is you've spoken with him since then, so now you'll know what I'm talking about," said Mrs. Appledore. "I daresay he's been filling you in on his own personal history of Illthwaite. Vigilante village, that's how he sees us, right? The place where they killed Billy Knipp 'cos everyone knew he was a nasty little tearaway; and got rid of my man, Artie, 'cos he wanted to sell up here and take me back to Oldham. Above all, of course, he probably hinted that they took young Mary Croft and dropped her into Mecklin Moss rather than risk her marrying the local bobby."

"He might have said something," said Sam. "If he did, what's the party line?"

"Billy Knipp came off his bike swerving to avoid a troop of boy scouts trekking along a lane he was driving down too fast. Only decent thing the lad ever did. Seventeen witnesses. As for my Artie, it was his second coronary that killed him. After the first he was told to lose weight and give up the fags. He did neither. One witness. Me."

"And Mary Croft?"

"She was another wild one. Only took up with young Noddy to disoblige her dad, who she hated. Got on well with her stepmother, though. That's why it was her she rang to say she was OK after she took off to London. God knows what she got up to down there, but a few years later, when the old man died, her stepmum sold up and went off to join her and split the inheritance. There was only about eight years between them and they settled down to run a *taberna* on the Costa Brava. Still do, from what I hear."

Sam recalled the retired policeman's story. How his eyes had misted as he described that last passionate kiss which he'd been so sure meant the girl had already decided to come to Candle Cottage on the appointed night and give herself to him. But if what Mrs. Appledore was saying were true, then its passion had been that of farewell.

"But why didn't anyone ever tell Mr. Melton?" she demanded.

"Tell him what? He was moved on not long after Mary disappeared. Did well for himself. Got married. Not much point turning up on his doorstep and telling him and his lady the truth, was there? It wasn't till he bought Candle Cottage and came back here after he retired that we realized what had been festering in his mind all these years. We should have told him then perhaps, but Mr. Dunstan said it would probably kill him. A man by himself needs a reason to get out of bed each morning and, if you take it away, he probably won't bother. Whether we were wrong or right, I don't know. But I do know you should take a big pinch of salt with you whenever you visit Candle Cottage."

"Don't worry, Edie," said Sam. "I've learned my lesson in Illthwaite. Whoever I'm talking to, I'll add salt by the bucket-load. Look, I've been thinking about what you said last night. OK, I take your word for it that Sam Flood's not in the frame. So, looking back, who do you think is? Could it have been Jim Gowder?"

Edie shook her head, in doubt rather than denial.

"He was a funny bugger, that's true. But he was genuinely broken up by Madge taking ill and dying. She was the best thing that happened to that family. Mind you, her being sick so long meant he wouldn't be getting his regular comforts, and that turns some men queer. But a kid like little Pam . . ."

"And anybody else? Was there anyone around who specially fancied kids?"

"You don't think we'd have put up with any of that!" said the landlady indignantly. "Mind you, with men there's always been some as don't much mind what age a woman is so long as she's got two legs to open."

"Yeah, we've got plenty of them too. But anyone in particular?"

Edie shook her head again.

"No one I'd put that on."

Sam was unconvinced.

"How about the vicar, Rev. Pete's father, I mean? My gran stayed at the vicarage, didn't she? So he'd have had his chances. And he was a widower, so nothing on tap."

"No! Not Rev. Paul. The way he preached he'd have had all young women corked up and all young men doctored!"

"Sounds a bit obsessive to me. And he was one of the ones keen to get my gran out of the country."

"Out of the vicarage, certainly. Getting her on that boat to Australia was mainly down to Mr. Dunstan."

"Who was a bit of a lad himself in his young days, by all accounts. And in his not-so-young days. Was it just a charitable impulse that made him elect my gran as an honorary Catholic orphan?"

"Old Dunny?" said Mrs. Appledore, aghast. "Sam, you can't go around firing off accusations in all directions."

"Why not? Let's see who runs for cover. Come on, Edie, are you saying Dunstan never tried his charms on the sexiest girl in the village?"

"Yes, well, maybe he did show an interest when I first started behind the bar. But most of them did! That's my point. I was bursting out all over from early on. When you had what I had, you soon learned it was easy to get the customers all heated up just by undoing a button and leaning forward. Dunstan was no different from the rest."

"Maybe," said Sam. "But I'll keep him on my list. Anybody else you can finger?"

"I've not fingered anyone yet, so far as I'm aware," said the landlady firmly. "You'll have to learn how to fathom men for yourself, lass. At least I'm glad to see you and Mr. Madero seem to have got things straight between you."

Jesus, thought Sam. We didn't make that much noise!

She said primly, "We are friends. But I'm not sure I can stand up to the competition, even if I wanted to."

Mrs. Appledore let out her merry laugh.

"Competition like Frek Woollass, you mean? And here's me thinking you Aussies liked a real challenge!"

This should have been jokingly flattering, but the stress had been on *real* and a hint to Sam was like an autumn leaf to a kitten.

"You saying she's a lezzie?" she pounced.

"Oh yes. Doesn't flaunt it like some. And I think she enjoys a bit of a laugh when some fellow who doesn't realize fancies her. Shall I bring you more coffee?"

"No thanks," said Sam, digesting this information. "Though if you've got a bit of that chocolate cake left . . ."

The landlady took the cake out of a cupboard and carved a generous slice.

Sam took a bite. It was even better than she remembered. Did Mig know Frek was gay? she wondered. Of course he did! she answered herself. Probably found out yesterday, which explained a lot about last night. Did it matter? Of course it didn't!

Through the crumbs she said, "Edie, I was wondering about Thor . . ."

"Now hold on! You're not suggesting . . ."

"No, no. I meant, you and him seem pretty friendly together . . ."

"And you're wondering why I didn't blame him?" said Edie, who was also pretty good at cutting to the chase. "Don't think I didn't think about it back then. Taking advantage of a kid and all that. A scapegoat's always handy when you're feeling guilty. But my whole point in everything I was in relation to Sam was that I weren't a kid, so it would have been really pathetic for me to start claiming I was just to wriggle out of my share of the blame. And to tell the truth, Thor was so ready to heap all of the blame on himself that I almost resented it! Funny things, folk, aren't we? In the end I asked him if he hated me for what I'd done. He said no, of course not, and I said I didn't hate him either. And that was the choice we had. We could either hate each other or we could take comfort together in recalling how much we both loved him. We settled for comfort."

"And that's all?"

"Has to be. We tried sex once. It was no use. We were both watching the door."

Sam nodded. She could understand that. But there were things she couldn't understand.

"So why do you think Sam came to the pub that day?"

"I told you what happened earlier," said the woman impatiently. "I'd put myself on a plate for him and he'd turned me down. Didn't stop us being in love."

"So you reckon he was coming to . . . what? Apologize and persuade you he was right? Apologize and screw you? Which?"

"You don't wrap things up, do you?" said Mrs. Appledore. "I don't know, and I doubt I ever will, not unless you've got some way of making contact with the dead!"

There was a cough from the doorway. Mig stood there and for a second Sam was tempted to reply, *Funny you should say that, Edie . . .*

"Come in, Mr. Madero. Do you fancy a piece of cake?" said Mrs. Appledore.

Sam, who'd just taken another bite, waved her slice to signal recommendation.

Mig said, "No thank you. Can I use the phone, Mrs. Appledore?"

"Surely. I'll leave you to it."

She went out. Sam made to follow her.

"It's OK," said Mig. "It's not private. I'm just ringing Max Coldstream to tell him to forget about publishing my translation of Simeon's journal."

"You're giving it back to the Woollasses then? Why?"

"It belongs to them if anybody. I can't expect other people to be honest with me unless I'm honest with them."

"You've just worked that out? Left the seminary before you reached the ethics course, did you?"

"Maybe I failed it," he said, smiling at her.

He looked so happy. She thought, oh shit. Someone else's happiness was a big responsibility.

She said, "About that spare hour, you'll have to kill it by yourself. I'm going to Candle Cottage to see Mr. Melton."

His disappointment was painful to see, but not so painful as the speed with which he tried to hide it.

"That's fine," he said. "Well, I'm sure we'll run into each other later."

He thinks it's a brush-off, she thought.

And then: if I do want to brush him off, this is a good moment.

She directed her thoughts back to the previous night.

She'd wanted company. She'd got company.

She'd wanted a diversion from her troubled thoughts more certain than Carroll's *Pillow Problems* or Goldbach's Conjecture. She'd been diverted.

And, in the end, she'd had a great time.

Again would be nice.

For her.

For him it would be commitment, which spelled complication. Mig might hop around like a wise old wallaby, but in this respect he was little more than a joey.

What the hell! she thought. So long as she enjoyed the hopping, she could deal with a bit of complication.

She said, "I'll probably come up to the Hall later. There are questions I want to ask that old bastard too."

Not enough. She saw it in his eyes.

She went to him, stood on tiptoe and kissed his cheek, leaving some cake crumbs there.

Still ambiguous, she saw. You might get as much from a nun.

Hell, if he wanted unambiguous, let him have it.

She put her hand on his inner thigh and squeezed hard.

"Keep practicing the counting," she murmured.

Then she broke away from him and half walked, half danced out of the kitchen, chewing on her slice of cake.

He watched her go, his heart bursting with delight. He wanted to run after her and suggest that without further ado they dropped everything that had brought them here to

Illthwaite and went away together. But it was easy for him, he reproved himself. The injustice to his family was five hundred years old. Her pain derived from something in living memory, and its perpetrators were probably still living also.

He put his hand to his cheek, picked off the crumbs he felt there, and licked them off his fingers.

Then he went to the phone and dialed Max Coldstream's number.

11

A villa in Spain

As Sam made her way to Candle Cottage, her super-analytical mind had plotted Madero's thought processes with a degree of accuracy which might have worried him.

He had described his efforts to subdue his natural young appetites in an entertaining way, but his comic narrative had not been able to conceal the huge expense of will which had gone into repressing and rechanneling these energies.

Now at last the fruit which his own choice had for so many years put completely out of his reach had fallen into his hands, its taste all the sweeter for the long delay (and perhaps also for a disappointment with Frek). At the moment, in the afterglow of that bliss, he could not entertain the notion that their coupling had been sinful. Indeed this experience seemed so intense that it figured as the single most important thing in his life.

She told herself he would certainly be feeling exactly the same if it had been Frek Woollass he'd been able to have his wicked way with.

Not that his way was all that wicked. Not yet. But, as she'd told him, he was a fast learner and it might be fun being his mentor.

Then, because her powers of analysis did not permit self-deceit, she took a further step back and gently mocked herself for trying to assume the safe role of experience guiding the steps of innocence.

She liked the guy!

Why? Here her powers of logical analysis failed her. He was so many things she didn't go for. Physically she preferred the blond Anglo type, like her namesake the unfortunate curate as he appeared in Winander's painting. As for the inner man, there were so many counts against him, it was hardly worth counting! He was serious, and spooky, and religious, plus he'd traveled a helluva long way down the road to becoming a Catholic priest.

She tried to imagine her pa's reaction if she took Mig home.

The wine might help. A bottle of El Bastardo to whet the appetite, followed by a couple of Vinada's gold-medal Shiraz to wash down the grub . . .

But first she'd have to get Pa to sit down at the same table, which wouldn't be easy, even though she could now assure him it definitely wasn't a priest who'd knocked up her grandmother.

She'd made no effort to contact home since her talk with Betty. She needed to get this business sorted completely before she did that. The bastard who'd abused that poor little kid had lived round here. The Gowder twins' dad seemed number one suspect, and he had gone beyond justice, at least beyond hers if not Mig's. But, dead or not, she wanted to be certain. And that was what she should be focusing her mind on now, not her own romantic entanglements.

The door of Candle Cottage stood open. She stepped into the living room, calling, "Mr. Melton, hi!"

"And hi to you too, Miss Flood."

He came out of the kitchen carrying a tray set with two mugs, a coffeepot and a plateful of biscuits, mostly dark chocolate. He'd remembered. She was touched. He might be, in the local parlance, a bit cracked, but she found she quite liked Noddy Melton. However she looked at it, she still felt it was a crying shame no one had ever told him that his lost Mary was alive and well and living in Spain. But it wasn't her call. She had enough on her plate without taking onboard that responsibility.

As she sat down, without thinking she took her sun hat off and laid it on the arm of her chair.

He regarded her skull birdlike, head cocked to one side.

"When I first joined the Force they encouraged haircuts like that," he said. "I take it the lady in Newcastle told you they cut your gran's hair off?"

"With shears," she said. Then added, "I never mentioned Newcastle."

He shrugged, self-deprecatingly. Apologetically. That was the giveaway.

She said, "And you knew I was a mathematician before I told anyone. It was you who searched my room!"

"So you did notice? Sharp. I'm sorry. I was curious. And as I think you've discovered, you need to be nimble on your feet and willing to cut corners to keep ahead of the game in Illthwaite. Sorry. But I've no way, legal or illegal, of discovering what you found out in Newcastle, not unless you care to tell me."

She told the whole story again. This was the third time. The first had been to Edie Appledore and that had been like reliving her own experience of hearing it. The second had been to Mig and that had been a kind of cathartic sharing, bringing her to a closeness which made all that followed possible.

This time it felt, perhaps not unfittingly, like a statement made to a policeman.

He nodded when she'd finished and said, "I thought it might be something like that. Not the detail but the timing. After the first time we talked, I got to thinking, there's too much going on here for there to be no connections. The name; the circumstances of the curate's death; above all, Illthwaite. The only thing which stopped it making any sense was your dates. Spring 1960. If somehow you'd got that wrong, then we'd got ourselves a whole new ball game. Everyone leaves traces, even kids. If she lived in Illthwaite even for a short time, she'd be on the school roll."

"I thought of that but the school closed down a couple of years back."

"Schools die, records don't. Oh, they might be dusty and spidery, but they'd still exist somewhere. I made a phone call. Yesterday morning I got a call back."

"Useful friends you've got," said Sam.

"Who said anything about friends?" said Melton. "You don't get to the top of most heaps without knowing where a lot of bodies are buried. Here's what I found out."

He handed her a sheet of paper. It was headed *Pamela Galley* and contained all the details she'd got from Edie Appledore.

Not wanting to downgrade his efforts, she said, "This is great."

He gave her a sharp look and said, "You knew this already, didn't you?"

"Yeah, I did. Sorry. But I'm really grateful. What else have you found out?"

"I ran a check on Jim Gowder this morning. Wife ill, sexually frustrated, young girl available in house. It's classic. The record shows convictions for drunkenness, affray and failure to pay rates. But nothing sexual. Without any background of similar offenses, you might find it hard to get him in the frame after all this time, if you made it official."

"Official? Went to the cops, you mean?"

It must have sounded as if she thought this was pretty way-out because he smiled and said gently, "You've taken a big step in that direction already, my dear. In fact, once I'm convinced an offense has taken place, I really ought to make it official myself."

"What would happen if you did?"

"Coming from me, and concerning Illthwaite, probably nothing," he said sadly. "But if *you* pressed, they'd have to take notice. On the plus side, once a prima facie case of sexual assault on a minor was established, they could require all likely suspects to supply DNA samples which would be checked against yours."

"And on the minus?"

"Publicity," said Melton. "Once the press got hold of this—and get hold of it they would; the modern police force has more leaks than a Welsh allotment—they'd be all over you, not to mention your family, as well of course as Illthwaite. Illthwaite has it coming, but it wouldn't be pleasant for your folk. You'd need to think about it."

Sam thought about it for long enough to eat two chocolate biscuits.

Finally she said, "You're right. I'd need to talk to my pa and ma first. Could the police make people give samples?"

"If they're alive and suspect, yes," he said. "With Jim Gowder they'd need either to dig him up or get the twins to volunteer a sample. As for the curate, that's more difficult as he was cremated. There's always the stones he weighed himself down with, but they're so smooth and they were under water for many hours, I'd be surprised if they helped."

Something came into Sam's mind then went out again as she said, "Doesn't matter anyway. I'm pretty sure he's not in the frame."

"You are?" He looked at her curiously. "I'm surprised. He's an obvious suspect, and in detective work, the obvious is so often right."

"Can work the other way in math," she said.

She wanted to tell him what she knew about the curate's reasons for killing himself, but it wasn't her secret to tell. She found she really was feeling bad about the old boy. He'd put himself out to help her, even bought some dark chocolate biscuits, and all she'd done was discount his number one suspect and let him know she'd discovered her grandmother's identity without his help.

"That's me done, I'm afraid," said Melton rather sadly. "I had hoped to amaze you with my discoveries and my theories, but I fear I've brought you here for nothing."

She said, "Thanks a bunch for all your trouble. And for the yummy biscuits."

"Please, have another. Or two, if you like."

"I'll take one for the road," she said, standing up and putting her hat back on. "Thanks again. Like I say, I need a long think before I make this official. I started it and it feels like I ought to see it through myself."

"Your decision," he said. "But tread carefully, my dear, before you start throwing accusations around. Get it right, someone could turn nasty. Getting it wrong can be nasty too. Remember what happened here in Candle Cottage. I still feel that poor devil's pain some dark nights when I'm sitting here alone. Good job I don't believe in ghosts!"

"Me neither," said Sam.

On the other hand, she thought, Mig Madero probably didn't believe in Hilbert space. And his spooks had got him as far along the path of revelation as her calculus.

At the front door, they stood together on the threshold and enjoyed the touch of the sun on their faces.

"Another couple of months and I'll be in permanent shadow," said Melton.

He saw the expression on her face and laughed.

"No, my dear, I'm not being morbid. I just mean that once we get into November, the sun never gets high enough to touch this end of the valley. It might bother some people, but I don't mind. Unless you lose it for a space, you can never feel the delight I feel when quite suddenly early in March I look out to see the first finger of sunlight touching my garden."

"That's lovely," exclaimed Sam. Impulsively she leaned forward and kissed the old man's dry cheek.

"Careful," he said. "You don't want to shock the vicar."

"What he doesn't see won't harm him."

"God sees everything and the vicar has a direct line to God."

"You don't like him?" asked Sam, detecting satire.

"On the contrary, I think he's a very decent man. Compared

with his father, whose main concern was what was going to happen to us miserable sinners after death, Rev. Pete concentrates on taking care of the living. He'll be missed when he's gone. And no more Swinebanks to follow. We'll probably get some menopausal matron—no offense."

"None taken," said Sam. "You said *we*. Like you feel you're one of them."

"After all my years here, how else should I feel?" he said, smiling.

"Yeah." She found herself thinking indignantly, it's not right he's never been told. Everyone's got a right to know the truth about what most concerns them. Someone ought to have told him long ago. Ought to tell him now.

His bright little eyes were fixed on her face as though seeing her thoughts.

As she opened her mouth—not yet knowing exactly what was going to come out, a not uncommon situation when the indignant fit was upon her—he put one finger up almost to her lips and said, "Yes, my dear, I shall live out the rest of my days here quite happily, an itch on the Illthwaite bottom which they might from time to time feel like scratching but which they will hardly use surgery to remove. After all, if I weren't here, keeping an eye on things, what reason would I have to get up in the morning? And where would I go? Retire to a villa in Spain perhaps to shrivel up in permanent sunshine?"

A villa in Spain!

He knows! How can he know? He can't know!

The thoughts tumbled across Sam's mind like leaves in a west wind. Again she opened her mouth, again not knowing what she would say, and again he was there first.

"Goodbye, my dear. And good luck. And use your ears. Fingerprints, DNA, these are fine, but frequently all the forensic us hardworking detectives get is words. What people say, what they don't say, what they say other people say. Look for inconsistencies. These too are tracks. The muddier we try to make them, the easier they are to follow."

Was he warning her off? She didn't know, couldn't ask. And in any case his advice, and his comments about the vicar, had brought something else to mind.

An inconsistency.

She said, "Just one thing more. About Sam Flood, the curate. Young Pete's statement said he was in his room and the curate shouted up to him that the Bible class was canceled. That was all the conversation they had, right?"

"Yes, I think so. In fact I'm sure so."

"And he didn't mention anyone else coming to the house after lunch?"

"No, definitely not. Why do you ask?"

"Just getting things straight in my mind. No big deal."

Which was probably true. If God was the last prime number, human beings were the first irrational. No, worse than that. The square root of two was an irrational number, but at least you knew that if you squared it, you got back to two. And if you wanted to actually *see* it, all you had to do was draw a pair of one-inch lines at a right angle. Human behavior, however, subscribed to no such laws. An inconsistency in a mathematical proof was fatal. But inconsistency in human evidence could mean nothing at all.

Or, as in the case of Gracie and the year of sailing, everything.

"Goodbye, Mr. Melton. Take care," she said.

"You too, my dear. I mean that. Take real care. You're exploring dangerous territory. The door to the past opens north. The devil lives there."

She went down the short garden path, out of the little wicker gate, and crossed the road. On the other side she paused and looked back.

He was still on his threshold. With his head cocked on one side and his lurid waistcoat, he resembled a robin scanning its territory for insects or intruders.

She gave him a wave. He didn't wave back but turned and went into the cottage. It was like losing sight of a friend as you embarked on a long and perilous voyage.

12

The devil's door

As Sam approached the great iron gate of St. Ylf's she saw it stood open and there was a vehicle parked outside. She'd only seen it once before but she was sure it was the Gowder twins' old pickup.

At the gateway, she hesitated. Though still without concrete evidence that one of the twins was responsible for her fall beneath the tower, she didn't relish the prospect of running into them again without witnesses. But she needed to talk to Rev. Pete. If he wasn't in the church, she'd do a quick turnaround and head back out, she promised herself.

She set out up the path. There was no sign of Gowders in the graveyard. When she reached the church door, she made sure its gothic groan came out at full pitch, and called as she pushed, "Hi there. Rev. Pete. It's me, Sam Flood."

No reply came, but there was something in the silence which gave notice of a listener as much as any words.

Taking a deep breath, she stepped inside.

The gloom wasn't anywhere near as deep as she'd expected. The reason lay straight before her.

The Devil's Door stood open.

Through it she could see the Wolf-Head Cross. Before it crouched a man.

Or perhaps, because she saw at once it was the vicar, and because it was the sacred symbol of his religion that towered above him, perhaps what she meant was *knelt* a man.

But what she thought was *crouched.*

She moved toward him, again saying, "Hi" as she passed through the Devil's Door.

He reacted to her voice, half glancing round, and by the time she got close to him he was pretty definitely kneeling.

She heard the sound of a rackety engine starting up and, looking back through the two open doors to the churchyard gate, she saw the Gowder pickup moving away.

Swinebank struggled to his feet. Sam noticed his knees were stained with grass, the price you expected to pay for outdoor praying. But to get your left shoulder and thigh in the same state required a devotional contortion not usually undertaken by Protestants.

"Miss Flood," he said, rather tremulously.

"Sorry to disturb your praying, Vicar, if that's what you were doing . . . ?"

She let the question hang.

He tried a smile and said, "You must think me eccentric, but it is a cross, after all . . ."

She looked up at the towering artifact and the wolf grinned back down at her.

"Maybe," she said. "Though to me it looks the kind of thing you're more likely to slit a goat's throat in front of than do a Christopher Robin. You OK?"

"Yes. Yes, I am. Is there something I can help you with?" he said in a peremptory tone which sounded more affected than real.

She shrugged. If his sermons were so bad his parishioners beat up on him, it was none of her business.

She said, "I wanted to ask you something about what happened a long time ago. More than forty years. The day my namesake, Sam Flood the curate, topped himself."

She admitted she might have phrased it better, but his reaction seemed over the top. There was anger on his face, and loathing. It took her a moment to realize they weren't directed at herself.

She said, "I'm sorry if I'm bringing back bad memories. I know all about them, how they can hurt. There's just something I need to clear up . . . about Mr. Flood . . ."

"I killed him, you know," he said abruptly.

Jesus! she thought. Not another one taking on responsibility for Saint Sam's death!

"I don't think so," she said gently. "He was on the edge and he went over, no one's fault, certainly not yours."

"What do you know about it?" he demanded.

"Not much, but at least I'm trying to bring stuff to light," she retorted.

He stood stock-still for a moment then said, "You're quite right. Light, it's time for light. Keeping things hidden never does any good. Like Sam's memorial. All that grows up as cover is filthy weeds!"

He went to the wall behind the cross and started dragging out the briars and nettles. Soon his hands were red and bloody, but he didn't stop till the inscription was clear.

"There," he said, standing back. "It's been too long. I'm glad you came back, Miss Flood. When I heard you'd gone away, I felt relieved. But I knew it was only a respite. Like a calm patch in the middle of a storm. You take a deep breath and you think, well, that wasn't so bad. But you know inside that the storm's only taking a breather too and will be back at you before you know it. Shall we go into the church and sit down and talk?"

His voice was calm, the calm of acceptance, of submission even. But Sam recalled Melton's warning not to take risks.

"Out here and standing suits me fine," she said.

While she was pretty certain most of Swinebank's anger was directed at himself, you never knew precisely where you were with these religious guys. Except maybe Mig. OK, perhaps she was silly to make an exception just because she liked the guy and had slept with him, but somehow she was pretty sure he wouldn't hear the voice of God telling him, *It's sacrifice time, and if you don't have a goat, a redheaded girl will do!*

Rev. Pete she wasn't so sure about. Pretty sure, but not enough to want to go into that dark scary church with him. Out here she reckoned she could leave a guy in skirts for dead from a standing start.

"Very well. Before our Wolf-Head Cross. That may be fitting."

She followed his gaze.

There it stood, packed full of messages from the past, maybe messages for the future. She thought on the whole most religions were crap, but religion wasn't the same as belief. They called this a Viking cross. She didn't know a lot about Vikings but she had a picture of them as large bold-faced men, doers not dreamers, undaunted by ferocious storms and mountainous seas, always ready for a scrap. What they believed in must have derived from what they were, and when they settled here they'd decided this cross would make a necessary statement of that belief. So there it was, paying lip service to the rules and repressions of this new intangible god who'd crept up from the south with the insidious inevitability of global warming, but at bottom making a plain statement of things as they were, an assertion of their own individuality, as true and uncompromising as a mathematical proof.

Her heart jolted in her breast at the feeling that finally the time of truth was close.

But her voice was calm as she said, "Pete, let's start at the beginning, shall we? Couple of questions first to get you going. Why didn't you tell the police that Edie Appledore had been visiting Sam the day he died? And what was it you went to his room to talk about?"

He turned to look at her almost with exasperation, as if she were interfering in some well-ordered, perfectly thought-out scheme.

"Oh no," he said. "The day Sam died wasn't the beginning. The beginning was when little Pam Galley, your grandmother, was orphaned and came to live with the Gowders. Or maybe it was when Madge Gowder was diagnosed with cancer. Or maybe it was the day she gave birth to the twins."

"They were here when I arrived, weren't they?" said Sam. "What were they doing? Threatening you?"

Some certainties just arrive, and then you spend days at the blackboard working out where they came from.

"Yes, they were here," said Swinebank dismissively. "It's not important."

He had, she realized, a story to tell, a story which had been bursting to come out for decades. At last its time was close and he was impatient for the moment of release.

"OK," said Sam. "Shoot."

He closed his eyes. Was he saying a prayer? And if he were, what for?

His eyes opened and fixed themselves on her face and he began speaking.

13

Pete Swinebank

Let's start with Pam Galley coming over to Skaddale from Eskdale. That was in the autumn of 1960, not long after Sam Flood started here as curate. She came to the village school with the twins. She fitted in all right, didn't talk a lot. We watched the way the twins treated her. That was the touchstone of survival for us lads. So long as you didn't cross the Gowders, you'd be all right. They weren't cruel to her or anything. They just treated her like she was some kind of animated doll. She did more or less exactly what they told her. Sometimes they'd play silly tricks on her, like telling her to stand out in the rain during playtime while the rest of us were sheltering. But it was too easy to be fun for long. Generally they just ignored her.

Not long after she came to Illthwaite, she started menstruating. The twins knew, living in the same house, and they told us. They were our sexual mentors. Living in the country, you pick up on the animal basics pretty early, but when it came to translating the facts of life from the byre to the bedroom, it was the Gowders who spelled things out. Sometimes their spelling was pretty terrible. If you did it standing up, the girl couldn't get pregnant, and if you did it in the churchyard, your willy would fall off, that sort of thing. But no one ever argued.

They stated pretty authoritatively that once a girl started bleeding, she was ready for tupping. Their word. Not that little Pam offered any incentive to tupping compared with some of the other more developed girls. And not that any of us boys had much real notion of the mechanics of human tupping, apart from some very confused and overheated fantasies. This was 1960. In rural Cumberland, it might as well have been 1930.

The Gowders I should say have never seemed very personally involved with sex, either as adolescents or grown men. Maybe it's because they've always formed a sort of self-contained unit. They were only interested in sex because they saw how much most of the rest of us were fascinated by it, so being the acknowledged experts gave them yet another form of dominance.

Midway through December Madge Gowder, the twins' mother, who'd been poorly for a long time, took really ill. It was cancer. They said reassuring things to the kids, of course, but all the adults must have known she was dying. It was a bright hard spell, lots of sun but very cold. We used to go up on Mecklin Moor to play. It's a wild place, there's lots of old stone circles up there, and lots of wild legends about what went on in them. And of course there's the Moss, where on a dark and misty night they say the ghosts of every creature that's drowned there come out to taste the air again.

Not far above the Foulgate track before you reach the Moss itself there's a place where two rock slabs have rolled together to form a sort of cave, and this was the spot us lads thought of as our den.

That day in January 1961—it must have been the first week, we still weren't back at school—there were five of us up there. Me, the Gowders, Pam Galley, and Gerry Woollass.

Here in Illthwaite the squire's children had always gone to the village school till they were eleven or twelve and then moved on to boarding school. There was no distinction made in lessons, but in the playground, maybe because I was the vicar's son, Gerry and I often kept pretty close together. The twins could easily have persecuted us for being different. Instead, maybe because it demonstrated their supremacy even more, they made us subordinates in their gang. It was an invitation you didn't refuse. In fact I felt quite excited and privileged as I swore a rather bloodthirsty oath of fealty and secrecy about all the gang's activities.

We brought some bits of wood for a fire, knowing we'd not find much up on the moor, and soon we had a decent blaze going. We pooled what scraps of food we had to make a picnic—some biscuits, a bit of cheese, a bar of chocolate—and the twins had brought a bottle of beer and a bottle of cider and some cigarettes. With Foulgate being a house of sickness, they'd been able to raid their father's drink store without being noticed. They'd also got a magazine which I presume belonged to him too. By contemporary standards, it was pretty innocuous, but the photos it contained of nude women posing with beach balls, that sort of thing, set our young minds swooning.

Then one of the Gowders asked if we'd ever seen the real thing. We had to admit we hadn't. And he said, would we like a look? Not knowing quite what he meant, me and Gerry said, yes, we wouldn't mind. And the twin turned his head and called to Pam.

We'd almost forgotten she was there. I think she'd been given some squares of chocolate and she just sat a little way behind us, dead quiet, waiting till the twins would take her home.

When the twin told her to take her clothes off, she looked at him blankly.

Then he said something like, it's all right, you won't get cold, here make room for her by the fire. And it was as if that was a kind of reassurance, as if the only thing to worry about was being cold. So she took her clothes off.

For me there was little or no connection between the women

in the pictures and this skinny little scrap of white flesh shivering by the fire. I don't think the Gowders were particularly aroused either. Like I said, they never showed much direct personal interest in girls. They were more like farmers showing off a prize yow at a show. But Gerry Woollass was different. Maybe he was more developed than the rest of us, or maybe he'd had more than his share of the cider and beer and tobacco. But it was clear that he was excited.

When they saw this, one of the twins said, "Would you like to touch her? You can if you like. You can touch her with your thing if you like."

Again, I think it just amused them to get the squire's boy so completely out of his own control and into theirs. The girl was just a means to an end.

After that things moved very quickly. Little Pam didn't struggle, she just did what the twins told her. Gerry was so excited it didn't last long. The mere act of pushing into her set him off. She screamed but not too loud, choking it back as if she didn't want to anger the twins. Gerry made more noise than she did. In the space of less than a minute it was all over, Gerry was buttoning himself up, Pam lay there quiet, but there were tears on her cheeks. And drops of blood on her legs.

I just sat and watched. I had a sense that something terrible was happening, but I wasn't a brave child. I'm not making excuses. I was what they call nowadays a bit of a wimp. I suppose that was what made me willing to put up with any indignities the Gowders heaped upon me. Being one of their gang meant the other boys treated me with respect.

So I was very willing to let myself be reassured by the way the Gowders acted afterward. They told Pam to get dressed, even helped her. And they gave her the rest of the chocolate and borrowed Gerry's handkerchief so she could dry her eyes and wipe her legs, and they threw the rest of our little store of fuel on the fire, and talked about our plans for the rest of the day as if nothing had happened.

Gerry suddenly stood up and said it was getting late, he had to go home.

He didn't look well. I think that maybe with him being brought up a strict Catholic, some notion of having committed a dreadful sin was already eating away at his mind. I could understand this. There was plenty of hellfire preaching in my upbringing, and behind all that reassurance I was letting myself feel, I think I too was already feeling the heat of those diabolical flames. I heard myself saying I was expected back at the vicarage too.

One of the twins said indifferently, "Off you both go then, long as you don't forget the gang promise."

Some threats don't need to be spelled out.

But some guilt is stronger than any threat.

Gerry didn't return to the village school for the following term. It was said his parents had decided he needed to be tutored privately to make sure he was fully prepared for starting at his boarding school in the autumn. I was too naive to suspect then that it had anything to do with what had happened. All I knew was I was left without anyone to talk to. Worse, I was left without having in view someone I could think of as the real culprit, which was a thought I might have been able to shelter behind when I started worrying about hellfire.

As for Pam, someone might have noticed something if she'd been returning to a normal household. But Foulgate had been a house of sickness for some time. And on that dreadful day, from what I've been able to piece together, when Pam got back to the farm, she must have made her way straight up to Madge's bedroom. Perhaps she wanted to tell her what had happened. Who knows? Certainly Madge would have been the only person Pam would have turned to.

It doesn't matter anyway. All I know is that when someone else went into the room a little time later, they found Pam sitting by the bed, holding a dead woman's hand.

Children back then were required to be seen and not heard

at the best of times. At the worst of times, they were expected to be invisible as well. Pam Galley was always a particularly quiet child. If anyone actually noticed any extra sign of withdrawal or distress, they had more than enough explanation for it in this second grievous loss following on in pretty close proximity to the death of her own parents.

Me, I tried to forget. Things weren't helped when some time later Sam Flood, our curate, insisted on bringing little Pam out of the Gowder house and settling her in the vicarage until such time as her future could be decided. I can recall overhearing fierce arguments between Sam and my father and Mrs. Thomson, our housekeeper. I would have put money on my father and Mrs. Thomson winning any argument—they both terrified me—but Sam wouldn't let himself be beaten down, and to my horror I came down one morning to find Pam sitting at the breakfast table.

At school, the Gowders didn't talk about what had happened either, but they kept me pretty close, and made it clear that resigning from the gang wasn't an option. To Pam at school they were as pleasant as it lay in their natures to be, but she didn't even seem aware of their existence. Not that this was noteworthy as she didn't show much awareness of anyone else's existence either. The teachers and everyone were really worried about her, and when word got round that one of Mr. Dunstan's religious charities had found a place for her with a family in Australia, everyone was delighted, saying things like that was what she needed, a complete change of scene and a settled family background, weren't we lucky that the squire was such a man of influence? Everyone except Sam Flood, that is. He was still asking questions, and raising objections, but finally even he got persuaded, and Pam vanished from Illthwaite.

You'd have thought that Pam's removal would have made things easier for me but it didn't work like that. On the contrary, I found things got worse and worse. At least having her around gave me the reassuring visual evidence that she appeared to be just the same as ever. But now she'd moved out of my sight into my imagination.

I would be woken in the night by the sound of that one scream she let out. And then I'd lie there listening to the silence. Her silence. Eventually I started to find that any silence that stretched for more than a couple of minutes became her silence, as if she were close by, withdrawn, suffering, but always present.

If my father had been a different sort of man, I would have spoken to him. But I knew what to expect if I did and that was one fear I had no strength to overcome.

The obvious alternative was Sam Flood.

He was a man from whom loving kindness emanated almost visibly.

His concern in the business of Pam's future was always to find what was best for the girl, what would give her the best chance of happiness. My father, on the other hand, urged on by Mrs. Thomson, wanted nothing but to get her out of our house and our lives. As for Squire Dunstan, even then I had serious doubts about the purity of his motives. Fair enough, this Australian business might be a genuine opportunity for the girl, but it was also a great chance to move a potential source of embarrassment to his family to the other side of the globe.

Of course I had no idea she was pregnant, and I don't see how he could have known either.

Sam was caring, involved, fearless, and also my friend. He was the first adult I knew who treated me as an equal.

Even with all this going for him, it took a long time for me to pluck up courage to speak. I could only guess at the consequences, and nothing in my guess was good for me. The anger of my father, the wrath of the Gowder twins, the possible involvement of the police—these were likely to follow and these I would have to bear.

If I could have foreseen the actual outcome, I would probably have held my tongue forever.

I looked for a good moment, kept on finding excuses to decide this time or that wasn't ripe, and finally on that Sunday, almost without thinking, having seen my father and Mrs. Thomson leave for the church to take Sunday School, I went to Sam's room and banged at his door.

It was Edie Appledore who opened it. I think if she'd stayed I would probably have lost my nerve and kept quiet. But she just pushed right by me and went straight down the stairs, and I started talking and told Sam everything in one incoherent burst.

At first he just looked at me blankly as if he wasn't taking it in. But finally what I was saying seemed to register and he sat me down and made me go through it again.

He was very calm on the surface but I could see that, underneath, my story had had a powerful effect on him.

All he said to me, however, was, "Thank you for telling me this, but I wish you'd spoken sooner. Never postpone a good act, Pete."

I felt hugely rebuked. I suppose I had looked for absolution, even reward for my courage in speaking. Not that I felt brave. The minute I got it off my chest, I started thinking about the Gowders.

Sam told me to go back to my room, he needed to be alone to think.

After maybe fifteen minutes, he tapped at my door and told me he would be canceling the Bible class as he had to go out.

Fearfully I asked him what he intended doing about what I'd told him.

He said there was someone he wanted to talk to first, then he'd decide.

And he left.

About ten minutes later the doorbell rang. I opened the door to discover the Gowders. It was like finding the Furies on your doorstep! I must have gone pale as death, but they greeted me as they usually did and said they'd come for the Bible class but, seeing it was canceled, wondered if I'd like to come out to play.

If I'd had the slightest suspicion they knew I'd been talking to Sam, I would have slammed the door in their faces. But they seemed so normal, and I thought it would just make them suspicious if I said no, and I didn't want to be around the house when my father returned and started asking questions about Sam's reasons for canceling the Bible class, so I said yes and went with them.

What a mistake! A moment's thought would have told me they must have encountered Sam on their way to the vicarage, and that he was unlikely not to have taken the chance to try and double-check my tale.

I found out the truth as soon as we were up on the moor, well out of sight and earshot of the village. One of them seized me from behind, the other put his face close to mine and demanded to know what I'd told the curate.

At first, in my fear, I tried to claim ignorance of what they meant. I got punched in the stomach for my pains. I then started telling them some watered-down version, and in the midst of this I took advantage of a weakened grip to break free and make a dash for it up the fell. Over twenty yards I was the quicker, but as I slowed they came on relentlessly. I decided that there was no future in trying to flee uphill so I turned and started racing down the steep slope, leaping from boulder to boulder till inevitably I missed my footing and went crashing to the ground. When I tried to push myself up, I realized I had damaged my wrist and done something very unpleasant to my ankle.

Worse, I was back in the Gowders' clutches.

With the way I was feeling, further threats were unnecessary. I told them exactly what I had said to the curate. After which they conferred for a while before telling me I should keep my mouth shut from now on and try to take back as much as I could next time I saw Sam. Failure to keep silent this time would result in further accidents which would make my present pains feel like a French kiss.

And then they helped me back to the vicarage.

The district nurse was summoned. She said I should be got to the hospital instantly for X rays. They kept me in overnight, and by the time the police got round to talking to me, I knew all about poor Sam's death.

Now I had even more on my conscience.

It seemed clear to me it was my fault. He must have felt the horror of my story so much that his mind flipped.

When the police talked to me, my father was present. They didn't stay long. I got very upset. And I said nothing beyond the bare facts that Sam had told me the class was canceled so I went out to play. How could I say more with my father there and the threat of the Gowders waiting outside?

So began my second silence, which I thought might last forever till I came into the church the other day and saw you standing by the font with water dripping from your hair, like a revenant from a shipwreck.

Which is what you are, Miss Flood. A ghost come back to haunt us. A ghost come back to tell us our crime was even more terrible than we knew. A ghost come back to summon us all to judgment. May God have mercy on our souls.

PART SIX

THE HALL

Check every doorway before choosing your entrance.
There's no way of knowing
what foes may be hiding in hall at the table.
You can't be too careful.

"The Sayings of the High One" *Poetic Edda*

1

Up a gum tree

When he arrived at the Hall, it seemed to Mig Madero that the wolf-head knocker looked keener than ever to bite the hand that touched it, but he was saved from putting it to the test.

As he reached forward, the door swung open. Mrs. Collipepper stood there.

"Good morning," he said. "I have an appointment. With Mr. Dunstan."

"Then you'd better come in," she said.

She led him into the house and up the stairs. As he followed he found himself observing as on his previous visit the rhythmic rise and fall of her buttocks, and there came into his mind a picture of her naked, on her knees, heavy breasts penduling, as she retrieved the scarlet robe from the floor.

He was delighted to observe it didn't have the slightest effect on him. Whereas if he let his thoughts slip to a certain skinny figure with less flesh on it than one of the housekeeper's thighs, it was amazing how quickly his thoughts became very languid indeed . . .

It was both with relief and reluctance that he found himself hauled back to the here and now by the sound of a savage blow being dealt to the study door by Mrs. Collipepper's fist.

When there was no reply she hammered again.

"He sometimes falls asleep," she observed over her shoulder, as if feeling some explanation were needed.

"That must be inconvenient," Mig heard himself responding.

She turned those watchful gray eyes on him, as if in search of innuendo.

"At times," he added. Which only made things worse.

He found he was storing up the story to tell Sam.

He was saved from further ill-judged attempts at mitigation by a voice crying, "Come in!"

Mrs. Collipepper opened the door and announced, "Mr. Madero."

Mig stepped by her, saying as he passed, "Thank you very much."

"That's OK. Sorry about your sherry," she said. Then rather spoiled the apology by adding as she moved away, "Too sour for a trifle anyway."

There was, he thought, in the history of this woman material for . . . what? A romance? A comedy? A tragedy? A social history?

Dunstan said, "Have a seat, Madero. I trust I find you well today."

He was seated at the desk on which lay a scatter of papers. He was fully dressed despite the, for him, early hour. But his face looked rather drawn, as if he had paid a price for this interruption to his usual routine.

"I'm very well," said Mig.

"And the Australian girl?"

"She is well too."

"I'm glad to hear it. She stayed at the Stranger, I take it?"

"Yes," said Mig shortly, keen to get off this subject.

"And did she reveal to you any further details about the cause of her distress?"

"Why should she make a confidant of someone she met only two days ago?" asked Mig with a disingenuousness the Jesuits would have been proud of.

It didn't seem to work.

"Extreme experience in foreign places often throws strangers together," said Dunstan. "Thus travelers encountering in the wilderness would huddle close at night for comfort and protection. In view of what you have both discovered since arriving here, it would not be surprising if you and Miss Flood felt an impulse to huddle together. I speak figuratively, of course."

There was no insinuating note in his voice, but Mig felt his cheeks growing warm under that keen slate-eyed gaze, and suddenly Dunstan smiled as if at a spoken admission.

"Mr. Madero, forgive me. I had no thought of embarrassing you. Nor indeed should you be embarrassed. Youth's the season made for joy, and the Church would be completely out of touch with reality if it didn't admit and make allowances for that."

How the devil have we got here? Mig asked himself in amazement. Silence is admission, but denial would feel like treachery!

Dunstan was still talking: "It certainly seems from all reports that Miss Flood has an engaging if original personality, plus, as you indicated last evening, a First in mathematics from some colonial establishment and a placement at Cambridge. Do you happen to know which college?"

"Trinity," said Mig shortly, wanting to move off this topic.

"Very fitting. The alma mater of Newton. Also, though rather less noteworthy, of myself. I should like very much to make her acquaintance. Perhaps I could call on your good offices to arrange an introduction . . . ?"

He really is like an old Prince of the Church, thought Mig. Worldly-wise, insinuating in courtesy, evasive in debate, and almost certainly ruthless in decision.

"Mr. Woollass," he said, determined to get away from Sam and back to his own affairs, "I have something for you here."

From his briefcase he took Father Simeon's journal and laid it on the table.

Dunstan glanced at it with what looked like token interest and said, "Of course. The journal. I thank you. And I too have something which I feel might interest you."

He picked a large leather-bound volume off his desk.

"I think I mentioned this to you at our first meeting. My grandfather Anthony's history of this part of Cumberland. He acted, you will recall, as assistant to Peter Swinebank in the preparation of his *Guide*, sparking a lifelong interest in the highways and byways of the past. You will have read the Reverend Peter's account in the *Guide* of the waif boy whom Thomas Gowder took into his care, which kindness he repaid by murdering the husband and ravishing the wife? That this youth is the same fugitive whom my ancestors aided in their turn now seems very probable. And after long thought, I find I am happy to accept your intuition that he was your ancestor."

"Thank you," said Mig. "And I hope we can both take as given Miguel's account of what really happened at Foulgate that night."

"Oh yes. In fact, as I was about to point out, the inhabitants of Skaddale had a deal too much common sense to take as gospel anything a neighbor like Andrew Gowder asserted. Which brings me to my grandfather. His *History* is more concerned with the broad sweep of events and their philosophical analysis rather than domestic particularities. In the main body of his text, the incident wins no more than a passing reference. He was however one of those scholars who cannot bear that anything, once discovered, should be lost. A large proportion of his book takes the form of footnotes which are generally, I fear, much more engaging than his central argument. There is one such note here in which he says . . ."

He opened the book at a marked page and, using a magnifying glass, began to read a footnote in minuscule print which Mig could see occupied nearly half of a page.

"Though the present writer is only concerned with matters of broad interest in the development of the county supported by proper documentary evidence, it is often helpful to our understanding of the atmosphere of any given time and place to note the extremes of local rumor and legend, especially when as here they stand in mutual contradiction.

"One such rumor asserted that the waif boy was in fact a thirty-year-old emissary of Philip of Spain, selected because his youthful appearance might aid him to pass unchallenged, and sent to make contact with the disaffected Roman Catholics of northern England and offer financial and military assistance in any proposed rebellion. Ship-wrackt on the Cumbrian coast, he played the innocent child till such time as he might find a way to pursue his mission.

"The counter story was that the boy was truly nothing more than a gypsy by-blow, politically entirely insignificant.

"What is undisputed is that, some dispute having arisen between him and his master, possibly involving Mistress Jenny Gowder, he knocked Thomas to the ground and fled in fear. Upon which (the local gossips whispered) Andrew Gowder, the younger brother, known to be fearful lest Thomas's marriage to a young and healthy woman should eventually produce a surviving heir and deprive his own sons of their claim on the farm, seized the opportunity to slit his brother's throat and then pursue, capture and despatch the alleged culprit before he could speak in his own defense.

"Thus we have on one side domestic rivalry, on the other international espionage, the whole issue muddied by what some held was divine or diabolical intervention when the fugitive's body vanished after the alleged crucifixion.

"Is it possible there may be some connection here with

the recorded capture in July 1589 of a 'Spanish emissary' in Lancaster where he lay awaiting passage out of the country? He died under torture, though not before he had allegedly confessed to having spent some months in the North spreading sedition. Names were mentioned, but none that had not already come under the gravest suspicion. Some indeed were already held and later executed. This suggests that this 'confession' was in fact one of those frequently cobbled together by the interrogator (in this case the notorious pursuivant, Tyrwhitt) to cover the fact that his too vigorous approach has resulted in the death of his victim before any truly significant information could be extracted."

He finished reading and looked up at Mig.

"It is unfortunate," he said dryly, "that as well as sparking an interest in local history in my grandfather, the Reverend Peter also seems to have passed on his rather ponderous style. I'm sure, however, that you picked up on the significant elements here. Exculpation of your ancestor. And the reference to our mutual friend, Francis Tyrwhitt."

Mig's gaze met the old man's. What a portrait this would make, he thought. The young man eager for knowledge being led forward by the old tutor intent on passing on the torch of learning which he has tended all his long years . . .

Load of crap, he heard a shrill Australian voice say in his mind. The old bastard's chasing you up a gum tree. So grab your chance and piss on him!

He said, "I brought along the document this morning because I believe that returning it to its rightful owner is the only honest way to proceed. I hope that you will agree and now do the same with the document that you removed from the Jolley archive."

Once more, just as he tried to grab the initiative, the old man slid away from him. Instead of the expected indignant denial, Dunstan's response was a delighted, "Bravo! You've worked it out. But do let me hear your exquisite reasoning. I love to follow the workings of a fine mind."

It was hard not to feel flattered.

Mig said, "It's been clear from the start that you know a great deal more about everything than the rest of your family. It was this knowledge that made you curious to see me when Gerald was reluctant to let anyone stick their nose into Woollass family business after the visit of Liam Molloy."

"The Irishman. Yes, I recall. Sad business."

"Sad for him, certainly. But I asked myself two questions. The first was, why should Molloy have come here unless he felt sure there was something to find? And the second was, why should you have been so untroubled by the prospect of my visit unless you were certain there was nothing for me to find? A large part of the answer in both cases was Jolley Castle."

Again there was no protest, just an encouraging nod.

"Molloy had been to Jolley," Mig went on. "I think what he found there was a detailed account of the interrogation of Father Simeon and its outcome. This is what brought him first to Kendal then to Illthwaite in search of any other information he might be able to garner to add even more spice and color to his story."

"How fascinating. But you've hardly had time to visit Jolley yourself to confirm the presence of this document, or even its absence," said Dunstan.

"I've done better than that. Max Coldstream got Lilleywhite, the new archivist, to burrow. Alas, he could find nothing relating to Tyrwhitt's torture of Simeon."

"A pity. Still, it's early days, especially with the archive in such a state of confusion," said Dunstan consolingly.

"Confusion? I didn't mention confusion. But of course, you'd know that because you went to see for yourself, didn't you, Mr. Woollass? The family were happy to let accredited researchers in, thinking perhaps that their occasional efforts might impose some kind of order without the expense of hiring a professional archivist to do the job. Well, they were wrong. And now the National Trust is having to pay handsomely. But amidst all the confusion left by the Jolleys was one little island of order: a box file containing letters requesting permission to trawl through their papers. Molloy's letter is there. And so, I learned when I talked to Max on the phone this morning, is yours, dated only a week or so after poor Molloy's accident."

Once more Dunstan cried, "Bravo! How well you have done. Now, let me see . . . yes, I've got it. Your conclusion is that, just as special circumstances made you feel justified in removing Father Simeon's journal from its hiding place, so I was justified in my removal of a section of Tyrwhitt's record. What will the world make of such a pair of *pícaros*?"

It was an ingenious *tu quoque* rejoinder which left Mig for the moment uncertain where to go.

Finally he opted for the politician's route.

When in doubt, be indignant.

"There's a significant difference," he said. "In fact and in law. I have restored Simeon's journal to the person with best claim to ownership. Whereas you . . ."

"Yes?"

"What have you done with the Tyrwhitt record? Burned it?"

"Good Lord. You think me such a vandal?" said Dunstan.

He even does indignation better than me, thought Mig.

"I don't know what you may be capable of. If not burned, then you'll certainly have taken care to hide it so well that no one will ever be able to discover it as evidence of your crime."

This sounded so forced and bombastic even to himself that he could not blame the old man for the flicker of amusement that touched his thin lips.

"Ah, the pleasures of being outraged! I remember them well though nowadays I enjoy them but rarely, having been warned by my medical advisor that undue excitation could rapidly summon me to a far more terrible judgment than any you can pass."

Does *undue excitation* cover your lunchtime siestas with Mrs. Collipepper? Mig wondered. A slow smile spread across Dunstan's face as though he heard the thought, and Mig felt himself flushing once more.

Forcing himself to speak calmly, he said, "There is no witness present and I assure you I haven't come along equipped with a hidden recorder. So perhaps at the least you would do me the kindness of telling me what the Jolley document contained."

"My dear young man, what do you take me for? You are as entitled to view the document as I am entitled to see the one you purloined. You're quite right. I have hidden it, but, *à la* Poe, in plain view."

He picked up a transparent protective folder from the desk.

"Here it is. Not hugely significant in the great scheme of things, in fact only of any real interest to those directly concerned, such as our two families. Take a look. I would value your opinion."

He put the open folder into Mig's hand.

Anyone who trumped you so effortlessly at every turn, you either had to hate or to admire, thought Mig ruefully. He hadn't yet made up his mind.

He opened the folder and began to read.

2

Like a dingo

Sam Flood moved at a pace which came close to being a trot down the center of the road leading from St. Ylf's to the Stranger House.

She was a missile in search of a target but not yet able to read the code in which its program was written.

After he'd finished speaking, Swinebank had broken the eye contact maintained throughout his story, turned away, and looked down at the memorial inscription.

Sam remained stock-still for what felt like an age. She had seen the look on the man's face before he turned. Shame had been there, and regret; but also huge relief that at last he had unburdened himself of his corrosive secret.

Deep resentment that he should be finding ease in what was causing her so much pain restored her movement in the form of an anger whose force set her body shaking.

"And that's it?" she burst out. "Nearly half a century for your second silence, and now you're starting in on your third?"

Swinebank turned back and looked at her helplessly.

"What more can I say? Ask me anything you like, I'll try to answer. I've got no excuses to offer. Not for myself anyway. Just heartfelt apology. To you above all. And your family. And to my parishioners. I've let them down too. All these years they've felt they shared the blame for the death of the best man they ever knew. He came among us for a while but we weren't anywhere near good enough to keep him here, that's what they think, that's why they clammed up when you started asking questions about someone called Sam Flood."

Suddenly Sam was sick to death of hearing about her namesake.

"Sam Flood, saintly Sam, that's all I ever hear from you people!" she said. "You think it was his tender bloody heart trying to cope with all the wickedness he saw that made him top himself, don't you? Well, you'd better get disenchanted! It was a lot closer to home than that. It was catching his best mate screwing his best girl that tipped him over. Yeah, something as banal and commonplace as that. Sexual betrayal. If you're a Latin lover, you kill them both! If you're an English curate, you kill yourself! Either way you don't end up getting canonized!"

She realized Swinebank was looking at her in amazement. She'd let out Edie and Thor's secret without thinking. But so what? They were both adults, they could take it. It was time for all of Illthwaite's sordid little secrets to see the light of day.

She went on with undiminished force.

"He was a grown man, he could make choices. It's my gran who's the only real victim here. She was just a kid. She got raped and nobody noticed. She got posted off like a fucking parcel to the other side of the world and nobody gave a toss. And when she got there, she got treated worse than shit, and still not a single hand was lifted to defend her. That's what you should be feeling guilty about. I can survive living in a world where some nutty parson tops himself. It's living in a world where what happened to kids like my gran can happen that makes me want to spew my guts!"

"I don't understand," said Swinebank. "What are you saying?"

He was looking bewildered, but there was something else there too.

Sam thought, I've given the bastard hope. He's thinking, maybe Saint Sam's death wasn't his fault after all!

She forced herself to think rationally. Make sure you've got all the equations worked out on the board before you let go.

She said, "Why didn't you tell anyone you'd seen Edie in Flood's room?"

He said, "I did. I told Dunstan Woollass."

"Woollass? Not your father?"

He laughed. There was no humor in it, a little sadness, a lot of bitterness.

"I told him the story about going out to play and having an accident. When he came to see me in the hospital next day, he told me that Sam was dead. He said he expected the police would want to interview me and he asked if I had anything else to say. I said no. That's where my father got his ministry wrong. He made himself more terrifying than God. But after he'd gone, Mr. Woollass came to see me. It was easy talking to him, especially as he knew all about everything . . ."

"How? How did he know?"

"Gerry had told him. Once I realized he knew what had happened, it all came out. When I ended by saying it was me who was responsible for Sam killing himself, he was marvelous. He said there must have been things going on in Sam's mind we didn't know about. He said that all men have secrets they want to keep. Like me, like my secret. Some men were strong and could keep them and lead a good life even if their secret was bad. My secret wasn't very bad, he said. I'd just been a witness. Gerry had been punished, both his father on earth and his Father in heaven had seen to that. And Pam had been taken care of. As for the Gowders, he'd deal with them. It wasn't my secret that had made the curate kill himself. It was his own."

"He said that?" Sam was puzzled. Intrigued too. This old guy she still hadn't met seemed to hover over everything that went on in Illthwaite. Maybe he was indeed the heavenly as well as the earthly father! "And did he give any hint what the curate's own secret might have been?"

Swinebank said, "He said he didn't know, no one could truly know another man's thoughts. But it must have had something to do with not being as good as he wanted to be, as other people thought he was. I'd told him about seeing Edie there, and he said it probably had something to do with this. Sex was one of the most pleasurable routes to hell, he said, but it got you there just the same. But now poor Sam was dead and beyond our judgment. And unless Edie herself came forward and told about her visit to the vicarage, it would be a kindness to her, and a help to Sam's memory, for me not to say anything about it. Edie kept quiet, so I did too. God forgive me for being so weak."

He looked so pathetic that Sam's scornful rejoinder died in her throat. He'd been eleven years old, terrified by his father, soft-soaped by Dunstan Woollass. They were the real villains who got little Pam Galley out of their hair by parceling her off to Oz.

Swinebank was still desperate to compound confession with explanation.

He said, "I've tried to atone. I've devoted my life since to giving this parish the loving side of my faith that my father chose to ignore—"

"You're bringing the tears to my eyes," interrupted Sam. "You'll be telling me next Gerry Woollass has been devoting his life to good works too."

"In fact, he has," said Swinebank. "And in face of much personal grief. His wife left him, and his daughter has turned her back on his faith in every way possible. If atonement isn't possible, there's not much point to the existence of either of us. After your revelation last night, I cannot imagine how he's feeling now."

"You can't? You think the news that when he raped a kid all those years ago he not only got her pregnant but caused her death too might have put him off his breakfast?"

She glared at him, promising herself, if he says anything more about atonement I'll nut him!

He said, "Gerry must answer for himself. No man can read another's heart. We all must make our own decisions."

"And what decision were you going to make if I hadn't turned up?" she demanded. "Public confession? Even though the Gowders were putting the silencers on you again? That's why they were here, wasn't it?"

He said, "They are worried. They reacted. Action, reaction. That sums up the Gowders, morally, intellectually. Judging them by normal standards doesn't work. But they're not altogether bad."

"That's very Christian of you, Pete," she said. "It's up to you if you want to forgive them for breaking your wrist when you were a kid and shoving you around this morning to make sure you continued to keep quiet. But when it comes to forgiving them for making my gran strip and egging on Woollass to rape her, I don't think it's your call. Where've they gone now? To give Gerry Woollass a kicking to make sure he doesn't talk?"

"I doubt it," he said wearily. "They rely on old Dunstan to keep Gerry in order. Of course, what happens when the old man dies is something else. I think Gerry really hates them, for what they made him do . . ."

"Made him? You don't make someone commit rape!" she burst out indignantly.

"Without them it wouldn't have happened," he said. "But he hates it also that, because of him, his father has taken care of them over the years. Gerry has devoted himself to charitable works, but as far as the Gowders are concerned if the workhouse and the treadmill still existed, he would happily see them consigned there."

"And he'd be with them if I had my way," said Sam. "And that would still be charity."

She turned on her heel and walked away, taking the direct route through the Devil's Door. It felt right.

She didn't look back. She felt some sympathy for Pete Swinebank. He'd been a child. Twice he'd looked to an adult for guidance. First the curate, then Dunstan Woollass. Both times things had gone wrong. So, she could admit sympathy but she couldn't offer absolution. He'd stopped being a kid long ago and had still kept quiet. But the bottom line for Sam was, he'd been there when it happened, it had been within his power to tell them no, they shouldn't be doing this, to threaten to tell his father, their fathers.

OK, he'd been very young and he'd been very scared.

But she knew beyond any shadow of doubt, and with no sense of self-righteousness, that in the same circumstances at the same age, she herself would have screamed and yelled and done everything in her power to bring things to a halt.

Her mind was in a turmoil as she strode along. Conflicting ideas spun round and clashed . . . head straight up to the Hall for a confrontation . . . find somewhere quiet to sit and work things out . . . talk to Mig (where did that one come from?) . . . get in her car and drive far away from Illthwaite . . .

It occurred to her that her namesake, Saint Sam, must have trodden this same road with his mind in a similar whirl. He'd opted for talking with the person he felt closest to, and look where that had got the poor bastard!

By the time she reached the pub she was no nearer resolution. Through the window she glimpsed people in the bar. She didn't want convivial company, she didn't want to sit in her tiny room alone. If Mig had been there, upstairs or downstairs, she might have gone in, but he was up at the Hall. Talking to Dunstan Woollass.

Her great-grandfather. The great god of Skaddale who'd used his power to banish little Pam and despatch her on her fatal journey.

She crossed the road to the bridge, and looked down into the dimpling waters of the Skad. The shadow. The corpse. This was a place with its roots deep in a mysterious and mythical past. But no more so than back home. When it came to mumbo-jumbo, Ma and her people could run rings round this lot. And, so far as she knew, the mythologies of Australia had proved pretty resistant to any attempts to work them into this Johnny-come-lately Christian stuff. Things seemed so much more clear-cut back home. Even the light was clearer. Here the sun still shone unchallenged as it approached its zenith, but all around, the sharp edges of the heights were being blunted by a translucent haze that threatened change.

She longed for some clear Australian light so she could see her way forward. Things here were so messy. Wrongs had been done, compounded by other wrongs, cover-ups, lies. She needed to get a grip. First rule of any problem was assemble your data. Who had suffered here? Pam Galley, total victim in every respect. Saint Sam the curate, who'd done his best for Pam, but whose best hadn't been good enough. Some might say that Rev. Pete too had suffered, and even Gerry Woollass, but any pain they felt was self-inflicted and, in the case of Gerry, she assured herself, far short of what he deserved.

And who had benefited? The ghastly Gowders. They'd orchestrated the rape and the only consequence for them was that they'd come under Dunstan Woollass's protecting hand. He'd probably assured them they'd go to jail if they blabbed and they'd survive in comfort if they held their tongues. No contest.

Which left Dunstan. The old man whom she only knew by report and reputation. Like God. Only this one really existed, and knew everything, and controlled everything. Except the future. He'd done everything to protect his family, and now, if Edie Appledore was right, his family was coming to an end. Perhaps there was a higher God who didn't care for a rival and chuckled to think, as he watched Dunstan's machinations, that Frek the lez would be the last of the Woollasses.

Except for me.

The realization came into Sam's mind the way the answer to a math problem often did. Simple, complete, as if someone else had spoken it.

Except for me.

A horn blew. She looked up to see a VW Polo half turned on to the narrow bridge.

Frek Woollass leaned out of the driver's window and called, "Morning. Sorry to disturb your meditations, but even with your figure it's going to be hard to squeeze by."

Sam stood up and made her way to the other end of the bridge. When the vehicle came alongside, Frek brought it to a halt again.

"Thanks," she said. "Are you all right? You look rather pale."

Sam looked into those calm gray-blue eyes. She knew now where she'd seen them before. They were her pa's eyes. Her own eyes. If there'd been any doubt about what Swinebank had told her, it fled. This woman was her . . . what? Her *aunt!* Jesus!

"I'm fine. Yourself?"

"Fine too. Are you just lingering on the bridge, or were you crossing it with a view to going up the Bank? If so, jump in."

Sam didn't have to think.

"Yes, I'm going up to the Hall," she declared. "A lift would be good."

She slid into the passenger seat.

"No gas guzzler today then?" she said as the Polo moved forward.

"The 4x4, you mean? That's Daddy's. He claims he needs it round here. For Cambridge, however, the smaller the better, as I gather you will shortly find out for yourself. Mig Madero mentioned you were going up. Something to do with math?"

Makes it sound like I'm going to be on a supermarket checkout, thought Sam.

"That's right. And you play around with this Viking stuff, right?"

"Right," said the woman, smiling. "The literature of Nordic mythology, folklore and legend, to be precise."

"So not much use then. Practically, I mean."

"I wouldn't say that. Study of old myth systems can remind us of a lot of things the modern scientific mind has forgotten."

"Like how to cure cancer by chewing nettles?" mocked Sam.

"Like understanding motive and cause and effect. What made Loki want to harm Balder, for instance, if that means anything to you."

"Oh yeah. Balder was the good god, right? Like my namesake, the curate—wasn't that what you told Thor Winander?"

"My my," said Frek. "You do get people to talk to you, don't you?"

"It's my sweet Australian nature," said Sam. "So what did make this Loki guy want to harm Balder? Because he was so good, maybe?"

"I don't think so. Because he was so . . . ineffectual. Snorri Sturluson—he was a thirteenth-century Icelandic scholar—tells us how lovely and good Balder was, but then he says that none of his decisions ever really changed anything. Loki was mischievous, often downright wicked, but whatever he decided to do got done."

"And that's a reason for killing someone?"

"It's a motive," said Frek. "Loki got his comeuppance as justice required. But even this isn't straightforward. The gods bound him in a cave with a serpent's venom dripping on to his face so that he writhed around in immortal pain. But with every convulsion, he causes the earth itself to quake, prefiguring the great earthquakes which are to be such a dreadful feature of Ragnarok."

"What the hell's that?" said Sam, thinking that on the whole she'd have preferred the nettle option.

"With one k at the end, it's the doom of the gods. With two, it's the twilight of the gods, a more poetic notion which appealed to the Romantic imagination. It's the end of everything, good and bad."

Sam tried to work out what this weird woman was saying to her. Sounded like the kind of stuff that her ma could have got her head round. Maybe Pa too. She heard his voice in her head.

Truth's like a dingo, girl. It'll run till you get it cornered. Then watch out!

"Everything's got to end," she said. "You can't stop doing what's right because you're scared of the consequences. Even gods should get what they deserve."

Frek laughed and said, "Brother will kill brother, incest and adultery shall abound, there will be an axe-age, a sword-age, a wind-age, a wolf-age, before the world plunges into fire. That's what an Icelandic prophetess said. How might a mathematician have put it?"

"There is nothing unknowable," said Sam. "We must know. We shall know. That's what a great mathematical prophet said. That'll do for me."

They were now coming up to the Forge. Frek came to a halt and blew her horn. The end of a vehicle was visible round the corner by the smithy. It looked to Sam like the Gowders' pickup. After a moment, Thor Winander appeared and approached the car.

He raised his eyebrows when he saw Sam, then winked at her and said to Frek, "Twenty minutes, we'll be there. You sure that Gerry's all right with this? He was pretty unfriendly when I was preparing the site."

"He's fine, I promise you," said Frek. "It will grow on him."

"If you say so. See you later then. Cheers, young Sam."

As Frek set the Polo in motion again, she explained, "Thor's promised to set up a carving he's done for me before I go back to Cambridge tomorrow."

For a moment Sam thought she meant the splay-legged nude and wondered where the hell she could display that. Then she recalled the Other Wolf-Head Cross.

"You didn't say who you wanted to see at the Hall," continued Frek. "Is it my grandfather? Or my father? Because if it's Daddy, he's not there, I'm afraid. He was driving Angelica back to her House this morning, and I'm not sure when he'll be back."

Sam, who'd never stood back from a confrontation in her life, was slightly ashamed to feel relief. She still had no idea how she was going to handle a face-to-face with the man who as a child had fathered her father on another child. If she met Gerry now, all she could foresee was a shouting match, with the Gowders and Thor Winander expected on the scene any moment to make up the audience.

"Your grandfather will do," she said.

"Will he? I'll need to check if he's up to it. His trip down to the Stranger was his first excursion in a little while, and one way and another it left him a little drained."

Sam thought, she knows something. Maybe not everything, but enough.

Frek went on, "He's talking with Mr. Madero this morning. Some academic matter, I believe . . ."

"Academic?" interrupted Sam, tired of obliquity. "Bit more than that, I'd say."

"Would you now?" murmured Frek. "Someone else who's opened up to you? How interesting. I wouldn't have thought you had a lot in common. Perhaps time together trapped in the darkness brought you close?"

They were turning into the driveway of the Hall now. Frek brought the car to a halt before the front door.

"You should be careful, my dear," she said, putting her hand on to Sam's knee. "There's not much future in falling for a priest."

She squeezed gently.

Sam recalled what Edie Appledore had told her and grinned. *There's a laugh in everything if you look,* was one of Pa's philosophical gems at moments of complete disaster. Sam had just had a vision of telling him the sad truth about his mother, and then adding, "Oh, by the way, the good news is you've got a half-sister who's a lezzie."

She lifted Frek's hand gently and said, "Mig's no priest, believe me."

"None of us can be sure of who we are until we put it to the test," said Frek.

"Tested and proved," said Sam, opening her door.

As Frek got out, she looked up. From the window immediately above the door a tall white-haired figure waved with a graceful economy of motion that would not have been out of place on a papal balcony. Sam felt his gaze register her too, then he turned away as Frek pushed open the front door.

"Come in," she said. "Let's go into the kitchen and have a cup of tea, then I'll check if my grandfather is able to see you."

But Sam's eyes were fixed on the staircase, computing where the entrance to the room above her head would be located. That solved, she was done with calculation. Time to let instinct have its head.

"You take tea if you like, Auntie," she said. "Me, I'm late for an appointment."

And then she was off running.

3

The Jolley archive

The document Dunstan Woollass put into Mig's hands at first reminded him of Alice Woollass's household ledger, which had also consisted of sheets of foolscap-size paper each divided into three columns by two neatly drawn vertical lines. But by contrast with Alice's bold firm hand, the writing here was both faded and cramped.

Observing he was having difficulties, Dunstan offered him the magnifying glass.

And now the detail of Francis Tyrwhitt's job log sprang out at him, and the impression of workaday domesticity faded into a background against which the horror of what he was reading stood out even more violently.

The first and narrowest column (about an inch) contained dates and times.

The second and broadest (perhaps four and a half inches) contained questions put and answers received.

So it must have been to open a filing cabinet in the office of a concentration camp and realize that here, neatly and efficiently stored, were the records of murder.

As he read, it became clear that this was no random application of pain but a carefully modulated progression, directly linked to the answers received.

It started on April 7th 1589.
At 9.15 A.M. the questioning commenced.

Q. What is your name?
A. Father Simeon Woollass.
Q. Where is your dwelling?
A. Where the Lord sends me.

Opposite this in the third column he read:

Insert needle under nail of 1st finger, right hand.
Scream. Prayer (Lat).
Remove needle.
9.20.
Q. What is your name?
A. Father Simeon.
Q. Where is your dwelling?
A. I wander where the Lord sends me.
Needles, 1st and 3rd fingers, r.h.
Screams. Prayers. Face white. Vile blasphemies (Eng.) Babbling. Piss & shit.
Face gray-yellow. Eyes rolling.

Three times the process was repeated, the needles withdrawn, the question re-put, and the unsatisfactory answer followed by more needles in more fingers, always on the same hand. The final ones were recorded as being heated till they glowed scarlet.

At 9.45 A.M. the same questions. But this time the answer was different.

A. Spain. I dwell in Spain. And at Douai in the English College. These are my dwellings. What more can I say?

Now came a pause with the single word *Water* in Column 3.

Then at 10.00 A.M. the process resumed.

Q. When did you come to England?
A. In the prime of 1588.
Q. Where have you stayed in England?
A. Nowhere. In fields in ditches in sheds.

Now the torture was renewed till finally an answer was given in the form of an address in Gray's Inn Fields in London which for a brief moment satisfied the interrogator.

Mig looked up. He was feeling Mrs. Appledore's fried breakfast moving uneasily in his stomach. He met Dunstan's sympathetic gaze.

"He comes over," said the old man, "as a most meticulous man. In preparation, in keeping records, in making physical and psychological judgments. You notice the careful note he makes of which fingers the needles are driven into. And he works only on the right hand. Father Simeon, I would guess, was, like most of our family, left-handed. Tyrwhitt would not want to maim the hand that might be needed to sign a confession."

"You sound almost as if you admire him," said Mig.

"Admire? No. But appreciate, yes. He was working on behalf of his faith, and I do not doubt that many of the refinements of his techniques were garnered from the annals of our own Church's long war against heresy."

"That makes them all right?"

Dunstan shrugged.

"It makes them understandable. When we are judged, Madero, surely our motives will be accepted in mitigation? But I'm interrupting your perusal of the document."

Mig scanned down. Tyrwhitt's basic technique of pain and reward, of following innocuous questions which Simeon could answer with more probing questions which he tried to evade, was varied only in the change from time to time of the instruments of torture and the parts of the body he attacked. When the right hand was, as he put it, *for the present played out*, he shifted his attention to the left foot, then the right eye, then the left ear. But nothing he did was life threatening. And whenever Father Simeon showed signs of escaping into unconsciousness, he received water and a respite from pain.

"Interestingly," observed Dunstan, "and by contrast with modern techniques practiced by most security agencies, there is no attack on the genitalia. Perhaps through experience Tyrwhitt had discovered that men whose vows of chastity made them, as it were, spiritual eunuchs did not fear in the same degree as the laity the threat of castration."

Mig ignored him and read on.

As the tortured man's powers of resistance weakened, the questions became cleverer, subtly implying knowledge already possessed, and inviting Simeon to protect the innocent from the fate he was suffering.

Simeon had been taken on the outskirts of Chester and Tyrwhitt was keen to get him to implicate a certain local Catholic, Sir Edward Ockendon, whose name was familiar to Mig as a recusant. But the pursuivant directed his questions with a clever obliquity, concentrating on the baronet's sister, as if she were the main object of his interest.

> Q. *What did the Lady Margery Ockendon say to you when you discussed the question of the Queen's edicts with her?*
>
> A. *I never spoke with Lady Margery.*
>
> Q. *Was Lady Margery ever present when you celebrated Mass in the chapel of her brother's house in Chester?*
>
> A. *I tell you, I know not the Lady.*
>
> Q. *Was the Lady Margery confederate with her brother Sir Edward in the supply of succor and protection to you during your sojourn at Chester?*

A. Will you not hear me? I know her not.

Q. Did not the Lady Margery by word and token make clear to you that she still held to the old discredited doctrines of Rome? Did she not regularly attend Mass with her brother in the family chapel? Would she not admit this if we put her to the question? Speak out. You hold her fate in your hands. Come, man, the truth! Or will you make me rip it out of her with pinchers and poignard?

A. I have told you, I never met the Lady Margery. As God is my witness, she was never present at any Mass I held in Chester.

Q. So, if she were not present, who was in attendance beside Sir Edward?

And so the implied admissions came. And with each, the next was easier. But never any mention of the Woollass family until near the end.

Q. Father, because I am satisfied that you have dealt fairly with me, I have no purpose to question you as to the actions and beliefs of any members of your own family, if only you will answer one last question, which is this. I have it on authoritie that you were in company of a notorious agent of the Hispanic king during your time in Lancashire. Do but say where I might lay hands on this enemy of our noble Queen and all is done between us.

A bargain offered. A real bargain. The safety of his own family weighed against the safety of a foreign fugitive, suspected of murder, and seriously injured already.

Eventually, inevitably, the answer came, that this agent lay in a house in Lancaster, waiting till a ship could be found that would bear him home to Spain.

Mig looked up to find Dunstan's gaze, benign, compassionate, fixed upon him.

Perhaps, he thought, if that answer had not been given, Miguel Madero might have returned home to see his bastard child, leaving Tyrwhitt to visit his wrath on the Woollasses, whose family line might well have been cut short.

In which case the old man wouldn't be here, and he himself wouldn't have needed to come here, and . . .

It was pointless multiplying possibilities, though Sam would no doubt have an equation to cover all eventualities. He recalled her hand squeezing his thigh as she took her leave.

He said briskly, "And was there anything in the rest of the Jolley records that gave a further account of this so-called agent?"

"A note to the effect that a Spanish emissary of King Philip was taken in Lancaster, that he confessed to having been in touch with certain notorious recusants, but died under examination before he could give details or sign a written deposition. This is almost certainly the same episode which my grandfather refers to in his footnote."

"And you believe this was probably the fugitive youth your family helped—my ancestor, Miguel Madero?"

"Who else? I would guess that, when Simeon finally left Illthwaite, he took the injured boy with him. He must have been a considerable encumbrance to one who was himself a permanent fugitive. Those who provided refuge on their journey into Lancashire probably had their own theories as to the identity of this wounded foreigner. Rumors grow; eventually Tyrwhitt hears that Father Simeon is traveling in company with an Hispanic agent. When he picks up Simeon alone, he is fired by the prospect of a great coup in using him to capture this important Spaniard who by now had been exaggerated into a member of the nobility and a personal emissary of King Philip."

"That he was none of these things must have been evident to his interrogator within a very short time," said Mig.

"Shorter than you think," said Dunstan. "He was said to have died under examination. It's clear that Tyrwhitt was far too expert to torture people to death. No, I suspect that the poor lad was almost dead already when he was taken. He'd been crucified, for God's sake, and the journey to Lancaster had probably undone any progress he'd made while in Alice's care. My guess is he died almost immediately, might even have been dead when taken, so Tyrwhitt claimed what kudos he could by fabricating a vague confession, adding weight to the case against other known suspects."

The old man shook his head as if to dislodge the images crowding in on his imagination, then rose abruptly and went to the window, thrusting it open to admit birdsong and a warm breeze which rustled the papers on the desk.

"Fresh air," he said, breathing deeply. "Beware drafts, my doctor says. They can blow you to heaven. But what can heaven be, compared to this? How I love this place, especially at this time of year with the whole valley changing beneath me. You can keep your New England tints, they're for the eye. Old England's palette lays its colors on the heart. Change and renewal. Ever changing, ever the same. Sorry, Madero, sometimes sensibility gets the upper hand over sense, even in a dry old stick like me."

He turned to face into the room and said, "So what do you, the outsider, think of our little valley, now you've been here a couple of days?"

"I like some of it very well," said Madero, wary of this change of direction.

"Good. We have a lot in common. Devotion to the faith. Love of family. Appetite for scholarship. Respect for truth. All most praiseworthy, but when we find two or more of them in opposition, what then? Personally, where my family is concerned, I have too great a sense of pride to want the world picking over our bones. What say you?"

"Let us be precise," said Madero. "You are suggesting we should repress both these documents?"

"What would suffer if we did? Scholarship? We both know a great portion of the scholar's life is spent dropping buckets into empty wells and drawing nothing up. So we add a little nothing to the nothing. Where's the harm?"

"What about truth, respect for which you claimed we hold in common?"

"What is truth?" demanded Dunstan. "That Simeon broke under torture? Or that in fact Tyrwhitt got very little out of him? Turning him loose wasn't a reward for betrayal but a psychological ploy to make the world think he had utterly betrayed his religion. A priest executed is evidence of the strength of faith. A priest released implies its weakness. It worked, though nothing was ever directly proven against Simeon. It took three centuries for my family to clean away the muck that Tyrwhitt smeared across our name. What will happen now if another hack like Molloy gets hold of this?"

"I hardly think it will make headline news in the national press," said Mig dryly.

"It will make news in places that matter to me and my family," said the old man. "Well, another half-century and that will probably matter no longer. The Woollass name will have vanished from the earth. Let them say what they will then, but for the present, I will fight with all my strength against such a manifest injustice."

"Injustice? He told them where they would find my namesake," said Mig.

"Who had been saved and succored by my family, by Simeon's family. Who had been carried down to Lancaster by Simeon at what must have been great risk to himself. Who he probably thought would have been smuggled out of the country long since! It can only have been his increasing debility which made it impossible to move him. There is little to reproach Simeon with here."

"He reproached himself," said Mig. "He could not face my family and give them news of their loved one's fate."

"He attempted to approach you, according to the story you told Frek," said Dunstan. "If you truly believe his spirit has been in torment all these years, then let him now at last have his peace, forgiven by you and forgotten by the world."

It was an appeal which fell on receptive ground. The passionate need to know which had been Mig's emotional dynamic since his first involvement with Illthwaite seemed to have faded. He had felt its absence yesterday morning up at Mecklin Moss. Was this what all those years of pain and vision and misunderstanding and misdirection had been about? There must have been easier ways for him to be directed toward the truth! And what was he going to do with this truth now he had reached it? There was no one to punish, unless perhaps the Gowders for being descendants of the dreadful Thomas and Andrew. What kind of justice was that? And even if he did feel like visiting the sins of the forefathers on their very distant children, did not that mean that by the same token he should be thanking Dunstan Woollass rather than arguing with him?

He surprised in himself a longing to sit down with Sam and discuss these things. What on earth did that signify? He'd known her in the social sense for just three days and in the biblical sense for a single night, yet here she was, the one person in all the world he wished to share his innermost feelings with! Was this what was meant by sexual obsession? No, there had to be more than that. If he felt himself at sea intellectually, it was in part because his emotional world now had a new center to which all his energies were drawn. Could it be that it was to this that all the signs and portents of his life had been directing him? To his encounter with Sam?

It was an absurdity. Perhaps, because it put his own pleasure and happiness before anything else, even a blasphemy.

Dunstan, as if to give him space to pursue his internal debate, had turned to look from the window again.

"Ah, here comes Frek," he said, waving. "That's nice. She wouldn't want to miss you, I'm sure. And I think she's brought your friend."

Mig's heart leapt but he refused to be diverted. He said, "Is there any indication where my ancestor's body was buried?"

Dunstan looked over his shoulder and said, "I'm sorry, no. The only consolation must be that, as he was not a priest and was never condemned by trial, he would not have suffered the customary mutilations. But I doubt if he received an individual burial. Probably he would have been thrown into the common pit to which the bodies of criminals and paupers were committed. But do not worry. You of all people must be sure that God knows where he rests."

Mig stood up. His mind told him it was over even though he felt no sense of completion.

He tossed the Tyrwhitt document on to the desk.

"Do with it what you will," he said.

"You are sure of this?" said Dunstan, turning from the window. "You do not want to show it to Dr. Coldstream and discuss it with him?"

He's playing with me, thought Mig. Just as Frek did. It must be in the blood.

He wasn't sure of anything except that he wanted to be out of here.

"Yes, I'm sure," he said.

He picked up his briefcase and headed for the door.

Before he could reach it, it was flung open and Sam burst into the room.

He felt joy. No puzzlement, no doubt, no uncertainty, just sheer unadulterated joy which for that moment banished all those other negative emotions. If she had run to his arms he would have embraced her without reserve.

But she didn't even acknowledge his presence.

Behind her stood Frek, looking for the first time in their acquaintance slightly flushed and out of breath.

Sam advanced till she was only a couple of feet in front of the old man she'd seen looking from the window.

"You're Dunstan Woollass?" cried Sam. "Of course you are. I recognize the eyes. You know who I am?"

She ripped the hat off her head as if the sight of her disfigured skull would aid identification.

"I believe I do," said Dunstan with great courtesy. "I've heard a great deal about you and I've been looking forward to meeting you and learning more."

"More than you want, maybe," she said. "But it's not me we're here to talk about, it's you. Dunstan Woollass, this is your fucking life!"

4

The truth of blood

They sat around the kitchen table.

Dunstan was at its head. On the right with her back to the window was Frek. Opposite her was Mig Madero.

Sam sat at the bottom end, facing Dunstan. Behind him she could see Mrs. Collipepper making coffee. It was hotter here than out in the autumn sunshine.

All this was down to Dunstan.

In response to Sam's aggressive flippancy he had said, "My life? Excellent. But that may take some little time and the atmosphere in here is a touch crepuscular and rather too chilly for my old bones. So why don't we descend to the kitchen, which the Aga always maintains at a nice temperature? The kitchen is the heart of a well-run household, don't you agree, Sam? May I call you Sam? How are you enjoying your visit to our little backwater? How do you like our valley? Do you feel any connection with it? I should be interested to know."

By God, he was a cool customer, thought Mig. Set the tone, keep it well mannered and English, put a proper distance between yourself and this strident little colonial! He waited with interest and some concern to see how Sam would reply.

"I feel like I've stepped through a north-facing door and met the devil," she said quietly.

It took Mig's breath away. It even disconcerted the old man for a moment.

Then he smiled and said, "Ah yes. You've done the church tour, I see. Or has Frek been treating you to those old legends she values so much? But, as I always say to her, it's all a matter of approach. It's possible to step through a north-facing door and find yourself facing south. Let's go down, shall we? Frek, my dear, your arm, if I may."

Downstairs in the hall, Mig had offered to leave.

The old man said, "No, no. I have Frek to support me, and it would be unfair if Sam didn't have a near and dear friend by her side."

Once at the kitchen table, Sam sat in silence, waiting to see if the housekeeper was to be included in the permitted audience. Mrs. Collipepper set the coffee down in front of Frek, said, "I'll see to your fire, Mr. Dunny. It'll need banking," then left.

Sam, recalling Mig's laughing reference to the old goat's midday "nap," wondered if this was some kind of code.

"Now, my dear," said Dunstan to Sam. "The floor is yours."

Keep it simple, thought Sam. And keep it cool and controlled.

"I've been talking to Pete Swinebank," she said. "He tells me that in January 1961 he was present on Mecklin Moor when your son, Gerald, raped my grandmother, Pamela Galley, who was eleven at the time. I believe that not long after this happened your son confessed to you what he'd done."

Mig could hardly believe what he was hearing, hardly begin to take in its implications. It was less than two hours since he and Sam had parted. Where had this devastating information come from? More importantly, what had it done to her and where was it leading? He looked at her with love and concern. She didn't even glance at him. Her gaze was fixed on the old man, challenging him to deny it.

Frek continued pouring coffee as if nothing remarkable had been said.

Dunstan nodded vigorously, like an old tutor confirming the accuracy of a point well made in a seminar.

"Yes, that's right, he did. But I was not the first to hear the sad tale. He told it first to his confessor, who urged him to make a clean breast to me. I reproved him, I punished him, and I removed him from Illthwaite lest his continued presence should cause the injured child more pain. But I knew my responsibilities did not end there. I took advice. Finally, feeling a deep obligation to take care of the poor girl's long-term welfare, I made what seemed then the best possible arrangements to guarantee her future."

He sat back with the look of a man who'd fought his corner for virtue in an unresponsive world and Sam felt her vow of control under early threat.

"Her future?" she echoed. "Yeah, you guaranteed that all right. All miserable eight months of it which she spent in pain and terror a world away from home among a bunch of insensitive and psychopathically cruel strangers."

Her voice spiraled upward but she managed to hold it down beneath those near-ultrasonic levels it could reach at times of untrammeled emotion.

He leaned toward her a little, his face expressing concern, his eyes warm with compassion and sincerity.

"My dear, I do not doubt the truth of what you say for one moment," he assured her. "What I have learned since—what we have all learned since—demonstrates how wrong we were, all of us at this end of the process, in our estimate that any short-term pain would be more than compensated by the long-term benefits. If anyone here knew the truth of what was going to happen to so many of these children when they reached your shores, do you think we would have permitted it to happen? I certainly had no idea. As to the fact that the child was pregnant, you must believe I was utterly ignorant here. She was carrying my grandchild, for God's sake! Do you think I would have permitted my own blood to be born twelve thousand miles away and left in the care of strangers?"

The old bastard's doing indignation! thought Sam. How the hell is it happening that I'm sitting here all calm and this slippery sod's getting indignant?

To hell with control! Now's the time to start screaming!

But before she could begin, Mig spoke in a mild but measured tone. He found he was looking at Dunstan Woollass from a new and unflattering angle. Removing historic documents to protect your family name was a venial sin, harming no one. But protecting your family name at the expense of an innocent child was very different.

He said, "I think we may accept that you didn't know the girl was pregnant, Mr. Woollass, but that's hardly the point. Surely if you were as concerned for her future as you claim, you would have made arrangements for regular reports on her welfare to reach you. Even if not detailed, I don't see how they could have avoided mentioning the fact that the girl died in childbirth within a very few months of arrival in Australia."

The response came not from Dunstan but from Frek.

She said, "All my grandfather would require was a general affirmation that all was proceeding according to plan. If at some point, early or late, someone saw fit to dilute the truth, then that's hardly my grandfather's fault, is it?"

"You mean, not mention the baby's birth and the mother's death?" said Mig incredulously. "That's not dilution of the truth, that's criminal misrepresentation!"

Sam had had enough. She wasn't here as a spectator in some debating chamber.

"Shut up, both of you!" she yelled. "You're here to listen, not to join in."

"Quite right, my dear. This is between you and me," said Dunstan, glaring reprovingly at his granddaughter.

Oh, but he's good! thought Mig, observing the ease with

which the old man lined himself up with Sam. What must he have been like in his prime!

For a moment Sam looked a touch disconcerted to find herself allied with Dunstan, but she had a directness to match his dexterity.

"Anyway, all this crap about who told who what is irrelevant. As soon as Pam Galley's boat sailed, that was it for you, wasn't it? End of story. Happy-ever-after or dead-in-a-ditch, didn't matter. You just didn't want to know. You'd got things tidied up here. The Gowders must have been easy once you'd spelled it out in words of one syllable. Big trouble if they blabbed, an easy ride if they kept quiet. As for Pete Swinebank, you probably worked out he'd be too scared to talk to his dad. You didn't foresee that what they'd done would eat away inside him till finally he spilled it all out to the curate. But even that fell right for you when the poor sod took himself off the board. And there you were when Pete got the news, a sympathetic authority figure telling him what he wanted to hear, that the best thing he could do now was keep his mouth shut."

Dunstan was nodding vigorously again.

"You put things very clearly, my dear. Your mathematical training, I suppose. Except that you have not brought motivation into the equation. I wished to protect my son. He was a child too. Back then we did not have the complex network of counselors and child psychiatrists we have today. What we did have was the Church, and it was to the Church's care in the form of a Catholic boarding school that I committed Gerry in the hope and belief they would steer him right, and enable him to mature into a decent and moral man, which all the evidence suggests they have done."

He paused as if to invite comment on his argument. There was the noise of an engine outside and through the window Mig saw a pickup arrive. On it, supported by the Gowder twins, lay the Other Wolf-Head Cross. Its huge eye seemed to leer into the kitchen, as if deriding what was happening there. Thor Winander was driving. He swung the wheel till the vehicle faced the kitchen. Catching Mig's eye through the window, he gave a cheerful wave, then began backing the pickup up the slope to the scooped-out niche which Mig had noticed as he walked down from the Moss. So, no marble Venus but something equally pagan.

No one else in the room seemed to have noticed. Dunstan resumed talking.

"As for the girl, little Pam, I did exactly the same for her as I did for Gerry. I committed her to the Church's care, in the honest belief that removing her from the scene of so much distress and helping her start a new life under the tutelage of the Church's officers and agencies would bring her to a healthy and prosperous womanhood."

This was breathtaking stuff, thought Mig. Hadn't the man said he'd read Law at Cambridge? What an advocate was lost when he opted not to practice!

"You really fucking got it wrong then, didn't you?" exclaimed Sam.

"Yes, I really fucking did," said Dunstan.

The echo of her profanity came across not as reproof or parody but as another strut in the bridge he was trying to build between himself and his accuser. And the process continued as, with his unblinking gaze fixed on Sam, he repeated his pleas in a low, urgent voice, discarding flowing periods and fancy turns of phrase.

"I admit my first priority was always my own family. I had no idea the child was pregnant. It never crossed my mind. But I don't need to tell you this, do I? Your own powers of reasoning will have got you there. I put my family first, and if I'd thought for one moment Pam Galley might be carrying Gerry's child, then she would have been family too. As you are, my dear. As you are. And, hard though it will be for you to believe it at this moment, I cannot tell you how much that knowledge delights me."

This beat all. And it wasn't mere advocacy, thought Mig. He means it! He loves Frek, but when he looks at her, he sees a dead end. Now he sees those same unblinking Woollass eyes looking back at him from the face of a woman whose sexuality he knows, courtesy of my schoolboy blushes, is not in doubt. And he doesn't just want to defend himself, he wants to conquer.

He glanced across the table at Frek and read in her face that this was how she understood the situation too. Did she care? That he couldn't read.

Behind her through the window he saw that Thor had got out of the cab and was supervising the Gowders as they maneuvered the Wolf-Head off the pickup. Still no one else at the table seemed to have noticed what was happening outside. In Sam's case this was probably as well. Sight of the twins could only be a distraction, and she had plenty on her plate dealing with Dunstan.

He could see that the old man's response had to some extent wrong-footed her. He guessed there was a lot of her priest-decking father in her. In a tight spot he didn't doubt Sam could throw a damaging hook too. But neither violence nor mathematics was going to see her through this present situation.

He wanted to speak to her, but knew it would be a mistake. Later perhaps there would be a time for words of comfort and advice, when they were alone and close . . .

His heart swooned at the prospect.

Dunstan had bowed his head as if in prayer. Now he sat up straight. His eyes bright, his voice firm, he did not look a man in his eighties.

He said, "You will want to think about what you've discovered, what I have said. And from what I've learned of you in the short time of our acquaintance, you'll want to confront Gerry. My son. Your grandfather."

"Too true I will!" snapped Sam. "He can run but he can't hide."

Mig saw Dunstan wince slightly at the banality, but all he said was, "I don't believe he's doing either. I know for a fact that after your revelations in the Stranger, he suffered a great perturbation of spirit. He spent much of last night in prayer with Sister Angelica. In our faith only a priest can administer the sacraments, but there are times when a troubled soul needs the ministrations of a wise and spiritual woman."

"You mean he screws nuns as well as little girls?" snapped Sam.

Mig was shocked, but mingled with the shock was a degree of admiration and pride. She is indomitable! he thought.

Dunstan, however, threw back his head and snorted a short laugh.

"I don't believe that is a habit he has got into, if you'll forgive the tasteless pun."

Unexpectedly he stood up and moved round the table as if he wanted to take a closer look at Sam. She rose too and, head tipped back to compensate for the disparity of height, met his gaze unflinchingly, diamond striking against diamond.

"Do not take it amiss, great-granddaughter, if I say that in you I see something of myself," he said softly. "You will pursue an end no matter what gets in the way. You will not rest till you have worked everything out, no matter where it takes you, or how long."

"Right to the last decimal point," she said.

"And if it is one of those what I believe you mathematicians call irrational numbers which have no last decimal point?"

"Then I'll keep going till what I believe you call God says it's time to stop."

"That's a voice we all need to listen out for," he said gravely. "I am truly sorry for everything that has happened, and for all of its consequences. Except for yourself. I cannot say I am sorry for that. I do believe that's Gerry arriving now."

The transition from intense emotion to casual comment was perfect, denying Sam the chance to offer any sharp, puncturing response. Instead she turned as they all did to look out of the window.

The Range Rover was drawing up alongside the house. Gerry Woollass got out. He didn't look into the kitchen. All his attention was concentrated on the activity up the slope. He walked toward the three men who had managed to slide the Wolf-Head off the pickup. Presumably its base was now over the prepared site and all that remained was to raise it into position. This was no easy task even for three strong men. There was only room for one of the twins to stand at the front and push while Winander and the other hauled at the ends of a canvas sling wrapped around the huge bole.

Later Sam and Mig learned from Winander what was said.

Gerry, in Thor's words, looked like death warmed up.

As he approached, he growled, "I see you've brought that abomination then."

"Thought you and Frek had got all that sorted," replied Thor.

"No. I gave in weakly, as I have always done. But that's at an end. You and your minions can take it away. And that will be the last time I ever look to see you Gowders on my property. You're finished here, you understand what I'm saying? It's over. Now you must answer for yourselves. To God and to man. If the Law doesn't punish you, then surely the Almighty will."

It was, theorized Thor when he knew the whole story, mere rhetoric, spoken by a man dizzy from lack of sleep, his emotional being a maelstrom of guilt and remorse, and fear too at the path of confession and penitence which lay ahead. There was in fact and in law no case for the Gowders to answer. Even if some kind of charge could be devised after all these years, at the age of eleven in a rape case they were below the threshold of criminal responsibility. But such subtleties were not a part of the twins' thinking. Their measure of what they had done was not a legal still less a moral one. It was the reward they had reaped from their silence, the patronage of

Dunstan Woollass without which they would almost certainly have ended up, in their own outdated term, "on the parish."

What they now heard from Gerry, that the truth was coming out and their protected status was over, simply confirmed what Sam's outburst in the pub had threatened. They were in deep trouble.

The Gowder under the Wolf-Head, which sloped out from the bank at an angle of forty-five degrees like the figurehead of some monstrous ship, was unable to react except with a threatening glower.

His brother, however, shot out a huge hand as Gerry turned away and grasped his sleeve, saying, "Now ho'd on, now ho'd on," still having enough strength in his other arm to do his share in steadying the Cross.

Probably Gerry's intention was merely to shake himself free from this abhorrent touch. But as he flung out his arm to dislodge the grip, the back of his hand caught Gowder full across the bridge of his nose. Blood spurted, tears came to his eyes. Strike a fighting dog and it will strike back. With a bellow of rage, he flung himself at Gerry.

The loose end of the canvas sling whipped round the Cross and Thor's own weight sent him toppling backward.

To the onlookers who saw all this in terrifying dumb-show, it seemed as if the monstrous Wolf-Head, freed at last from long restraint, leapt forward in its eagerness to destroy its nearest captor.

Even now if the other Gowder had simply hurled himself sideways he might have come off scot-free or at least escaped serious injury. But a lifetime of triumphing in all trials of strength inspired him to hold his ground.

Thor, prostrate, could only watch in horror. The other twin, grappling with Gerry, turned his head and saw too late what was happening. His brother held the monstrous bole of wood steady for perhaps two seconds, which was at least a second longer than most other men could have achieved.

And then he fell backward, still embracing the Wolf-Head, which crashed down along the whole length of his body.

His arms flew wide, he spasmed for a moment, then he lay there, stock-still, to the kitchen onlookers' eyes like a man crucified upside down.

All this in less time than it takes to gasp a prayer.

After that it was all confusion, with everyone rushing around, and most of them guessing that not all the activity in the world could make the slightest difference.

Winander and Mig and the other Gowder, now forever Laal, dragged the Wolf-Head clear. Thor proved himself a man for emergencies, trying every technique of resuscitation, but it was soon clear to everyone except his brother that the crushed man was dead. He knelt by the body, pleading with it, urging it, screaming at it, to return to life. He resisted all efforts to move him away and he was still there when the small local ambulance came ululating up Stanebank.

Accepting, as though hope remained, that the hospital was the best place for his brother, Gowder finally allowed the paramedics to lift the body into the ambulance. As he climbed in beside it, Thor tried to accompany him, but felt himself pushed back, not roughly but firmly.

"Nay," he said. "Just me. We've got nobody, we need nobody."

Then he turned his terrible gaze, which had something of the Wolf-Head in it, on to the three Woollasses who stood close together and said, "This is thy doing."

It defied logic, it expressed no threat, yet the words fell on the listening ears like a sentence spoken by a black-capped judge.

5

Invitations

As the ambulance's warning wail faded down the valley, Sam looked toward the Woollass trio, standing close together, Dunstan in the middle, Frek and Gerry on either side.

Maybe that's where I should be, she thought. I'm one of them.

Revulsion from the thought made her put her arm round Mig's waist and he needed no second invitation to pull her close to his side.

Sam and Gerry had come near to each other during the melee after the accident, they had even made eye contact, but not a word had yet been exchanged. This didn't feel like the right time. But when would be a right time to say whatever they had to say?

Thor looked from one group to the other as if sensing but not yet comprehending the gulf between them.

Then the kitchen door opened and Mrs. Collipepper appeared.

"Mr. Dunny, you get yourself in here afore you catch your death," she commanded. "I'm surprised at you, Miss Frek. Can't you see he's not well?"

The old man did indeed look very frail, but Mig found himself wondering if this too wasn't just part of the consummate performance he'd witnessed over the past hour.

It certainly resolved the situation. Gerry and Frek began to assist Dunstan toward the kitchen. Imperiously he shook them off on the threshold, looked back at Sam and said, "We should talk further, my dear. This afternoon, when we have all had time to recover our composure. Come to tea. Four-thirty sharp."

For Mig and Sam the precise domesticity of the invitation was a tension-breaker. As the kitchen door closed, they looked at each other and had difficulty stifling their giggles.

"I'm glad you find something funny in all this," growled Thor.

"I'm sorry," said Sam remorsefully.

"You don't understand," said Mig.

"Then come down to the Forge and explain it to me," said Thor, opening the door of the pickup.

Sam started talking even before they were out of the Hall driveway. She felt strangely calm now, as if the death of whichever Gowder it was had been cathartic. She felt the same calmness in Mig, pressed close against her on the seat. Perhaps, cocooned in this calm, they should carry on down the Bank to the Stranger House, get into their cars, and simply drive away, leaving Illthwaite and all that it had done to them behind.

But as she told Thor in simple lucid terms what she had discovered that morning, she knew that the calm was merely an interval, a gathering of strength for some final onslaught.

He brought the vehicle to a halt by his front door and sat in silence, staring straight ahead as she completed her story.

Then he smashed his fist on the dashboard and exclaimed, "Dear God! The poor kid. And that happened here and none of us knew anything about it? Dear God."

"What would you have done if you had known?" asked Sam.

"For a start, I'd have made sure the kid was properly taken care of, not packed off to the sodding Antipodes!" he exclaimed.

It was a good answer, the best answer.

Now he turned his full attention on her.

"Sam," he said. "I'm so sorry. This must be terrible for you. I'm sorry."

"What for? It's not your fault."

"It happened here and we let it happen, and after it happened, we didn't find out about it. I'm sorry for that. And I'm sorry you've been messed around, and I'm sorry you've had to . . . Jesus. You must hate this place and everybody in it."

She considered this for a moment then said, "No."

"No?"

He didn't sound as if he believed her.

She said slowly, getting her thoughts in order, "Where's the logic in that? What happened to my gran was terrible, all of it, what happened here and what happened back home. So if I hated everyone here then I'd have to hate a helluva lot of people back home too. And every tyke in both places."

"Yorkshiremen?" said Thor, puzzled.

"Roman sodding Catholics," said Sam. "Which would include my Aussie granpa and gran. And one or two others who aren't so bad."

She glanced at Mig who said, "Sam, I'm so sorry."

"You too? So which of you pair of sorry plonkers is going to do something useful like getting me a stiff drink?"

They got out of the pickup and followed Thor into the kitchen where he picked up a bottle and some glasses before leading them out into the cobbled courtyard.

"Might as well enjoy the sun while we've still got it," he said.

Above them the sun, just past its zenith, still shone out of a clear blue sky, but away to the west where the sea lay, huge storm clouds were now bubbling up.

They sat at one of his wrought-iron tables. Thor poured generous measures of Scotch. Raising his glass, he said, "To better times."

They drank. No one seemed inclined to talk further. Sam's eyes kept straying to the piece of wall against which the Wolf-

Head had stood. She recalled how she'd found it menacing, repulsive—and compulsively attractive.

She said suddenly, "Until the moment it fell, I wanted it to fall. Once it happened, it was terrible. I wanted it all reversed. But before, when I laid eyes on the Gowders, I hated them so much it was like I caused it."

Now they'll say, *There, there, don't be so silly,* she thought.

Mig said, "I felt the same. At least you were hating the same people that caused your family harm. My hate was four hundred years out of date."

Thor said, "You're both wrong. Anyone in the dock, it's me. Industrial accident, employer's responsibility. I can't even say I wasn't aware. I've gone on long enough about lifting gear and safety harnesses and not relying on the Gowders' brute strength. Drink up."

Mig accepted some more, but Sam put her hand over the glass.

"Need to keep a clear head," she said. "It would be rude to turn up to tea at the Hall legless. In fact, maybe I should get back down the Stranger, grab a bite to eat and build up my strength."

"Don't think that's a good idea," said Thor. "I'd guess the Stranger's buzzing this lunchtime, and there'll be just one topic of conversation after the show last night. Plus once news of the accident gets round the village . . ."

"How's that going to happen so soon?" asked Mig.

"This is Illthwaite. They'd hear the ambulance siren, plus Noddy Melton monitors the emergency channels. They'll know already. You don't want to walk into that. You'd better have a bite of lunch here with me. OK?"

They didn't argue.

"Can I help?" asked Sam as Thor rose.

"Careful," said Thor. "Haven't they heard about us new men in Oz?"

They watched as he went into the house.

Sam said, "I'm glad we're here. He's what we need. He shows you can get over the past even though you never forget it."

"You'll get over all this then?" said Mig.

"Absolutely. You?"

"I hope so. But it's hard to say until I'm sure what 'all this' entails."

"I thought you were all done."

"It doesn't feel like it. Or maybe it's just that I can't feel it's over for me until I'm sure it's over for you."

His expression was so full of affection and concern that she said, "Mig, look, it's important we get things straight . . ."

"I know. I shouldn't act like a lovesick adolescent who thinks one night of passion must presage a lifetime's deep and meaningful relationship. Right?"

"Close," she said, smiling. "I'd have said something like, lighten up, for Godsake, let's see how things look away from this place. But maybe the way you put it is better. Look, I like you, I admit it. Must be chemical, I suppose, it's certainly not rational. Set you down on paper, I wouldn't hang you in a dunny. But in the flesh, I don't know, I feel I've known you a long time, if that makes sense."

"It makes sense to me, but if I start on again about feeling we were both sent here for a purpose and it's the same purpose, you'll probably break that bottle over my head."

"You see? Like I said last night, you're a quick learner."

They both laughed at the memory.

Thor, emerging from the house with a tray, said, "How good it is to see the little victims at their play. This is the best I can do."

It was a pretty fair best. Cold beef and pickles accompanied by crusty wholemeal bread and creamy fresh butter.

"I rang the hospital. They weren't very forthcoming. All they'd say was the ambulance had just arrived and it would be some time before the medics had made an assessment. And I had to tell them I was the Gowders' uncle to get them to tell me that. I'll try again in half an hour. Not that I expect to hear anything but what was obvious to all of us."

This dampened the mood again and they began their meal in silence. Eventually Thor made an effort at conventional conversation which the others joined in, rather stiltedly at first, but soon it began to flow and eventually it was possible to think for half-minutes at a time that they were just a group of friends enjoying a snack in the sunshine.

Dessert was tangy cheese, apple pie and strong black coffee.

After half an hour, Thor excused himself and went back inside. When he returned he looked very serious once more.

He said, "I rang the hospital again. They confirmed the poor bastard was dead on arrival. Then I asked about Laal. Normally they'd be very cagey talking about the living, but they were worried enough about him to be glad there was someone outside taking an interest. It was like I'd forecast. They had a hell of a job getting him to take it in. They had to let him see the body. For a while he just sat there in a stupor. Then suddenly he stood up and left."

"Didn't they try to stop him?"

"Would you try to stop a Gowder? Anyway, they had no cause. But the way he looked, they were worried."

"So where's he gone?" asked Mig. "Did he say anything at all?"

"Just three words as he got to his feet," said Thor. "*They did it.* That's all. As for where he's gone, he'll head for home, where else?"

"Shouldn't there be someone at Foulgate to meet him?" said Sam.

"Yes. I'll go myself," said Thor. "But no hurry. He's got no vehicle, public transport in these parts is irregular and round the houses. And only a very saintly or shortsighted driver would stop to give a Gowder a lift. I rang Edie at the Stranger too. She'll pass the news on in the bar which, as I forecast, is absolutely packed. That means everyone will keep an eye open."

"What will they do if they see him?"

"Why, help him, of course," said Thor, surprised. "He may be a monster, but he's our monster."

Thor resumed his seat. Mig stood up and said, "Can I use your bathroom?"

"If you mean bog, there's one downstairs, through the kitchen, turn left."

As Mig disappeared inside, Thor said, "Incidentally, Sam, I should have thought sooner, if you want to use the phone, feel free. You might want to talk things over with someone back home."

Sam glanced at her watch. It would be easy to say that it was too late, they'd be in bed, but she knew that would be just an excuse. Some time she was going to have to ring Vinada and tell them what she'd discovered. Part of her wanted to put this off till she'd had her face-to-face with Gerry Woollass. She'd no idea yet what she was going to say, but her awareness that it was her choice that had brought her to this point made her reluctant not to see it all the way through before reporting back home.

At the same time, her father was entitled to have an input. How he would react she couldn't guess. He'd spent all his adult life thinking it was probably some randy priest who'd forced himself on the young girl in the nuns' care, and he'd found a way to deal with that. After that first excursion, age sixteen, he had made no further attempt to solve the mystery of his parentage. She'd heard his reasons, but maybe he simply feared what he might do if he came face to face with the man.

Now he would have a name and an address and the whole sordid story.

Ma would be there, of course. Ma with her unique blend of common sense and semi-mystic insight.

The simple truth was she longed to hear their voices. Going round like the wrath of God was a lonely business.

She said, "Thanks. I'll do that."

As if sensing her hesitation, Thor said, "Won't it be quite late down under?"

"Yeah. But what the hell! Pa's the hardest guy in the world to knock off-kilter. He'll probably listen to what I've got to tell him, then turn right over and go back to sleep!"

She rose and strode toward the house, leaving Thor grinning with affection and admiration.

"Phone's in the hallway just outside the kitchen door," he called after her.

As she came out of the kitchen, she noticed the living-room door was open. Something glinted on the floor. She identified it as one of the lager cans she and Thor had tossed aside on her previous visit. Then the glint died as a shadow moved over it.

She advanced to look inside the room.

Mig was in there, standing in front of Thor's painting of the smiling youth in riotous spring, holding out the nest of fledglings.

"Striking, isn't it?" said Sam, entering the room. "And it's about the only thing in this place it's safe to admire. Anything else could cost you dear, but that's definitely not for sale. That's my namesake, Sam Flood, the curate. Mig? Are you OK?"

He had turned his head to look at her as she spoke and she was shocked to see how drained of color his face was. Perhaps, she thought, he'd asked to use the bathroom because he was feeling ill.

"I'm sorry," he said. "This painting . . . who did you say it was?"

"I just told you! The Reverend Sam Flood who drowned himself in the Moss. Why? Hey, you're not having one of your ghostly turns, are you?"

"No! Yes. I mean, in a way . . ." he said agitatedly.

It was to some extent a relief to hear even such a confused answer if it meant his condition wasn't physical. On the other hand, she felt she had enough on her mind without Mig being away with the fairies once more.

She said, "Maybe if you could be a bit more precise . . ."

"I recognize him," said Mig. "Is that precise enough for you. *I recognize him!*"

6

A face from the past

She swept the clutter of books and papers off one of the chairs which faced away from the portrait and by main force made Mig sit down. Then she perched herself on the arm beside him, took his left hand in both of hers, looked straight into his eyes and said lightly, "Don't see how you can do. He was dead before you were born."

"That, I think, is why I am able to recognize him," said Mig. His hand felt deathly cold, his eyes though fixed on hers didn't seem to be properly focused.

She said, "OK, Mig. I can do codes, but not this one. Let's hear it straight."

He said, "Do you remember me telling you about my childhood? Of course, you do. You remember everything. I told you of the time I was accosted by what I now think was the wraith of Father Simeon in the cloisters of Seville cathedral, and a young priest led me back to my mother. Then I saw the same young man again on my sixteenth birthday. He held out his hands to me like the boy in the painting. The very same posture. And in his hands he was holding some eggs."

"So, a coincidence," said Sam. "Which in mathematical terms can often turn out to be more probable than . . ."

"To hell with mathematics!" he interrupted vehemently. "It's not a coincidence! I don't just mean the posture and the eggs. What I'm telling you is that this is the same young man! The very same face, the very same smile, the very same everything. Beyond all doubt, this is him!"

Sam's heart sank. She felt the gap between them opening up once more. Ghosts and ghouls and things that went bump and apparitions of all kinds had nothing to do with the world she wanted to spend her life in. Truth was her goal in all things, and if the absolutes of mathematics were sometimes hard to reconcile with the uncertainties of diurnal existence, at least you could give it your best shot, which meant you didn't just pile up the detritus of mythology and superstition under the window, you opened the window wide and tossed it out!

"Come on, Mig!" she said. "Get a grip. Ask yourself, even if you believe all that supernatural stuff, why the hell should the spirit of an English Protestant priest have traveled all the way to Spain to haunt a Catholic cathedral?"

It was, she recognized even as she put it, a bloody stupid question. Once admit ghosts, then the laws of rational discourse no longer applied.

There was a faint chink of china from the doorway. Thor stood there, a trayful of dirty dishes in his hand.

He said, "I didn't realize you two had snuck off to hold a séance. What's all this about spirits?"

Sam looked from Thor to Mig and back again. This was in some sense holy ground to both of them, but you didn't acknowledge holiness by evasion and deception.

She said, "Mig sees ghosts sometimes. One of them looks like your painting of my namesake, Sam Flood."

She saw the jocular light fade in the big man's eyes and his knuckles whiten as he gently set down the tray.

"Indeed," he said in a cool controlled voice. "Then you asked a good question, Sam. Why on earth should our Sam's phantom decide to take a trip to Spain when there were people closer to home he had so much more cause to haunt?"

"I don't know! I don't know!" said Mig wretchedly.

"A case of mistaken identity, perhaps?" Thor went on. "I don't have any personal experience, but I daresay one ghost looks much like another."

"For Christ's sake, Thor, stop being so sodding English!" yelled Sam. "I know this is sensitive stuff for you, but it's the same for Mig too, can't you see that?"

Thor froze for a moment then, making himself relax, he said, "Sorry. This has been a hell of a day for all of us. Why should anything surprise me? Mig, tell us about your ghost."

Mig looked at Sam as if requiring her permission. She smiled encouragingly and he told his story, all of it, including the information gleaned from Simeon's document.

"I thought I was beginning to make some sense of it all," he concluded. "I've felt from the start that I was guided here. I think Sam was too, though no doubt she'll put it down to the power of inductive reasoning."

"I think if there's some divine power clever enough to get us both here, why the hell didn't it stop what happened to my gran in the first place?" she retorted.

"Children, children," said Thor, back in full control. "Young people who are fond of each other should never have serious arguments in the presence of a witness and out of reach of a bed. Mig, I have no idea what your visionary experience might signify other than you need psychiatric help. If we discount that possibility, then that leaves some sort of supernatural intervention which by definition is not susceptible to rational analysis. There was a hymn we used to belt out in St. Ylf's back when I was too young to resist the pressures of convention and the back of my dad's hand. It went on about the mysterious ways of God and concluded, *He is His own interpreter and He will make it plain.* In other words, wait and see."

Good plain common sense, but he was using it to conceal how deeply this trespass on his most deeply sensitive memories had troubled him, thought Sam. Her own instinct faced by any problem was to rip at it, tooth and claw, until she found a solution. *Nothing is unknowable.* But she was learning to tread more delicately.

Thor picked up the tray again and said, "I don't know about you two, but I think another little drink is in order."

He went out into the kitchen.

Mig stood up, said "Thanks" to Sam and tried to kiss her forehead. This struck her as a touch too avuncular so she raised her lips to meet his and gave him a bit of tongue into the bargain just to remind him who he was dealing with. He looked at her thoughtfully for a moment, then smiled, and turned to study the portrait once more.

"Hey, you're not going to go weird on me again," said Sam.

"No. I'm past that. In fact it was more the shock of recognition than any sense of the supernatural. That's the odd thing. I could understand it better if I did get that kind of feeling as I looked at the picture, but I don't. And when I was up at the Moss yesterday, standing there looking out over the place where he drowned himself, you'd have thought I would have got something. But there was nothing other than a normal reaction to such a dreary place."

Sam said, "Describe it."

"The Moss? Why, it's just a huge flat area of lank grass, the kind of spiky olive-colored stuff that grows on swampy ground. From a distance it looks as if you could walk over it, but as you get closer you see it's dotted with pools of black water, some hardly more than puddles, others large as ponds. The only brightness is the occasional patch of livid green, some kind of lichen, I think. Again, it looks solid enough, but if you put your weight on it, your foot goes right through into foul black mud, as I found to my cost. Which reminds me, I haven't returned the clothes I borrowed from Thor."

"What about stones? Rocks?"

"I told you," he said, puzzled. "It's wetland. A morass. When you get back to the solid ground there are some huge boulders, terrifying things, God knows where they rolled down from. But there's nothing on the Moss itself, or if there is it's buried so deep you'd need a submersible to find it. Why so interested?"

Sam was saved from answering by the return of Thor with three tumblers filled with Scotch. Mig took his gratefully and downed half of it in a single draft.

Sam said, "No thanks, Thor. Like I said, I want to keep a clear head. I'll get myself some more coffee though."

She went into the kitchen, refilled her mug from the cafetiere, but didn't return to the living room. Instead she went out into the courtyard. What she was looking for was exactly where her eidetic memory told her it was, the tub of polished and many-colored stones standing in a corner. She put her hand into the tub and plucked three of them out, one gleaming white, one dusty red, one gray-blue, like the Woollass eyes.

Like her own eyes.

"There you are," said Thor behind her. "Mig suddenly remembered he'd been heading for the loo when he strayed into the living room and saw the picture. And you were on your way to the phone, weren't you? Changed your mind?"

"Decided it's a bit too late," she said. "Thor, these stones . . ."

"Nice, aren't they? You like them? Trust a sharp Aussie to pick the one thing unchargeable to my artistic magic. Nature did all. To wit, the sea. There's a couple of beaches and one bay in particular which abound in such lovely pebbles. I suppose I could charge you for my time in collecting them. But no, I feel a generous fit coming on. Help yourself, my dear, help yourself!"

"Thanks," said Sam. "So what do you use them for?"

"Pebble mosaics mostly, our rough Cumbrian answer to the glittering pavements of Byzantium. Curiously enough, the first one I ever did was up at the Hall, to mark the elevation of old Dunny to a papal peerage or some such thing. It took the local fancy and there are many homes in Skaddale where you can see the result. The Woollasses have always been the glass of fashion and the mold of form . . . Sorry. I'm being crass. I was forgetting . . . you know . . ."

"That it's my family you're talking about?" said Sam. "That's OK. I'm going to be facing them shortly, remember? The better prepared I am, the better prepared I'll be. So Dunstan got a title from the Pope?"

"Oh yes. His father was delighted. Even more pleased, I heard, than when his boy was awarded the Military Cross in the war. God and Caesar, no question who came first in old Rupert's eyes."

"So he's a hero too? I can imagine him leading a cavalry charge!"

"I think you're thinking of the wrong kind of war," said Thor. "No, he didn't dash about in a lovely uniform waving a saber. On the contrary; as he was in the SAS, I suspect he did more crawling than dashing, and more quiet garrotting than noisy swashbuckling."

"Did you do a mosaic for his medal too?"

"No, despite my evident antiquity, I wasn't quite into my artistic stride in 1945," laughed Thor.

"No, sorry. But the papal award thing, when did you do that?"

Thor thought a moment, then the animation went out of his face.

"That would be 1961," he said shortly.

"In the spring? In *that* spring?"

"Yes, as a matter of fact. But what does that signify?" asked Thor, regarding her suspiciously.

"I suppose it helps explain Dunstan's defensive tactics when he heard what his son had been up to," said Sam. "Family just honored with his title, and I'm sure Mig said something to me about Father Simeon getting an approving mention in some Vatican statement—that was probably at the same time. So, the Woollass family on the up and up, a nasty old rumor finally put to sleep—old Dunny must have shit broken glass when he learned his son and heir had committed rape!"

It made sense, even though it was mainly verbiage to divert Thor from the real trend of her thinking. Sense or not, he was still regarding her doubtfully when the phone rang in the house.

He turned and went inside, passing Mig emerging from the kitchen into the courtyard.

Sam slipped the stones into her bumbag and gave him a welcoming smile.

He said, "Sam, I was wondering. When you go back to the Hall, would you like me to come with you? Your decision, of course. I just want you to know I'm available."

"If I'd thought for a second you weren't, I'd punch you in the throat," she said. "I think I need to see them alone. Especially Gerry. But it would be nice to know you were in screaming distance. Anyway, we've still got well over an hour. Tell you what I'd like to do . . ."

Before she could finish, Thor reappeared.

"That was Edie," he said. "Fred Allison, local farmer, just dropped into the Stranger. He hadn't heard anything about what happened this morning, but when he did, he told Edie he'd picked up Laal Gowder a few miles down the road from the hospital and dropped him outside the pub. He never said a word all the time he was in the car and, when he got out, he ignored Fred's invitation to come in and have a drink but crossed the bridge and went along the riverbank as if he was going up the fell path to Foulgate."

"Well, that's good. At least he's got back safe," said Mig.

"It's what he might do now he's back that bothers me," said Thor.

"Harm himself, you mean?"

Thor barked a humorless laugh.

"Doubt it. Not big on self-destruction, the Gowders. But when it comes to simple destruction . . . Look, I think I'd better head round there. He shouldn't be alone and he's used to me talking straight to him."

"Do you want us to come?" said Mig.

"Perhaps not," said Thor. "Somehow I don't think the sight of Sam is going to calm his troubled mind."

"Of course not. Sorry. I wasn't thinking," said Mig.

"That's why you almost became a priest," said Sam kindly. "Not thinking's a condition of service. Tell you what you can do, Thor. You can drop me and Mig off up at the top of Stanebank. I fancy a breath of air and he said he'd take me up to Mecklin Moss."

Mig looked slightly startled at this news, but Thor said, "OK, if that's what you want. Let's go then."

A few moments later they were in the pickup, rattling up the track. There was no sign of life as they passed the Hall. Perhaps, thought Sam, they've all done a runner.

On second thoughts, it didn't seem very likely. Dunstan didn't strike her as the running type. Frek neither. As for Gerry, perhaps by the time she'd finished with him, he'd be wishing he had run while he still had the chance!

A couple of minutes later, Thor brought the pickup to a halt.

"Here we are, folks," he said. "Though what you're going to do in that dreary place, I can't imagine. Unless you'd like to borrow a groundsheet, that is."

He managed a twinkle, but they could tell he wasn't looking forward to whatever awaited him at Foulgate.

They watched the pickup bump away along the track.

"He's a good man, I think," said Mig softly.

"Yes," said Sam. "I do believe he is. But now he's gone, I suppose I'll have to rely on you for guidance. Beggars can't be choosers. Lead on and show me this Moss."

7

A gift of stones

They set off up the narrow sheep-trod toward the Moss. As they got nearer and the character of the place became more and more apparent, Sam said, "Thor wasn't exaggerating when he said it was dreary."

"I did tell you. Yesterday when I was here at least I could lift my eyes to the hills, but not much point today."

He was right. The storm's battle plan was clear. It had sent its cloudy columns probing out of the west to occupy the high ground and now most of the surrounding hills were visible only as dark islands in a sea of billowing grays. Directly above them the sun still shone, but it gave at best a lurid light. The shadows they cast seemed to move around them with an independent life. The wind had dropped and the air felt menacingly heavy.

"Good day for Ragnarok," said Sam. "With as many k's as you like."

"You've been talking to Frek," said Mig.

"Well, she is my auntie," said Sam, trying to keep things light. But her attempt fell flat, even for herself, and they walked on in silence over increasingly boggy ground till Mig stopped abruptly and said, "This I think must have been the site of Mecklin Shaw."

"The wood where they crucified your namesake," said Sam. "And up ahead where those big pools are, I presume that's where my namesake was drowned."

"I think so. There is nothing to mark either spot," said Mig.

"Oh, I don't know," said Sam. "Seems well enough marked to me."

He turned to face her, looking very serious.

"Sam, what exactly are we doing here?" he asked.

She said, "Look around you. See any stones?"

He looked, with a little satirical exaggeration.

"Stones? No. I don't believe I do. I should have thought your scientific mind would have worked out that anything of any weight would have sunk into this stuff eons ago. Why do you keep going on about stones?"

"Because," she said with the patience of a teacher explaining something to a slow child, "the inquest record says that Saintly Sam, the curate, had filled his pockets with stones to make his body sink more quickly when he topped himself."

He put his hand to his brow as if to massage away a headache.

"What inquest record?"

"The one on Sam Flood, dummy!"

"You've seen it? But how . . . ? Why . . . ?"

"I've got connections," she said, echoing Noddy Melton. "So where did the stones come from? That was one question no one seemed to ask."

"Why should they?" he said dismissively. "He probably picked them up as he came up Stanebank. I didn't pay much attention, but I seem to recall the surface of the track consists largely of fragments of rock. I presume that's what *stane* means. Stone."

"Thanks for the linguistic lesson," said Sam dismissively. "I did pay attention. Yes, you're right. Fragments, lumps, slivers, broken pieces ground down over the years. Nothing like these."

She reached into her bumbag and grasped the stones she'd removed from the tub in Thor's yard. Then, cupping them in her hands, she held them out for Mig to examine.

It was, she felt, a minor *coup de théâtre*. The way Mig reacted, it could have been the end of *Don Giovanni*. She reminded herself he didn't get out much.

He was staring transfixed at the shiny smooth ovoids. When he spoke, there were two false starts before the words came out.

"What are these?" he asked.

"These are the kind of stones Sam had in his pockets to weigh him down. I've seen the actual stones, and believe me, they look just like these."

She spoke triumphantly, but Mig's reply was uttered so softly he seemed to be speaking to himself.

"Stones," he murmured. "Stones, not eggs."

"Sorry?" she said. "What the hell have eggs got to do with it? Not much point stuffing your pockets with eggs if you want to drown."

He raised his eyes from her hands to her face and said with a quiet urgency, "When I saw the portrait at the Forge, the only thing that wasn't quite the same was that he had a nest in his hand, full of fledglings bursting out of their eggshells. My ghost was showing me what I thought were whole eggs, and big ones too, more like hens' or ducks' than songbirds'. But now I see it wasn't eggs he was showing me . . . it was stones . . . like these stones . . ."

She shook her head impatiently. Here she was doing important detective work and all he could do was go drifting off into his dreamworld.

She said, "Look, the point is, where did curate Sam get these stones from? One possibility is he picked them up from the Forge, which is where I got these three. Thor uses them, or used to, in making some kind of mosaics. He did one up at the Hall way back. In fact he worked on it in the spring of 1961, around the time it all happened—Pam being shipped off to Oz, the suicide . . ."

Mig had made a visible effort to focus all his attention on what she was saying.

"Hold on," he said. "Are you suggesting this poor devil was still so much in control of himself that he decided on his way up the Bank that it might be useful to weigh himself down, so he made a diversion to have a look for some suitable ballast? Surely if such an idea did occur, he'd simply have grabbed handfuls of broken stone from the track before he turned off and headed up here?"

Sam looked at him approvingly.

"There is a brain in there after all," she said. "You're dead right. That's what he'd have done. So?"

He looked at her hopelessly and shrugged. She felt like shaking him. His mind had spent so long wrestling with the mystery of apparitions and messages from beyond that he couldn't follow a trail of reasoning as clear and as simple as $2n = 4$. She wished she had a blackboard so she could spell it out.

But in truth she knew that it was only now, up here, in this place, that she was beginning to let herself spell it out completely.

She said very clearly, "He must have had a reason for diverting. We know that he knew Thor wasn't at home because he'd just caught him shagging Edie down at the Stranger. It's just possible he might have visited the Forge to find something to aid his suicide that would leave a clear message to Thor. If so, he made a lousy choice. And from what I've heard of him he wasn't that kind of guy. So that leaves the Hall."

"But why should he visit the Hall?" asked Mig.

"Don't you listen to anything unless it's in a burning bush or can walk through walls?" she demanded. "Here's what we know. Sam goes to the Stranger to see Edie. Why? To talk about their future? Wrong. He goes there because young Pete has just told him that the little girl he'd tried to take care of, my grandmother, had been raped and that Dunstan's motive in shipping her off to Australia, far from being charitable, had been to get her as far away from Illthwaite as humanly possible before she could open her mouth. Sam is furious, on the kid's behalf, and on his own because he's been made a fool of. Catching Edie on the nest can't have improved his state of mind. But I don't believe he'd be suicidal. He'd be angrier than ever. I think he was heading up Stanebank to have it out with Dunstan Woollass!"

There. The first half of the blackboard was full. She looked at her calculations and found no flaw.

"But didn't he meet Dunstan driving down Stanebank or something?" said Mig.

"That's the evidence Dunstan gave. Said hello, thought the fellow looked distracted, reported this the same evening, soon as he heard the curate had gone missing. What a load of garbage! Think about it: was Sam Flood going to pass the man who'd dumped on little Pam and shut young Pete up with a nod and a hello?"

"You think that he confronted Dunstan?"

"Yes. And not on Stanebank. I think he went up to the Hall. Perhaps Dunstan was getting his car out of the garage. They quarrel. Perhaps Saint Sam is a bit more intemperate than usual. He had cause. And then . . ."

She paused, metaphorical chalk in hand, suddenly reluctant to record her logical conclusion on the metaphorical blackboard.

Mig, she guessed, was there too, but it was her calculation, he wanted to hear her say it.

"And . . . ?" he prompted.

"Dunstan tries that old silver tongue of his. It's got him out of worse scrapes than this. But this time it doesn't work. Sam's not in the listening mood. As far as he's concerned, it's next stop the cops. He turns to go, Dunstan lays a hand on his shoulder, probably just to hold him back so they can talk more, but Sam's so wound-up by everything, he lashes out."

She paused again, and now at last Mig helped her out.

He said, "So they fight and Sam ends up dead, is that what

you're saying? But does it really make sense? Sam was so much younger, and can you really see Dunstan getting mixed up in a vulgar brawl?"

"Dunstan was no old man in 1961," said Sam. "Rising forty and probably fighting fit. And the kind of fighting he was fit for wasn't just a barroom punch-up. Thor told me he was in the SAS during the war, and got himself a medal for killing Germans!"

Mig said, "There's a portrait of him in uniform at the Hall."

"There you are then," said Sam inconsequentially. "So he'd probably have no problem. Quick squeeze in the right place and the poor sod's lying there unconscious. Well, that's how they do it in the movies," she added, seeing Mig regarding her dubiously.

"And then . . . ?" he said. "And then . . . ?"

"Think about it. Now he's got a real problem. Does he wait till Sam wakes up, then try reasoning with him again? If he fails—and in the circs that's where the clever money would be—he faces a police investigation of his son, and a public humiliation for himself and his family."

"No," said Mig, shaking his head. "I can just about accept a struggle in which Sam is accidentally killed, but what you're suggesting is cold-blooded murder."

"Sam was alive when he went into the Moss," said Sam bluntly. "I've seen the autopsy report. He died of drowning. I think Dunstan decided the only way forward was to get rid of him. Quick thinking, isn't that what they teach them in the SAS? He thinks of the Moss then decides it would be best to weigh the body down. Thor's unused stones are lying around, perhaps he stored them in the garage. They're a good size for stuffing in pockets. He then dumps him in the back of his jeep and heads up the track to the Moss. He finds a pool, probably holds the poor bastard's head under till he's sure he's not going to revive. Then he watches till the clothes get sodden and the weight of the stones pulls the body down out of sight."

She finished. Part of her wanted Mig to agree with her reasoning. But another part, aware that to all the other crimes she was laying at the door of her newly found family she was now adding murder, wanted him to laugh and set about demolishing her calculations.

He stood with his head bowed. In prayer? She hoped not.

Then he raised his head and she saw in his eyes that she, or something, had convinced him.

"This is a terrible thing," he said.

"You agree with me then?"

"Yes. Now I understand why Sam's apparition held out the stones to me. It was a message I couldn't understand, one that I would never have understood without you. That's why we were both brought here."

Bloody typical! she thought. It wasn't her immaculate reasoning that got him agreeing with her but the way it fitted in with his mumbo-jumbo!

She felt a huge exasperation welling up inside her, but recognizing it as that kind of exasperation compounded with affection which she had previously only felt when provoked by her ma or pa or, bless her memory, Gramma Ada, she battened it down. This wasn't the time or place for a falling-out, especially on a side issue.

The main point was she'd reasoned herself into making a good case that her namesake, Sam Flood the curate, had been murdered, and the man she now knew to be her great-grandfather was the killer. *Eu*-bloody-*reka!*

"So what do we do now?" said Mig.

She liked the *we*. Exasperating he might be, but at least he wasn't ducking out.

She said, "I don't know. There's no evidence, just logic, and law's got nothing to do with logic."

"What do you want to do?" he asked gently.

"I want to go away and forget about all of this stuff," she heard herself saying. "But I know I can't. These ideas about

Saintly Sam just muddy the water even more. I'd like to set them aside completely till I get things straight with regard to Gerry. In fact, I wish I'd never got into the Sam stuff at all. But now I know what I think, I've got to tell Thor and Edie at least. They've spent forty years blaming themselves for Sam's death. They've a right to know what we think really happened."

He put his arms around her and drew her close.

"You know, despite all your efforts to hide it, you're a good old-fashioned moral . . . woman," he murmured.

"Yeah? If you'd said girl I'd have kneed you in the crotch, and how moral would that have been? Let's get away from this place. It gives me the creeps."

They turned and made their way back downhill. As they neared the track they saw the pickup approaching from Foulgate, moving at a speed which wasn't good for its suspension.

"Thor's in a hurry," said Sam. "Perhaps he got a dusty welcome."

She waved her hand, expecting the vehicle to slow down, but if anything it came faster.

It was Mig who spotted it first.

"That's not Thor driving!" he said. "It's Gowder!"

Then it was past them in a cloud of dust and swinging round the curve that marked the descent to the Hall.

"Oh shit," said Sam. "Where's Thor? What do you think's happened to him?"

"Only one way to find out," said Mig. "Come on."

He set off at a fast jog along the track toward Foulgate.

"Don't you think we should try to warn them at the Hall that he's coming?" panted Sam, for the first time finding herself stretched to keep up with him.

"No way to warn them, he'll be there long before we could get close. No, we need to check that Thor's all right," said Mig grimly.

She checked his logic and found, rather to her surprise, that it was totally without flaw. Then Mig's concern for Winander proved infectious and images of him lying in the farmyard with his head stove in began to fill her mind.

It was with huge relief that she heard Mig cry, "I think I see him!"

She strained her eyes through the gathering gloom of the impending storm and saw way ahead a figure moving toward them. Another couple of seconds confirmed it was Thor and a few moments later they met.

There was no sign of blood, but there were the beginnings of a livid bruise on his right temple and he looked as if he'd been rolling in dust and mud.

"Did you see him?" he yelled.

"Yes. He went past us like a bat out of hell," said Sam. "What happened?"

"The bastard thumped me!" said Thor. "I met him coming out of his barn. I tried to speak to him and next thing I was flying through the air. Then he got into the pickup, turned it round and took off. He'd have backed it clean over me if I hadn't rolled out of the way. Come on, we need to get down to the Hall!"

"Why? What do you think he's likely to do there?" gasped Mig as they set off jogging back along the track.

"God knows," said Thor. "All I know is when I saw him he was carrying an axe and a jerrycan full of petrol, so I don't think he's going for tea!"

8

Ragnarokk

Afterward all Sam recalled, not without shame, of running along that seemingly endless track was the pain in her legs and lungs, her shock that she was finding it hard to keep up with a sexagenarian and an invalid, and her determination that she wasn't going to be beaten.

The shame derived from her later realization that what motivated the two men to break their pain barriers was unselfish concern for the inmates of the Hall. Perhaps, she tried to explain to Mig, it was a gender thing. She, being a woman, found it impossible to imagine the worst Laal Gowder might do. They, being men and thus tarred with the same brush, had no delusions.

Even to herself it did not sound a reasonable argument.

But they all shared an equal relief when at last the twisted chimneys of Illthwaite Hall came into sight.

A few moments later, as they reached the viewpoint where Mig had paused the previous day, Thor stopped. The others, taking their lead from him, came to a halt too and peered down the fellside toward the house.

The pickup was parked close against the wall, its driver's door wide open. Up the slope opposite the kitchen window they could see Laal Gowder. He was standing alongside the great carved trunk that had killed his brother, swinging a long-handled axe with practiced ease and driving its head into the fatal wood.

Into Sam's mind came words from the Reverend Peter K.'s *Guide*:

> *Experienced woodmen found their axe-edges blunted. Finally Barnaby Winander, the village blacksmith and a man of prodigious strength, swung at the cross with an axe so heavy none but he could raise it. A contemporary account tells us that the razor-sharp edge rang against the stump with "a note like a passing-bell," the shaft shattered, and the axe-head flew off . . .*

No such problem, diabolic or human, here. No bell-like sound either. Just a solid *crunch!* as the blade drove deep into the bole sending woodchips flying off to left and right.

"He's decapitating it," said Thor. "He's taking the Wolf-Head right off."

"But why?" asked Mig, which seemed to Sam an odd question for a religious guy to ask when a paid-up atheist like herself had no problem with following the superstitious irrationalities of Gowder's psyche.

"Because it killed his brother," said Thor. "I always knew that sodding thing was evil. I should never have listened to Frek. At least Gowder is taking it out on something inanimate . . . Oh shit!"

A figure had appeared at the kitchen window. Sam couldn't make it out, but Thor had no doubt who it was, nor of the possible consequences.

"It's Gerry," he said. Then he bellowed, "Stay inside, you stupid bugger! Don't come out!"

Even Thor's mighty shout could hardly have reached the man in the kitchen. He vanished from the window. Sam looked toward the kitchen doorway, then realized she could only see the top of it because the pickup was parked so close to the wall. The door opened, but the vehicle blocked exit. There might have been space for someone as skinny as she was to crawl out alongside the wheel, but not for a thickset man like Woollass.

There was a cry of triumph, more an animal howl, as one last blow from Gowder's axe separated the Wolf-Head from the bole. But he wasn't finished yet.

Dropping his axe, he picked up a petrol can and started to pour the fuel over the snarling head.

Again words scrolled across Sam's mind:

Faggots of bone-dry kindling were set all around the stump, flame was applied, the Winanders got to work with the bellows they had brought up from their forge, and soon whipped up a huge conflagration. Yet when all had died down and the ashes were raked away, there the stump remained, just as it had been before . . .

But once more, if this were that same Other Cross, its powers of resistance seemed to have died over the years. Laal Gowder brought a box of matches out of his pocket, struck one and let it fall. The petrol ignited with a whoosh and in a few moments it was clear that the old dry wood was burning away merrily. No, not merrily, thought Sam. Somehow the shimmering diaphane of flame made the carved Wolf-Head look as if it were writhing and snarling in the heart of the fire.

Mig put her thoughts into words.

"It's more like he's bringing that thing to life than destroying it," he said.

"I think we'd better get down there," said Thor.

But before they could resume their descent, events in the drama which they were viewing from the distant gallery began to spiral out of control.

Gerry had reappeared at the kitchen window and opened it

to shout something at Gowder. In the bedroom window immediately above they could now see the figure of Dunstan, unmistakable with his mane of white hair above his cardinal red robe. Sam thought she glimpsed someone behind him. Mrs. Collipepper? It would be like the man not to let the drama of the day interfere with his refreshing "nap."

Laal Gowder seemed to find the sight of one or both of them, and perhaps the words that Gerry was shouting, an unbearable provocation.

He stooped down, seized the flaming Wolf-Head in both hands, raised it high in the air, and hurled it through the kitchen window. Gerry fell back out of sight. And Gowder, his axe in one hand, the petrol can in the other, scrambled on to the sill and squeezed through the open window.

Now the three spectators were running again. No time for commentary now, no breath to spare even for exclamations of shock, they ran as humans have always run, toward danger even when they know that tragedy is inevitable.

It took at most three minutes, probably less, for them to be turning into the driveway, but in that time the age of the wolf had come and it was not to be denied.

In the kitchen Gowder had gone berserk. A blow from the axe, fortunately from the flat of the blade not its edge, drove Gerry Woollass to the floor. Before he passed out he saw the enraged man hacking the furniture and fittings to pieces, but, with a heightened instinct for destruction, aiming the worst of his violence at the kitchen range, severing all its input pipes and releasing an unstoppable supply of gas into the air.

Then, it later became clear, he had run amuck through the rest of the house, trailing petrol till the can was empty, then using his axe to reduce everything he encountered to firewood.

To the three figures running down the drive, the attractive front elevation of the Hall looked the same as it had looked for almost half a millennium. Only the smoke billowing up from the far end gave normalcy the lie. But as

Thor flung open the front door there was a muffled explosion as the gas in the kitchen ignited, sending a blast of hot air driving deep into the building, and the trail of petrol laid by the crazed Gowder sent flames leaping joyously upward to seize on paneling and beams whose wood had been drying out for centuries.

Buildings like these, wrote the chief fire officer in his report, were often bonfires waiting to be lit. A circular warning of the dangers, detailing the protective measures available, had been sent out to all owners the previous year. Frek Woollass had been keen that its recommendations should be followed, but her father had looked at the estimated cost and declared that the money could be put to much better use in the community. Thus, opined that keen ironist Thor Winander, had Gerry's compulsion to atone ultimately brought about the destruction of his ancestral home.

But such philosophical niceties had no place in the minds of the three new arrivals as they burst into the entrance hall, which was already filling with smoke.

Sam had no firm idea what they should or could do now they were here, but Thor like a Hollywood action hero had no doubt of his priorities.

"The old man's upstairs," he said, making for the staircase.

"What about Gerry in the kitchen?" said Mig.

"Either he got out or he's a goner," said Thor over his shoulder.

It was an analysis too clear to need debate. The kitchen was the volcanic center of the eruption which was threatening the downfall of the whole building. Nothing could survive in there.

The thought trailed across Sam's logical mind that Gerry's death would remove the problem of their first confrontation. She brushed it away angrily and in its place popped the question whether Thor would be so keen to dash to old Dunstan's aid if he knew what she suspected about his involvement in Sam Flood's death.

This too she erased as irrelevant. But the question she couldn't get out of her mind as she went up the stairs behind the two men was the same question she'd found herself asking in the wake of the other Gowder's death beneath the Wolf-Head—*Is this all down to me?*

The fire was moving laterally at a steady speed, but in its natural direction, which was upward, it went like a rocket. Dunstan's bedroom was almost directly above the kitchen. Already there was fire there, banked high in the hearth to keep his old bones warm. And according to Mrs. Collipepper, as the coils of smoke started coming up through the floorboards, the old man stretched his hands out to them as if welcoming the extra heat.

She tried to lead him out of the room but he pushed her away. Now Frek burst in and attempted to add her strength to the effort. Dunstan resisted them both, showing remarkable strength.

Then he said to the housekeeper, "For God's sake, Pepi, if you want to help me, get her out of here. Quickly. No point in us all dying."

So Mrs. Collipepper had turned her attention to Frek and dragged her out of the room, just as Thor and Mig and Sam came round the corner from the landing.

It was clear at once there was no hope of getting to the old man. The room was a maelstrom of fire and smoke. It was incredible that Dunstan still had anywhere to stand, but when the curtain of flame opened a fraction, Sam saw him quite clearly, upright by the window, as if taking one last look at the landscape he so loved.

She heard herself crying his name. He couldn't have heard her, but he turned his head.

She never knew if it was an optical illusion, or maybe a created memory, but she always recalled that he seemed to smile as if in recognition and mouthed something. The smile and the mouthing were probably both simply a rictus of pain as the heat began to melt the flesh from his bones. But in her memory she read his lips, and this was what persuaded her the memory was real. For surely a created memory would have had old Dunstan uttering some sort of confession, perhaps begging for forgiveness?

Instead, which she never told anyone except Mig, what she saw him saying was, "Sorry about the tea."

Then she felt herself pushed aside roughly by a figure it took her a moment to identify.

Scorched, smoke-blackened, with a huge gash across his temple which the heat had cauterized, it was Gerry.

He screamed, "Dad!" and would have rushed into the room if Thor hadn't flung his strong arms around him and grappled him back.

At the same moment the floor collapsed, Dunstan vanished, and there was no room left to rush into.

With the vibrant urgency of one who had been learning the line for years, Thor said, "Let's get out of here."

He hauled Gerry along by main force. Frek seemed close to collapse and Mig followed Thor's example and dragged her along the corridor. At last he's got his hands on her, thought Sam. And she's the nearest she'll ever get to being hot stuff!

It seemed to her that she might have spoken these wild words aloud and she glanced at Mrs. Collipepper as they hurried along behind the others. Their eyes met for a moment, blue gray looking into gray blue.

Oh God, thought Sam, remembering there'd been three generations of Collipeppers housekeeping at the Hall. Not another Woollass by-blow!

At the head of the stairs they could see the hall below was full of smoke. Thor yelled something at Mig, who grabbed hold of what remained of Gerry's jacket while hanging on to Frek with his other hand. Mrs. Collipepper thrust Sam forward into contact with Frek, herself seizing Sam's trailing hand.

Then they dragged what air they could into their lungs and,

with Thor leading what felt like a crazy conga, they plunged down the stairway.

Heat on the skin; smoke in the nostrils, the eyes, the lungs; staggering, falling, recovering; all the time fighting the urge to lie down and simply let it be over; if this was the kind of hell Mig truly believed in, thought Sam, how did he manage to get out of bed in the morning?

Then she died.

She knew it was death because she'd burst into that heaven she didn't believe in. She felt cool air playing on her face and when she breathed it was the same nectar that poured down her throat, flushing out all the ashy filth in a bout of lung-racking coughing which was the sweetest pain she'd ever felt.

She released her grip on Frek, collapsed to her knees in a parody of thanksgiving which wasn't altogether parody, and opened her eyes.

The action hero had done it. They were in the middle of the lawn in front of the house.

The others lay about her, coughing, gasping, retching. Gerry looked the worst affected. The rest were already like herself recovering enough to pay heed to each other. She caught Mig's eye. He mouthed "You OK?" and she nodded and they smiled at each other.

Then she turned her head to look at the Hall.

They had made it out just in time. The kitchen end of the house was sending tongues of fire licking up at the low storm clouds which were boiling overhead. Behind windows along the whole length of the rest of the building they could see flames dancing like guests at a wild party.

Some blast of air—or perhaps Mrs. Collipepper acting like a good housekeeper to the end—had closed the front door behind them. Inside it must already be burning. They could see the paint bubbling off the woodwork as they watched, and now the wolf-head knocker was snarling at them out of a corona of fire.

Frek used Sam to lever herself upright as if to get a better view. Sam reached up and took the hand on her shoulder and held it there. Mig rose too and stood beside Frek.

"I'm sorry," he said.

"What for?"

"The house . . . your grandfather . . . Look, the way it happened, it was unforeseeable, I'm sure . . ."

Frek coughed a laugh.

"You think I'm worried because he died unshriven, with all his many sins, carnal and otherwise, upon him? Forget it. He died in flames like a Viking, with his most precious belongings burning around him, as Odin himself ordained. No forgiveness necessary in that belief system. A man is judged by his best, not his worst, and a hero's welcome awaits heroes."

She squeezed Sam's shoulder as if in acknowledgment, then went to kneel by her father, who was being tended by Thor and Mrs. Collipepper.

Sam rose to stand beside Mig.

Above them the clouds gobbled up the last morsel of clear sky and met in an almost simultaneous flash of lightning and clap of thunder. The front door of Illthwaite Hall fell out on to the pebble mosaic and a blast of fire-bright air strong enough for Sam to feel its heat shot out and upward to be absorbed by the mighty storm raging above.

"There he goes, the old bastard," said Sam, flip as always in face of irrational fear.

"Yes, I think he probably does," murmured Mig, putting his arm round her shoulder. She noticed that with his other hand he was crossing himself. A mocking quip began to form in her mind but aborted long before it got anywhere near its term.

Above them, the clouds finally opened and the rain began to fall, in fat intermittent drops to start with, then in hissing torrents, and, though Sam would never admit it even to Mig, it felt like a blessing on her shorn and scarred and heat-scoured head.

PART SEVEN

AFTERWARD

That's it. I've told you more than I've ever told anyone else. I really can't think of anything else you might want to know.

Make of it what you will.

Prose Edda Snorri Sturluson

1

What more?

So what is there left to tell?

It would be nice to say that Sam and Mig walked off into the sunset and lived happily ever after, but while Mig's fondness for Hollywood movies might have made him dream of such an ending, Sam had other agendas, mainly mathematical, in which sunsets didn't figure.

First, however, she had to work things out between herself and her new relatives.

Gerry Woollass was the only one of the survivors of the Illthwaite Hall conflagration who needed extended hospital treatment. It was a couple of weeks before he and Sam had their face-to-face. Prior to it, Mig had gone on about the healing power of forgiveness, which she thought was a bit rich coming from the native of a country which had practically made revenge a national dish. Anyway, she said, forgiveness wasn't really in her gift, coming third in the queue behind her father and little Pam herself.

The meeting itself was strangely unsatisfactory. What was the point, Sam asked, in going after a guy like one of the Furies when everything you laid on him he'd already laid on himself with an even bigger shovel? Not only that, he now blamed himself for his father's death and the loss of the Hall.

In the end, following the specific advice of her ma and the tacit advice of her pa, she moved on, and might even have developed some kind of warmer relationship with Gerry if his guilt hadn't been such a bar. On the whole she felt she would probably have got on better with Dunstan if he'd been the survivor. Ruthless, arrogant, passionate in belief, coldly rational in execution, there had been something in him that appealed to something in herself. It wasn't an altogether comfortable notion, but at least his death had meant she could lay to sleep her theories about his part in the curate's death.

She did, however, share them with Thor and Edie. She stressed she had absolutely no proof, but strong probability was enough for this ghost-tortured pair. Finally they could acknowledge the powerful natural attraction they felt for each other, but having reached years of discretion, they took such care in the planning of their first (which is to say their second) sexual encounter that it was at least two hours before the whole of Skaddale rejoiced in the news that Thor and Edie were at it.

Mig insisted that Rev. Pete should be given the full story too. His argument that the restoration of Sam Flood to his true place in the annals of St. Ylf's was the main purpose of what he called their summoning to Illthwaite cut little ice with Sam. But Thor and Edie were in enthusiastic accord with his proposal, and so it was on the next anniversary of the curate's death, a proper memorial stone, carved by Thor, was consecrated to his memory in the aisle of St. Ylf's.

It took Sam a little time to accept Frek's repeated invitation to tea at Cambridge, but when she did she found she rather enjoyed it, especially once she realized that Frek's introduction of her as "my Australian cousin who happens to be a mathematical genius" sprang as much from genuine pride as it did from a desire to take the piss. She was helped to this conclusion by reasoning that Frek was hardly going to risk offending someone who could cut the ground from under her feet at any time by saying, "Actually, she's not my cousin, she's my auntie."

Anything else? Oh yes. Laal Gowder was presumed to have died in the fire, and some ashes were found which were probably his. But Illthwaite being Illthwaite, a legend soon grew that he had in fact escaped and was living a solitary, half-animal life on the high fells where there were soon plenty of locals ready to claim they'd glimpsed him trudging through the mist, with his axe over one shoulder and half a slaughtered sheep over the other. Eventually this story was conflated with the legend of St. Ylf, but that was much further into the future than this brief rounding-up and winding-down cares to venture.

As for Mig, it took him some time to be persuaded that there was no place for him in Sam's immediate plans. Even then he did not give up hope, but kept in constant touch. His thesis never got finished, which Max Coldstream said was a shame. But with the destruction of so many original documents in the Illthwaite Hall fire, it would have been a sadly diluted affair.

Eventually he got involved once more in the family business, taking on overseas marketing, which Cristo thought was great so long as it kept his brother overseas and a long way from Jerez.

Mig's hopes for a romantic future were nurtured by Sam's rather surprised discovery of just how reluctant she herself was to let the relationship fade into nothingness. Though there was much about him that still exasperated her, she felt a closeness to him that not even mere sexual attraction could explain. So they stayed friends—occasionally, if the moon was full, the air balmy and the wine red, passionate friends.

Noddy Melton went to Spain on holiday, and had a snack in a certain *taberna* on the Costa Brava, and let the grossly overweight chain-smoking English *patrona* buy him a drink. When she asked about his background, he told her he was a retired insurance salesman from Slough, paid for his food by cash, and returned to Illthwaite in such a mellow frame of mind the locals opined he should go on holiday more often.

Talking of travel, when Sam went back to Vinada during the long vacation, Mig invented a necessary business trip which took him to Australia at the same time. Exasperated, flattered and amused in equal proportion, Sam finally introduced him to her parents. Lu took to him at once, saying she could feel the spirits liked him. Sam's pa greeted him with, "You the bastard who makes the Bastard? You'll not sell a lot out here. Too thin and sharp." But even he, after a while, had to admit that, in spite of all the contraindications, there was something about Mig that drew him to him, though God alone knew what it might be, and He wasn't telling.

But if you know where to look He may drop hints.

It is Christmas 1589.

In a smoke-filled hut in Eskdale in Cumberland, Jenny, widow of Thomas Gowder of Illthwaite, sits and nurses her infant child.

She is expecting a visit from her brother-in-law, Andrew, and she is not expecting him to come laden with gold and frankincense.

As the baby sucks greedily at her breast, she recalls her last sight of Miguel, the waif boy, after she had cut him down from the tree. As he staggered away on his makeshift crutches, he had looked back at her once in the corpse-light of dawn, and she had felt a huge shame that she was not brave enough to stay with him. But she knew that it would almost certainly mean death not only for herself but for the child she had only just become aware she was carrying.

Whose it was, she did not know. Had Thomas in one of his brutal sexual assaults finally planted a fertile seed? Or was it the fruit of those joyous escapes from her daily miseries in the arms of the foreign boy?

Even her return to Foulgate and her acquiescence with Andrew's version of the night's events did not guarantee safety.

She was certain in her heart that Thomas had been alive but unconscious when Miguel fled, and that Andrew, seeing the chance to take over the farm for himself and his sons, had been responsible for his brother's death.

Having done that, he was not going to let a little thing like a sister-in-law who might be carrying his brother's legitimate heir stand in his way.

So she kept quiet about her condition and after a short period craved his permission to return to her family in Eskdale, which he gave most willingly, glad to see this reminder of his brother removed from Foulgate.

In Eskdale as her condition became increasingly more difficult to hide she had turned to her first cousin, Michael, five years her senior and the man everyone thought she would marry till the eyes of her more distant and much more powerful Skaddale cousin had fixed upon her. A quiet, thoughtful man, he had listened to her story, then proposed that they should marry and he would declare the child his own.

News of the intended marriage only two months into her widowhood had necessarily been sent to Illthwaite. Andrew had turned up at the wedding, ostensibly to offer his blessing, but Jenny had felt his sharp piggy eyes fixed on her waistline.

And news of her labor at the end of November, barely seven months after the marriage, must have set the dreadful machinery of his Gowder mind clanking to a dire conclusion.

He waited a couple of weeks. Infant mortality rate in the first few days was high. With premature births it was near one hundred percent.

But the child was flourishing and now Andrew was coming to see for himself.

The baby has finished feeding. Softly she croons it to sleep. But she does not set it in its cradle, holding it close in her arms as she hears the noise of a horse outside.

A few moments later Andrew comes through the door.

"Give you good day, sister," he says. "And this is the child."

"It is, brother Andrew," she says.

He stoops to look closer, then seizes a brand from the fire and holds it over her head so that the flickering light falls full on the baby, waking it.

Already the features are becoming individualized. Full, dark eyes, a fine rather sharp nose, well-defined cheekbones, a light golden skin, and Jenny's own bright red hair, though still sparse, promises a rich harvest on the noble head.

There is no resemblance in even the smallest detail to the solid brutal face that squints down at it.

Satisfied, Andrew stands upright as a thin, slightly built man comes into the hut.

"Give you good day, cousin," he says softly.

"And you too, cousin," says Andrew. "I have been admiring your fine child. And what will you call him?"

It is Jenny who answers.

"Michael," she says. "After his father. Michael Galley."